THE FELICITOUS

MATT FORGIT

This book is a work of fiction. Any reference to historical events, real people, or real places are used fictitiously. Other names, characters, places, and events are products of the author's deranged imagination. Any resemblance to actual events or places or people, living or dead or undead, is entirely coincidental.

ISBN 979-8-9853874-2-1

First published September 2023

Cover design and artwork by Matt Keller at matthewkellerart.com

To Katie, who had me at "Kelly Clarkson"

To Lisa, who'll get it because she's farthest
from the phone

To Shannon, who would make a phenomenal
final girl

To Steph, my Sanderson sister

And always to Matt,
my best dude friend of a cousin, for everything

"The only ones left to mourn

The last witnesses to the execution

Suspended in time by a puppeteer with blood on his hands

Little broken dolls that go on dancing after the music has stopped."

—Trailer narration for *Three on a Meathook* (1972)

CHAPTER ONE

It was neither a dark nor stormy night.

Dr. Melinda Winthrop and her daughter Casey arrived home around the same time as Melinda's husband, Dean. Melinda, a psychiatrist, worked with Casey. Melinda had always been close to her father and wanted to go into the same field as his. She was so proud that Casey had the same aspiration. A long line of psychiatrists in one house.

Melinda and Casey saw patients at their clinic while consulting with local hospitals and mental institutions. The women loved their jobs but needed a mental health break of their own after diagnosing others' maladies day after day.

For the upcoming weekend, they had organized a family vacation to North Sea Cottages and were heading out the next morning. There was still a list of things to do before they left.

The sun had gone down, but that didn't stop Melinda and Dean's teenaged sons, Lewis and Duncan, from ziplining down the hill behind their house with their grandfather, Arthur. They had built an entire obstacle course in their back yard, including a rope-climbing wall, giant ring toss, cornhole boards and bags, and a fort atop the hill as their home base.

Dr. Arthur Wainwright, Melinda's father, sat in a lawn chair at the top of the hill. He was strong and steady for his age but didn't like to stand for long periods of time. He was retired after a fifty-year career in the mental health business, specializing in cults, serial killers, and patients with severe psychotic, violent tendencies. He had published many articles on the subject in medical journals, as well as written a few books on the subject. He was considered an expert in the discourse on many unseemly, not-dinner-table topics. These days, he wanted

1

to enjoy time with his daughter Melinda and his grandkids.

Duncan had his phone out, trying to catch some Pokémon Go and chattering about how the science behind *Quantum Leap* was unsound. Lewis secured the zip line to make sure it wasn't coming loose, checking the pulley, cable, and harness. In the wintertime, they turned the hill into a gigantic ice luge. The summer weather found them engineering the zipline.

Lewis was in his last summer before he'd leave home for college while Duncan was headed into his senior year. Lewis and Duncan were best friends, always constructing and creating structures together. Lewis didn't know what he'd do without Duncan in the fall.

Lewis wore a Gene Loves Jezebel T-shirt, while Duncan wore a Cutting Crew shirt. They had recently discovered their parents' large record collection and searched Amazon and eBay for all the shirts to match their newfound musical treasures.

"What do you think the worst inanimate object to be is?" asked Lewis.

"Hm," pondered Duncan. "A Flintstones vitamin. Oh, worse, a plunger. That's got to be a sad life. What about you?"

"I think it would suck to be an eraser. Not like *Eraser*, the Arnold Schwarzenegger movie. That would actually be kind of cool. But an eraser. Your whole purpose is to clean up other people's mistakes and then they grind you down into dust. What a thankless existence."

"Did you know there's two hundred and sixteen species of owls and eleven are found in Maine?" Lewis said. "Owls know things. They carry secrets. Like in *Harry Potter*."

"Do you think the 'Give a hoot, don't pollute' one lives here?"

"Maybe the Tootsie Roll owl," Lewis said as he grabbed on to the zipline handlebars and prepared for a ride.

"Grandpa, remember that story you used to tell us when we were kids?" asked Duncan. "About the night crap."

"The Nachtkrapp," Grandpa Arthur said. "The legend of the Nachtkrapp. It's a giant raven who leaves its nest every night and searches for children to eat. If you look directly into his eyes, you'll go insane or get really sick or even die. It flies around, looking for children who won't go to bed. It comes in their windows and steals them away in the night, bringing them back to its nest and eating them limb by limb, saving the heart for last."

"Great bedtime story, Grandpa," Lewis said and took off down the cable to the shed.

The first thing Melinda and Dean noticed as they walked up to their front door was their out-of-place front yard decorations. Normally, their yard was filled with perfectly-placed outdoor ornaments, from windchimes to concrete geese, toilet planters, lawn gnomes, and mechanical singing Fraggles from *Fraggle Rock*.

They had all been knocked over, as if a giant storm came and threw everything out of place. The day had been temperate and calm. Melinda presumed her boys were roughhousing and took out the decorations, but in typical fashion, didn't put them back.

Dean carried grocery bags full of meat and cheeses from the market downtown, where he worked as a butcher in the deli. He was a part of a barbershop quartet, a Civil War reenactor—he preferred to be called a "living historian,"— and had lived in Hartwell his whole life.

He plopped the bags down on the kitchen counter. The plan was for grilled steaks and a cheese and cracker board for dinner with the kids. A big dinner before they left for their trip. Dean loved his grill. He would grill soup if there was a way.

He walked to the back deck to turn on the grill and waved at his sons as they careened down the wire attached to a tree on the edge of the forest ridge and ended at their shed. The Winthrop family owned several hundred acres on the outskirts of Hartwell, Maine, surrounded by fields, forest, and few neighbors—though that could describe many of the families who lived there.

Like many of the houses in Hartwell, the Winthrop home was warm and cozy and well lived-in, having been in their family for generations. Melinda put on her Eddie Rabbitt *Horizon* vinyl record and kissed her husband as he came inside to grab his favorite tongs, the sounds of "I Love a Rainy Night" filling the house.

"Do you like my new plates?" Dean asked Melinda, holding them up for her to see. "I got them on QVC. The Lacey Chabert collection. I also got the Dierks Bentley steak knife set."

Melinda laughed to herself. This was one of the many things she loved about her husband. The big, burly butcher with the macho exterior who bought Lacey Chabert plates on QVC. The man who told everybody that his favorite movie was *The Departed* when she knew it was really *Did You Hear About the Morgans?*

"Have an orange. You don't want to get scurvy," Dean picked up an orange from a big bowl on the kitchen table and handed it to Melinda.

While Dean started on the steaks, Melinda went out to fix the lawn display. She heard her sons and father laughing and yelling in the back as they ziplined. She didn't notice the figure standing in the doorway on her front porch, watching her. She bent down to pick up the fallen arrangements and the familiar groan of the porch floor caught her attention.

When Melinda looked back at the porch, the front door was closed and nobody was there.

Inside the house, Casey sat at her computer desk in her room, checking her email and catching up on current

4

psychiatry articles. She changed her outgoing email and voicemail messages to state that she would be away and would return all correspondence the next week. She had never moved out of her parents' place even though she could have.

After being away at school for four years to get her degree, the past few years of being around her family made her happy. Casey was getting her PhD in psychiatry at Briggs College. In the meantime, she could see patients like her mother did, though she was not a fully-fledged psychiatrist yet.

Her attention turned to an unlabeled flash drive on her desk. Where or who she'd gotten the flash drive from was a puzzle—perhaps it was for work. Maybe patient files her mom left for her? Old papers from school? Curious, she slid it into a port in her computer.

A link to a video popped up on her computer screen. Casey clicked on it.

It was a grainy video shot in night vision. She instantly recognized the location as the inside of her house. There was no sound. The camera's point of view moved slowly throughout the house, from room to room, capturing footage of each of her family members sleeping soundly in their beds, completely unaware of the intruder's presence. Her room was last. The camera focused on her slumbering. The person filming zoomed in on Casey's face as she snored obliviously while the stranger in her house recorded.

The video ended abruptly. Casey sat back from her computer, stunned. She went through a list of friends and pranksters she knew. Who could possibly think this was a funny joke to play? She didn't want to think of the alternative—that someone they didn't know, whose motives weren't clear, had invaded their personal, private space.

A flash of red caught her eye. Casey spun her chair toward her closed bedroom door. A long, bright red piece of yarn was hanging through the keyhole. A small, shiny key was tied to the end, as if it was an anchor.

"Lewis? Duncan? Not funny, you boneheads," she said as she got out of her chair and stood before the door. She reached out to grab the red yarn. Before she could touch it, the yarn yanked back and the key lodged itself crookedly in the keyhole.

Casey threw the door open. There was nobody there. She peeked out into the hallway, up and down. Only the sounds of her father rummaging around downstairs in the kitchen drifted through the house to her. She went back into her room and looked out her window at her brothers goofing off outside.

Downstairs, Melinda prepared the plates and silverware for dinner as she decompressed from her day. This was her favorite time of the day. All the family together at dinner, all the background noise and static pushed to the back of her mind. She paused and stared out of the kitchen window for a moment, collecting her thoughts.

There were eyes staring into the house from the trees.

They glowed an unnatural yellow, reflecting the artificial light from within the Winthrop house. The thing was far away from the window, but even in the distance, Melinda could see it wasn't an animal. It was too tall, too massive. The eyes moved in the dark, as if stepping in between the trees and brush.

Then they were gone.

Melinda squinted; her eyes had not adjusted to the darkness outside. She flipped the overhead light off to get a better look.

There was nothing there. Nothing outside except her sons having fun with their grandfather. It had to have been some kind of animal. There were all types of wild animals in the woods in Hartwell.

Boom!

Melinda turned toward the loud bang against the window glass.

A stark white face stared right into hers from the other side of the window.

She squealed and jumped back, throwing the light switch back on.

There was nothing at the window.

Smack!

Something smashed against the window, causing it to crack. A long, winding tendril of breakage cut through the glass. Melinda gasped and backed away. She needed to get Dean.

Melinda felt something—a person, a thing—pressed against her back as soon as she stepped away from the window.

She spun around, face-to-face with the figure. Melinda didn't have time to register all its features.

No time at all as the hunting knife in its hand came down on her. Over and over.

Lewis stood at the top of the hill, getting ready to make another run on the zipline. Duncan was at the shed, waiting for him. They only had one line at the moment—after destroying the others in ill-fated engineering experiments. Lewis couldn't see where Grandpa Arthur had gotten off to, but the pathway was clear and he was ready to ride.

His attention turned to the sound of snapping twigs and crunching leaves off in the woods behind him. He peered into the trees, unable to see much. The sounds were getting closer.

Lewis jumped back. A shadow passed from behind one tree to another, not even a hundred feet away in his eyeline. Lewis reached out for the handle to the zipline.

At the bottom of the hill, Duncan waited on his brother. He thought he saw Grandpa Arthur walking around the side of the house. He called out to him but got no response.

Swish!

The zipline coasted down the wire from the hillside, stopping at the top of the shed. Lewis's Amity Island *Jaws* hat was snapped around the zipline handlebar, swaying in the breeze.

"Lewis?" Duncan called up toward where he last saw his brother. Only the sounds of the forest answered.

Duncan trudged uphill to the top of the tree line, annoyed at the trick his brother was trying to play on him. This would be his last run down. He'd had fun but he was hungry and not in the mood for Lewis's games.

He noticed something in the distance, atop the hill, within the woods. It was clearly his brother, awaiting his moment to jump out and scare him. Lewis didn't know that Duncan saw where he was hiding.

"I can see you, dummy!" Duncan shouted into the darkness.

Lewis didn't reply. Or move. Duncan stepped deeper into the forest. Something wasn't right. The ground crunched and squished under his sneakers as he got closer to where Lewis stood.

Lewis was propped up against a tree, his eyes wide open. Blood soaked the front of his chest, still oozing in rivulets down his coat, puddled in the leaves at his feet. Once Duncan was close enough to really see his brother, he saw the multiple stab wounds that Lewis had succumbed to.

Duncan fell backward onto the ground in disbelief. He gathered himself quickly, jumping to his feet. He turned to run and came face-to-face with his Grandpa Arthur, who had been tied up and strung by his hands and feet between two trees like some kind of giant marionette.

8

Grandpa Arthur had been eviscerated; all of his insides spilled out in a pile on the forest floor.

Duncan ran down the hill, losing his balance and falling most of the way. He scrambled to his feet, dusting himself off. He was halfway to the safety of his house.

Bang!

A trap door built into the ground, like some kind of military bunker or trapping pit meant to catch animals, flew open. Duncan was practically on top of it. He screamed out as he felt an axe slam into his leg.

The figure stood inside the trap. The hole in the ground was only a few feet deep, revealing the figure's upper torso. It was dressed in a ghillie suit.

It wielded the axe in its camouflaged hands. Duncan tumbled to the ground, his leg taken off at the knee beside him.

The figure reached forward and pulled Duncan into the pit with him, slamming the door shut. Duncan's screams and struggles were brief, barely audible from within the restrictive confines of the manmade trap in the ground.

Dean heard commotion while he was bringing the steaks from inside to put on the grill. He didn't think much of it. He was used to the boys being rowdy with their grandfather. He didn't notice the figure standing behind him as he cooked. Or that it slipped into the house undetected.

Clunk.

A small thud from Arthur's room caught Dean's attention.

"Arthur?" Dean called out. "You okay in there?"

Dean pushed the door to Arthur's room open. All of Arthur's files, papers, and photos—saved and stored away from years of work and writing—were strewn all over the floor. Someone had torn through them, clearly looking for something.

A word was smeared on the wall in large letters, written in red that was still wet and dripped down over the white paint. Blood?

ERICA

Dean rushed back to the kitchen. Everything had gotten so quiet. Where was everyone? He ran into the dining room and unleashed a horrified moan of terror.

Melinda, Casey, Lewis, Duncan, and Grandpa Arthur's corpses sat placed around the dining room table. All arranged wide-eyed, bloodied and mutilated, staring directly at him.

Written on the dining room wall in his family's blood was one word:

ERICA

Dean didn't have the chance to run or call for help as a skewer from Dean's own grill thrust through his back. It burst out of Dean's chest, blood spraying all over the table. Dean looked down at the skewer as it retracted, then felt it burst through him a second time.

The figure positioned Dean in a seat at the table. It had decapitated him and stuffed his head inside the hollowed-out midsection of his torso. Dean's eyes were still open, gazing out lifelessly. The figure walked out the front door into the darkness of the night.

It returned moments later, unraveling the black medical tool roll on the table, filled with sharp, shiny surgical equipment.

It began its work on the bodies.

CHAPTER TWO

Four boxes.

Some clothes, books, photographs, and her favorite sponge.

That's all Annie Porter was taking with her. She didn't want reminders of her life in Boston coming with her. Her life there was over now. Time for the next chapter in the book of her life. The upside was that she no longer had to put out any of the gifts she didn't like when her friends came over; the presents she hid away until she knew she was having company and didn't want to hurt any feelings.

Her friend Sloane, a woman she'd met in her bereavement support group and a wonderful real estate agent, had worked tirelessly to help Annie find a suitable new place to call home. Someplace quiet. Once Annie saw the listing for a ghost town called Gull Valley, the pull could not be denied.

Sloane had asked her a hundred times if she was sure this was where she wanted to be. But it was the right call and she wasn't going to become a hermit, so Sloane made sure Annie got a good deal and arranged for a relatively easy and unencumbered move.

"But what about the mountain people?" Annie's beloved Aunt Dolly asked, completely seriously, as she opened her box of wine in Annie's now-empty kitchen.

"The who, now?" said Annie.

"The mountain people. The people who live in caves and wilderness in secret, hidden away from society. They rob and murder travelers and passersby for their belongings and for food."

"That's not a real thing. That's an urban legend about Sawney Bean."

11

"They kidnap the women to help propagate their clan. They're completely cut off from the rest of the world. They're like the Amish but with more inbreeding and bloodlust."

"All myths and fables. None of that is based in fact, Aunt Dolly."

"Yes, it is. And you'd be perfect for them. You are a foxy treat! It's real. Remember that documentary we watched about it on HBO Max?"

"That wasn't a documentary. That was the movie *Wrong Turn*."

"You're going to become like those Grey Gardens ladies, living out there all alone in isolation," Aunt Dolly told her as Annie stacked the four boxes next to the front door of her now-bare apartment.

Annie had sold off all of her furniture, artwork, kitchen appliances, and electronics. Although she'd loved Gary more than her own life, she couldn't bear to keep his things or stay in the apartment they'd lived in together. His earthly possessions weren't him anyway. They were simply painful reminders of what she'd had and lost.

"This is all you're taking with you, Annie?" said Aunt Dolly. "Well, you never were much for sentimentality."

Annie had always felt like a loser in life. Gary had made her feel like she'd won for once. That was over now. Annie's mind was in a constant battle between anxiety and depression; each day, one or the other would win, but neither ever completely sat the game out.

"What are you going to do if something horrible happens and there's nobody around to help you? What if a bunch of ZZ Top-looking marauders and buccaneers come kidnap you and force you to work at The Eager Beaver as a stripper dressed like Xena: Warrior Princess, dancing to Def Leppard's 'Pour Some Sugar On Me'? That happened to Pam's niece, you know. Remember Pam, the chatty dental hygienist? She ended up arrested on *Live PD* for stealing a bunch of those five-finger body glove shoes when she was all cracked out. Her eyes were like pinwheels! Pam's niece, not Pam. That would be weird. Pam really shares a lot when she's cleaning my teeth."

"I guarantee that never happened, Aunt Dolly. 'What if's' are a special kind of torture. Besides, I'm forty-six. Nobody wants me to strip for them. And why would you describe my kidnappers like they're guitar-playing pirates? Anyway, if I was going to be an exotic dancer, I'd pick 'Scotty Doesn't Know' from the movie *Eurotrip* as my song."

Dolly Haskell had always had a flair for the dramatic. She'd lived a colorful, unusual life. She was what they would've referred to as a "broad" or a "dame" in the old days. She was a nun when she was younger, then left the convent to marry four separate times. In between, she'd been at marches for women's rights, civil rights, and gay rights. She'd traveled the world, seen empires and political parties rise and fall, hung out at Studio 54 with Andy Warhol and Donna Summer, and danced in the street when the Vietnam War ended.

She'd partied for days in foreign countries with Stevie Nicks, Diana Ross, Ann and Nancy Wilson from Heart, and the guy from Amy Grant's "Baby Baby" music video. She'd met and spoken with luminaries and visionaries like Maya Angelou, Jane Fonda, Gloria Steinem, five past presidents, chancellors at every Ivy League school in the nation, and Elle Macpherson.

At seventy years old, Aunt Dolly was more vibrant, energized, and full of life than most people half her age. And somehow, through all of her adventures, she'd always managed to be there for Annie, from giving advice to attending Annie's oboe recitals.

Aunt Dolly had also raised Annie since she was only eleven years old. Annie's mom was Dolly's younger sister. Both of Annie's parents had struggled with depression, alcoholism, and drugs during Annie's entire life, until they died in an accident. Aunt Dolly had stepped up and taken custody of Annie, raising her as if she were her own daughter. Until Aunt Dolly became her guardian, Annie had been in and out of foster homes and seen the depravity and horror of addiction and neglect firsthand; not to mention the degradation and apathy of the foster system itself.

Aunt Dolly had saved her from all of that; helped her gain self-worth and self-esteem, confidence, and direction. Annie would never forget any of that—which was why she tried to be careful with Aunt Dolly's feelings. Tried, but not necessarily succeeded.

"In times of trouble, you know what I always ask myself?" Aunt Dolly asked. "What would Claire Danes do?"

"I don't think Claire Danes and I share the same problems."

"Aren't you afraid at all? To be out there, all alone, all by yourself? What if something happens to you and there's no help available? We'll find you three months later, sitting in a lounge chair, your face eaten by stray cats."

"There's a groundskeeper and a caretaker who come into town and takes care of the property, Aunt Dolly," Annie reassured her, although Aunt Dolly's serious, pinched face didn't seem reassured. "He and his team are going to help me with repairs and fixing the place up."

She was well-prepared. She'd done the research. She'd read books and watched YouTube tutorials on how to live in a ghost town. There were thousands of people who lived in seclusion. She'd already had the land stocked with what she'd need—amenities, tools, food, equipment, light, heat, electricity, gas, gear, supplies, internet. She'd bought several generators (and studied how they worked and how to properly use them), stocked up on stored goods and items, and had maps of the layout, landscape, and terrain. Like a doomsday prepper, living in a remote, fortress-like compound, but less fraught and intense. It was all already awaiting her arrival in Gull Valley.

And whatever she didn't know, she would learn.

"Yesterday, on my way to my meeting, I saw a guy clipping his toenails on the train, a woman taking a dump on the sidewalk, a guy yelling at a bag of Vidalia onions he was holding, a woman shaving her dog in a laundromat, and not one, not two, but three fistfights. I don't want to be a part of this world anymore."

"It scares me when you talk like that," Aunt Dolly said, taking bigger and bigger sips of her chilled white wine.

"I don't mean I don't want to be on this earth anymore. I just want to make a change. I need a break from this life. To try a different life. I want to live. I just don't want to live this life here anymore. Can you understand that? I need do this."

"For how long? Isolation drives people mad! We are meant to be with others."

"I don't know. Gull Valley is mine now. So, for however long I feel like it. I can leave whenever I want. I'm only two hours away from you. You're acting like I'm a teenager who has never been away before. I'm not moving to The Land of Oz. You have all your best friends to keep you company and do your *Buns of Steel* workout tape with."

It was the farthest Annie had ever lived from Aunt Dolly since she went into her care. She tried to remember that while Aunt Dolly worried and paced.

"Two hours," Annie said. "You can drive up and back in a day. By the time I get all settled in, I'll have your very own house all set up for you to stay in, just for you."

"I hate the thought of you out there all by yourself. With no one to protect you. With nobody to talk to. I don't want you to turn into one of these cuckoo bird survivalists like The Liver King. You know I always want you to be like Cher."

"I can protect myself, Aunt Dolly. You made sure of that. I have a computer, so we can Zoom or Skype any time. My phone works and you know I'll call you all the time," Annie said, then smiled widely at Aunt Dolly to comfort her. "And I'll always carry Cher's wisdom with me. I believe in life after love. I believe the children are our future. I believe the truth is out there. I believe that mimes are all secretly serial killers and everyone should carry emergency cheese on their person at all times. But I also believe that the biggest lesson in life is that just because you're a good person, it doesn't mean good things will happen to you. So, I have to go."

"What if you run out of food? I've seen you at a buffet. You ate the macaroni necklace you made for me when you were little. You get hangry and crazy when you don't eat. There's no delivery or Grubhub or DoorDash all the way out there. Do you know the HALT acronym?"

"I love eating," Annie said wistfully. "I love food. Cheese tortellini with red sauce and meatballs, Chinese food, garlic hummus with sea salt pita chips, black bean salad with vinaigrette, Girl Scout Cookies—especially the peanut butter ones and Caramel deLites."

"Hey, Ina Garten, come back. I feel like I didn't prepare you enough, teach you things you need to know," Aunt Dolly continued, snapping Annie out of her daydream. "You don't know how to do archery or how to fix a car or plumbing or how to use an egg timer or what to do if you fall into quicksand or a peat bog. I never took you to Disneyland. Remember when you got hit in the face with a football? What will you do if that happens again?"

"That wasn't me. That was an episode of *The Brady Bunch*. You taught me lots of things, Aunt Dolly. I know what upside-down pineapples mean and I know never to buy a timeshare. And I know I love you and you're just trying to shield me from mistakes you think I'm making. But this is what's best for me right now. I need you to respect that. I can take care of myself. And there's this crazy contraption called the internet, where I can find lots of information on how to do things. One click on

WikiHow and I'll be making checkered tile floors out of rubber cement, popsicle sticks, and a hot glue gun."

"Remember—if you ever get lost in the woods, change your voicemail to your location, so that even if you don't have reception, the search and rescue team will hear your message and be able to find you," said Aunt Dolly. "And never walk down stairs with your hands in your pockets."

Annie's friends had told her not to go. Not to leave behind the life she had built for herself in Boston. Not to give up a good career, a stable job, a comfortable apartment, a network of support, and the conveniences of a big, thriving city. Not to "run away," as they put it, not to hide from the bad things in the world.

"What happened to Gary was awful and cruel and wrong," said Aunt Dolly. "Life isn't fair. But I don't want you to base irrevocable life decisions on this one horrible event. I don't want this terrible tragedy to be the thing that defines your life now. I want you to remember who you are. You're the girl who waves at kids and dogs, who cried at the end of *The Hot Chick*, who made me my own Bloody Mary-scented Yankee Candle for Christmas, who feels bad for ugly houses when she sees the advertisements on billboards offering to buy them, who used to circle every book in those Scholastic Book Fair paper flyers so I'd get you all the books. Don't lose that girl. Gary wouldn't want that."

"I also used to be the girl who thought maybe, just maybe, she'd get a happy ending," Annie said flatly. "Gary was murdered, Aunt Dolly. Justice wasn't served. I have to go on with my life without him now. We don't always get what we want."

"Everybody wants a happy ending," said Aunt Dolly. "And I don't mean that in a gross sex way. You can still have yours. What's the best feeling in the world?"

"The feeling you get when you get out of the pool or the ocean and dry off and put your clothes on."

"Don't lose that feeling, Annie," said Aunt Dolly.

"You had that one in the chamber, ready to go."

"What is a dream that you still have?"

"To recreate the prom scene in *Pretty in Pink* when Molly Ringwald enters the school while OMD's 'If You Leave' is playing."

"That's my girl," Aunt Dolly said, hugging Annie so tightly that Annie thought she'd never be allowed to leave. "Don't run away from the people who love you, okay?"

She wasn't running away. She was making the best decision for her own mental health and happiness. She wanted to put her former life behind her, to start anew. Things were different now than they once were. She didn't want to be a part of the general public anymore, making meaningless small talk and witnessing the population's thoughtless and selfish behavior. She didn't want to doomscroll on social media any longer, to be inundated with bad, depressing news. She'd had enough doom to last a lifetime. She had her reasons. She refused to constantly justify them, even if it was to people she loved and who had her best interests at heart.

Annie made a comfortable living writing science fiction novels and short stories. She could do that anywhere. The peace and quiet of the countryside would be beneficial to her writing. She wasn't super rich or famous, but she had sold enough books under her pen name over the years to support herself, and Gary had left her a sizeable amount of money between his life insurance and his will.

The next morning, Annie packed those four boxes into her car before sunrise and drove to her new home.

CHAPTER THREE

Nineteen buildings spread out in a walkable proximity and split on either side of a long dirt road, three thousand and eighty acres of land, and dense woodland constituted the entire abandoned town of Gull Valley, Maine. It all belonged to Annie now. It had been eleven months since she'd signed the paperwork and moved into the main house, where she ate and slept. Hartwell, the nearest town, was twenty-seven miles away. She had the solitude and distance from the general population that she'd sought.

She had everything she needed in Gull Valley. Most of the buildings were stuffed with old furniture and various remnants from the city's past. It gave her something to do with her time. She planned to renovate, remodel, and restore each building, one by one. It was a project that posed many challenges and obstacles, but she was willing and able to put the effort into rebuilding the place she now called home.

The infrastructure was situated in the center of majestic mountains and sprawling woodland. The houses stood in the middle of the valley, in an enormous gorge made by years of running rivers and shifting glaciers. The riverbed was completely dehydrated; no rivers or lakes ran through what used to be bountiful and lucrative territorial waters. Large, old-fashioned windmills were spread over the region, untended to in favor of the invention of water turbines used by bigger cities. The water supply came from a newly-updated well near the tree line, covered with a windowed well cap.

Since its founding in 1852, Gull Valley had functioned as a mining town, school, campground, hippie commune, farmland, ski resort, retreat for hikers and campers, as well as just a place for people to live. In the past twenty years since its abandonment, it had become a destination and refuge for treasure hunters with metal detectors searching for profitable valuables, urban explorers, ghost town enthusiasts, history buffs, hunters, hikers, birdwatchers, transients in need of shelter, and kids looking for somewhere uninhabited to party.

Despite its great distance from the nearest town, Gull Valley had power lines and a cell phone tower that ran through, though service was spotty and unpredictable at best. And now it was her home.

She was a landowner. Landowner and sole resident of Gull Valley, population one. What had once been a forgotten ghost town was hers for the state's paltry asking price of fifteen thousand dollars. That made her the mayor, sheriff, fire chief, city manager, planning director, and economic development director all in one. She was the law and order in these parts. Town meetings consisted only of her attendance.

Eat dinner in her underwear? Done. Sing The Cranberries' "Zombie" or Whitney Houston's "I Wanna Dance With Somebody (Who Loves Me)" at the top of her lungs while painting? It was known to happen. Use a buzzsaw at midnight and not worry about neighbors complaining? Just fine. Watch *Sherlock* and *Supernatural* reruns until six in the morning and the sun peeked over the nearest horizon? More than once. There were no nearby neighbors. Only wild animals frolicking in the forest around her estate. They didn't seem to mind.

Of course, the woods, small mountains, rolling hills, and long-dried up lakebed around Gull Valley attracted campers and hikers, and there'd been the occasional wanderer or transient who stumbled through the town. Old ghost towns were a popular destination for the curious, but Annie had posted thousands of "No Trespassing" signs across the acreage, sometimes multiple warnings at the main entrances. As of yet, she hadn't any trouble with intruders. Most of them left as soon as she told them they were on private property, and she had Sheriff Meeker's number if she needed the authorities. None of her interactions with anyone had come to that yet, though Mr. Brisket told her to watch out for illegal hunters and poachers.

Annie used to love hiking. She'd lost the passion for it—like she had with everything from her writing to any and all of her hobbies—once Gary died. She would spend entire days walking and being in nature. She even had a special playlist for her hikes, including her four favorite Enya songs (didn't everyone have four favorite Enya songs?). She had taken a few walks lately, acclimating herself to her surroundings. It would take time to get back to what made her feel happy, feel alive again. Baby steps. Adjustment period, all that.

She'd gotten used to how cold, windy, and frosty it got at night, even after warm and sunny days. The weather was extreme—lots of rain, wind, unexpected snowfall, and cold fronts that came with living in a valley, surrounded by deep woods and mountains. She wasn't quite a mountain woman yet, but she was content that she could handle whatever came her way.

She had nothing to lose. She had lost everything already.

Annie was okay. She was going to be okay.

CHAPTER FOUR

The snap, crackle, and pop of the engine of George Squires's antique moped sounded a full five minutes before he pulled into the center of the gorge. As he'd done several times before, he dismounted and began yelling at the main house. He didn't even need Annie's audience. He wasn't dressed appropriately for the windy weather; though he was in long sleeves and brown pants, he had no heavy coat or hat.

George had the reputation in Hartwell as the town loony, as well as town drunk. When he came to Gull Valley, he was also town crier. He was Annie's very own harbinger of doom. Annie wasn't necessarily afraid of him; at seventy-five, he was relatively harmless and rather frail. But he was out of his gourd and loved to spout off prophecies of doom to whoever would listen. His faculties had diminished with age.

He'd hop on his moped and take the drive into Gull Valley about once every couple of weeks. Annie was used to it by now. She almost expected it. He lived in an assisted living facility, but his granddaughter Marcie looked after him when she could.

On his first surprise visit, Marcie came racing into the gorge in her car, apologizing profusely to Annie for George's arrival. She gave Annie her phone number, just in case George ever got too lost or out of control.

"You are not alone here!" George shouted into the void. "They never rest! They'll never let the past die! You are next! They come in with the tide!"

"Morning, George," said Annie, standing in the doorway of the main house. She had been eating eggs benedict with spinach and bacon at the kitchen table, listening to the latest episode of the *Tell Me About Your*

Book podcast when she heard the sputtering of George's moped approach.

She knew to speak to him in a calm, even tone. "There is no tide. Big flaw in your narrative here."

"They wear their skins! They'll take yours, too!" George continued, barely acknowledging Annie's presence.

"Do you want something to drink, George? Some coffee?"

"You shouldn't be here!" George rambled on. "Nobody should be here! This land was built on terror and madness. Blood is the only thing it wants!"

"Do you want to come in and warm up?" Annie called. "I'll get out the good doilies. We can watch a movie if you want. Have you ever seen the music video for Mary-Kate and Ashley Olsen's 'Gimme Pizza'? Even if you're not medicated when you watch it, you'll think you're high."

"Leave this place! Leave while you still can! Leave before the past catches up to you!"

"Okay, George. Good talk. Thanks for coming. There are refreshments in the lobby."

"This place is evil! Evil!"

Annie went back inside to her eggs as George wandered out in the open, hollering at the heavens. She texted Marcie to let her know that George was visiting, and would she mind coming to get him? Marcie texted back immediately, saying she was already on her way.

Annie went about her day while George ranted and raved in the distance. By the time Marcie arrived, George was nowhere to be found. His moped was still there. But no George.

"I'm so, so sorry about this, Annie," said Marcie. "He's supposed to be at the center but he keeps fooling them into thinking he's in his room. Today he put a bunch of those giant Jenga blocks under his covers and sneaked out. He would've been such an amazing escape artist. What a missed career opportunity."

"It's all right. I'd probably worry about him if he didn't show up every few weeks to preach the gospel that only he can."

"Grandpa and his madcap romps. He was upset because he wanted salt cod fritters and hash browns, and then they gave him Jell-O with shredded carrots in it, so he said his caretakers were trying to kill him."

"To be fair, only monsters put shredded carrots in Jell-O," said Annie. "Last night, I got one of those two-pound trays of shrimp and ate the whole thing by myself. I used to keep a can of frosting in my desk so I had a snack when I wrote."

"I'm equally horrified and impressed by that," said Marcie. Her eyes swept the surrounding area. "Where did he get off to?"

Marcie Squires was in her mid-thirties. Dark-haired, easygoing, and secretly talking Riverdance classes on Wednesday nights at the local community center, she worked at a consignment shop in Hartwell while she got her master's degree in business. She obviously loved her grandfather dearly. Marcie was the kind of person Annie and her girlfriends would be friends with.

Annie and Marcie walked past the houses, calling for George.

"Oh God, he could be anywhere," Marcie said, clearly trying not to panic. "Grandpa?"

They saw a figure wandering by the tree line and instantly headed in that direction.

"George!" Annie cried out, while Marcie yelled, "Grandpa!"

The figure disappeared out of sight as Annie and Marcie got closer to the trees. They called for George to no avail. They saw no one as they peered into the woods, though it would be difficult to see into the dense and seemingly endless forest.

24

Their heads whipped around at the sound of dead leaves crunching beneath someone—or something's—feet.

"Grandpa!" Marcie shouted.

The women stepped farther into the woodland, listening for any sound that would betray George's location. Animals chittered and scampered as the whoosh of wind reverberated around them. Annie hoped it was the noises of woodland creatures and not some forest monsters or cryptids.

"What is that?" Annie said, pointing toward the top of one of the trees.

A mutilated, gutted deer carcass was stuffed high above their heads, within the mass of brown branches. It had been disemboweled; its guts and innards spilling, its blood congealed down the side of the tree. Its black eyes stared lifelessly down upon Annie and Marcie.

"There's something you don't see every day," Marcie said, her voice wavering.

"How did it get all the way up there?" Annie had read about the wildlife that populated Gull Valley—black bears, red fox, gray fox, bobcat, Canadian lynx, coyote, the extirpated gray wolf, and eastern cougar comprised the majority of carnivores in Maine. None of them were known to stash their kills high above the ground—in treetops, no less.

It looked purposeful, not random. Not an abandoned kill stolen away and saved for later. The way it was arranged—it was like a gruesome, macabre warning. Abandon all hope, ye who enter here. You are not welcome.

Annie had only a moment to notice the symbol carved into the tree at eye level. Some of the deer's blood had filled it in, making it even creepier.

An image of a capital E fused to a capital K, like an emblem or spooky hieroglyph. Like something out of a movie about secret societies or alchemists.

25

George's scream jolted them from staring up at the rotted husk of the deer. It wasn't coming from within the woods. It was coming from the houses.

"Stay away from me, you devil!" George bellowed. "You demon! Get away from me! No! No, I won't! I won't go with you! I won't go!"

Annie and Marcie ran toward the sound of his voice. George burst out of the front door of the main house, stumbling toward them.

"I told them they can't have me," George rambled. "I told them. I told them I'm not one of them."

"Okay, Grandpa," Marcie said, putting her arms around him and exchanging a sympathetic glance with Annie. Marcie guided her grandfather toward her car.

George stopped, his eyes burning on Annie. "Don't ever whistle. Something may hear you and whistle back. They hear everything we say! They see everything we do!"

Annie was used to George's ranting and raving but he had never been this escalated before. For the first time, she was actually a little afraid of him.

"Do you want some water?" Annie asked feebly, then scolded herself for such a dumb question. Why do people think getting someone a glass of water when they're upset helps?

"It knows you," George hissed at Annie. "Don't look for it. They're angry that you're here."

Marcie got him into her car and gave Annie a wan wave. The sound of her car motor faded as Annie watched her leave the town. George's moped remained vacant in the middle of the dirt road that ran through Gull Valley. Annie put it in a parking space next to her car and Mr. Brisket's truck.

Music wafted quietly on the air. It was a hymn. Solemn, grand voices like a religious chant, singing over the sounds of a pipe organ and woodwind instruments.

26

Annie wondered if Mr. Brisket was listening to music. She'd never known him to do that. He had always worked without any outside noise or distractions. Annie's curiosity was piqued by the mellifluous tune, though her chest had slight pinpricks of fear. She didn't know why.

She followed the song down the road, passing each house, trying to pinpoint the source of the singing. The hymn grew louder and louder as she reached the double doors of the church.

She stepped inside. The music filled the room, echoing off of the ornate stained-glass windows and empty wooden pews. Melted candles lined the shelves next to a pulpit. Dust particles floated in the air, magnified by the sunlight shining through the doors. The entire room had a musty, wet smell.

Annie felt cold and unwelcome there; though it was a house of God, it gave off the opposite feeling. It was forbidding and glacial inside. Nothing about it felt like happy, good things happened there.

She walked between the pews, searching for the music's origin. She approached a giant, baroque wooden door. She pressed her ear against it, hearing the hymn through the door.

Was that Loretta Lynn's "In the Garden"? Annie's mother used to listen to that song on repeat when she was having one of her manic episodes.

She'd walked on eggshells around her parents. Her mother would put Annie in the tub with scalding hot water and scrub Annie's skin raw with a washcloth, muttering, "Not clean! You're not clean!"

She would lock Annie in the cold, dark, musty basement with The Under-the-Stairs Man, an imaginary murderer who lived beneath the staircase. Annie's mother had invented him in her own twisted mind, telling Annie he would kill her and steal her soul. Annie was a child then; she'd been convinced The Under-the-Stairs Man was with her as she screamed and cried, banging on the door for her mother to let her out.

Don't think about this, Annie told herself.

Annie pushed against the door to open it. It wouldn't budge.

The song stopped.

Annie paused. Listening to the quiet.

Clunk!

Wooden slats, once leaned against the walls, crashed to the floor behind her. Annie jumped back, startled.

She tried to open the door again. It didn't move an inch. Mr. Brisket had a skeleton key. She made a note to herself to have him unlock the door.

Her eyes fell upon the long-extinguished candles, their wax covering the shelves. Aligned on the shelves behind the votives were glass mason jars partially filled with now-rusty water. Inside each of the mason jars were small black-and-white photographs from the past, of people Annie had never seen before. Smiling, happy faces, posed in front of suburban homes or with friends and family. Each of the pictures was different, with unconnected individuals in each picture. As far as Annie could tell, none of these people knew each other.

Annie reminded herself not to let her imagination run wild. She'd bought a centuries-old ghost town. There were bound to be lots of weird, freaky things there. People, after all, were weird and freaky. That was part of the deal.

Annie headed back to the entrance of the church, pausing at the dried-out holy water font. She shuddered when she saw the inside of the circular stoup.

It was filled with extracted, rotted teeth.

CHAPTER FIVE

Since Annie had moved, she hadn't written a thing. She stared at her computer screen, hoping for inspiration. It never came. She knew Gary wouldn't want her to give up on her writing career, but she couldn't force herself to make the words appear on the blank page. Her next book was overdue to her editor and she'd been avoiding any and all meetings and contact from her agent.

Annie's agent had told her that she'd best make herself available for a Zoom call ASAP or else. Or else what? Annie wasn't sure. But she knew she had to have some pages or an idea to show, even if it wasn't her best work.

She was fortunate to make her living as a science-fiction writer. That was all she ever really wanted to be. Her books always had elements of space opera, romance, and thrills, and had built up an audience over the years.

She was going to do what her therapist always told her not to—avoid everything. But before that, she was going to eat her feelings. She went to the kitchen to search for leftover sour cream blueberry pie. After she ate and did her avoiding, she headed outside.

Her favorite building was the roller-skating rink. It was the first house, aside from the main one where she lived, that she'd had Mr. Brisket, Ms. Click, Jack, and Ben work on. They had repainted, cleaned, and repaired what they could for now.

She had no clue whose idea it had been to set up a roller-skating rink. Maybe a failed business venture? Maybe relinquished from the days of disco past? Whatever the reasoning, she loved whoever came up with it.

It had a countertop concession stand with a popcorn machine, soda fountain, snack bar, and a few tables, and red-laminated chairs at booths and banquettes. Shelves for shoes and roller skates, a small employee area, lime green-colored landline phone hanging on the wall, a foosball table, and an out-of-commission *Addams Family Values* pinball machine. Everything needed more mending and shining, but it was a usable—even cheerful—space.

When Annie needed to clear her mind and think, whether to relieve stress or collect her thoughts, she laced up her roller skates, plugged her computer into the electrical system, and blasted her jams over the giant speakers.

Annie locked the entrance to the roller rink and queued up her (as of yet, incomplete) Divas playlist— Debbie Gibson's "Only In My Dreams," Paula Abdul's "Vibeology," Madonna's "Into the Groove," Mariah Carey's "Fantasy," Rihanna's "Don't Stop the Music," Lady Gaga's "Just Dance," Britney Spears's "Stronger," Kylie Minogue's "Can't Get You Out Of My Head," Laura Branigan's "Solitaire," Janet Jackson's "Nasty," Cyndi Lauper's "She Bop," Kim Wilde's "You Keep Me Hangin' On," Belinda Carlisle's "Heaven is a Place on Earth," and Beyoncé's "Crazy In Love." She pressed play and skated over the smooth concrete floor, taking a deep breath as the music enveloped her.

Annie smiled to herself beneath the flashing neon, the glitterball sending sparkles over the rink floor, and gel-covered lights illuminating the room in reds, blues, greens, and yellows. Everything shone and reflected in the mirrored walls encircling the skating area. She felt like Olivia Newton-John in *Xanadu*. Like Linda Blair in *Roller Boogie*. It was nice not to feel like the sad, widowed lady for a moment.

As usual, her thoughts as she glided over the circular rink turned to Gary.

How Gary would laugh when she'd hysterically say, "Look at this bump under my arm," as if every ache, pain, and malady was the beginning of her end. How she'd hide his blood pressure medication in pieces of cheese or

30

peanut butter because he'd always forget to take them. How he set her Google word alert for the word "fart," so anytime an article on passing gas came up, she'd get a notification on her computer. How every time they watched the news, he'd say, "People who use the term 'moral compass' don't have one." Their day trips to Salem, Castle Island, The Lizzie Borden House, and Nubble Lighthouse. How he always said that he and Annie were going to be a sexy middle-aged couple, like Kelly Ripa and her husband.

The time he gave her a Sponsor a Highway certificate in her name for her birthday, thinking it was a genius gift. The time they were babysitting Alice's son, who asked for a bedtime story, so Gary read the blurb on the back of an *Olympus Has Fallen* DVD to him. How his favorite bands were The White Stripes, Talking Heads, Jimmy Eat World, Simple Minds, and Cheap Trick, although he never stopped listening to his beloved Time-Life Guitar Rock CD series. The way he couldn't stop himself from saying, "Pew, pew!" any time they played laser tag or Nerf guns with the nieces and nephews, telling everyone his spy name was Kale Caesar. How much he wanted to meet someone who worked for the postal police ("Stamp cop!" he would exclaim), as if it was the coolest job he'd ever heard of. How he was the only person in the world who seemed to remember the Molly Ringwald sitcom *Townies* and started a letter-writing campaign to get it released on physical media.

How he laughed. Gary had laughed all the time.

It was the small things about him that she missed the most. Although there were lots of milestones and big events they'd celebrated, it was the little details of their day-to-day life that she didn't want to forget. They would've celebrated their nineteenth anniversary this year, ten of them as a married couple.

Gary had been gone for two years. Two long, painful years. Annie never knew how quiet their apartment could be without him, how empty their once-shared space could feel. There were no words to describe the loneliness and grief that consumed her, especially the first few months when she'd had to readjust to life without him. She had been so alone and full of rage at the degenerates who'd stolen his life and his presence from his loved ones.

Annie had never been the type of person who had to have a man in her life to function. But this was different. She chose a life with Gary. Their lives were completely intertwined. He was the biggest part of her existence. And he had been taken away. Beaten and tied up and sealed in a blue plastic oil drum with holes in the sides so water could get in and sunk to the bottom of the Charles River.

Gary used to play YouTube videos of people vacuuming to make Annie think he was actually vacuuming the floor. He used to—

Who was that?

Someone—or something—stood off to the side of the concession area, visible as she skated past the opening from the rinks floor. A figure in a long black coat, hat, and scarf. Face obscured, half of its silhouette hidden by the wall.

She spun her head around as she skated. The figure was gone.

Crackle.

The speakers began to fizz and sputter, making firecracker noises. Static covered the music as the song waned in and out. The lights began to dim and fade.

She saw the figure again as she skated by. In a different spot, still partially obscured.

The song fizzled out as the speakers popped and sizzled. Mazzy Star's "Fade Into You"—Annie and Gary's wedding song—began to play.

She hadn't changed the music. The flashing lights around her became confusing and menacing, like the room was closing in on her. Her surroundings felt chaotic, overwhelming—like she was being swallowed by it. Her wedding song distorted in her mind as if it were a funeral dirge.

Boom!

The speakers exploded. The music stopped completely. The lights continued their up and down dance. Annie stopped skating, doing a 360 around the room.

There was nobody there.

CHAPTER SIX

Annie had gotten into a nightly routine. Before sundown, she'd go from building to building, making sure there were no squatters or other people taking up residence without her knowledge. She'd examine whether there was anything out of place. She'd double check that each window and door was locked and closed shut. She would triple check every corner, every closet, under the beds, and inside cupboards, ensuring that she was well and truly the only one who resided in Gull Valley. When it was time for bed, she'd type her password code into the keypad of the security box next to the front door. Access would not be granted to night callers.

It was her town, after all. Population one. She was the only resident, and she planned to keep it that way.

Mr. Brisket had warned Annie about how dark it got at night in Gull Valley, but the blackness that surrounded her felt almost impenetrable. The houses and structures that reflected the sunlight only hours ago were now so obscured by inky, opaque darkness that she couldn't even discern the outline of the edifice closest to the one she chose as her home base.

The only thing worse than the oppressive darkness was the ominous silence. Though there were sporadic sounds and calls from animals in the woods around her home, at night all of the noise seemed to stop. The faint hum of the generators permeated the eerie tranquility, but it was as if all of the animals and woodland creatures went into hiding as soon as the sun set. On the occasions there was a noise, every single sound resonated and reverberated as if on a speaker system; its location never entirely discernable, like its origin was somehow coming from every direction all at once. Sounds Annie could sometimes identify as an animal, others she had no clue as to who or what it came from.

And the shadows. Always the shadows. They danced around the buildings and at the tree line, moving as if they were desperately trying to avoid detection. As if they were ducking out of sight and didn't want to be noticed. Yet they were everywhere in the dark—black silhouettes against the even blacker night.

It was at nighttime when Annie truly realized how thoroughly alone she was. How far away from the closest town, the nearest safety of civilization, the bustle of people her move to Gull Valley had made her. How her old life and the person she used to be were no longer. How restless she was, searching for answers she would never get.

Even though she'd lived there for eleven months, she still hadn't gotten completely used to the sights and sounds of the nightfall around her. She thought of what Mr. Brisket, a man of few words, told her—always leave the outside lights on at night, and always lock your doors. Advice that seemed like an ominous warning, though he was clearly only concerned for her safety in a deserted land. But she chose to live there. She chose to stay. She'd learn to adjust to her new location and its mysteries and charms. She wasn't going to leave.

Annie stood in her front doorway, looking out into the surrounding night. Her gaze fixed on a spot next to the church, where she swore she saw a figure. It stood completely still, its features hidden and indistinguishable under the pervasive cloak of darkness. It could have been a trespasser; maybe a stray animal that wandered in from the forest around them. As Annie focused on the figure, the darkness played tricks on her eyes and became one imperceptible black space. She shook her head and laughed at herself, committed to the thought that her mind was conjuring an intrusive image where there was none. It was just the night.

Just the night, Annie.

CHAPTER SEVEN

Thump thump.

Annie awoke with a jolt, as if unseen hands had shaken her to consciousness. Her face was wet with tears; she couldn't tell if they were happy or sad ones. She was caught for a moment in the period between her dream and the hard truth of reality, as she realized she was in bed alone. The space where Gary would've slept was empty and cold.

The only sound in her room was the humming of the oscillating fan. She couldn't sleep without the constant buzz of her fan going.

In that instant, all of the memories flooded over her. The pit in her stomach came to life again. The realization of her situation sank into her bones. The how and why Gary wasn't in bed with her. The when, the where, the how long it had been since he'd lain beside her, reading Grady Hendrix's *The Final Girl Support Group* as she did an internet deep dive into the Max Headroom signal hijacking.

And the who—the who that were responsible for why Gary was gone. Those evil people who now sat in prison, getting free health care and three square meals a day. Those who were career criminals and should not have been walking the streets on the night Gary was murdered, who had received lenient sentences their whole miserable lives, so were free to do what they did that horrible night. Those who stood before the court, saying their empty, hollow words about how sorry they were for what they did and how they deserved forgiveness and a second chance. How they wanted to spend holidays with their families and children—holidays that Gary would never celebrate again. How they were "mentally ill," as if that made their horrific act okay, and they needed help—a lame excuse and desperate ploy that they pushed during trial but was never taken too seriously. Everything except them taking responsibility for their own actions—it was society, poverty, bad upbringings, poor parenting, life was unfair. The blame was everywhere else but themselves. The murderers who snuffed out Gary's life like he was nothing still breathed, could see their loved ones, and would be free eventually.

Gary was never coming back.

They weren't sorry for what they did. They were sorry that they got caught.

Annie couldn't fathom the idea that there was one person who was so evil and vile that they'd plan to rob and murder a stranger, let alone a group who shared the same lack of humanity. It was bad enough to know there was one psycho out there—but somehow, they'd found others who thought like them and had no hesitation in carrying out violent, corrupt acts.

And scum like that always had children, didn't they? The irony.

Annie's mind conjured up images of Gary at the bottom of that cold, dark river. What he must have been thinking and feeling. The sheer panic and terror that must have overwhelmed every fiber of his being. The knowledge that he was going to die a cruel, unusual, depraved death. Did his mind call out for help to a god that didn't answer? Did he think about her, how he'd never see her again? These thoughts swirled in Annie's brain constantly. He was gone; forever a victim, a statistic, his existence wiped away forever. Everything he'd ever said and done was erased from the earth, though not Annie's memory, by one chance encounter. He was a memory now. A painful one.

And for what? Thirty-eight dollars and an Apple watch he'd bought on Amazon.

She'd felt sadness and longing before, but after Gary's death, the feeling was like nothing she'd ever experienced. The absolute depth of pain, the abyss of despair and heartbreak. There weren't words that could properly explain.

It was just her and her half-empty bed now. She had never been a big sleeper, even when she was with Gary. These days, she was lucky to get two or three decent hours of sleep. Most of her sleep was restless and filled with nightmares about Gary. Him crying out for her to help, with those pleading eyes and pained expression. Him getting farther and farther away from her, as she ran to catch up to him. But she never did.

The upside to her insomnia was the abundance of time to renovate the town. She had hundreds of projects still on her to-do list. She had nothing but time now.

Thump thump.

Since she'd moved in, she'd had to adjust to the strange noises the house made at night. There were many times when she heard people talking to each other in hushed voices, coming from other rooms in the house. The thumping sounds that emanated from within the walls, as if somebody was pounding on the wood. Then there were the items that would go missing and reappear in random places, or objects that had moved somehow overnight, although Annie knew exactly where she'd put them. The sound of footsteps in other rooms, even though she was the only person there.

Each time, she checked that the storm shutters were secure, that the house was locked up tightly, and that nothing was out of place. She couldn't find an explanation. Not a rational one, anyway. Her mind conjured up the ideas of ghosts, spirits, phantoms, and apparitions haunting the centuries-old landscape. Surely people had died in her house. Maybe their souls were still here. She wasn't ready to entertain that thought in a serious way.

Once, she opened her closet to find a pale, faded yellow dress hanging among her clothes. The dress, which was clearly once bright like sunrays, had its color eroded over time and seemed to be made from an itchy, unflattering combination of burlap and polyester.

Annie's wardrobe consisted mostly of jeans, T-shirts, and flannel shirts; she'd never been a clotheshorse or fashionista and only kept a few dresses when she moved. There was no explanation for how the dress appeared in her closet. Annie reasoned that Ms. Click may have thought it was hers and hung it up for her.

More disturbing was when she was taking old pictures, photographs, and paintings off of the walls after she moved in. One black-and-white photograph, which seemed to be taken sometime in the 1970s, featured a group of men, women, and children smiling for the camera. All of the men wore the same shirt-and-pants combination, and all of the women wore the same dress type—exactly like the yellow dress Annie had found in her closet on a hanger.

Old houses have quirks, her Aunt Dolly told her. *You haven't been yourself and you've been through trauma, your mind may be forgetting things or imaging things*, her friends told her. *Trauma manifests in a myriad of unexpected, sometimes overwhelming, but controllable ways, and this could be a residual effect*, Dr. Crews told her.

Yet the scratching sound in her walls, right near her bed, made her sit straight up and listen intently. This wasn't a manifestation. Not her imagination. Rats? She'd seen them around the buildings and had once watched a terrifying documentary on how they were legion and traffickers of chaos and destruction.

Please don't be rats. I don't want to be eaten by a giant rat with beady red eyes and cheese breath.

Tap!

A plunk against her bedroom window made Annie turn to look outside. The moon was still up, daylight a few hours away. Her bedroom was on the second floor, so she wasn't expecting to see someone there—though the thought had crossed her mind.

Creak.

Did someone just walk past her bedroom door, down the hallway? Annie shuddered and steeled herself. She was alone. Her mind, her vivid imagination, her think-the-worst brain was playing tricks on her. That was not a shadow of a figure that passed by her open door.

Was it?

Click.

The light in the bathroom down the hall turned on, its rays peeking into the darkness of Annie's bedroom.

Click.

The light turned off.

Click.

The light turned on again.

Annie reached between the nightstand and her bed to grab Jason Statham (her baseball bat), slowly climbing out from underneath the sheets. Trying to be as quiet and undetected as possible.

She did not see the figure—crouched in darkness in the corner of her room by the top of her bed—stand in the darkness behind her, watching her exit her bedroom.

She crept into the hallway, eyes focused on the light that streamed from inside the bathroom. There was no shadow to accompany it, no sign of a person, no noise.

She took one step, two, three, toward the bathroom door. She was almost at the door frame.

Click.

The light turned off.

Annie grasped Jason Statham tightly in her hands, steadying her breath, trying to quell her pounding heart. The house was completely silent.

Click.

As soon as the light flicked on again, Annie jumped in front of the bathroom door, the bat raised and ready to strike.

There was no one there. No person, no unnamed thing, no maniac prowler. The bathroom window was latched shut. The shower was empty. No one behind the door.

Annie let out a relieved sigh, laughing at herself. It was only faulty wiring or an electrical glitch, she told herself. She double checked the bathroom cabinets for any intruder, but everything was normal. As normal as it could be.

"Front door open," the security system intoned in its robotic voice from the computer speaker downstairs. "Front door open."

Annie charged down the stairs, ready to pounce on whatever stranger danger had disrupted the sanctity and security of her home.

The front door was, in fact, wide open, but there was no sign of any forced entry or random weirdo skulking about her home. She quickly shut and relocked the door, checking the security video feed to find out who was milling about her house. One of the cameras was angled directly above the front door.

Aside from the occasional animal that strolled past, there was no human activity. She saw the moment the front door opened inward, as if of its own accord, but nobody exited her house. As if the wind had just blown it open. There was nothing, no one, on the Ring doorbell camera.

It was a windy night, Annie reassured herself. The house was quiet and calm, no other indication of intruders or anything out of place.

Despite her relief that there was no evidence of any hostile presence in her proximity, Annie wondered how all three locks on the door were unlatched, allowing the wind to blow the door open. She was certain she had locked the door.

Her phone buzzed. She held it up, seeing she got a text message.

From Gary. Gary Rourke, her husband. Her husband who had passed away almost two years ago.

It read: *I can't wait to see you again. It's so lonely here.*

Annie didn't cry or scream, though all of the nerves and organs in her body cried out for it. She was numb. Her thoughts raced and went blank at the same time. This wasn't possible. This was a sick, cruel joke. She had gotten rid of Gary's cell phone before she moved.

She wasn't going to get any sleep now. After she combed the house, turning every light on in every room as she and Jason Statham searched for the mysterious home invader, she gave up and made herself a pot of coffee.

She tried to call Gary's cell phone, but all she got was an automated message saying, "The number you have reached is not in service. Please check the number and try your call again."

Holy shit, I am crazy.

Annie would've loved to hear Gary's voice again, even if it was only his outgoing message on a long-disconnected cell phone. Even under these strange circumstances.

She stared at the giant, empty fish tank on the shelf. Currently, it was filled with an empty popcorn tin, some door knockers, and a pair of festive New Year's Eve party glasses that had the date "2000" emblazoned in sparkly boldface over the frames.

Annie wrapped herself in a big comforter and watched *We're the Millers* then *Sisters*—the Tina Fey/Amy Poehler movie, not the scary one. No way was she watching

42

anything scary. She ate cold pizza that she dipped in canned queso sauce, letting the Roomba vacuum up the crumbs. She only got off the couch once she saw the sunrise break over the horizon.

CHAPTER EIGHT

Eudora Click, Mr. Brisket's associate, worked in estate sales. She had taken on the responsibility of helping Annie tidy, wash, polish, and de-gross the houses in Gull Valley. She went through many of the personal effects left by previous inhabitants and put them in boxes for Annie to sort through. She organized, catalogued, and took stock of inventory found.

Ms. Click wasn't a maid or a housekeeper, but her particular set of skills came in handy for this large project. She used to work for a housecleaning business, specializing in hoarders' houses, and had contacts who brought giant metal waste containers and took them later to landfills. Gull Valley was their newest project.

"I made some turkey tetrazzini for you," Ms. Click said, as she put a plastic container of food in the refrigerator. "I made you an icebox cake too, it's in the freezer."

It wasn't Ms. Click's job to feed Annie, but she would occasionally show up with prepared meals. Annie wondered if it was Ms. Click's way of making sure she was eating properly.

A thin, pleasant woman in her early seventies, Ms. Click arrived three times a week to assist Annie in whatever indoor tasks, cleaning, and arranging she needed. Like Mr. Brisket, she wasn't extremely talkative. Annie figured it was a generational thing—the older folks being hard workers and all that.

That day, when Ms. Click arrived, she noted how peaked Annie looked and insisted she go upstairs and get back in bed. Ms. Click was going to work on the inside of the office that day. She would be sorting through the plentiful stacks and filing cabinets of paperwork and junk that had been left there for decades upon decades.

Ms. Click pushed aside a box filled with dog and cat collars, tongue depressors, empty cleaning supply bottles, ripped up wrapping paper, stacks of old newspapers and magazines, and Alyssa Milano's *Teen Steam* workout videocassette. Annie didn't want to think too hard about what happened to all of the animals whose collars somehow ended up empty in Gull Valley.

Annie hadn't quite made it off the couch. It might have been that she was overtired, or she just wanted to talk through her experience from last night, but she uttered a question to Ms. Click that she felt would certainly make the older woman believe she was truly insane.

"Ms. Click, do you believe in ghosts?"

Ms. Click paused from taking inventory of old the books and various music media on the shelves in the main house's living room.

"Ghosts? Oh yes, there's ghosts all around us," Ms. Click said matter-of-factly. "When my son was little, like two or three, he would wake up at three a.m. screaming and holding his head and saying, 'My head! My head!' We'd ask if his head hurt, and he'd say, 'No, Mama, I can't find it.' Years later, we found out the man who'd owned our house before us had his head cut off in a freak accident in our garage. And my mother swore that our toaster was haunted growing up. Make of that what you will."

Annie stayed silent and waited for the rest.

"Gull Valley is about 176 years old, if my math is correct," Ms. Click continued. "There's so much history here, and so many souls have passed through. When the riverbed dried up years ago, they found thousands of bones and people's remains. It's bound to happen. This whole place is a graveyard, in a sense. In the really old days, in the wintertime, the ground was too frozen to bury their dead, so the bodies would be wrapped in burlap and stored beneath the buildings until the spring. The land, the trees, the ground—they soak up all the feelings and

45

memories and events that happen. They echo and vibrate through them, even now. It seeps into the ground and stains the land. They remember what came before, even if we don't. Think of all of the people who have come through here, visited—many not respecting this place at all, throwing raves and parties. It leaves a mark. Did you see something last night? Is that why you look about as happy as a wet dishcloth?"

"Is that even a saying?" Annie asked.

"Not the takeaway here, dear," Ms. Click shook her head. "Just like my daughter. Full of piss and vinegar. You could call Sheriff Meeker and have him come by. I'm sure old Harv would love driving in from Hartwell and going on a ghost hunt. I guess the question is, do you believe in ghosts?"

"Metaphorically or literally?"

"I don't think they care much if you believe in them. They're still there. People in town, many of them won't step foot in Gull Valley. They say this land is cursed."

"If this land is cursed, why do you come here then?"

"I don't believe in curses." Ms. Click held up a compact disc. "Is this yours? Hoobastank. Never heard of them. I'm more of a Mannheim Steamroller gal."

"Not mine," said Annie. "But if you find any Vengaboys, keep it."

Ms. Click came a little closer to where Annie sat on the couch. "It's a primordial, ancient fear—to be scared of the dark, of the unknown, of strangers. Just remember, there's nothing in the dark that isn't in the light. Except vampires."

Ms. Click's tone was so serious that Annie couldn't tell if it was her attempt at making a little joke. She couldn't figure out why, but at that moment, she felt closer to Ms. Click.

"Is there a Mr. Click at home?"

"Oh, he went on to his eternal rest years ago. The Lord rang the bell and he answered. He and I worked with Stewart—Mr. Brisket—on lots of projects. We worked here several times over the years, actually. We worked for the previous owners, the ones who were here right before you. And a few owners before that. He always thought people who lived out here were crazy, but I'd tell him it was none of our business why and they must have their reasons. Isn't that so?"

Annie nodded. This was the longest conversation she'd ever had with Ms. Click.

"Would you look at this?" Ms. Click said with awe. She held up a well-worn, tattered book with a blood red cover. "This is one of the manifestos The Felicitous wrote in the 1970s. Wow, I never thought I'd see one of these. You're probably too young to remember them, but they lived here for quite a few years."

"I've heard of them, but I don't know much about them."

"They weren't as famous—or infamous—as some of the other counterculture groups of that era, but they had quite a few members, if I remember correctly. Nobody in town wanted anything to do with them. They all thought they were a bunch of dirty, free-love hippies. And I guess they were. They had their own self-sustained community here, like a little village. They protested against the government and the war and advocated for civil rights. They were a response to the hypocrisy and constraints of conservative America—a rejection of traditional family values. At least, that's how they started off."

"What happened to them?"

Neither Annie nor Ms. Click were aware of the figure that stood silently at the top of the staircase on the second floor as they talked. Whatever it was—human or otherwise—waited perfectly still, not making a sound as it listened to them talk. Though the sun was rising, the second story had many dark places to hide in plain sight.

"Nobody knows. They all disappeared. Sometime in the 1980s. They lived here, and there were lots of rumors about nefarious and sinister things they were doing, and then one day, poof! They just vanished and haven't been heard from since. I mean, most of them would be either really old now or dead. This book contained all their ideas and rules and tenets. They'd pass it out to get more followers. Almost like how people use social media to get someone to join an MLM nowadays. They were 'spreading the word,' as they said. I guarantee there's tons of true crime podcasts out there on the subject if you're interested. Wow. Gar Mooney would love to get ahold of this. He's the history professor over at Briggs College."

"Wait," Annie said. "Why were people in Hartwell so afraid of them if they were a bunch of bohemians and beatniks? Because of the era? Because they were different and people are afraid of different? Because flower children and nonconformists named Eucalyptus and Frampton are so scary?"

"You're simplifying something you don't know much about," Ms. Click said. "It was a long time ago. Things were different back then."

Ms. Click held up several more compact discs and vinyl record albums (none that belonged to Annie) to weigh in on—The xx, Patty Griffin, Aerosmith, Liberace, The 1975, Keane, Mumford and Sons, Creedence Clearwater Revival, Greg Laswell, The Lumineers, Maggie Rogers, Bastille, Lord Huron, Oh Wonder, First Aid Kit, Milky Chance, Broods, Arcade Fire, Peach Pit, Hozier, The Innocence Mission, The Rolling Stones, Beastie Boys, The Human League, Fiona Apple, Beck, Yo-Yo Ma, Punch Brothers, Straight No Chaser, The Trans-Siberian Orchestra, on and on.

The "trash" pile was way larger than the "keep" pile, not because Annie didn't appreciate the found music, but because her goal was to downsize and declutter. She made a mental note to look into Amazon and eBay—among other sites—to set up a seller account. Gull Valley was full of things she could sell and maybe make some money from. She now had a surplus of antique wall sconces that she didn't want or need.

"It may just be an old wives' tale," Ms. Click said as she tossed a No Doubt record aside. "But if you put a bowl of water in the center of your kitchen table overnight and your house is haunted, supposedly the water will be bubbling in the morning."

Ms. Click stopped talking and went back to sorting through the books and records, signaling that their conversation had come to its end.

CHAPTER NINE

Annie had Sloane on speakerphone while she got dressed for her day, throwing on blue jeans and a well-worn flannel over her Letters to Cleo T-shirt. Ms. Click was at the office working and Annie triple-checked that every door and window in the house was locked up, even though it was bright and sunny outside.

Annie's mind was preoccupied. She kept thinking about how Aunt Dolly always told her that there were no villains in life. Everyone was just trying to get by. "You're the villain in somebody's story," Aunt Dolly would say. There were always shades of gray. Nothing was simply black and white.

But Aunt Dolly had been wrong. There were villains. Gary's murderers were villains. There was no excuse, no justification, no reasoning for what they'd done, except the evil in their hearts and blackness in their souls.

Annie had never realized how dark and vile the world was. Even with all of the bad things that had happened to her, she'd always held on to hope and the idea that better days would come.

Bad things—truly bad things, like murder and the absolute destruction of a person's security and safety— were something that happened to other people. Something that someone would read about in the news or see on television. It didn't come knocking on her door.

Until it did.

Nowadays, Annie felt like she was covered in those "fragile" stickers that movers and delivery people placed on packages.

What was the point of loving people? They would only be taken away, like they always had been for her. What was the point in loving someone, knowing they were only with you temporarily? Knowing that at any moment, someone or something could come along and destroy it all?

There were plenty of animals who felt no attachment to their offspring and simply survived without feeling or emotion. Why couldn't she be like them? Why were humans the ones who suffered from the pain of loss and heartbreak and longing, fear and terror, and the realization of how horrible things could truly get?

"Okay, here goes," Sloane said, bringing Annie out of her thoughts. "*The White Lotus*, *Upload*, *I'm Sorry*, *Special*, *Veep*, *The Americans*, *Derry Girls*, *The Righteous Gemstones*, *Better Things*, *Loot*, and *Modern Family*. Are you writing this down?"

"Mmhmm," Annie said, her hands completely devoid of paper and pen.

Sloane Doyle had become a great friend. Sloane listed the television shows she recommended so Annie could distract herself from melancholy. She appreciated Sloane's tireless efforts to lift her spirits, especially since Sloane had her own grief.

When they'd met in their bereavement group, Sloane shared that her husband and children had been killed in an accident. Like Annie, she'd been trying to repair the emotional and mental damage. Neither woman was always successful, but it was good that they had each other to lean on. A shared commonality of sorrow and anguish that they hoped their loved ones would never experience.

Annie went through a period of a few months where she developed agoraphobia and would not leave her house. Sloane had asked Annie to come meet her at her real estate office for lunch, or to take a walk in Boston Commons, but Annie couldn't do it. So, Sloane would send huge grocery orders from Wegman's to Annie's house and have Italian subs from J. Pace and butterscotch pies from Betty's Pies on Goldbelly delivered, just to make sure she was eating.

There'd been a particularly terrifying incident, where she hallucinated that Gary was alive—rather not alive, but undead and in their house. Walking around, dripping wet, covered in detritus and mud from the bottom of the river he was killed in. Half-aware, half-zombie-like, stalking Annie throughout their home.

It had happened more than once. Dr. Crews informed Annie that this was not a far-fetched or unheard-of trauma response. Annie couldn't trust her own mind. The hallucination was a catalyst for her to leave and start somewhere anew.

As soon as she told Sloane about it, Sloane dropped everything and came over with red velvet cake, *Bob's Burgers* Mad Libs, and Richard Simmons' *Sweatin' to the Oldies* tape and made sure Annie was eating, laughing, then working off all the sugar they consumed.

Thankfully, Annie's friends loved Sloane and accepted her wholeheartedly into their group. If Annie loved Sloane, that was enough of a recommendation for them.

"You ever wonder about these people who propose to their significant others at people's weddings? Who does that?" asked Sloane. "Or announce their pregnancies? Talk about main character syndrome. May those people walk the road ahead of them barefoot and may the road be made of loose Legos."

Sloane had her own real estate business in Boston and didn't talk about her deceased husband and children often. It was her own way of coping with the loss. Annie never pushed the subject. She was just grateful to have someone who understood her. As much as Annie loved her group of friends, they didn't know what it was like to lose someone the way she had.

"I think I'm going to try and make dishwasher salmon. Have you seen this recipe online?" Sloane continued. Sometimes her way of dealing with her harder days meant a stream-of-consciousness chattering. "Have you ever smelled your keys? They smell super weird. And have you ever thought about how many passwords we have for so many websites? I'm rambling today. I have a lot of clients who are really, really pushing my chaos buttons."

"That's okay," said Annie. She had already filled Sloane in on her frightening night. They'd decided that Annie would call Dr. Crews and make sure the medications she was on weren't having hallucinatory side effects and that Annie would buy a carbon monoxide detector, just to be on the safe side. There had to be logical, reasonable explanations for all the weirdness she'd been experiencing. "Have you done your daily affirmations and breathing today?"

"Yes. I'm still trying to breathe. I danced it out to Lisa Lisa and Cult Jam's 'Head to Toe' when I got dressed this morning, wrote in my journal, practiced gratitude, did a mud mask, packed up my husband's tie collection and mock turtlenecks, watched a little bit of Swayze in *Road House*, and admitted to my Telehealth therapist that I have an unexplainable and overwhelming sexual attraction to Guy Fieri. And I don't mind saying that I look pretty good today. And I have to go. Client meeting. Are you going to be okay? Are you practicing your self-care and mindfulness?"

"Yes, I'm fine, I promise." Annie laughed. "Thank you for everything, Sloane. If I get overwhelmed, later I'll make a blanket fort for a safe space and smell the fall leaves scented dish soap Ms. Click got me."

"You should get a dog. You're all alone out there and it'd be a great companion. You could train it to steal cheese at picnics. Do people get the zoomies or just animals?"

"I'll think about it. Sometimes lately, I feel like if I woke up in a tub of ice missing a kidney like that old urban legend, I wouldn't even be that upset about it. It would be such a good excuse to have a nice vacation."

"Remember, we fake it until we make it. We basically gaslight ourselves into happiness. Stop, drop, and roll, but into happiness. We are our repeated behaviors."

"That sounds healthy. Have a great day, Sloane. Love you."

"Love you," Sloane said, ending the call.

Annie pulled back her sheets and comforter to make her bed. She drew back, struck with fear and confusion.

Beneath the covers was a mound of dirt, rocks, sticks, tree bark, and various flora from the forest. She didn't do that. There was no way. She had not gone crazy. Someone had to have been in her house. There was no other explanation.

She wasn't crazy. She wasn't crazy. She knew it.

Her next call that day would be to Dr. Crews.

CHAPTER TEN

Annie sat at the kitchen table in the main house, the uneaten apple turnover she made for breakfast sitting on a plate before her. She was determined to shake away any bad thoughts, any fears, all of last night's weirdness. She could, she would, she should, she told herself.

Annie thought about a night she and Gary were on the couch, watching an episode of *Girls*. In it, Hannah and Jessa went to a restaurant that specialized in dozens of different flavors of rice pudding, and nothing else.

Gary sat straight up and said, "There's a place that only sells rice pudding? We're going!"

It confirmed to Annie what she already knew—anyone that excited about rice pudding was the right one for her. Gary was meant for her.

She smiled and laughed to herself, running her hands along the tabletop.

She'd refurbished the table when she moved in, along with several other pieces that remained when she arrived. The buildings in Gull Valley were littered and filled with old furniture, clothing, gadgets, outdated electronics, stuffed animals, outmoded phones, appliances, artwork, books, jewelry, watches, pictures, wallets, passports, driver's licenses, photo IDs, keys, old money, maps, blueprints, vintage china sets, toys, and thousands of remnants from the previous owners who'd come and gone.

People's hopes and dreams; their pasts, connections, and links to the lives they once had in Gull Valley—Annie saw it in the forgotten objects. Sometimes she'd invent stories for the fictional people inside her head based on the things they left behind.

She was still in the process of taking inventory, uncovering whether or not any of these items had value, deciding what things could be saved and reused, and which ones would be thrown into the bonfire.

Her computer was on. She should get some work done, but she had no inspiration or motivation. That had all been ripped away from her after Gary died.

She had a Zoom meeting in a half hour with her "girl gang," as Gary had always called them. The women who she'd been friends with since college—Jess, Sally, Laurie, Alice, Ginny, Chris, Trish, Nancy, Kit, and Rachel—who supported and loved her no matter what. They'd seen each other through the good and bad times; the relationships, promotions, life changes (big and small), challenges, deaths, divorces, careers, children, and everything else, down to the silly, minute details of everyday life.

Annie's forty-seventh birthday was rapidly approaching. That day's Zoom call was undoubtedly to convince her to come to Boston and celebrate with them. She appreciated it, though her answer would be a firm but loving "no."

A series of loud knocks at the door snapped Annie from her thoughts. She figured it must have been Mr. Brisket, Ms. Click, or Jack and Ben, the handymen he brought with him to rebuild and restore the structures in Gull Valley.

When she opened the door, her smile faded. There were five costumed kids on her front porch, holding out empty plastic pumpkin buckets.

There was an awkward moment of silence while Annie tried to make sense of what was going on.

"What in the blue frick?" she said, louder than she'd intended.

"Trick-or-treat!" the child dressed as an astronaut said, raising his empty pumpkin bucket. Annie couldn't see any of their faces beneath their cheaply-made papier mâché masks. Next to the astronaut stood a vampire, a ninja, a dinosaur, and a robot.

Pinned to the shoulder of each of their costumes was a small, vintage black-and-white photograph. Each photo had a different person featured, though the subjects of the photos all shared dead-eyed, hollow stares at the camera.

She leaned out of the door frame to see where these children's parents were. There was nobody else outside— no cars, no other grown-ups. Mr. Brisket hadn't arrived back from town yet. The nearest neighbor was on the other side of the mountains. Despite the mild, unseasonably warm October weather, it would still be a treacherous and lengthy hike into Gull Valley due to the rocky, foliage-dense terrain, which kept most people from impromptu jaunts into Annie's radius.

"How did you get here?" Annie asked. "Where are your moms and dads?"

"Trick-or-treat!" the astronaut repeated, shaking his pumpkin bucket at her.

"You know it's not Halloween yet, right?" Annie said, keeping the door as a buffer between her and the children. She couldn't read their expressions beneath the crudely colored and pasted masks they wore.

"Is this a joke? Who put you up to this?" Annie asked hopefully, to no answer. She thought of telling them that they were on private property, but she doubted it made any difference to them.

The children shook their pumpkin buckets at her in unison.

"Hold on," Annie said, shutting the door and heading to her kitchen. Her mind raced. Who were these kids? Why did they think it was Halloween? Why did they make her feel so uneasy? Why did she feel like if she didn't give them something, there would be dire consequences?

She couldn't find any candy or sweets. She hadn't done her weekly run into Hartwell to get groceries and supplies or check her P.O. box for whatever books and household necessities she'd ordered from Amazon. She rummaged around in the cupboards for anything suitable, all the while unnerved by the children at her doorstep.

The children were still holding out their Halloween buckets when she opened the door again. She didn't want to get too close to them, so she launched the items as best as she could directly into their buckets—cans of creamed corn, Chunky soup, little jams and jellies from Stonewall Kitchen, cans of Hormel baked beans, Dinty Moore beef stew, and boxes of Rice-A-Roni. The children stood motionless for a moment, staring at Annie.

"You should get home before it gets dark," she said, trying to control any tremble in her voice. "Your parents are probably worried about you."

They didn't make a sound. They stared up at her for an uncomfortable amount of time, then turned, buckets full, and walked toward the tree line. They were headed away from civilization. Toward the thick forest full of bountiful, bright foliage.

Annie watched as they stopped at the edge of the tree line. The astronaut, vampire, ninja, dinosaur, and robot turned slowly, gazing in her direction. Their emotionless, crude masks gave Annie a shudder through her body. What were they doing?

She waited in the doorway until they made their way into the forest, disappearing out of view. With a giant exhale, Annie locked the door behind her and started back toward the kitchen. She paused when she saw it.

A smiling jack-o-lantern sat on her coffee table, staring right at her. She sucked in a frightened breath.

Her feet kicked something. She looked down to see an empty pumpkin bucket. Just like the ones those kids were holding before.

Annie looked over her shoulder and scanned the room, trying not to overreact or panic, then ran to the windows and peered out into the daylight. Nobody was there.

"And that is how horror movies start," she whispered to herself in disbelief.

She made a mental note to ask Mr. Brisket to do a double-check for errant campers or hikers in the woods. She hadn't heard any quad four-wheelers or motor vehicles in the distance. Those kids couldn't have gotten to Gull Valley on foot, could they? Unless there was some kind of camper or RV in the woods she hadn't heard or seen. Maybe a family passing through. There were tons of trails and paths in the forest surrounding her property. Technically, the forest was also hers by deed, but she was too stressed out and paranoid from her visitors to press that issue.

Annie checked the tree line through the windows several more times before she returned to her apple turnover.

CHAPTER ELEVEN

Jack Henderson and Ben Russell always brought their fully-stocked toolboxes, extra wood, and various home improvement gadgets every day to work on the seemingly endless list of repairs, renovations, and refurbishments required to restore Gull Valley to its original glory.

Since the weather had cooperated that day, both men worked on repainting the guest houses, often referred to as the living quarters. After that, they'd get started on mending any holes in the roofs and floorboards.

Mr. Brisket instructed them to take any loose, unusable wood and scraps to the woodchipper, where he was decimating rubble and waste.

Jack and Ben were in their mid-thirties and fit from years of strenuous construction and remodeling work. They knew Mr. Brisket from various jobs he'd hired them for over the years, but this was the biggest and most important one he'd tasked them with so far.

They'd been working at Gull Valley for eleven months now. When they first started working for Annie, they couldn't get as much accomplished as they wanted because of the harsh winter weather. After the warmer days of spring and summer, they accomplished many of the tasks they were assigned but still had an endless to-do list. Each of the buildings were in various stages of remodeling and rebuilding.

The nineteen buildings consisted of the main house (where Annie lived), the mess hall (a cafeteria-style kitchen with a giant pantry), church, bathroom area with multiple showers, main office, storage facility, woodshop garage filled with tools and woodworking equipment, infirmary (a medical center with a vintage apothecary sign on the front door), laundry room (with several washers and dryers), roller-skating rink, movie theater (complete with medium-sized movie screen, plush red theater seating, and a concession stand), library, schoolhouse, one boiler room-like building that housed the generators (a main one and several back-ups), and five guest houses, each of which had eight separate bedrooms.

The fifth guest house was situated closest to the tree line. In between that distance was a junkyard, filled with scraps of metal, wood, barbed wire, and old appliances, pieces of cars, electronics, housing, siding, and the like, all of which would be taken to the county landfill trip by trip, or repurposed in Mr. Brisket, Ms. Click, Jack, and Ben's reconstruction of Gull Valley.

Through Jack and Ben's handiwork (and Mr. Brisket and Annie's assistance), these buildings were coming back to life.

They'd done everything they could to get the place up and running, from carpentry, reupholstering old furniture, digging holes, fixing the water lines, rewiring the electrical, installing the security system of cameras and flood (and motion detector) lights outside the houses while setting up in-home security alarms on the doors and windows of the main house, and removing any mold or asbestos. They were nowhere near done. Many of the buildings needed heavy-duty overhauls. Annie had hired Jack and Ben indefinitely. As long as she was paying for it, they were just fine with the work.

They restored a fenced-in garden area with decorative arbors, next to large communal picnic tables beneath a wooden pergola. They set up trail cameras along the paths in the woods that took photos on a timer, ideally to snap cool shots of the local wildlife.

There was a spacious parking lot next to the garage, where Jack and Ben parked their jacked-up pick-up truck. In another six months, Gull Valley wouldn't seem like the lonely, creepy ghost town everyone described it as.

Word spread that Annie had bought the town. People were naturally curious as to who she was, what her deal was, why she'd bought a ghost town to live in alone. Jack

61

and Ben never really had a definitive answer for them. Annie kept mostly to herself, and they noted that she often came across as sad and detached. Most of their conversations, though polite and friendly, were about what repairs or work she needed done. She always had food and beverages for them, got them gift certificates to Lowe's Home Improvement store for Christmas, and waved every morning when she saw them before she went on her walks, so Jack and Ben never took her disposition personally.

Jack and Ben had been best friends since they were kids. They even dressed similarly; their work clothes consisted of toolbelts, paint-stained jeans, brown Carhartt boots, and T-shirts. Jack sported an AC/DC shirt, while Ben donned a Dokken *Dream Warriors* one. They lived and worked together. Jack secretly hoped they'd be featured on *Maine Cabin Masters* someday.

As they headed to the schoolhouse, Jack lit a cigarette and said, "Hey, what does 'fungible' mean? I do not get cryptocurrency."

"Replaceable by another similar item," said Ben.

"Did you know that television stations used to make commercials and emergency broadcasts ahead of time, in case some horrible event happened, like war or a bombing or global catastrophe? They'd have their news anchor do mock transmissions in preparation for terrible disasters."

"By the power of Grayskull, what is this?" Ben said, stopping at the porch to the schoolhouse.

A set of black footprints lead up the steps to the door. They look as if they'd been burned into the wood, a foot-shaped pattern singed into the floor.

"You're cleaning that," said Jack, pushing the schoolhouse door open.

The schoolhouse was a quaint, rundown relic from the 1900s. It was easy to picture a classroom full of kids learning with their schoolmarm. The room was littered with disused rulers, pencils, books, notebooks, and a 1910

Farmer's Almanac haphazardly splattered on and in wooden desks.

A poster pinned above a corkboard was entitled "Emotions," and featured corresponding facial expressions to the proper feelings.

Several black-and-white class photos lined the walls. In many, the teachers' and students' faces had giant X marks through them. Some people's visages had been burned away by a flame, leaving black stains on top of their bodies. An arithmetic poster hung on the wall, ripped and dusty, beside the photos and kids' drawings and paintings.

Jack inspected one of the crayon-colored sketches, of a boy with his family and dog, standing beneath a smiling sun.

"Hm," he said. "I don't really get the artist's point of view on this one. What's the focus? What's he saying here? Is he celebrating the nuclear family, or condemning it?"

The teacher's desk was cluttered with homework assignments and class lists of a bygone era, with desiccated apple husks spread over the teacher's notes.

Across the blackboard, written in chalk, was a word:

ERICA

"Hey, look! Do you need a neti pot?" Jack said, holding up a teapot-sized container. "You get all those springtime allergies, this could help."

"No, Jack, I don't want a used neti pot," Ben said, completely grossed out by the thought.

Ben fixated on the staircase in the corner that led to the second floor. They were made from alternating half-treads, each stair cut in half and staggered, made to dictate which foot someone ascended with.

"These are witches' stairs," said Ben. "My grandma told me about these. It's an old New England folktale. It's an old superstition that witches couldn't climb them, so if they came into your house, you could hide upstairs until the sun came up and the witches had to return to their houses in the woods."

"You know I hate stuff like that," Jack moaned. "Don't tell me that kind of stuff. Remember when we first started working here and somebody had smeared all the doors with that red goo or whatever it was? Like they were marking the place."

"All right, next movie night we can watch *Sweet Home Alabama* or whatever else you pick so you don't have to hire a professional cuddler to be your thunder buddy at night," Ben said. "Now I don't know if I should tell you about lizard people. Supposedly, they walk among us."

"What?" said Jack, already horrified.

"What?"

Creak.

The floorboards above them groaned as if someone were walking around above them. Jack and Ben went silent.

"What if that's a witch?" whispered Jack.

"Shh!" said Ben.

"What if they're trapped up there by the witches' stairs?"

Creak.

"Hello?" Ben called up the staircase. "Mr. Brisket, you up there?"

No answer. Only silence. Ben took a big breath and turned back to Jack.

"*Rrrraaaaawwwwwrrrrr!*" Jack roared. He was dressed in a giant dinosaur costume, reaching out his clawed arms toward Ben in a monster pose.

Ben jumped back, startled. "Not funny, you gray poop! You mosquito! Where the hell did you get that?"

"You're really good at insults, Ben." Jack's voice was muffled under the large dino head. He pulled it off,

64

laughing. "Ah, someone must've left this here. It smells like the inside of a tauntaun."

Ben laughed. "You better hope whoever left that here didn't have some communicable disease or skin condition. There's probably bacteria in there that's going to turn you into one of those *The Last of Us* fungus people."

Jack shuddered, panicking. He hurriedly began to rip the dino costume off of himself. "Do we have any hand sanitizer?"

Plunk.

Plunk.

Plunk.

A red-and-blue ball bounced down the witches' stairs and landed at Ben's feet.

"That's gonna be a 'no' from me, dog," Ben said, as he rushed Jack out the front door.

Neither man saw the lower half of a figure appear on the stairs as they ran out. Only the figure's legs were visible, stopped on the staircase; its upper body blocked by the ceiling.

It didn't descend the staircase any farther.

Ms. Click glanced up from the pile of boxes she had stacked in guest room one, watching out the window as Jack and Ben fast-walked away from the schoolhouse.

Jack was still half-inside the dinosaur costume, trying to shimmy out of it as he attempted to keep pace with Ben.

"What in the ever-loving applesauce are these two idiots up to?" Ms. Click said, shaking her head, then went back to cleaning.

CHAPTER TWELVE

Though it was a blustery day outside, Annie wanted to paint over some of the graffiti that was sprayed over several of the buildings in Gull Valley. She brought a bucket of white paint and a brush to the office and began to paint over a large, black, spray-painted message that read *Gad loves you!*

Annie laughed. Gad? Gad loves you? Who, Josh Gad? Who writes this stuff, his PR people? Fans? Why is he worried if I know he loves me?

She was aware that the graffiti artist meant "God," but she still chuckled every time she saw the misspelling. Too bad the spray paint didn't come with a spell check. It would be forgotten, painted over soon.

Next, she'd tackle the *Cival War is Coming!* graffiti next to the Josh Gad PR.

Cival War? Was it a war on spelling? Should she bring a dictionary and Grammarly app to the battlefield? Would librarians and scholars bring the Dewey Decimal System and heaviest books to the fight?

Annie didn't hear the car that pulled up and parked in the parking lot, but she did see the unfamiliar man and two children wandering around her property, over by the movie theater. He seemed to be looking for someone or something, while the kids ran around the spacious dale, giggling and playing.

"Can I help you with something?" Annie called out curtly, headed toward him.

The man smiled and waved, walking toward her. They met halfway across the gorge. Annie tried not to sound too welcoming. She didn't appreciate trespassers.

"I'm sorry. Do you work here?" the man asked. He was tall, in his late forties, with salt-and-pepper hair and beard.

"Who are you?" Annie asked, not in the mood for small talk.

"My name is Cal Reardon," the man said, shaking her hand. Though Annie was trepidatious, Cal gave off a very warm, friendly vibe. He pointed over at the two kids darting between buildings. "Those two rascals are mine. Ruby and Rex. Ruby's eight and Rex is six. They're my partners in crime. I didn't realize anyone was here. I thought Gull Valley was abandoned."

"I'm Annie Porter. I own Gull Valley."

"Oh, I'm so sorry. I'm trespassing. I thought all the signs saying, 'Keep Out!' were put up by people from Hartwell. We just wanted to take a look around. I'm actually doing research on Gull Valley for a book I'm writing. I'm not actually a writer, though. I'm a tech geek. I'm trying something new. Kind of like John Goodman in *King Ralph*. I figure, like the kids say, 'YOLO.' We have to YOLO so we don't get FOMO."

Annie felt at ease with Cal's affable energy and big smile.

"I tried to YOLO once. When I was a kid, I went swimming less than a half hour after I ate. It was quite a scandal. I was the talk of the neighborhood. I was always an edge lord."

"That's incredibly heroic. I look forward to the documentary they make about you someday."

"Thanks. I was thinking more of a Hallmark movie, with Pamela Anderson playing me, clearly. I'm a big fan of her work on *VIP* and think she could really capture my essence," Annie said. "Now, not to be completely rude, but what can I help you with?"

"I really didn't mean to intrude," said Cal. "I just wanted to take a look around and get some pictures. We can leave if you want."

His two kids ran over and sidled up next to him. Ruby carried a stuffed Squishmallow unicorn in her hands. Her coat was adorned with Celine Dion pins and buttons. Her winter knit cap had the word "Celine" written on the brim. She had a big smile and bright blonde hair that peeked from under her beanie.

Her brother Rex was a chubby-cheeked bundle of energy, grinning up at Annie. He held a potato in his hands.

"That's Rex's potato," Cal said, noticing the question on Annie's face. "It's his best friend. They go everywhere together. Even to church and bed. We were playing hot potato and he really got into it."

"Hot potato!" Rex said, laughing hysterically.

"Yes, I have considered calling a child psychologist, but also yes, I was a way weirder kid. I used to carry around a spatula. His name was Mr. Spatula."

"I'm weird?" Rex said.

"No, no, not at all, bugaboo. You're super cool and awesome, like a Zamboni driver."

"Zamboni!" said Rex, holding his potato up to the sky in celebration.

Annie beamed at the kids. She and Gary loved children but had decided against having any. Not with the parents Annie had. She didn't want to pass on any of her broken genetic legacy. She and Gary wanted to travel and grow old together. They were okay with that. They made for a great aunt and uncle team. They'd give all their love to their nieces and nephews, blood related or friend related. That had been the plan anyway.

"Do you have a dog?" Ruby said.

"No," said Annie.

"Do you have a cat?" Ruby said.

"No," said Annie.

"Do you have a spider?" Ruby said.

"Well, not on purpose," said Annie. "I'm sure these old buildings have lots of them. As long as they leave me alone, I'll leave them alone."

"Annie!" Jack called from the doorway of the library, a look of concern on his face. "You good?"

"Yes, thank you, Jack!" she called back to him. Jack nodded and went back into the library to work on whatever project he'd been at today.

"Ruby and Rex like helping their old dad out on all his projects," Cal said proudly, hugging both kids to him. Ruby and Rex smiled widely, their little eyes beaming up at Annie.

"Do you like Celine Dion?" Ruby asked Annie. She unzipped her coat to show off her Celine Dion T-shirt. "Look at my shirt!"

"Well, of course I do. Who doesn't? Cool shirt!" Annie answered.

"I have all of Celine's songs on my Apple music. I have seen her in concert three times now. I'm the president of her Celine Kids fan club. Do you want to hear me sing 'It's All Coming Back to Me Now'? That's my favorite song of hers."

"Uh, maybe later?"

"She likes Celine Dion!" Ruby attempted to whisper to her dad, but it was louder than her speaking voice.

"You're a really bad whisperer!" Cal teased her in exaggerated sotto voce. He turned back to Annie. "We were watching an Olivia Rodrigo video on YouTube and a Celine video popped up right after. She's been obsessed ever since. We listened to the Celine Dion Spotify station the whole drive over here. You 'stan' Celine, right, Carrot? That's what you kids say."

"Dad," moaned Ruby. "Nobody says that. You're weird."

"I figure there's much worse things out there she could be into," Cal laughed, then tried to have an aside to

Annie. "She's been asking a lot of questions about S-E-X lately—thanks cable and kids at school—and I'm in a boat without oars here."

"I can spell, Dad, and I know what that is," Ruby said.

"Oh yeah, well, what is it then?" said Cal.

"I'm not telling you," Ruby said, turning back to Annie. "Do you think I can shoot my music video here?"

"Sure," Annie said, not entirely convinced. "Let me talk to your dad about it."

"We're a very musical family," said Cal. "I play bass in a Toto cover band. We're called Risotto."

"This is Betty," Ruby said, holding out her unicorn for Annie.

"Well, hello Betty," said Annie, petting Betty's soft head.

"I'm the photographer," Rex said proudly, holding up a camera that was almost too big for his hands. "It's my job to take pictures of this place. Dad is paying me in Minecraft Lego car kits."

"As you can tell, they're both painfully shy," joked Cal. He looked down at Ruby and Rex. "Why don't we get out of Annie's hair? We can go to the Circle K and get some scratchers and see if we won millions of dollars. What do you think? Then we'll go to Denny's and get a Grand Slam breakfast. Do they still have those?"

"No, you're fine," Annie relented. "Feel free to look around. I'd appreciate it if you didn't wander through the buildings. There are people working and it could be dangerous for the kids. Um, were you and your kids here earlier? Five kids showed up at my door in Halloween costumes."

"I only have two kids."

"There were five—you know what, never mind," Annie stopped herself. No need to unleash her crazy on a stranger.

"Are you going to be our new mom?" Rex asked.

"Whoa, buddy," Cal said. "Let's not scare Annie away. We usually wait until the second time we meet a lady to ask her that. Sorry about that. They never see me talk to any women besides their Aunt Lyla. You're like a beautiful mythological woodland creature to them."

"Do you have any kids?" Ruby asked.

"No, no kids," smiled Annie.

"Come on, guys, you're killing me here," said Cal. He grinned over at Annie. "You can unsubscribe to these two anytime you want. But I'm stuck with them. Right, you monkeys?"

Cal hugged and tickled both of his kids. Ruby and Rex burst out laughing.

"Are there any bears around here?" Rex asked seriously.

"Yep, there are," said Annie. "But there's no grizzly bears in Maine. And most bears are active from April to November, so you're safe. They're mostly hibernating right now. Besides, I've never seen one around here."

"I don't like bears," Rex said. "They do drugs and drugs are bad. And then they eat your face."

"He saw the commercial for *Cocaine Bear* and now Rex has a phobia of bears, huh?" Cal said, squeezing Rex. "I guess I can thank Cocaine Bear himself for helping teach my children the dangers of drugs. Coke is so '80s anyway. You know you're not supposed to be watching scary stuff anyway, Rex. Like the other night, when I caught you watching that Edward Krueger movie."

"It's Freddy, Dad," Rex said with a sigh.

"This Halloween, Ruby is going as Celine Dion and this guy is going as the giant critter ball from *Critters 2*. Rex is a little horror movie buff. He loves the scary stuff. Again, thanks cable! We have to listen to John Williams's *Jaws* theme when you go to bed at night, huh?" Cal said proudly. He addressed the kids. "You hungry? You want to go get some pizza with peas and mayonnaise on it?"

"Nooooooo!" Ruby and Rex both giggled.

"What do you call the bad guy with the mask in *Halloween*, Rex?" asked Cal.

"Herman!" Rex answered decisively.

"That's his name? You sure?" Cal prodded.

"Yes, it's Herman," Rex said, giving Cal a look as if he had two heads. Rex turned to Annie. "Do you know the story about the girl who always wears the ribbon around her neck? Her head falls off!"

"Hey, spoiler alert!" said Cal.

"I don't like scary stuff," Ruby said, clutching Betty tighter.

"That's okay," Cal said, pulling Ruby closer to her. "You're a sensitive soul. Ruby's more of a *Shrek*, *Wreck-It Ralph*, *Moana*, *Ratatouille*, *Tangled* kind of gal. We watched *The Goonies* and you got scared, so you had to sleep with Dad for the next two weeks, huh?"

"Can we have a lemonade stand out here?" asked Ruby, preferring not to recall the terrors of *The Goonies*.

"I don't think you'd get many customers this way, Carrot," said Cal.

"Can I put paper lanterns up on a string between the buildings?" Ruby continued.

"Maybe some other time," Cal said. "We should probably get out of Annie's hair. Thank you for letting us talk your ear off. I'm going to take these two to the fish spa and have the fish eat the dead, dried skin off their feet."

"Eww! No, Dad!" Ruby and Rex protested.

"You guys can stay a little if you want," Annie said. She didn't feel like Cal and the kids meant any harm. "I mean, get your pictures. You probably know more about this area than I do."

"That's okay?" Cal asked hopefully.

"Yeah, yes, of course. It's okay. It's just me here. There are no townies here 'cause I'm the only one. And Mr. Brisket, Ms. Click, Jack, and Ben—they're helping me rebuild, but they're all really nice people."

"Okay, kids, go play!" Cal instructed Ruby and Rex. He shouted after them as they took off. "Do not go into the woods and stay where I can see you! Best behavior! I love you! Hearts and farts!"

CHAPTER THIRTEEN

Jack and Ben moved heavy boxes out of their way as they made space for floor repairs. As Ben lifted one of the boxes, its contents tumbled out all over the floor. He hurriedly shoved the scattered papers and items back into the box, pausing when he uncovered what looked like a scrapbook.

"What you got there?" Jack said.

Ben opened the scrapbook. Each page was full of old newspaper stories on The Felicitous, alongside black-and-white photographs of members of the cult. The pictures ranged from snapshots of the cultists smiling and communing with each other to their many protests and staged public dissents.

"The Felicitous," said Ben. "That sounds familiar."

"Look at these stories," Jack said, pointing to the headlines. The articles were a mixture of salacious gossip rags and more reputable news sources.

Felicitous suspected in massacre at local wedding

I rented my guest house to a former cult member!

Living in fear: How one member of The Felicitous escaped

How well do you know your neighbors?: Cult members infiltrate society

Break-ins and burglaries tied to The Felicitous

Calista Asylum doctor's family missing

The Felicitous: Happy campers or depraved murderers?

Missing hikers in Gull Valley estimated in the hundreds

Who is Laird Hubbell?: A peek behind the curtain

Home invasions linked to cult members

Former cult member performs murder-suicide of own family

Bodies found in Gull Valley with bizarre markings, ritual slaying suspected

The ghosts of The Felicitous still haunt me: A survivor's account

Hartwell residents unsettled by cult member's new home in Gull Valley

"What are you two up to?" Ms. Click said from the doorway behind them.

Jack and Ben smiled at Ms. Click. She was always kind to them, though they both got the impression she found them rather dim.

"It's an old scrapbook about The Felicitous," Ben said, showing it to Ms. Click. "Someone kept all of these old reports and pictures."

"It says here that they were a Bigfoot UFO Satan sex cult," Jack said.

"None of that is true," said Ms. Click. "Don't believe everything you read."

"It says here that they sacrificed babies and inbred with each other and ate people," said Jack. "And that they spilled blood to feed the land. Oh! And that Laird Hubbell had two penises. Maybe one was good and one was evil."

"Does that sound reasonable or logical at all, Jack?" Ms. Click said. "There's a lot of memories here. You can throw that in the burn pile."

"Are you sure?" said Ben. "This feels like a part of history."

"It's a part of history a lot of people want to forget," Ms. Click said. "People don't like to be reminded about painful memories."

"Did you live around here when The Felicitous were around?" said Jack. "My mother used to tell me stories about them to scare us."

"I did," Ms. Click said. "People used to warn us to lock our doors and hide our kids when they'd come around. The townspeople in Hartwell used to blame every bad thing that happened on them. People say a lot of things."

Ms. Click lowered her eyes toward the scrapbook, as if to double down on her request to destroy it. Jack and Ben looked over the scrapbook once more. Ben tossed it into the box.

"Why don't you boys come help me with the generator?" Ms. Click said. "I need you to make sure it's in peak working condition."

"Yes, Ms. Click," Jack and Ben both said and followed her out.

"You know, you're the reason why she thinks we're morons," Ben whispered to Jack.

A figure emerged from its hiding spot. It walked over to the window and watched Ms. Click, Jack, and Ben as they walked away.

It reached into the box and took the scrapbook.

CHAPTER FOURTEEN

Jordan Caffrey was taking a break from the pressures of work and stress of daily life. He had been a nature lover and an avid camper and hiker his entire life but had never been to the forests of Gull Valley.

Until now.

He was happily overwhelmed by how expansive it all was, how the woods seemed endless. And they were—miles and miles of green trees and brush with trails in every direction.

Jordan had camped in the woods the night before but decided to go off trail for his second night. Using the daylight and a compass, he strayed from the main path and walked through the trees, searching for the perfect desolate area to camp at.

He did not notice the two people chained to trees as he walked by. They had been left there, in the middle of the woods, to die and never be found. Their bodies were practically skeletons, their flesh and meat having been picked apart by woodland animals.

Jordan paused when he came across the tiny, fenced-in burial ground. Most of the tombstones were simply wooden crosses with people's names etched into the slats. The majority of the death dates were between the late 1960s to the 1990s. He had no clue who any of the people were; he had never read about the makeshift cemetery in any of his research on traveling the Gull Valley woods.

Jordan made a mental note not to camp too close to the graves and carried on for another hour, selecting a relatively flat circle of land to set up his tent.

There was no one around for miles. Jordan wanted it that way. He wanted complete isolation and to be as far away from the human race as possible. He had his cans of pork and beans and his water; he didn't need much else. He had done dozens of solo camping trips before.

As he put his tent together, Jordan wasn't afraid or nervous to be alone and so far away from civilization, from help, from people.

He resumed his search for a perfect campsite.

CHAPTER FIFTEEN

Cal snapped photographs on his iPhone as Annie walked with him around the property. She explained which building was which, and offered whatever information she knew about each house, which wasn't particularly much.

"What do you do for a living, Annie?" asked Cal.

"I'm a science fiction writer."

"Oh, wow, that's impressive. Anything I would have read?"

"I don't know. What have you read? My biggest seller was *Beyond the Black Hole*."

"*Beyond the Black Hole*," Cal repeated thoughtfully. "Okay, Annie Porter, I'll have to buy that one. Sounds awesome."

"Oh, I don't write under the name 'Annie Porter.' I use a pen name. My literary agent said 'Annie Porter' sounded too much like the name of a character in a Meg Ryan romantic comedy. It'll be under 'Errol Greaves.'"

"Errol Greaves? That is a serious name."

"Science fiction sells better if people think a man wrote it, unfortunately for me. I told her that Ursula K. LeGuin and Octavia E. Butler would disagree, but I had no power and wanted to be a writer. I use my husband's picture in my 'About the author' section."

"Errol Greaves? He sounds like a swashbuckling space pirate. I'd want to be a guy named Errol Greaves."

As Annie and Cal walked, a figure watched them from inside the church, its face close to the window but obscured by the reflection of the sunlight against the glass. It radiated rage and anger, eyes filled with hatred and rancor.

Annie and Cal stopped outside the main house.

"Is there a specific reason you're writing about Gull Valley?" Annie asked.

"Uh, actually, a documentary crew reached out to me," Cal said, putting his phone in his pocket. "I'm sure you know that there used to be a cult that lived here. They didn't call themselves a cult, but that's what they were. Um, well, my parents were in the cult. The Felicitous. I was actually born here. That's how I met my wife. Her parents were cult members here too, and years later, we met at a group run by cult deprogrammers. I mean, neither of us was in the cult or believed in any of that nonsense, but we had friends and family who still did, even though The Felicitous disappeared sometime in the 1980s. Ah, God, is this freaking you out?"

Annie didn't really know if it was or not.

"Oh man, I'm freaking you out," Cal sighed. "I'm sorry. It's a lot, I know. I've dealt with it my whole life. Well, you should know that you'll probably get some correspondence or a call from some filmmakers who want to film here. They've reached out to family members and friends of the people who believed in The Felicitous. My parents got out—they left a while after I was born—but there was always something 'off' about them my whole life. They're both gone now."

Annie still didn't say anything. She was listening.

"You should know I'm relatively normal. I'm a little weird, but good weird. I wear bolo ties and play the baritone horn and buy Groupons for Cirque de Soleil and my favorite song is 'Waiting for a Girl Like You' by Foreigner, just like everybody else."

Annie chuckled to herself. Cal had good energy and an honest, positive vibe. And she knew all about weirdness and trauma. She tried to set her judgment and fear aside.

"Good weird," Annie said. "I relate to that. I grew up with my Aunt Dolly mostly. She raised me. My parents were also very 'off.' It's not easy. Can I ask you a personal question? You said you met your wife at that deprogramming meeting. Are you guys still married?"

"Oh," Cal said. "She passed away a couple of years ago. It was a really bad accident. Closed casket and all that. It's been really tough on the kids. But it's given me time to practice all-time classic Dad lines like, 'I'll give you something to cry about!' and 'Don't make me pull this car over!' My wife, Mara—she was an amazing lady, but she had some problems she was dealing with. Don't we all? She loved those kids. There's always been speculation whether her accident was intentional or not. Oh wow, I'm sorry. I'm just dumping all this insane information all over you. I'm an over-sharer. It's a really bad quality. I can't even help myself. I just open my mouth and can't stop the verbal diarrhea. I always say I'm going to be a man of mystery and just make small talk. Instead, my brain spews out my life story in detail."

"Really? I couldn't tell," said Annie. It was nice to have someone to talk to, to take her mind off things. She liked Cal's good-natured energy. She needed some of that herself.

"When things get really bad, I thank my lucky stars and remind myself that at least my kids aren't ugly," laughed Cal.

"I get it," Annie said. "Sometimes I think I'm just a sick, sad, depressed pretzel, all twisted up inside. Maybe we all deserve a booze piñata—something we get to take out all our frustrations and aggressions on, then at the end, we get alcohol."

"Do people still do the sprinkler when they dance?" Cal said, trying to break the tension with a joke. He got more serious for a moment. "Do you mind if we visit again? I'll give you my number and I promise I'll text beforehand. We'll try to stay out of your way and not destroy anything. I mean, I can't promise anything with these two hooligans. If you want, we'll bring over snacks and a movie to say thank you. Have you seen *Surrogates* with Bruce Willis? That's one of our favorites."

"Dad! Dad!" Ruby and Rex shouted as they ran back toward him and Annie. "We saw so many birds!"

"Birds aren't real," Cal teased them. "That's how people spy on you!"

"Look what we found!" Rex said. He held up a wooden totem with the symbol of the E and K.

"We didn't find it!" said Ruby. "The man gave it to us."

"He told us not to tell anyone," said Rex.

"Dad doesn't count," Ruby protested.

"What man?" Cal asked, trying to mask his worry. "What man, Rex? Ruby?"

"The man over there," Ruby smiled, pointing toward the tree line. "He was hiding behind a tree and said he had something to give us. He said he wants us to meet his friends."

Annie and Cal immediately craned their necks and squinted their eyes to see the tree line. From their distance, they couldn't make out any figures or strangers. Only the leafy green trees, their branches clacking together in the wind.

Cal held his iPhone up and opened the photo app. He zoomed in as far as the camera would allow, granting him the ability to see the tree line. He didn't see any unfamiliar individual—not that he expected the person to be familiar.

"I don't see anybody," he said. "You guys aren't making this up, right? We talked about fibbing. Like when we play Taco vs. Burrito and you make up your own rules so you can win. We don't tell lies in this family, right?"

"Swedish Fish and Bugles are part of the four major food groups, Dad!" Rex insisted, clearly holding on to a lie he was still sensitive about.

"It could have been Mr. Brisket. He gathers branches and chops wood for the woodpile over there," Annie said to Cal, although she didn't sound convinced. She addressed Ruby and Rex. "Was he young or old?"

"He was old, like you and Dad!" Ruby said.

"What's 'eclectroshock'?" asked Rex,

"Electroshock," Cal said. "It's...when you get a perfect bowling score. Where did you hear that word?"

"The man said the doctors gave him eclectroshock," Rex said. "He must have really high bowling scores."

"Yeah, that guy, he's quite a bowler," Cal said uneasily.

"Can we go bowling today?" Ruby said.

"The man said the doctors gave him a lom-bom-tom-be, too," said Rex.

Cal and Annie listened while actively searching the area with their eyes. The man? What man? Who was this man?

"Did this man mention if he had LSD in his corn flakes this morning?" Cal said.

"What?" Ruby and Rex said.

"Hey, guys," said Cal.

"What?" Rex and Ruby said.

"Knock knock."

"Who's there?"

"Interrupting cow."

"Interrupting co—,"

"Mooo!" Cal cut off their response. Rex and Ruby burst into giggle fits.

"What does this man look like?" said Annie.

"I don't know," said Rex. "He's got big eyes."

"Are you sure this isn't an imaginary friend you guys are making up?" asked Cal.

"He's real!" Rex said. "He said he lives in the woods and he doesn't like us being here."

"Well, this got creepy fast," Cal said. "We passed Creepy Lane a long time ago and now we're on Diarrhea Boulevard."

"He said he'll come by our house later and knock on the window to let us know he's there," Ruby said.

"No one's coming to the house, Carrot," Cal said.

"What if he wants to visit?" said Ruby.

"Then you tell him he smells like shame and bad decisions and crocodile pee and he'll run away crying," said Cal.

"Crocodile pee!" laughed Ruby.

"We are all together and the only visitor you'll have tonight is a big bunch of cows jumping over the moon and taking you to Sleepyville," Cal said.

"Dad, cows don't jump," said Ruby.

"Hey, guess what?" said Cal.

"What?" Ruby and Rex said.

Cal let out a huge, atomic fart. "Did you hear that duck? I think there's a duck somewhere on Annie's property! Where is it?"

"Daaaaaaaadddd!" Rex and Ruby said, bursting into another giggle fit. Cal looked over at Annie, a little embarrassed at himself for farting in front of her.

"Whatever works, right?" Cal shrugged. Annie shrugged back.

"I'll have a talk with Mr. Brisket and Jack and Ben," Annie said. "If it's them playing a prank, I'll tell them to cut it out. I can check the trail camera later to see if there's any hikers or campers who thought they were being funny here."

Annie told herself that's all it was. Gull Valley had tons of outdoorsmen come through every day. She couldn't stop that, even if she owned part of the land.

"Okay, it's definitely time to go now," Cal said, taking the totem out of Rex's hand.

"Please, can we keep it?" Rex moaned.

"No," said Cal. "This is not yours. It belongs here."

"No fair! You never let us have anything!" Rex stomped his feet.

"I know, I know, your lives are so hard," Cal said. "Like when you got to go to the wave pool with the boogie boards I got you, and when we went to meet Forky from *Toy Story 4*, and got you all that silly string, and bought you all your Pound Puppies. Call the wahmbulance. Nine-wah-wah! Kids with the saddest lives in the world, party of two! Your table is ready!"

"Okay, Dad, we get it," said Ruby. She leaned toward Annie and utilized her whisper-voice, which was not a whisper at all. "Dad's going to take me to the Barbra Streisand concert when she goes on tour. She's my second favorite after Celine. He doesn't know we're going yet."

"Yeah," sighed Cal. "Most kids her age are into Barbies and horses. We've seen *Yentl* 704 times."

"I know all the words to 'Papa, Can You Hear Me?'" Ruby said. "I'll sing it for you!"

"Maybe later, Carrot. Say goodbye to Annie. We gotta go." Cal arched his eyebrows at his beloved offspring. "There's a sixty-year-old gay man living inside my eight-year-old daughter."

Cal handed Annie the totem and she put it in her pocket.

"I know this is off-topic, but is the moon ever going to collide into the earth?" Ruby said, her face deadly serious.

"What? No. What? Who told you—what?" Cal said. "Let's go. Stop worrying about the space time continuum or whatever Ms. Frizzle and *The Magic School Bus* is telling you. Great books, by the way."

Annie laughed. "It was really nice to meet you, Ruby and Rex."

"Will you be okay with some lurker in the woods?" he asked Annie.

"I'm sure it was just Mr. Brisket," Annie said. She wasn't sure.

Cal gave Annie his business card and thanked her, rounding up his kids. Ruby instinctively hugged Annie. She hugged right back. They waved goodbye cheerfully as Annie watched them walk back to their car. She overheard Cal ask the kids if they wanted to go to Jimmy John's for subs, to which they enthusiastically responded.

As soon as the car started, the sounds of Celine Dion's "The Power of Love" blared on the speakers through the closed windows. Annie laughed to herself. She waved as their car pulled away and disappeared into the ether that was the miles-long single-road exit out of Gull Valley.

CHAPTER SIXTEEN

Annie decided to get her weekly shopping trip in Hartwell done early, since the events of the previous night unnerved her. Interactions with other humans would do her a world of good. Simple transactions and nothing heavy or stressful.

She spent the day checking out Hartwell's local businesses. An antiques store called Curious Goods. A local, old-fashioned, retro vintage curio shop named Slausen's Lost Oasis, to browse through comic books, trinkets, candy, jewelry, hardware, home goods, snow globes, historical reproductions, and the like. She wandered around at the Park Plaza Mall and stopped to get an Orange Julius, then off to Walnut Lake Market for Chipwich and Drumsticks ice cream treats for later.

When she arrived back home, a pepperoni and onion pizza in her hands for dinner, Annie found a piece of paper—clearly torn from out of a book—pinned to her front door. She read it with trepidation.

Tenets of The Felicitous:
1. *Bishop Laird's word is the one and only*
2. *Rejection of government and societal laws and mores*
3. *Community is key*
4. *Our way of life is to be protected by all means necessary*
5. *We are best as a whole*
6. *Remorse, guilt, and shame are useless emotions*
7. *Personal possessions belong to all*
8. *Traitors will be exiled*
9. *Music, art, and knowledge are celebrated*
10. *We are your family*

Annie crumpled the page in her hand and threw it in the wastebasket. She didn't know if someone was messing with her or if she had gone off the rails. It would do her no good to let her brain think up every twisted scenario around every strange event.

Annie set herself up on the couch in the cozy entertainment room the previous owners had built and she remodeled. She went through the leftover DVDs and Blu-Rays to find something to watch and take her mind off of dark thoughts (she considered *Knight and Day*, *Uptown Girls*, *Failure to Launch*, *Bride Wars*, *Date Night*, *Untamed Heart*, *What Happens in Vegas*, *Garden State*, *Little Miss Sunshine*, or *Four Weddings and a Funeral*), sticking to films without excessive violence or scares, or films that reminded her of Gary. Annie was afraid if she watched something grim or gory, it would somehow trigger "off-balance" feelings in her, and she needed to relax.

She threw the *P.S. I Love You* DVD directly in the trash bin. Not because she disliked the movie, but because it was way too close to home.

She recalled what Ms. Click told her earlier in the day. After she made sure the house was securely locked and shuttered, she filled a large glass bowl with lukewarm water and placed it on the center of the kitchen table. She felt completely ridiculous doing it. But who was to know except her?

She settled on a double-feature of *The Princess Bride* and *One Crazy Summer*, then fell asleep on the couch seventeen seconds into the first movie. As Annie slept, she was unaware of the presence in the room with her. Its shadow cast across her as it moved throughout the room. She never stirred as the figure made its way through her home, keeping its existence hidden from her.

Annie sat up startled, sucking in a deep breath. It took her eyes a moment to adjust to the pitch blackness around her. She was still on the couch.

All of the power and lights had gone out while she was asleep. The house groaned and creaked from the wind outside, setting Annie's nerves on edge. She'd have to restart the generator.

Drip.

Drip.

Drip.

The sound of a leaky faucet, water hitting a hard surface, echoed and plinked through the house.

Faint light emanated from the kitchen. Annie didn't see anything else unusual but she was certain she hadn't left a lantern or flashlight on. She pulled her blanket off and stepped quietly onto the floor.

Her feet kicked something when she stood. She jumped at the sound of a clunk and rattle. She turned the light on her iPhone on, shining it on the ground.

Every one of the photographs she'd hung—of her, Gary, her friends, Aunt Dolly—had been stacked by the couch. She had kicked them when she got up, sending them scattering.

She swept the room with the light. She was alone. Her attention was brought back to the light in the kitchen. She made several small, deliberate steps toward the light source.

Drip. Drip. Drip.

Her mind raced. Was someone there? Was it really ghosts? Was some psycho waiting around the corner to strike? Was someone trying to drive her out of her house? Maybe a former owner or someone who used to live there who had nowhere else to go? Someone who was trying to drive her crazy?

Was it Gary? Could his spirit actually be reaching out to talk to her, letting her know he was there with her, wanting her to know he was all right and she would be too? Or was she slowly losing her mind?

It didn't matter at that moment. She crept around the corner and choked back a cry.

On the kitchen table was a birthday cake. Forty-seven candles, all lit and only slightly melted. White frosting, two layers.

Written on the cake in blood red gel were the words *Happy Birthday Annie.*

The manifesto Ms. Click found, written by The Felicitous, lay right beside the cake.

The bowl of water was overturned on the table. The water trickled on to the floor, creating the pervasive "drip" sound.

Another light, off in the distance outside, made Annie rush to the window. Off by the tree line, a beam of light flared quickly then stopped. Again and again. Start, stop, light then darkness. Like Morse code.

As if someone answered, another light—this one across the valley gorge—flicked on and off, like the two lights were having a conversation back and forth.

She considered grabbing the telescope, another leftover curio from a former owner, to see what was out there.

Bang!

Something slammed hard against the side of the house.

Fuck this. She snatched up her coat, car keys, and credit cards and dashed outside. She didn't even care if the door was locked behind her.

She stopped dead in her tracks.

There were several footprints—almost too many to be from only one person—in the mud around her house.

"Nope," she said out loud, rushing to her car.

Annie drove to Hartwell and checked into a nice hotel. As she got underneath the covers of her temporary bed, her phone lit up. It was a text message from Gary.

It read: *Why did you leave me here all alone?*

Though it was nearly four a.m. and nobody she knew would be awake at that hour, she sent texts to her girlfriends and Aunt Dolly to let them know where she was staying and that they needed to have a Zoom meeting to discuss the disturbing events of the past two days.

CHAPTER SEVENTEEN

Jordan Caffrey had put out the fire at his campsite and settled into his tent hours ago. He had texted his wife and kids to let them know he was safe, though the cell phone reception was spotty at best in the almost two-hundred square mile expanse of the Gull Valley forest.

Jordan had kept his clothes on and slept atop of his sleeping bag that night. He couldn't pinpoint why but he'd had an eerie, unsettled feeling all day. Despite his uneasy feeling, he convinced himself that he was being silly and paranoid. He would relocate his campsite once the sun rose.

Though tired, he restlessly dozed in and out of sleep. Jordan's mind kept going back to the deadfall trap he'd passed earlier in the woods. A large boulder was balanced on top of sticks; underneath, an animal carcass in the center. In theory, the trap was set by hunters to trick animals into feasting on the animal's remains and triggering a mechanism that would cause the sticks to give way and crush the prey beneath the falling rock.

Yet the one Jordan saw was much bigger, much more elaborate, than ones meant to capture and kill smaller prey. It looked set up to catch something larger.

Something larger, like a human being.

Jordan tried to clear his mind and sleep. He had never been afraid of the woods before. He wondered why tonight, of all nights, that fear crept over him like a snake wrapping around his body. Jordan wasn't afraid of wildlife or the supposed spirits the haunted Gull Valley. He feared people more than any of those things.

After a few minutes, his eyes opened wide. He heard the unmistakable sound of footsteps and movement in the forest around him. Not the sounds of playful animals frolicking or foraging but the deliberate, definitive sound of something on two legs walking around.

Jordan realized that the woods were strangely devoid of animal activity. He hadn't heard any of the nocturnal animals for hours. The only noise was of branches and dry brush crackling beneath someone's feet.

He was well aware of how sound traveled in the woods, especially at night. But this was different.

Crunch.

Crack.

The sounds of someone approaching were too close for Jordan to dismiss. In the pitch darkness of his tent, he fumbled for the zipper to the opening flap and slowly raised it. Jordan peeked out of his tent, scanning the area for any indication that he wasn't alone.

He found it.

Though the two lights he saw bouncing up and down in the distance weren't particularly close to his campsite, the likelihood of other people camping that far in the forest and yet that close to him was extraordinarily small. Jordan felt a chill trickle down his back.

The night was so dark that even the closest trees were barely visible. The two lights, which looked as if they came from lanterns, bobbed in and out. Jordan strained to hear any voices but only heard the footfalls traveling through the brush.

Something inside of Jordan told him to hide. He slipped out of the tent as silently as he could, taking only his backpack and flashlight with him. He would come back for his things later. Jordan didn't turn the flashlight on.

Every step he took sent a crackle echoing through the night. Jordan hid behind a large tree, peeking around it to see the two lights getting closer to his campsite. He could not make out the figures holding the lights. Neither was speaking.

Jordan cursed himself for leaving his guns at home. He had a hunting knife, which he clutched tightly in his hand. The people could not have seen him. It was far too dark out.

Could they?

Jordan did not see the arm that stretched out from behind the tree, the hand that reached to touch his face. The arm retracted itself as quickly as it emerged.

Jordan held his breath, afraid to make any noise. He watched as the two lights weaved and searched the black forest for hours. He remained in his hiding place.

By the time the lights faded away and Jordan heard the footsteps disappear farther away into the forest, he was so exhausted that he fell asleep against the tree.

When the sunlight broke through the woods in the morning, Jordan's eyes fluttered open. He had almost forgotten about the terrors of the night before.

Until he saw the two decayed, mutilated corpses situated on either side of him.

Jordan leapt up, choking back a cry. Someone had put two rotted carcasses next to him during his slumber.

He ran back in the direction of his campsite, intent on gathering his things and leaving Gull Valley Forest.

As Jordan's campsite came into view, he stopped in his tracks and covered himself behind a tree.

Two men in animal skull masks and black suits were at Jordan's campsite, rummaging through his belongings. They tore his tent apart with knives, tossed his gear over the cold ground, and destroyed whatever they found.

The two men stopped and looked in Jordan's direction. Jordan hastily ducked down and cowered, crawling toward a fallen tree.

Jordan made it to the other side of the downed tree, hidden from view. He knew he had to figure out an escape plan.

Above him stood one of the animal skull-masked men. Jordan heard the snap of twigs behind him and stumbled to his feet to run.

Jordan ran directly into the other animal skull-masked man. He was sandwiched between the two strangers.

A third skull-masked man appeared from behind a tree, holding up a video camera. He was recording everything.

Before Jordan had a chance to run again, the man behind him grabbed Jordan's forehead with one hand and inserted a leucotome—an ice pick used in pre-frontal lobotomies—into Jordan's eye. The man rummaged around the inside of Jordan's skull with the leucotome as Jordan spasmed and shook. Blood seeped from Jordan's eye.

Jordan's last thoughts as the blade seared into his brain were of his wife and children. Would they find his body all the way out in the middle of the forest?

Jordan watched helplessly as one of the men used Jordan's own blood to write the word *Erica* on the side of his destroyed tent.

Then everything in Jordan's mind went silent.

CHAPTER EIGHTEEN

Mr. Brisket texted Annie in the morning, after he, Jack, and Ben inspected every building themselves. There were no intruders, no signs of robbery or destruction or other malfeasance.

Annie reluctantly returned to Gull Valley, determined she would either find out if she was indeed being haunted by restless spirits or if she needed her head examined. Dr. Crews gave her a new prescription for different medications. Annie was hopeful that would alleviate some of her bizarre encounters. She hadn't ruled out a nervous breakdown or stress-induced hallucinations.

What would be worse—that she was imagining everything or that she wasn't?

Annie was showered and dressed for the day, bundling herself in a scarf, alpaca fleece hat, and puffer coat. Though it was a temperate day, the wind swept and swirled through the valley down from the mountaintops. She was avoiding calls from her editor about the next book, writing her list of what she wanted Mr. Brisket, Ms. Click, Jack, and Ben to start on in the coming weeks. There were so many things that actually needed to be done to renovate the buildings that Annie preferred to focus on them one at a time, otherwise it felt too overwhelming.

She wanted a fence (electric or otherwise) put around the property, as well as some barriers to protect from floods. She instructed Mr. Brisket to buy some sandbags since Gull Valley was at risk of flash flooding, despite the fact that the river that ran through it had dried out decades ago.

Before she left for her daily tasks, she went to the woodpile on the front porch to grab some wood and throw it in the fireplace. Though the two-story main house where she lived had heat, it was old and drafty. Keeping a fire going in the fireplace helped the house stay warm.

She knew she had to check in with Dr. Crews but didn't feel up to it. She had tried some of the ultimate positive thinking exercises Dr. Crews had recommended to her, but they weren't working quite yet.

Annie had picked Hanson's "MMMBop" as her cheerful start-the-day song. She did thirty minutes with her light therapy lamp every day. She kept a gratitude journal, wrote postcards to her friends and family, made daily affirmations that she was worthy and everything would be okay. She put happy pictures of her and Gary in good times all around the house, all his degrees and achievement certificates hung on the wall next to his smiling, handsome face. She put more happy pictures up around the house as well, of her and her girlfriends, and of her beloved Aunt Dolly, the woman who raised her. Sometimes, Annie would look up at the sky on a clear day and talk to Gary like he was still there.

Though she'd lived in Gull Valley for eleven months, she spent most of her time in the main house. She had barely made any dents in cleaning and decluttering all the other buildings, aside from the movie theater, a couple of the guest houses, and the roller-skating rink. She pictured having all of her friends over to watch *The Devil Wears Prada* or *How to Lose a Guy in 10 Days* on the big movie screen, then a night of disco roller boogie. The thought of that made her smile, even if temporarily.

It was a daunting task to remove all of the wayward belongings, personal items, trash, knickknacks, and assorted, collected objects and artifacts that remained on the property. Sometimes Annie wondered about each item; what their owner's story was, how did they come to land in Gull Valley, where they ended up, what was the history and timeline of their arrival and departure from the land she now owned.

Annie could have opened her own thrift store with the forgotten objects she'd found. Most of the pieces ended up as kindling for the bonfire. There was no major trash pickup in this end of the world, so all waste and discarded treasures were burned.

She was in the process of cleaning out guest house number five. All of the guest houses had a number attached to their side and an upturned horseshoe nailed into the wall above the front door.

Annie didn't like how quiet the guest house felt. She clicked a few buttons on her phone and David Bowie's "Let's Dance" began to play. Gary had loved David Bowie. Annie wanted to listen to songs that reminded her of Gary. She placed her phone against an old mug on the countertop in the common room.

Each of the guest houses had a shared space before the hallway that led to the bedrooms, consisting of a common room with a tiny table, several chairs, two couches, a small kitchenette with a fridge, and mini-bar.

Pinned to the wall in the sitting area were a knitted "Bless This Mess" sign, 1996 sixteen-month puppy calendar, and autographed picture of Kim Basinger. Beneath them rested a rusted anchor. A grandfather clock, no longer ticking away, was nestled in the corner. On the porch stood a vintage, old-fashioned Dr. Pepper soda machine, disused and out of the pages of a history magazine. It was twenty-five cents for a soda.

The house, like all the others, was littered with trash, spoiled food and drinks, and yellowed papers. The floor needed sanding and buffing. The 1970s-style, seafoam green, decorative floral wallpaper was peeling and flaking off, its pastels now discolored to an ash and soot-covered gray-brown. Tangled fish netting was strewn about the ground, next to discarded Yoo-Hoo bottles, Zagnut candy wrappers, Good Humor Strawberry Shortcake ice cream bar packages, empty liquor bottles and beer cans, multitudes of crusty clothes and shoes, books, maps, and various fishing, hunting, hiking, kayaking, spelunking, boating, and backpacking equipment and gear.

Annie had found about seventy-four sleeping bags between all of the buildings. She hated the thought that her home had a reputation as somewhere roaming, lawless voyagers could wander into. Some passers-through were surely travelers seeking shelter, but Annie didn't feel comfortable with that idea. It was her place now—there would be no guest ledger or welcoming committee.

Each house had that musty smell that came with neglect and disuse. The wind outside was too wild to open the doors and windows to let some fresh air in, so Annie accepted she'd be inhaling stale air all morning. It would take all day to clean, sweep, dust, and hose down all the surfaces and flooring. Some days, she felt like there wasn't enough Lysol or Clorox Wipes in the world to make these spaces inhabitable again. Thankfully, Mr. Brisket was the kind of caretaker who knew his way around power washers and industrial floor cleaners and vacuums.

Had the general chlorine smell not been so overpowering, she may have zeroed in on the odor of the decayed bodies stuffed and tied into sleeping bags underneath the floorboards.

As with each of the guest houses, each room had a dresser, bed, closet, mirror, and small desk. Room eight had a red racecar bed, as if it were once a child's room. Several rooms had moldy waterbeds, all of which were promptly jettisoned in favor of regular, newly deloused and disinfected mattresses.

Like all of the other houses, the walls were adorned with old paintings, graffiti, writing, scribbles, and drawings from the people who'd passed through. A mixture of shoddy artistry by vandals and people's once-valued possessions.

Photographs decorated the rooms and hallways. Mostly black-and-white (though some color) photos, spanning over a century, of schoolchildren with their teachers, land proprietors, families, campers, and various other guests and owners who'd come before her. Who'd

99

somehow been a part of Gull Valley. Next to the doorway hung a framed photograph of a sullen-looking woman, her eyes sad and longing, as if all she wanted to do was escape her life and confines.

Why did people look so much older than they were back then?

Annie took all of the sheets and comforters—the ones that were salvageable, unstained by mildew and other gross bacteria—to the laundry room and started the wash.

While the comforters and sheets laundered, Annie gathered all of the boxes of items left behind by travelers and visitors that Ms. Click had loosely packed for inspection. After sorting through to see if there was anything valuable, Annie had filled an entire blue garbage bin with abandoned items.

Worn-down Minnie Mouse and Daisy Duck plush stuffed animals. Several hardcover *Where's Waldo?* books. A blonde, pigtailed, chubby-cheeked Cabbage Patch Kid. Old Maid card game from the 1980s. Leann Rimes maxi-CD single of "How Do I Live?" dance remixes. Red-and-white-striped windsock that looked like The Cat in the Hat's hat. Hundreds of cracked, broken twinkle lights. Earrings still on their plastic Claire's display cards. Calligraphy kit with special writing utensils and a booklet on penmanship. Snausages box, half-full. Columbia House mailers, advertising CDs and cassette tapes for the low price of one penny. Rolled up, tattered bomber jacket and crushed blue velvet baby doll dress. *Super Troopers* DVD. Magnifying glass pendant necklace. The Stuffer. Package of twisty straws. Pool noodles. Back scratcher. Banana hammock. The Brownie Batter Grabber. Joe Dirt Funko Pop doll. Ship-in-a-bottle. *The Art of Golf Antiques* book. Inactive baking-soda volcano, like somebody's middle school project. Volleyball net. Empty Mrs. Butterworth maple syrup bottles. The Slap-Chop! Bingo spinner cage. Etch-A-Sketch. Unmailed fan letter to Tilda Swinton. Paper shooting targets for gun ranges. A two-dollar-off coupon to Virgil's Videos. The Bangles'

"If She Knew What She Wants" forty-five RPM record, complete with picture sleeve and German writing on the back. Wonder Sauna Hot Pants. Hundreds of Crocs, in every color of the rainbow.

Well, that's more for the fire, Annie thought. Her mind wandered, thinking about people's possessions. What they said about a person. What the things they left behind said about them. She thought of Gary, and how he'd left her behind, through no fault of his own.

Annie didn't notice the face in the window behind her. Someone, or something, watched her unboxing and sifting through the pieces of Gull Valley's past. It watched as she mumbled to herself, then stood up to go to another room.

It followed her along the outside of the guest house, peering in at her as she made her way to the other rooms. She never caught sight of him. She was completely oblivious to the person, or thing, that stared at her through the windows.

She headed to the front door, on her way to the laundry room to put the sheets, comforters, and pillows in the dryer. It kept its distance from her, hiding itself behind anything and everything it could, making note of her every move.

Annie exited the laundry room and had a sudden strange feeling overcome her. A feeling of unease she couldn't place and had no reason for. She scanned the area around her, not sure what—or who—she was looking for.

There was nothing there.

She resumed her clean-up in guest house five, filling black garbage bags with detritus and debris, sweeping the hallway. She wasn't into any of the Marie Kondo shit, but most of what was left in the houses definitely did not spark joy. She knew hot garbage when she was buried in it.

Clunk.

A dull thud from room number eight stopped Annie from her work. She looked up from the broom and dustpan, watching as the door slowly creaked open, though there was no one else in the building with her.

"Mr. Brisket?" she called out, knowing he was rewiring the sound system in the roller-skating rink on the opposite side of the gorge.

Annie cautiously made her way to room eight, gingerly pushing the door open. The windows were closed, so no draft caused the door to swing by itself.

A beaten-up box, one that wasn't there before, sat on top of the red racecar bed. Annie scrutinized the space around her. She was alone. At least she'd thought she was alone. How did that get there?

She knelt down in front of the bed and examined the box's contents. Hundreds of photographs of people of all ages, in front of the buildings and landscape of Gull Valley. All of the photographs were of the same era. Men, women, and children laughing, dancing, playing instruments, building their homes, gathered together.

Beneath the photographs were other pictures attached to patient's medical files, all stamped with faded words— Calista Asylum for the Criminally Insane. Several of the people looked completely ordinary, even sane. There were others, though, who looked as if they had not slept in years and would eat someone alive. Their eyes were like black pools, soulless orbs of nothing but darkness and hatred and evil.

More photos. A black-and-white picture of Calista Island Asylum from the 1900s. Some in color, of the asylum in all its imposing glory, when it was fully functioning and housed thousands of people. Doctors and nurses in starched white uniforms, stethoscopes around their necks. Emaciated, skeletal patients. Doctors performing surgery on a patient strapped down to a gurney. Security guards restraining a raving, screaming inmate.

Feral-looking patients who stared directly into the lens of whoever's camera had taken these pictures.

Arcane, outdated medical equipment. Patients being sprayed down with water by guards wielding a giant fire hose. A long, dark, desolate tunnel with little light emanating from the other end. Doctors smoking cigarettes and holding glasses filled with whiskey, smiling and laughing. A weeping woman with a bouquet of roses in her hands, standing at the lobby desk alone, waiting for someone to help her.

Most of the photos looked as if they had been taken without the subjects' knowledge or permission. As if the photographer was on a secret mission, capturing the horrors and evils that the asylum housed.

The last picture was of a group of people who were posed as if they were at Sears to have their dysfunctional family portrait taken. Annie gasped. She recognized one of the women, from the photo in the doorway. However, in this picture, the woman was in a frilly pink dress with several bows, standing quietly in the center of the photo. She wasn't smiling. She had no expression on her face— only the vacant, hollow stare she wore in the doorway photo. The mystery woman was surrounded by men and women of varying ages, all formally dressed. None of them were smiling.

The figure stood in the doorframe behind Annie, observing her as she flipped through her findings. Watching her expression as she tried to put pieces of a puzzle together. She was too engrossed in the contents of the box to see its long, lanky, dark silhouette in the doorway, looming over her like a monster hovering above its prey.

She scoured through the transcripts and files, her mind racing as she read about their maladies and ailments, mostly psychological and mental. Forms sanctioning lobotomies, hydrotherapy, and electroconvulsive therapy. The files were mostly from the 1950s and 60s, each one signed by the same four attending physicians—Dr. Arthur Wainwright, Dr. Andrew Liu, Dr. Meghan Chittle, and Dr. James Salehi.

Annie's eyes widened as she pulled a crumpled, used straight-jacket out of the box. Beneath it lay oxidized and rusted dental forceps and a blood-letting fleam, among other antiquated and outdated medical equipment that she didn't know the names for.

Annie let it all fall to the floor. She jumped up and left guest house five, needing some space and time to rationalize what she'd discovered.

The figure stayed out of sight as it watched Annie half-walk, half-run toward the main house.

CHAPTER NINETEEN

Annie got into bed that night, after walking the perimeter of the buildings and securing every lock as tightly as possible. She was still rattled over the strange occurrences she'd had the past couple of days.

Every creak and moan of the house settling made her pause.

She propped herself up on her pillows and took a deep breath.

Before she'd retired for the night, she'd lined the hallway to her bedroom with bubble wrap. The entire floor, covered with it, taped to the ground. If someone or something was haunting her, their footsteps would make the bubbles snap and crackle, alerting her to a presence.

Did ghosts walk on the ground like living people? That may have been a flaw in her plan. What did those people in the *Paranormal Activity* movies do?

Oh yeah, they all died.

Annie listened to the soft buzz of her fan and tried to clear her mind.

Cal had texted earlier with a proposition. He asked for her assistance in writing his book on The Felicitous and Gull Valley. He cited her superior writing skills and experience in the world of books, from creation to selling. The upside was Cal had already done heavy, in-depth research, from interviews with former cult members and experts ranging from police officers to mental health experts, to collecting every newspaper and magazine article, television broadcast, photograph, and correspondence between the former members that he could find.

Annie was intrigued. She hadn't given a definite answer. The idea of writing a book about the land she now owned fascinated her. She would have to do her own research and connect threads herself, but she was never afraid of hard work. She smiled, a little thrill shooting through her. She'd be a regular Nancy Drew, investigating and exploring, finding the truth.

There was so much she didn't know. So many layers and levels of involvement, emotion, and events that neither she nor Cal had understood or uncovered. But a project like this may help to distract her and revive her love of writing and creating.

The biggest thing holding her back was the fact that she didn't know Cal well. They'd met once. He seemed kind and genial, but she'd need to get to know him better. Not romantically—she had zero interest in dating.

Annie picked up the book on her nightstand—the manifesto written by the members of The Felicitous.

On the inside cover of the book, the word *Erica* was written over and over, in different colors, fonts, and handwriting.

Page one was their mission statement—*To create and facilitate a world without government, restrictions, oppression, and fear. To reject social norms and expectations, fostering a community of like-minded individuals and families who will be free from the shackles of tyranny, persecution, and repression. To defend our right to live our lives in the manner that best suits us. To be a good neighbor to each other, acting as one symbiotic and harmonious unit that shuns the horror, lies, war, poverty, cruelty, and surveillance of modern society. To build a self-sustained, self-sufficient Utopian civilization, untethered to the outside world. To worship, obey, and be in the service of their land and our leader, Laird Hubbell.*

We shall not back down from the monsters, usurpers, and liars who threaten to steal the foundation of our beliefs, lives, and souls.

Beneath the mission statement was a symbol—the E and K. The same symbol that Annie and Marcie had seen carved into the tree earlier.

She flipped the page to the tenets of The Felicitous, which were simply the mission statement ideas in bullet point. Annie had seen them already anyway, on her door.

Annie opened her laptop and typed in "The Felicitous" into her browser.

Thousands of articles emerged. Firsthand accounts, historical summaries, timelines, opinion pieces, testimonials from former cult members and families of people who left them to be a part of The Felicitous, news articles from around the globe.

Images of The Felicitous in their specific 1950s and 1960s clothes—men in black suits and ties with white button-down shirts, women in housewife-y dresses. Of Laird Hubbell and his family, before he left them to create The Felicitous.

Crime scene photos of murders, robberies, bombings, kidnappings, and disappearances that The Felicitous were implicated and suspected in, though never definitively proven.

Videos of The Felicitous dancing in Gull Valley. Laundry hanging from clotheslines. Fruit and vegetable gardens near a flowing river. How different it looked back then.

More videos of The Felicitous at anti-war rallies, Laird proselytizing to his flock, Laird and his followers attempting to convert new recruits, and behind-the-scenes, intimate peeks into their daily life—mundane aspects like the group eating together, sharing work duties, doing their chores, making pies and cakes to sell at the Farmers Market.

Videos of strange sightings, alleged ghost encounters, and weird figures and creatures captured on camera by hikers and YouTube explorers in Gull Valley.

Annie closed her laptop. It was too much information. Was this how Veronica Mars felt when she investigated?

Kristen Bell, give me strength.

Annie wanted a Diet Pepsi and a meatball sub but knew if she had anything to drink, it meant she'd have to get up twenty times during the night to pee.

She conjured up images of things that made her happy. Gary on the Fourth of July, running around with all their friends' kids with sparklers in their hands, laughing and giggling. The feeling of relief she got when someone approached the elevator in her building as she pretended to press the "hold door" button and the doors shut before the other person could get in, sparing her an unwanted stop and chat. Jon Favreau shirtless in *Couples Retreat.* Her favorite parts of her favorite songs—the best lines and notes that made her stay in the car, or stop what she was doing, just so she could hear them. She didn't care that Gary teased her because she loved Imagine Dragons' "Radioactive"—when that song came on, she wasn't going anywhere until it was over.

Annie pulled Wikipedia up on her phone, typing in the words "Laird Hubbell." The article featured a picture of Laird at thirty-three, captioned "Laird Hubbell in Gull Valley, 1973." He was tall and muscled with wavy, fair hair. He was dressed in a gray suit and robe combination, his lips pursed together in a stern smile.

The page was lengthy and detailed, though Annie knew that didn't mean everything in it was factual. It was Wikipedia, after all.

Annie read parts of the write-up aloud to herself. "*'Laird Hubbell, born May 17, 1945, to Clarence Hubbell and Millicent Burton Hubbell in Portland, Maine. The Hubbells were a wealthy family of business magnates whose ventures included steel and oil, meat-packing, and the booming railroad industry. Laird attended boarding school and was noted to have a genius IQ, excelling in all subjects and sports. Popular, charismatic, well-liked, and adept in leadership roles. Showed a distrust and dislike of authority and rules from an early age. Frequently orchestrated protests and dissent against what he and fellow students claimed were unfair and unethical practices. Spent several years in and out of The Calista Asylum for the Criminally Insane and other mental health facilities during his teenaged years. Became immersed in the idea of anarchy and active in resistance movements through a combination of events, including the changing social climate in the 1960s and the tragic death of several family members, friend, and father's work associates, of which he was the lone survivor. Best known as the creator and leader of The Felicitous, an infamous counterculture cult that began in the early 1960s."*

Annie's phone buzzed, taking her out of her reading.

"Hey," she said into the phone. It was Sloane calling. "This call may be monitored for quality assurance."

"Hey! Just wanted to check up on you," Sloane said through the line. "Today I had this horrifying realization—the 2020s are to the 1980s what the 1980s are to the 1940s. I spent the whole day in a daze, like I was on the Scrambler ride at the fair. I ate my weight in little things wrapped in dough with savory fillings. Soup dumplings, potstickers, pierogies, stuffed shells. Did you know that in German, there's a word to describe emotional eating? *Kummerspeck*. It literally translates into 'grief bacon.' You know what's rough? Being smart enough to know how awkward I am, but not being smart enough to be able to not be totally awkward. At work today, I had two speeds and nothing in between—either frenzied productivity and hyperawareness or barely functioning and wondering if everyone is mad at me because the second anyone's vibe is a millimeter 'off,' I'm convinced it's my fault and sense danger around every corner. It's a terrifying thought that my future depends on me and me alone."

"It is way too late for a patented Sloane-deep-thoughts-info-dump," laughed Annie. "And you are a beautiful, magical princess mermaid warrior made of glitter, unicorns, and double rainbows. Don't you forget it. Are you doing all right over there?"

"I am. I am. I think I'm a little lonely. The only company I have right now is *The Munsters* repeats on Cozi TV. What are you doing?"

Annie filled Sloane in on her day.

"Are we listening or problem-solving?" Sloane asked in her best Dr. Crews impression. "Do you want comfort or solutions?"

"I want to know how injuries I sustain in my forties take me ten times longer to recover from than when I was in my twenties. Now if I turn my neck too hard, I need muscle relaxers. I want to know if life is just one big elliptical machine, where I'm just climbing and climbing but never actually go anywhere. I want to know what kind of people actually bought and used the Better Marriage Blanket. I want to know who actually has bowls of fresh fruit on their countertop. I want to know what I do with my life now."

"You get up every day and you put one foot in front of the other. And you breathe. And you know that nothing else is ever promised."

"I've never had the awareness of time that I do now. Ever since Gary has been gone, I'm so painfully aware of every second. His death just made everything feel so much more real, but in the most horrible way. I don't feel happy that my ignorance has been shattered. I don't feel like, okay now I can make every moment count."

"I know. I understand. The only time I'm happy anymore is when I get to see my niece and nephew."

"Did you ever go to the library or get used books, and someone wrote some 'inspiring' message or platitude inside. Like, 'You got this!' or 'Don't give up!'. And it's just so fake and shallow, not to mention ruins the integrity of the book. Do you think those people give themselves five and post duckface selfies afterward, because they're so impressed with themselves? I want to punch the people who wrote those things in the face over and over, because they deserve to be put in lobster cages and forced to watch mukbang porn on an endless loop."

"What is muk—you know what, never mind. I don't want to know," Sloane said, waving her hand over her face, thinking of happy things. "Kittens, mittens, reversible hats, Baby Yoda, the comforting sound of rain."

Neither Annie nor Sloane noticed that the red camera light on Annie's laptop popped on. Her webcam feed was active. Annie's computer was on her desk, facing her bed.

"You know what my favorite episode of *Mr. Belvedere* is?" said Sloane. "The one where Wesley enters the spelling bee and is the favorite to win. But the other kid tells him some sob story about his life, so Wesley throws the match so the kid can win. Turns out the kid was lying to Wesley so he could get the trophy. So, when it's Wesley's turn to spell a word, he gets 'phlegm.' He goes up to the microphone and says, 'Phlegm. F-L-E-M,' and his dad stands up and shouts, 'Yeah, Wes!'"

Annie laughed. Sloane definitely lived in her own world. She wished she could be more like that.

She thought about the biggest, saddest lies she'd been told about getting older and life. When people aged and matured, they learned the hard way—the stupidest people were the loudest and tended to rule and ruin everything. Money did buy happiness, or at least afforded people more time and freedom, which in turn created more happiness. If rich people were unhappy, they could simply dry their tears with hundred-dollar bills. And everyone had regrets. The whole "no regrets" thing was a fallacy. And everyone who told her she'd need less sleep the older she got was wrong. Annie hated sleeping as a kid, but now all she wanted was more sleep, even though it eluded her. The party was in her bed (not in the sex way), not out at some club, bar, or overcrowded social event.

"Annie?" Sloane said. "You still there?"

"Yes. Sorry. Hey, can you do me a favor? Can you look up the names of the people who used to own this property? I'd like to contact them and ask them a few questions."

"I'm not sure that's completely ethical or legal, Annie. What's your plan? You call them up and say, 'Hey, how are you? Did you ever notice there's always fewer orange jellybeans than other flavors in a bag? Oh, and by the way, did ghosts and spirits haunt you every night? What's the phone number for the Ghostbusters? Oh, really, great!' Probably not the best idea."

"Well, when you say it like that, it sounds ridiculous."

"Why don't you ask your new friend Cal about all of that stuff? If he's done as much digging and research as you think, he'll probably have all of that information. Your new Cal pal. I'm your gal pal, he's your Cal pal."

"Okay, I can ask him, I guess. But will you take a little look into who owned Gull Valley?"

"I don't want to freak you out here, Annie. But don't you think it's a little weird that all this weird stuff just started happening to you and this guy Cal shows up? It's an awfully big coincidence, isn't it? I mean, it's a little suspicious. What do you know about this guy?"

Annie was silent for a moment. "Not a lot, I guess. No matter where I go, life is going to happen regardless of whether I'm prepared for it or not. I can't outrun it anymore. I'm not leaving Gull Valley and I'm not backing down."

"If this was a romantic comedy, I'd say it was destiny."

"My life is more of a horror movie these days."

"Okay, well, you know what we always say. When in doubt, dance it out."

Sloane cranked up the music in the background so Annie could hear through the wire. The Postal Service's "Such Great Heights" filled Annie's ear.

"Are you shaking it? Are you? Huh?" Sloane said.

Annie shook once then bid her friend a loving good night.

CHAPTER TWENTY

Annie was well into a deep slumber, the only sound in her bedroom being the hum of her fan.

She was unaware of the figure that stood between her headboard and the wall. Looming over her, staring down at her peaceful, sleeping face. Reaching its dark hands out to touch her, coming close enough to almost feel her skin but stopping short so she wouldn't wake.

Annie stirred, eyes slowly opening. She had been having a strange dream, in which she was at Target with Bear Grylls. He was making her pick things out that they could use to survive in the wilderness. If she picked the wrong thing, like she did when she picked out a romper, a ridiculous coffee table shaped like a hippopotamus, then a welcome mat, the customers all threw circus peanuts at her. Meanwhile, Richard Marx was in aisle five, playing "Right Here Waiting" on a grand piano as the three-breasted woman from *Total Recall* gave a demonstration on how "a little lemon juice does the trick" in getting stains out of things.

Her eyes adjusted to the low light, her bedroom only illuminated by the Oscar the Grouch nightlight she found among the endless piles of junk on the property.

Pop.

The quick, sudden bubble burst from the hallway zapped Annie to lucidity. She sat straight up in bed, her eyes fixed on her closed bedroom door.

She didn't breathe for a full minute, listening intently.

Pop.

She lurched forward, unsure of what her next move should be. She reached for Jason Statham, her bat.

Pop! Pop! Pop! Pop! Pop!

In rapid, angry succession, the bubbles burst from the hallway.

Annie leapt out of bed and edged toward the bedroom door. She was halfway between her bed and the door.

Scratch.

Scratch. Scratch.

Someone on the other side of the door was softly, deliberately scraping and clawing against the wood with their hands.

Annie hoped it was with their hands and not some horrible sharp object.

"Annie," a soft, almost timid, voice whispered. "Let me in."

Annie didn't scream. She threw the door open, the bat raised high in the air, ready to strike.

Nothing.

There was nobody there.

Annie flipped the hallway light on.

The entire hallway was empty.

She didn't know whether to cry or scream or breathe a sigh of relief. She must have been having some type of waking dream or been in some kind of fugue state.

At least that's what Annie told herself as she got back into bed. After she emergency emailed Dr. Crews, she popped two pills—one blue, one red—and watched *22 Jump Street* then *Barb and Star Go to Vista del Mar* while she waited for the sunrise.

At around 3:15 a.m., Annie swore she heard the distant echo of bells ringing, emanating over the valley from the woods. She didn't trust herself or her judgment. Instead, she focused on the television and tried to clear her head, saying silent prayers for the sun to arrive.

This was becoming a habit.

CHAPTER TWENTY-ONE

The sun was still hours away from rising when Victor Broome conceded that he was lost. His usually reliable GPS, complete with Arnold Schwarzenegger instructional voice, had stopped working somewhere between Boston, Massachusetts, and his destination of Portland, Maine.

Victor had insisted on taking the scenic route home. He wasn't tired, so he stopped at an all-night diner to have tuna melts and jalapeno poppers with his beloved mother, then set back on the road well after midnight. Along the way home, he encountered a rickety detour sign that diverted him from the backroads he knew into the ones he didn't.

Victor's mother Dinah slept in the passenger seat as he drove. He had surprised her with tickets to the Styx reunion concert at The Wilbur in Boston. Styx was Dinah's all-time favorite band and their songs were a soundtrack to Victor's childhood. Now that he was grown, he wanted to do something special for the woman who had been such an amazing, strong support system for him. Dinah was demure in stature but was the toughest person Victor had ever known.

Dinah's joyous tears when Styx burst into "Come Sail Away" told Victor everything he needed to know. He had made her happy. Dinah had spent her life in the service of others as a nurse at The Calista Island Asylum for the Criminally Insane in Neve, Maine. She was retired now, spending her days babysitting Victor's children and going on trips to the Christmas Tree Shops with her friend, Janice.

Victor's younger brother Jeremy was fast asleep in the backseat, sprawled across the cushions and snoring. It was a great, fun night. Victor needed more of that in his life.

Jeremy had left his wife and kids at home for the night, as did Victor. They wanted to take their beloved mother out for a night of celebration, sort of a long overdue "thank you" for the love she'd given them their whole lives. A night where it was the three of them again.

They were deep in the backroads of Maine, somewhere around Hartwell. Victor guessed that they were somewhere in the forests that connected to Gull Valley. They were surrounded by dense foliage and no light, except for the car's headlights. It reminded him of a scarier, gloomier version of The Arnold Arboretum of Harvard University, which he had visited a million times growing up. Victor wondered how many different types of trees were found in Maine.

The unpaved road ahead of him, which stretched endlessly as far as Victor's eyes could see, seemed so foreboding and desolate. There were no houses, no mailboxes, no signs of people anywhere.

When he passed the faded, decaying metal sign on the side of the road that read, "Hitchhikers may be escaped inmates," Victor made sure that all the car doors were locked.

They came to a fork in the road. Either direction seemed the same—more darkness, bushes, and trees. Victor took a breath and chose to go right, eyeing his GPS, hoping it would somehow spring back to life. He didn't ask for much; now would've been a good time for some luck.

After a mile or two, the headlights of the car illuminated something that made Victor's heart jump. He slowed down as he saw it.

There was a person on the side of the road.

It looked like a young woman, dressed in a vintage 1950s Peter Pan dress—big, flat, rounded white collar with ends that met in the front over a black-and-white tiny polka dot print.

A flimsy, dimestore plastic mask covered her face, secured by a thin white rubber band.

A witch mask—green skin, warts, and comically oversize, jagged teeth.

She looked like a secretary from another time. Like she was a ghost from a different era. Like she thought it was Halloween and put on a costume...then took a walk in a remote, unpopulated area filled with potentially dangerous wildlife.

Did she need help? Victor vacillated between stopping and asking if she was okay or hitting the gas and speeding the hell out of there, never to return.

Her witch mask told him that he should keep driving.

Victor grew up in Maine. And like all of the other New Englanders, he'd been told scary stories and folktales his whole life about the creatures, ghosts, killers, and otherworldly beings that haunt the forests and lonely stretches of road. Ghouls, goblins, extraterrestrials, and things with no name, not tethered to this realm or another, in search of blood and carnage. Searching, stalking the night for helpless victims to hunt, maim, and murder. Stories of lovers lane and secret spots in the woods that became crime scenes after something grisly and dreadful happened to a friend of a friend's mother's neighbor's cat-sitter's hairdresser's uncle's pool cleaner.

Nope. Not stopping.

Victor didn't see the thing strewn across the road a few hundred meters ahead of him.

A lump of flesh and bone that was once a living person, now a carcass of meat. Thick metal hooks attached to chains driven through its rotted flesh. One end of chain wrapped around a large tree to the left side of the road.

The other, on the right side, in the hands of an unknown entity. A stranger, waiting for the right moment to set their plan into motion.

As Victor's car approached, its headlights barely cutting through the insidious darkness, the stranger pulled tightly on the chain.

The force raised the fetid, lifeless corpse into the air like a jangly, uncoordinated scarecrow. A wobbly, off-kilter, giant marionette being pulled by strings. Its sunken-in eye sockets home to milky white, sightless orbs.

It hovered directly in the pathway of Victor's oncoming car.

The car's headlights shone around the body, casting shadows around its silhouette. Victor slammed on the brakes as soon as he saw it, but it was far too late.

Splat!

Bone, blood, fat, and body parts exploded and splashed over the grill and windshield of Victor's car as if he had detonated a bomb made of gore, sinew, and tissue.

Victor lost control of the wheel, sending the car careening into the closest tree on the right-hand side of the road. Smoke billowed from beneath the car's hood.

He didn't see the chains as they were pulled from off of the road, into the blackness of the forest. Erupted body parts soiled the dirt road, like some kind of meat puzzle that hadn't been put together.

Dinah jerked awake from the passenger seat, startled by the commotion and crash.

"Are you all right, Mom?" Victor asked breathlessly. "Jeremy? You okay?"

"Yes, are you?" said Dinah. "What did we hit?"

Jeremy clamored up from the floor in the back seat, where he'd rolled when the car came to its sudden stop.

"Somebody was in the road. They jumped in front of the car! A person," said Victor.

Jeremy looked in the side mirror, seeing some of the parts on the road. "They're not a whole person anymore."

"Stay here," Victor said, getting out of the car to inspect the damage.

His feet sloshed in the viscous blood and internal organs soaking the road. He surveyed the front of the car. It wasn't totaled but there was significant damage.

What was that?

Footsteps and branches breaking—like someone was running around in the woods—echoed in the nearby distance.

From all sides of the road.

Victor heard someone—or several people—circling the car around him, like he was in the center of bullseye.

Crack!

A loud twig broke right on the other side of the tree he stood at. Victor rushed back inside the car, closing and locking the door behind him.

"Victor!" Dinah said. "What's wrong?"

"Somebody's out there," he said, desperately trying to get cell phone service or make his GPS work again. He put the car in reverse but it wouldn't budge. "I think the front of the car is stuck into the tree. I have to get it loose."

"Who's out there?" Dinah asked, her eyes like saucers.

"I don't know, Mom. I heard people moving around. We have to get out of here. You move into the driver's seat and I'll try to pry the car off the tree, okay?"

Victor peered into the darkness through the driver's side window. He couldn't hear anything strange at the moment.

"I'm coming with you," Jeremy said. Jeremy had always been the more athletically-inclined, physically gifted of the two brothers. This gave him an inflated sense of strength and power over people.

"No, stay in the car," Victor said. "Stay with Mom."

In a burst of bravery, Victor jumped out and ran to the trunk, grabbing a crowbar. Dinah slid over to the driver's side.

Victor prodded and pulled at the twisted metal jammed into the giant tree trunk. Dinah had the car in reverse, though the wheels were sunk into the earth from Victor's sudden braking and the crash itself.

Victor cautiously looked all around him, listening as snaps and cracks emanated from the woods. He heard people whispering to each other.

Knock knock knock!

Three knocks on a tree, not too far away from where he stood.

Knock knock knock!

Three more, from a different direction. As if answering the first set of knocks.

"Victor," a faceless voice whispered from the darkness. It was right near him.

Victor's heart jumped into his face. He bolted back to the car, back to the driver's side, as Dinah sat herself back in the passenger seat.

"What? What it is?" Dinah said.

"We have to go," Victor said, the feeling of helplessness and fear gripping his entire body. "Jeremy, you have to stay here with Mom, okay? I'm going to try and get help. I can run to the nearest town. I've got to get whoever is out there away from you guys."

"What are you talking about?" said Jeremy.

Tap tap tap!

The trio turned to see someone staring into the passenger side window—right next to Dinah.

A tall, lanky man, dressed in a vintage black suit, black tie, and off-white button-down shirt. His face was covered by an overexaggerated, gray-and-purple-colored zombie mask, similar to the witch's mask—cheap-looking and found in any small-town drugstore.

They all screamed.

They heard the sounds of people skittering, running, circling their car. Like a pack of wild animals getting ready to pounce on their prey.

How many of them were there? They couldn't get a good look. The people outside were too fast and had the benefit of the immeasurable black night outside.

The zombie was gone. Disappeared back into the darkness.

Pop! Sssss...

Pop! Sssss...

Pop! Sssss...

Pop! Sssss...

All four tires on the car had been slashed and were leaking air. The car began to sink farther down to the ground. Victor, Dinah, and Jeremy scrambled to see who was outside.

"Stay in the car!" said Dinah.

"Victor," Jeremy said, pointing to the back window.

The witch girl stood in the road behind their car, at a far enough distance that she was only slightly visible beneath the moonlight and in the car's rearview brake lights.

"Who are they?" said Dinah. "What do they want?"

"I don't know, Mom," Victor said. "I love you."

Victor leapt out of the car, slamming the door shut behind him. He heard Jeremy and his mother call out his name.

He ran down the road, into the awaiting darkness. He ran until he couldn't see his car anymore. Crowbar in hand, he frantically scanned the area for the strangers. He could only hear the sounds of animals milling about, owls hooting, the chittering noises of woodland creatures.

Victor's eyes adjusted to the darkness. As he squinted, his eyes zoned in on a vehicle pulled over to the side of the road. He sprinted toward it, tripping over something on the ground.

A metal spike chain laid out across the road, stretching from one side to the other. A trap set for unsuspecting passersby, with sharp bladed spikes attached to a long chain.

The vehicle in front of Victor had surely driven over the spikes, as evidenced by the damaged tires.

He would see if the keys were still in the ignition. He'd drive this car on its rims if he had to.

Victor threw open the driver's side door and gagged, lurching backward.

The corpse of a young woman sat lifelessly in the driver's seat, her eyes staring straight forward. Her mouth frozen in a contorted, twisted mockery of a scream.

A tree branch impaled her through her seat. She was covered in deep, bloody cuts and wounds, as if she had been repeatedly skewered and punctured over and over.

The cut across her neck was so savage that her head was barely attached.

Across the car's windshield, scrawled in dried, dark red blood was one word:

ERICA

Victor gasped when he saw the outlines of approaching people down the road. He charged into the forest, away from the main path.

Back at Victor's car, Jeremy had moved himself into the driver's seat and fruitlessly attempted to back the car off of the tree. Dinah anxiously scoured the area for Victor—or worse, the masked deviants.

Dinah's eyes focused on a tree across from where they were trapped. Despite the darkness, she made out the figure of someone hiding in its branches. Whoever it was, disguised in the leaves and limbs, watched them.

"I'm going to push the car off of the tree," Jeremy said.

Dinah grabbed his arm. "No! Jeremy, stay here."

Jeremy didn't listen to his mother. With a cursory surveillance of the area, checking that there was no immediate danger nearby, he flicked the "unlock" button on the car.

Bang!

Dinah and Jeremy barely had time to react as the passenger door swung open. A male figure, dressed in the same black suit as the zombie-masked man, reached over Dinah and stabbed her in her chest repeatedly; a mad frenzy of bloodlust and rage. Dinah didn't even scream out, her voice squeaking out strained cries and gurgles. She saw the skeleton mask on the entity's face. She looked into the eyes of her killer but saw no sign of life in them.

It happened so fast that by the time Jeremy registered what was happening, Dinah had taken her final breath. She was slumped halfway out of the open passenger door, her seat belt keeping her from falling all the way on to the road. Jeremy cried out her name, looking around him for the person responsible. The trees and road were empty. Whoever killed her had disappeared back into the darkness.

The panic swept over Jeremy as quickly as his sorrow did. He was alone on a desolate road with a murderer somewhere nearby, watching him. He was in the crosshairs.

Jeremy bolted into the woods. He had to find Victor, to hide and wait for the sun to come up.

Jeremy's eyes searched the area around him, looking for any sign of someone following him. The leaves and sticks under his feet crackled and snapped with every step he took. He knew his position would be given away to anyone at his heel.

He struggled to see in the pitch dark. He ran directly into a mess of clear fishing line that was strung up between the trees like a giant spider web. Jeremy let out a cry of pain.

There were hundreds of small fishhooks attached to the fishing line. They dug into Jeremy's skin, slicing it open as blood poured from the wounds. He pulled at each hook one by one, attempting to dislodge himself from the trap he was caught in.

He saw the figures in the distance through the tangled fishhooks, advancing toward him steadily. Jeremy panicked, futilely attempting to rip himself free of his entanglement.

It was too late for him. The masked figures—witch, zombie, skeleton, werewolf, ghost, mummy, alien—pounced on him, surrounding him.

The male figures—zombie, skeleton, werewolf, and mummy—all wore the black suits, like a uniform.

The female figures—ghost and alien—were in 1950s dresses, similar to the one the witch wore. The ghost in a blush-colored swing dress with a big bow waist, the alien in a plaid one with a big white belt. Like unhinged housewives from black-and-white television shows—but bloodthirsty mad hatters.

Jeremy fell face-first into the dirt as the mummy kicked him in his back, digging its knees into his spine. The ghost whacked Jeremy on the head with a large ballpeen hammer.

He felt the rock in the zombie's hands bash into his head, rendering him semi-conscious. Then the noose as it wrapped around his neck, tightening around his throat.

The werewolf pulled the rope tightly, lifting Jeremy into the air, off of his feet. Jeremy struggled against the dizziness and fog in his mind, his legs kicking in the air in vain, trying to find something to stand on and get his center back. Blood from his head wound flowed into his eyes.

Jeremy choked and gasped as he tried to free himself. The werewolf had wrapped the rope around a rusty hook nailed into a large tree. The masked killers stood back to watch their handiwork as Jeremy kicked, flailed, and squirmed at his body hoisted off of the ground, the rope that constricted his neck taut around a thick tree branch.

The masked killers stood motionless and unaffected as they watched Jeremy thrash around like a goldfish out of its bowl.

The skeleton stepped forward, brandishing a hunting knife in his hand. He stabbed it into Jeremy's sternum and pulled down hard—slitting Jeremy open all the way down to his groin.

Jeremy screamed as his innards tumbled outward, spilling on the ground. The heat of his internal organs smoking in the cold night air. Jeremy's guts toppled into a large pile at the skeleton's feet.

The skeleton backed away, rejoining the others.

Victor was next.

Victor had no idea what had become of his mother and brother. He was deep into the forest, stumbling and falling over the rocks and roots he couldn't see in the dark, too afraid to turn on the flashlight on his phone, for fear it would give his location away.

He heard talking and noises in the distance but couldn't see who or where they were coming from. In the woods, everything echoed and it was impossible to make out their origin.

He walked straight into something that knocked him on his rear.

Victor looked up to see the carcass of a man strung high up off of the ground—his arms tied with thick ropes on to branches connecting him between two trees, left suspended mid-air for predators and birds to scavenge. The man's legs swayed in the wind.

Victor quickly turned his phone flashlight on. He had to see.

126

Stacked and collected around the tree trunks were people's personal belongings—from sleeping bags, blankets, camping equipment, and backpacks to wallets, identification cards, and destroyed cell phones.

The area was littered with hundreds of vintage dolls of every size and shape, plastic action figures, and crudely made figurines—black moss-and-twig bodies, red eyes—fashioned together with sticks and twine, hanging from tree branches and scattered along the ground.

Victor clicked his phone light off and ran a few hundred yards, then stopped in his tracks.

He had gone in a complete circle. Victor realized he was back at the dead young woman's car. The driver's side door was wide open.

He looked up and down the dirt road and saw nothing, no one; heard nothing. He stepped closer to the car. He was going to take it.

The dead young woman's head had been turned in his direction. Her blank, thousand-yard, dead-eyed stare fixated right on Victor. Her slashed neck only holding on to her head through gristle and stringy muscle.

Victor heard talking coming from within the woods. He sprinted to the young woman's car, slouching down and hiding himself in the shadows of her back seat.

He listened intently, trying to control and silence his ragged breathing. The voices dissipated, sounded farther away. He peeked over the edge of the door, only enough to look out the window.

Victor did not see the figure that emerged from the boot of the car as it slowly, methodically climbed over the backseat in calculated, hushed movements. Creeping closer to Victor. A male, dressed in a black suit, face covered by a green gas mask with two large, shiny eyeholes and long tube running down from the mouthpiece.

Victor turned to see the man right next to him. Before he could make any movement, the gas masked man shoved the long, sharp end of an ice pick up through the soft flesh beneath Victor's neck. The gas masked man made sure the steel bar penetrated all the way through to Victor's skull.

The gas masked man covered Victor's mouth with his hand as Victor shuddered and trembled. Victor's eyes rolled white into the back of his head.

Victor saw his own reflection in the glass eyes of the gas mask.

The plastic-masked strangers—witch, zombie, ghost, mummy, werewolf, alien, and skeleton—stood around the car to watch Victor die.

With the last gasp of his strength, Victor pushed the car door open and toppled onto the dirty ground. The wood handle of the ice pick was lodged under his chin.

The strangers descended upon him, stabbing and slashing Victor's body. As Victor took his final breaths, he felt the sting and pain of sharp instruments—knife, machete, hatchet, axe, sickle, scythe, pickaxe—penetrating his flesh, until his body gave up and he collapsed in a heap.

The alien brought a hammer down on Victor's head, as if to finish him off.

The strangers dragged Victor's body deep into the woods, propping it up against a dead tree trunk.

A crude, makeshift altar had been set up amid the trees, made up of sticks, stones, animal bones arranged in geometric formations and gruesome statues, and forgotten belongings scavenged from the forest. Desiccated, decayed corpses—some merely skeletons at this point—dressed in similar fashions to the strangers' attire, leaned against trees as if they were overseeing the scene. Old black-and-white photos nailed onto the bark and spread over the foliage, as if decorations for a makeshift home.

The masked madmen took turns smearing Victor's blood over the exposed wood grain, filling in the grooves on the symbol carved into the trunk—an E and K. The alien and the werewolf rang a rusty, ancient bell, as if

128

they were signaling to the ether that they'd been successful in their bloody mission.

The sun was going to rise in a couple of hours. The strangers had more work to do.

CHAPTER TWENTY-TWO

Annie hated surprises. She always had. It was no secret that she did.

So, when Aunt Dolly showed up in Gull Valley with her best friends Diane Fenwick, Martha Gaines, Brenda Mulhern, and Karen Belmont, with Brenda's assistant Eunice Trout in tow, Annie had to settle for internal screaming, instead of the external shriek she wanted to unleash.

They had so many suitcases and bags with them. So many. All that luggage. Annie wondered if they had plans to move in and hadn't told her. Annie's own Golden Girls had descended upon her home, with no immediate plans to leave.

"Ugh," said Brenda. "This whole place needs a pressure wash with a water tower full of Febreze. Say 'Beetlejuice' three times and he would be right at home here."

"Hi, Brenda," sighed Annie. "Welcome to my home. There's no concierge or room service, but we have a live-in masseuse and nail technician."

"Really?" Brenda's eyes lit up.

"No."

"The place looks great, Annie!" chirped Karen, throwing a side-eye to Brenda. "Cruella de Vil just hasn't had her nap yet today."

"It's your birthday surprise!" Aunt Dolly cheered as she hugged Annie tightly upon arrival. "It's like a giant slumber party! We brought a limbo stick, Boggle, our weighted blankets, Chinese finger traps, and our book for book club. This month, we're reading *The Meaning of Mariah* by Mariah Carey."

"Aunt Dolly, what are you doing here?" Annie said, careful of her tone.

"Well, none of us ladies have any rent to pay, or jobs, since we're all retired, so we figured why not come stay here for a while and keep you company?" Aunt Dolly said, completely oblivious to why it was a bad idea on so many levels. "I'm going to get so many steps in here on my FitBit. Look, I'm wearing the photo necklace you gave me when you were a little girl."

Aunt Dolly showed everyone the engraved locket around her neck, opening it to show a picture of tween Annie—braces, glasses, acne, crimped hair—inside. Diane, Brenda, Martha, and Karen all responded with an "aww."

"I made you a care package," Aunt Dolly said, giving Annie a box that contained a flare gun, road flares, stun gun, bear spray, GearLight LED flashlights, portable door locks, batteries, compass, muffin basket, and a Redbubble gift card.

"Aunt Dolly, I'm not preparing for nuclear winter," said Annie. She softened her tone. "Thank you. I love you."

"Wow, it is so beautiful out here," said Diane. "And desolate. You could totally bury a body out here and no one would ever know."

"Lord love a duck! I see you still dress like you're one of the lesbian lovers in *Fried Green Tomatoes*," Brenda said, giving Annie the elevator eyes up and down to the shapeless brown and white frock Annie wore for painting.

"Towanda!" Annie said weakly, attempting enthusiasm.

"Why does your face always look like that?" Brenda said.

"Like what?" said Annie.

"Like you're sucking on a lemon."

"I guess that's just my face, I guess. I don't—I mean, I'm dealing with a lot of things right now."

Brenda was one to talk. In Brenda's case, resting bitch face was quite literally just her face at any given moment.

"Ever since you moved to the woods to live like a vagabond in Endor with the Ewoks and dance around in fields to sad Natalie Merchant records and churn butter like some Amish person or whatever it is you're doing, your aunt has been torturing us by making picture collages of all of us," Brenda said. "We blame you."

"I'm running out of wall space for them," said Martha.

"We're all members of the dead husbands club," Karen said, putting her arm on Annie's shoulder, trying to comfort her. "This place could use some potpourri. Are the beds here Craftmatic adjustable?"

"You should paint this place purple," said Aunt Dolly. "Purple symbolizes royalty and luxury, as well as creativity and a realm of fantasy. You can get back to writing your books again."

"You could write an *Alien* book!" Karen said. "Did you know that in space, farts are highly flammable?"

"In space, no one can hear you fart," Annie said, nodding. "I'm this close to having AI write my next book."

"Are you working on anything new?" said Karen. That was Annie's least favorite question. Her creativity had dwindled significantly since Gary died. She didn't want to write, or do, anything.

"I'm going to write a story about a vampire who falls in love with a mortal girl but he's got an S&M room and then they are forced to participate in a battle royale for survival at a school for wizards," Annie said. "That will make me rich and be a best-seller."

"That sounds nice," Karen said.

"We've come to rescue you from exile, Robinson Crusoe," Aunt Dolly said.

"I'm assuming I'm going to have to feed you guys now," Annie said, feigning a smile.

"Oh, no, dear! We brought lots of groceries," Martha said, as Eunice wheeled in bags upon bags of food and drinks, as though the ladies had bought out all the bulk products at Costco and Sam's Club. "I hope you like ham and bananas hollandaise!"

"I don't know," Annie stammered, mainly to herself. "What's—what's happening here? I've lost all control. What in sweet Ryan Gosling's name is ham and bananas hollandaise?"

None of the women heard her. They were busy putting their belongings down and chattering excitedly with each other, so thrilled that they'd pulled off the surprise. They couldn't see Annie's imaginary thought bubble with the words "Oh, hell no," written inside in capital letters.

Annie situated the ladies in guest house number one, the only place unstained and renovated enough for visitors. Each woman would have their own room, though they'd share a bathroom. Plus, it was the most cleaned-up building farthest away from the main house where Annie slept, which worked for her.

CHAPTER TWENTY-THREE

While the ladies were busy making guest house one their current home base, Annie had a Zoom call with Trish Vaughn, one of the members of her girl gang.

"I'm just checking," said Annie. "If I lock all of them in their rooms while they sleep, I will go to jail, right? Like, I could make a judge understand why I had to do it. I think if a judge met them, they'd go easy on me. Can I file a preemptive motion of extreme duress? This is a total boner killer. Is adult onset murderous rage a real thing? You know, I raised Aunt Dolly and her friends the best I could."

"Any contract induced by physical violence is null and void," Trish said. "Sorry, Annie. I'm putting you in a time out. I want you think about what a special hell it is when someone makes you watch a video on their phone. Bonus points if it's one of those 'Wait for it!' videos."

Trish was a public defender for the Boston legal system, spending her days at the courthouse in Government Center. She was well-known for her pro bono work and passionate closing arguments. In her free time, she watched cleaning videos on YouTube, finding something soothing and relaxing about seeing people clean their couches, make their garbage disposal drains sparkle, and declutter rain guards, catch basins, and street sewer grates.

"The last time Aunt Dolly did something like this was for Brenda's fiftieth birthday party," said Annie. "I was told it was at a piano bar and the worst horror I'd see all night would be Brenda singing Black Eyed Peas' 'My Humps'—but instead, we went to an extreme haunted house at a carnival. We said we didn't want to go inside, and Brenda kept calling us 'chicken,' so we went in. Why does being called 'chicken' work on everybody? There was this one clown that chased us who looked like Pennywise from *IT*'s scarier, more deranged sibling. One of the guys in line pooped his pants. The phrase 'down to clown' has a completely different meaning for me. When I asked Aunt Dolly what she and the girls were thinking, she just said that Brenda loved haunted houses and fried dough. Note to self—don't tell Aunt Dolly my address ever again."

"Hey, that's your villain origin story!" said Trish, before her tone became serious. "Be kind, rewind. They're there because they love you so much. Don't add us to your shit list, but Aunt Dolly told all of us about her surprise visit."

Everything became clear for Annie. Sighing, she said, "When do you all get here?"

"Tomorrow morning. I love you! Don't be upset. Aunt Dolly and Sloane swore us to secrecy. We'll go get Boba tea and shiatsu massages and fangirl over online pics of Jason Momoa and get double exposure photos taken at the mall like the ones in the '80s, where your face is just floating in the sky."

"Sounds good. It'll be fun. I love you guys, too," Annie said, rethinking her stance on some surprises. She felt relieved and loved that she'd have some company after the eerie happenings she'd been experiencing. "In the words of the great Jessie Spano from *Saved by the Bell*, 'I'm so excited! I'm so excited! I'm so scared!'"

Trish laughed and cued up The Pointer Sisters' "I'm So Excited" on her computer so that she and Annie could have a dance-off before they signed out. No matter how sad or mad Annie and her girlfriends were, they never turned down an opportunity to dance things out.

CHAPTER TWENTY-FOUR

Annie gathered all of the groceries, amenities, and food items that Aunt Dolly and her friends brought. She stacked them in her four-wheeled folding shopping cart then pulled it to the mess hall. It would take more than one trip.

The mess hall must have been a relic from when Gull Valley was a campground. Cafeteria-style tables, drink station, and a space for silverware, plates, and napkins, as well as a shelved, open pass-through that allowed people to see into the kitchen area.

Annie headed into the kitchen to the giant pantry, where she stored all of her non-refrigerated foods and perishables. She laughed to herself, thinking she was turning into one of those bunker people who overstocked and prepared for disasters by hoarding food and toiletries. Everybody bringing her food reminded her of Gary's wake—which everyone insisted they should call a "celebration of life," but to Annie, it still felt like a wake—and the days after, where all of her friends showed up daily with prepared meals and tinfoil-wrapped dinners in large cookware.

Her mind turned to the odd events of the past few days. There was no need to tell any of the girls. Best not to mention it to them. She'd put a pin in it for now and let her new meds do their work.

She opened the pantry door wide—

Boom!

George Squires, the errant wanderer and prophet of doom, took two quick, hulking steps toward her from his hiding place in her pantry.

"Leave this place now!" George wailed. "It's here! It's close."

136

Annie lurched back, jumping out of George's way as he marched forward and shouted at the kitchen utensils and machinery.

"George!" Annie said, unsure whether to try and calm him down or get out of his way. She chose to stay back and texted his granddaughter Marcie as fast as her fingers would move.

"You shouldn't be here," said George, in a desperate attempt to speak to the imaginary monsters around him. "You'll be sorry. They're waiting for you. You're going to die out here. You're going to die in those woods! You came looking for hell, and you've found it!"

George stared at something Annie couldn't see. His eyes were fixed on something past the cafeteria area, out in the distance. He walked past her, out of the kitchen, through the mess hall, and into the open grounds outside.

Annie watched him leave. Her mind spun. Why did George keep switching how he referred to the phantom menace, flipping between "it" and "they"? Did he even have the faculties to understand what he was saying anymore? Could he be the one playing these pranks on her? He was the only person she'd seen around that wasn't supposed to be there.

Annie didn't know what she'd prefer—that Gull Valley was haunted or that it was a human doing these things to her. How about neither, she decided. She liked ghosts about as much as she liked people.

Which wasn't much.

CHAPTER TWENTY-FIVE

After speaking with Dr. Crews, Annie went through her phone to find Gary's most recent texts. To her dismay, they were gone. No evidence of them existed. Had she really imagined them? Could stress and anxiety, with the bonus of the medications she took, caused her to simply invent his messages?

She frantically searched and scrolled through the text messages, finding the last text Gary sent her before he died—

Be home soon. We know you have lots of options when choosing a husband and thank you for choosing Gary. Please exit through the gift shop. Love you.

P.S. Remember that movie Drillbit Taylor? How come nobody ever talks about it?

—but nothing after it.

Annie took a deep breath and laughed to herself. Gary was such a goofball. He was funny and smart, always putting effort into their relationship. She'd somehow invented all the texts after his final one—maybe because she needed him.

This was a good thing, she reminded herself. Gary wasn't tormenting her from the afterlife, his spirit doomed to live in a hellish limbo and purgatory. It was her. She was experiencing side effects from the pills and trauma. Annie made a note to call a specialist to check the houses for black mold. She had read it caused hallucinations.

She felt relieved. Why would Gary want to scare her? That made no sense. It wasn't who he was. She thought of sweet, logical Gary, and how if he was there, he'd tell her it was Occam's Razor—the simplest answer was true.

For the first time since she moved, she took out her and Gary's wedding photo album. She wasn't entirely sure she had the emotional bandwidth for it, but she wanted to see Gary's face again. She wanted to remember happier times.

Her phone buzzed. A text message from Cal, saying he had some photographs he wanted to show her. When was she free?

She put her phone aside. She'd text him back later. She wanted one more moment to look at Gary and his lopsided smile and floppy brown hair.

CHAPTER TWENTY-SIX

Aunt Dolly spearheaded the great crepes-making bonanza in the mess hall. She, Diane, Martha, Brenda, and Karen busied themselves making a dozen different types of crepes, ranging from savory to sweet. Eunice, Brenda's twenty-five-year-old assistant, was in charge of any heavy lifting and garbage disposal.

Annie peeked in to check on them, listening to their excited chatter in the flour-filled air as they grooved to Natalie Cole's "Pink Cadillac."

Brenda took one look at Annie's flannel, Red Hot Chili Peppers T-shirt, jeans, and Chuck Taylor sneakers combination and gave her a sarcastic thumbs up. "Oh yeah, much better. The boys will just come a-running now. You look like you're the third alternate to a band that makes music with water glasses. Go and think about what you've done."

"The factory is closed, Brenda," said Annie. "I'm not desperately seeking a replacement for the love of my life."

"Not looking like that, you won't," Brenda said. "You look like one of those people who microwaves fish in the office and eats hard-boiled eggs in small spaces."

"Okay, got it," Annie said. "I'm going to take a wild guess here and say you never went to those etiquette and manners classes the ladies signed you up for."

"Don't editorialize," said Brenda. "It's unbecoming. Nobody likes tall tales or sarcasm."

Annie was used to Brenda, as well as all of Aunt Dolly's best friends. She grew up with them. They had been a fixture of her life since Annie went to live with Aunt Dolly at age eleven.

Aunt Dolly, Diane, Martha, Brenda, and Karen had been friends since they were girls. They grew up together, having met in their small Massachusetts neighborhood. Their families knew each other. They spent their youth in each other's houses, navigating the trials and tribulations of life. As time went on, they never lost touch with each other, no matter where they ended up. They'd each eventually married and raised children of their own, who spent their time in the women's houses as they grew up. It was a community of family—one that protected, loved, and supported each other for seventy years.

Annie thought about all of the things she'd seen, heard, and learned from the women she grew up around. They'd provided security and sanity for her, as she'd come from an unstable and chaotic household filled with trauma, unpredictability, neglect, and abuse. She had escaped the havoc of her parents' addictions and learned what it felt like to be loved, wanted, and seen. Aunt Dolly, Diane, Martha, Brenda, and Karen treated Annie as if she were their own, even when she didn't want them to.

"Alexa!" Brenda interrupted Annie's reminiscing. "Alexa! Play 'Abracadabra' by The Steve Miller Band! Alexa! Alexa? Alexa!"

Eunice went over to a computer on the shelf and started fiddling with it.

"Alexa!" Brenda shouted again.

"Brenda, I don't have an Alexa," said Annie.

"She means me," Eunice said, shoulders slumped. "I'm Alexa."

"Alexa, tell us a fun fact about crepes!" said Brenda.

Eunice brushed her curly, shoulder-length blonde hair from her face and typed furiously on the computer keyboard. She read aloud from the screen.

"In French folklore, there is a tale that crêpes were born of a 'happy accident,' when a thirteenth-century housewife in Brittany accidentally spilled some buckwheat porridge from a kettle in the fireplace onto a flat cooking stone, but other sources put crepes much earlier on the timeline," Eunice said.

"What? I can't hear you!" Brenda snapped. "Do you have a bird in your throat?"

"That's not an expression, Brenda," said Diane. "It's frog."

"Frog?" said Brenda. "Why would someone have a frog in their throat?"

"And her name is Eunice, not Alexa," Diane said. "Be nice or I'm going to donate all your fancy jewelry and expensive clothes to charity. Think about it—poor people walking the streets, wearing your designer clothes and shiny broaches."

"You wouldn't dare, you old battle axe!" Brenda snarled. To Brenda, the thought of the unwashed masses having her prized material gains was a fate worse than death.

"I know where you live," Diane said.

Diane had played the role of Contessa Wilhelmina von Strathmore Windham Vanderpatch (and Wilhelmina's evil twin Lucretia) for forty years on the long-running soap opera *As the Wind Blows* until it's cancellation in 2013. Other than a six-episode arc on *Blue Bloods* in 2016 as a woman who was attacked during a tug-of-war tournament and fell in love with Tom Selleck, she had mostly retired from acting. The last audition she went on was for the Lifetime TV-movie *The Wrong Wedding Planner,* but she lost out on the part to Jackée. Lately, Diane had attended soap opera conventions and meet-and-greets, signing autographs for soap fans.

Diane wasn't an A-list celebrity or even particularly famous, though she'd amassed quite a fanbase over the years and still got fan letters for her role, a shocking number of them from prisoners. Soap operas didn't have the power to reach an audience like they used to, leading to the show's demise. When Diane was younger, she wanted to become an actress like her movie and television idols, like Janet Leigh, Kim Darby, Shirley Knight, Patty Duke, and Karen Black. She started her career in low-budget B-movies and long-forgotten grindhouse pictures, then landed her soap role. She'd done several made-for-television movies over the years, the most famous being *Not Without My Pressure Cooker.*

"Eunice!" Brenda wasn't quite done. "You move with the speed of a life-sized Mrs. Potato Head. One day we'll get you out of those skorts and Lane Bryant rags and Spanx and find you some troll that lives under a bridge to marry and you guys can finally write that book about ferns you've always dreamed about."

Despite Brenda's cranky demeanor, Annie admired many things about her. Brenda was a doer. The world was full of people who constantly claimed they were going to do things, but Brenda actually went out and did them. Every time she set her sights on a goal, she worked and scraped and battled until she won what she wanted. She'd had a long career in several businesses, from real estate to paper goods to fashion. She had been the CEO of the Quickdraw Oatmeal Company, the third largest breakfast conglomerate in New England. All of her endeavors were smashing successes, which in turn made her quite wealthy and fond of her money.

Why she needed an assistant in retirement was a mystery. She had no real need for one. Annie surmised it was simply for companionship and Brenda's inability to let go of being the boss.

Why Eunice, who was so sweet and pleasant, worked for Brenda was another mystery. Eunice was getting her PhD in human development with a minor in psychological anthropology, which possibly explained why she chose to work for a bossy, demanding tyrant. For Eunice, it was research into the mind of a deranged septuagenarian.

"How are you doing out here all alone, Annie?" Martha asked. "This place looks straight out of *The Leftovers.* It's so empty here. Like we're the last people alive. Are you lonely?"

"Alone, not lonely," said Annie, forcing a smile.

"I often wonder why bad things happen to good people," said Martha. "Is it fate? Bad luck? Wrong place, wrong time? Why do good people die when horrible, hateful, ignorant people live forever, never punished for the terrible people they are? It's so unfair. All of the people who die every day, all the victims who suffer while there's all these people who get away with bad things and are all alive and well and go on procreating. There's no justice in the world. But however you choose to deal with it, you know we all support you. We've seen the way you eat barbecue ribs and still love you, so you know we'll always be here for you."

Martha had worked for a sponge company until her retirement. She used to have everyone in the neighborhood come over for barbecues and badminton after church on Sundays. She was considered the unofficial mayor of their little community in their small suburb of Massachusetts, always there to lend sugar and sympathy to those in need. Martha was well known for dispensing level-headed advice and having an open-door policy at her house. She had many friends and acquaintances but her heart belonged to her children and Aunt Dolly, Diane, Brenda, and Karen.

"I often wonder if the 'Are you still watching this?' notification is actually helpful," Annie said. "Stop judging me, Netflix! If I want to watch seven hours of *Brooklyn Nine-Nine*, let me! You don't know my life. You don't know what I'm going through. Your judgment only sends me deeper into a shame spiral."

"You always do that," said Diane, putting her flour-covered arm around Annie. "You always deflect uncomfortable topics with humor."

"You should learn from your repeated mistakes and behaviors, Annie," Karen said. "Life is all about perspective. Instead of saying, 'Sorry,' say, 'Thank you.' Like, 'Thanks for waiting for me,' instead of, 'Sorry I'm late,' or, 'I get to go to work,' instead of, 'I have to go to work.'"

"Okay, I'll try it," Annie said. "Thank you for showing up unannounced at my home. I get to learn how avoid certain situations by stopping being so nice and starting saying, 'No.'"

"Sarcasm is the lowest form of wit, Anne Porter," Karen said. "You could have it so much worse. Think of the poor guy whose job it is to shave people's nether-regions before surgery or the person who has to clean dressing rooms when people take dumps in them."

"I don't need others to ruin my day," Annie said. "I can do that all by myself."

Karen was a former secretary and devoted housewife. There was always a cherry pie or upside-down pineapple cake cooling on her windowsill. She was obsessed with tornado preparation, convinced that even though they lived in New England, a tornado could strike at any moment. She always left a wooden slat over the washer and dryer when she wasn't using it. She would make her children squeeze into the washing machine and dryer and practice yelling for help, through the dryer duct into the wall connector, so that they could call out to be rescued if Karen ended up dead and the house fell down. Karen would always tell her kids, "Hurricanes flood! Tornadoes destroy!" More recently, she'd texted Annie in the middle of the night to ask what a 'fuckboi' was.

"Do you hear something?" Aunt Dolly said.

The sounds of Reba McEntire's "Fancy" filled the air. It emanated from the cafeteria area. Annie lit up as soon as she heard the chords. She knew what it meant.

"Right on time," Diane said, in on Annie's surprise.

Annie dashed out into the mess hall to see her people waiting for her. In particular, her best girlfriends—Alice, Chris, Ginny, Jess, Kit, Laurie, Nancy, Rachel, Sally, and Trish—waiting for her. More than waiting for her.

They were dancing to "Fancy" like they were the back-up dancers on Reba's tour. It was their special tune, symbolizing their solidarity, sisterhood, and empowerment. The women had created their own special choreographed dance to the song, perfected over years in bars and clubs in their twenties and thirties, and were reenacting it in the mess hall for Annie.

Annie watched on with a beaming smile. Her heart felt full. Aunt Dolly, Diane, Martha, Brenda, Karen, and Eunice stood behind her to observe the sacred dance routine. Annie waved at her girlfriends, who were busy dancing and lip-synching.

The rest of Annie's new arrivals, the men in their lives—Bill, Dave, Max, Ned, Richie, Sean, Steve, T.P., and Wes—cheered on the synchronized show. Annie teared up at the sight—all of the friends that she and Gary had collected over the years, the ones who had become their chosen family, there in Gull Valley.

Standing next to the men was Beverly, Ned's girlfriend. She and Ned had been dating for a year. Annie and her friends liked her but Beverly was most definitely the new girl in the group.

The only thing that was missing was Gary.

When the women finished their dance, the onlookers applauded.

Annie and most of her friends met in Film Club during college. They had spent countless nights watching movies and television shows, listening to music, going to concerts and bars, and talking about life, love, relationships, books, art, and pop culture.

They had all maintained their friendships with each other no matter where their lives took them. They shared what Annie felt was an unbreakable bond, forged by late night conversations, similar political and religious beliefs, and unmistakable affection for each other. And pop culture. Always pop culture, from the obscure and forgotten to the modern—though none of them were particularly up on most of the current trends. Pop culture—the language of Generation X.

They had the kind of friendship where everyone spoke openly and sometimes even over each other, without filter or embarrassment—many times with very little segue from one topic into the next. Their dialogue was a free-for-all. They were comfortable with each other to the point that they all knew nothing—not differing opinions, not disagreements, not jokes—would destroy their friendships.

Annie was turning forty-seven in two days. Like all of her friends, she was born in the 1970s. They were all members of the oft-forgotten Generation X. The people who grew up during that magical time when there were no cell phones or social media platforms. Who went from replacing vinyl albums with cassette tapes to replacing cassette tapes with compact discs to learning how Napster worked to music streaming services. Whose parents weren't home when they got home; latch-key kids who spent their evenings on their bikes and getting into whatever they could without their parents ever really knowing where they went, until dinnertime rolled around. Who called a number from their mustard yellow-colored landline phone so an automated voice could tell them the time and temperature.

The kids who grew up renting movies and not streaming them, waiting entire summers for their favorite television shows to come back, having parents smoke cigarettes in their faces, and teaching themselves how to set the clock on the VCR. A world without influencers, TikTok, Facebook, Instagram, instant gratification, participation trophies, Yelp reviewers, people filming themselves crying, and cancel culture.

What Annie would give to make a mixed tape again. Annie didn't think the world was any worse nowadays—especially with the advancements in medicine, technology, and electronics. It was just different. She missed the era when people didn't feel the need to express every emotion and feeling to the world just because they could hide behind their computers. She missed the days of limited TV stations and how every friend she had kept warm memories of some random, unknown movie they watched with their family a hundred times because it was always on one of the eight channels they had.

Annie had seen *Who's Harry Crumb?* approximately two hundred and twenty-three times while she was growing up. And the Jim Belushi/Charles Grodin movie *Taking Care of Business* that was constantly on.

"Is this my intervention?" said Annie, as everyone rushed to kiss and hug her.

All of her people were there for her, as they had always been. In that moment, Annie felt a happiness she hadn't experienced since Gary was alive.

"You said you were coming tomorrow!" Annie said accusingly to Trish.

"Well, we knew you needed us here, and we wanted a surprise within a surprise," said Trish.

"Sloane will be here later tonight," Ginny said. "She had meetings she couldn't get out of, but she told us to tell you that you're a goddess, an icon, an idol, a queen, and her hero and she'll be here later tonight."

"She's selling a house that has a sordid history, so she put a 'Not Haunted' sign on the sales board outside the house," said Jess. "Which, of course, is very convincing. Nothing lets people know your house isn't haunted more than a huge billboard claiming it's not."

"You look like a Portishead song," Nancy said, brushing back Annie's hair. "We came just in time."

"And we brought you these," said Laurie. She held up a white bag full of Doughboy Donuts chocolate crème-filled doughnuts.

"Oh my god, you guys do love me!" said Annie, taking the bag of her favorite treats from the doughnut shop, pizzeria, and deli ten minutes down the street from where she used to live in Boston.

148

"I brought you something too," Sean said, handing Annie a Gold Bond anti-chafe stick, a bag of marbles, and a Slinky. "My mother always told me you're supposed to bring the host housewarming gifts."

"Thanks, Sean," Annie said. Goofy Sean, always trying to make everyone laugh. "I'll save these for a special occasion."

"I wore my special Hulkmania boxer briefs for this," said Sean, pulling his jeans partially down to reveal his red undies with yellow writing.

"That's very nice?" Annie didn't know what the appropriate reaction was.

"Put your ratty drawers away, Sean!" Aunt Dolly said. "Everyone here has seen your bum more times than we ever wanted to."

Everyone laughed. Annie sighed, scanning the room to see her friends gathered together, almost as if she was double-checking that it was real. That they were really there.

"You're all here," Annie said. "I'm so glad you came. I know it was a hike."

"Do you know how much roadkill we saw on the drive up here?" Richie said. "It's like *Pet Sematary* out there."

"Sloane put out the Batman signal and we assembled," Kit said. "We all missed you. The girls told us to tell their Aunt Annie that they love her."

"We all met at the train station in Hartwell and took Ubers and Lyfts here," said Chris.

"I do not think our Lyft driver was amused by the journey out here," Dave said.

"Yeah, or the fact we had to listen to these five belt out 'Un-break My Heart' by Toni Braxton on the ride over," said Bill, pointing to Trish, Nancy, Alice, Ginny, and Sally. "I was doing mathematical calculations in my head to see how fast the car was going compared to how badly I'd hurt myself if I jumped out onto the road."

"You had a tear in your eye," said Sally. "We moved you with the power of our voices."

"That wasn't a tear! I don't cry. That was just extra testosterone leaking from my eyeballs!" Bill said. "And the only person who was crying in that car was the driver because your singing was like a thousand nails dragging across a chalkboard. I hope you tipped that poor man extra."

"This place is unreal," said T.P. "You own all of this? All my family owned growing up was our own burn barrel and some broken-down cars in our back yard. We were one rabbit cage away from officially being white trash."

"Yeah, Sloane got me a good deal," Annie said. "It's home."

"Annie, why don't you get everyone settled in their rooms and then we can all sit down and have some crepes?" Aunt Dolly said.

Aunt Dolly shooed them away as Annie guided her friends out of the mess hall.

CHAPTER TWENTY-SEVEN

Annie got Trish, Bill, Sally, Dave, T.P., Sean, Rachel, Chris, Ginny, and Wes settled in guest house number two. Ned, Beverly, Laurie, Max, Jess, Richie, Alice, Steve, Kit, and Nancy took guest house number three. The plan was for Annie's houseguests to get situated, then they'd all reconvene for crepes in the mess hall.

In the meantime, Annie went back to the main house and checked her email. She had a message from Cal with several photos and a file attached.

Cal wrote that he'd found some weird anomalies in the pictures he'd taken on her property the other day. She didn't finish reading his note before she clicked on the first photo.

Cal had marked up the pictures with red arrows and circles to point out what she should be looking at. Annie's eyes widened when she saw what he wanted her to see.

The first photo was a long-distance snap of the tree line. In between the trees stood several nondescript figures, their features partially blocked by the foliage.

The second photograph from a medium distance, of a sole figure standing at one of the windows of the church. It looked like a young woman, dressed in a black Victorian wedding gown.

The third photo was a blurry shot of a silhouette between two of the guest houses, as if someone was peering out from behind the structures.

Were Annie's eyes playing tricks on her? Was she seeing things that weren't there? She knew about pareidolia—where the mind attributes human characteristics to explain images and find shapes in random images.

Then again, it could have been Mr. Brisket, Ms. Click, Jack, or Ben. She wasn't really always alone in Gull Valley.

As if on cue, Mr. Brisket knocked on her door, startling Annie from her racing thoughts.

"I have the key for the locked room," Mr. Brisket said, handing over a key that looked like it came out of a Gothic horror novel.

"Thank you," said Annie. "I actually read online that skeleton keys are a myth. Who knew, huh?"

"Just call me if you need anything," he said in that weary way he always spoke, completely disinterested in small talk.

Though Mr. Brisket was seventy-five years old, he was surprisingly agile and strong. Annie imagined he'd been a hard laborer his entire life, or perhaps former military, from the generation where men worked in fields or mines all day and came home to the meals their homemaker wives had prepared. He had no use for human interaction, preferring Annie to give him a list of the day's chores so he could carry them out by himself.

"Okay, then," she said as he exited. "Good talk!"

Annie returned to her email. She read the rest of what Cal wrote.

Okay, not to be an alarmist here, but either you have uninvited guests on your property, or the spirits of The Felicitous still haunt Gull Valley. I know I sound like Stephen King here and I'm not trying to scare you, so here's a link to a book about The Felicitous and a gif of a golden retriever puppy learning to walk down a staircase.

Annie clicked on the link.

A new page brought up a book entitled *The Felicitous: A History of an Insidious Cult*, written by Dr. Arthur Wainwright, released in 2020.

Annie hit "buy now" on the Audible button. She would listen to the audiobook when she had time.

Ghosts? She didn't really believe in them. This was where her life had taken her? Should she laugh at the absurdity of the thought or cry that she was entertaining the notion that her home was overrun by cult ghosts?

Or was the proper way to say it, "the ghosts of cult members"? "Cult ghosts" sounded like the ghosts themselves were in a special club different from other ghosts and didn't do the things people thought ghosts usually did, like a bunch of dead cool kids who turned their noses up at mainstream paranormal activity and judged conventional ghosts.

Hipster ghost nonsense.

Why did Cal automatically assume that it was the ghosts of The Felicitous, given that the land was hundreds of years old and saw more than its share of varied owners, travelers, death, and madness?

Why did Cal's appearance coincide with all of the scary things that were occurring around her?

Stop thinking, Annie chided herself. *Turn it off.*

Either way, she was glad her friends and family were staying in Gull Valley with her.

CHAPTER TWENTY-EIGHT

Kit Granger and Steve Collver had two daughters at home, both under the age of ten, that they rarely spent overnights away from. As they unpacked their suitcase, they found some of the items their girls had secretly packed away for them—Steve's old Stretch Armstrong rubber doll from when he was a kid, a bag of half-eaten ketchup chips, and a Berenstain Bears book.

Kit was a licensed therapist with several college degrees, fluent in many languages, and once waved at the wrong person at Whole Foods and was so embarrassed, she never went back.

Steve owned his own construction company, wondered what awful thing had happened to create the expression "Keep your eyes peeled," and had a habit of falling asleep in his favorite chair at home with a sandwich in his hand.

"You're getting sad face," Steve said. "The girls will be just fine."

"I know. I keep thinking about them all trapped and alone in the house without us."

"They're not veal in a cage. Your sister is there. She'll take them out of the house."

"Last time she watched them, she and her husband ate cookies in front of the girls and didn't even offer them any!"

"Yeah, they're fucking weird."

"Anxiety and excitement are physically the same," Kit said, more to herself than to Steve. She was happy to be in Gull Valley to see Annie but missed her kids.

"Let's enjoy this weekend," said Steve. "A break from the never-ending cycle of rent, bills, laundry, and grocery shopping. The next best thing to never working again. It's my dream to give up the nine-to-five lifestyle. Corporations don't care about you. Take your days off."

"You're the boss of the company, Steve," Kit said. "You request your days off from yourself."

"Yep," said Steve. "And I'm an award-winning businessman."

"Are you talking about the 'Best Drywaller Ever' award?" said Kit. "The girls made that and gave it to you."

"You're just jealous 'cause you're not the best drywaller," Steve said.

Steve opened the closet door to hang up his shirts.

"Whoa!" he said, jumping back.

"What? What is it?" said Kit, standing next to him.

Inside the closet stood a mannequin. Its face was smashed, burned, and smeared with paint and weird symbols. It was dressed in a tattered, shredded suit.

A note was attached to the suit jacket pocket. It looked like a page from a diary or journal, written in cursive. Kit grabbed it and read aloud.

"'No one will protect me like Bishop Laird will. No one loves me like Bishop Laird does. There is no other god than Bishop Laird. I commit to follow his teachings until the day I die. I will die for my leader and my family. I vow to follow Bishop Laird's word of truth and destroy all infidels and non-believers that stand in the way of justice and righteousness. I shun the lies and deception of the world. My eyes are open to the truth Bishop Laird has shown me.'"

"Whoever wrote this is one of those people whose fingers are always covered in Cool Ranch Dorito dust," Steve said. "Those dumbasses who go on Reddit to ask stupid questions like, 'I ate an apple seed, is an apple tree going to grow inside of me?'"

"It's kind of scary," said Kit.

"It's wannabe supervillain nonsense," Steve said. "People are gullible. They lie so much, they start to believe the shit they're peddling."

Steve crumpled the note up and threw it in the trash.

"I'll get rid of this," he said, grabbing the mannequin out of the closet.

"Please do," Kit said.

CHAPTER TWENTY-NINE

Sally Forster and Dave Sanders put away their belongings in their temporary lodging. Sally stared at the framed poster of Burt Reynolds from his infamous 1972 *Cosmopolitan* centerfold, where he posed nude on a rug, that hung on the wall.

"Take your eyes off Burt and come back to me," said Dave, unpacking a stack of clothes and putting them into a dresser drawer.

He pulled an acid-washed, black jean jacket out of the drawer. It had a Good Charlotte patch sewn onto the right pocket.

"Do you think Annie would let me keep this?" Dave said, trying it on. "Look! It fits me perfectly!"

"I'm sure Annie will be okay parting with somebody's crusty, dirty, used old Good Charlotte jean jacket," said Sally. "That thing is not coming home with us. It's probably covered in emo tears, eyeliner, and depression."

"That's what you said about my mother when she came to visit last Easter."

Sally and Dave had been married for twenty years. They had three children. Sally worked as a children's book illustrator, while Dave was employed as an elevator inspector.

"I just don't want Annie to be upset with us," Sally said. "We've never been to Gull Valley. It's our first time seeing it. She's never invited us here. We kind of sprung this on her."

"She seemed really happy to see everyone," Dave said. "She's depressed and has PTSD from trauma. People deal with things in different ways, Sally. This might be the only way she knows how to regain some control over her life. We all love her. Sometimes, we have to let people we love make their own choices and come to terms with things in their own time. You can't 'mom' everyone, Sal."

"I'm not trying to dictate her decisions or pass judgment on her."

"I know, I know. It comes from a place of love and worry. You're like that with the kids, too. Did you notice that this place is as far away from water as possible? The lakebed is completely arid. I don't know if that was a conscious or subconscious decision on her part."

"I don't know what I'd do if something happened to you. I don't know how Annie does it. That's my worst fear, something happening to you or the kids. How do you recover from that? Do you ever think about that?"

"Yes, I've planned it all out. Once you're gone, I can finally run away and shack up with Greasy Dana from town. We'll live in a shanty by the sea, making money from our cotton ball art and raising chickens to sell their eggs to tourists, since eggs cost the same as rent these days."

"Ladies and gentlemen, the father of my children. Your brain is like a bad neighborhood. You shouldn't go there alone."

"You help your kids make jumpsuits out of Brach's Turkey Dinner Candy Corn one time and suddenly, all the mean parents in your magnetic poetry group treat you like you're the guy who carries around one of those thirty-two-ounce wolf urine jugs. If Lady Gaga did it, it would be called fashion."

"To be fair, you did start eating their jumpsuits in front of people. While the kids were still in them."

"I was hungry!"

"Our kids never ate paste or paint chips, so that's a win for our parenting. Also, why are you still in that magnetic poetry group?"

158

Dave thought to himself for a moment. "My worst fears are sharks, demonic possession, bedbugs, and getting old. If Hollywood ever makes a movie where a demonically-possessed shark gets infested with bedbugs and goes on a killing spree at an old folks' home, I'll never sleep again. Mine seems kind of dumb now though, compared to yours."

"You're an idiot," Sally laughed.

"You married me."

Sally dropped a pair of pants on the floor. She bent down to pick them up, seeing beneath her and Dave's bed.

Several large, sealed glass jars rested beneath the mattress and frame. With a grunt, Sally reached under the bed and pulled out four of them.

Inside each of the jars were faded, sepia-toned photographs with graying borders.

In each photo, the same man—maybe mid-thirties, shoulder-length hair, with a stern and serious expression on his face, dressed in an unusual gray robe and suit combination—stood behind a seated person, his hand on their shoulder. The seated people varied in each picture. The tall, lanky man was the constant, like a master lording over his subjects.

Sally held them up to show Dave. While the photos themselves weren't overtly frightening, there was something unsettling about them.

"Are these our welcoming gifts?" said Dave.

CHAPTER THIRTY

Chris Sawyer stared at herself in the full-length mirror that hung on the wall of her room. She looked at her reflection, her mind wandering.

As Chris and her friends approached their fifties, lately her thoughts had turned to the passing of time and how their lives had been so full of potential when they were in their twenties. The years had gone by so quickly. There were so many missed opportunities. How did they end up the way they did? It wasn't necessarily a bad thing. She simply wondered what the path not taken would've been like, and what she would have said to her younger self now that she had experience and wisdom.

No matter what path we choose, do we always regret it? Chris remembered how exciting and boundless everything seemed in her youth, when they were all forming their group of friends that grew and changed over the years. Were they now just like everybody else—trapped inside the lives they'd made for themselves, victims of their choices, older and hopefully wiser?

She used to feel as if time was limitless. Now the crushing dread of aging, and the realization that there were more summers behind her than ahead of her, weighed on her mind. They used to go to raves and stay up until six in the morning, eating disco fries at all-night diners.

Now Chris had favorite emojis, knew that "I before E except after C" was a blatant lie, got into debates over whether the Helvetica font was a professional choice for emails, and had perfected that smushed-smile face people make when they pass an acquaintance on the street—that face everyone makes when walking by someone that's not a friend, but not a stranger. Her favorite songs were now solely played on the oldies radio station. She didn't want to rock-and-roll all night and party every day anymore.

She wanted to sit on her comfy couch in her Snuggie and watch *Dr. Quinn, Medicine Woman* reruns.

Chris was a successful theater director, respected and well-regarded. She had a great career and friends she loved. She breathed in, smiled, and then her thoughts shot in a different direction.

She'd read articles about two-way mirrors but forgot how to tell if it was one. She put her finger to the glass, trying to recall if a gap between her fingernail and its reflection in the mirror was the good kind of mirror or the creepy kind.

Before she could ask Siri, she was interrupted by T.P. knocking gently on her door.

T.P. Mitchell was what would be called a "ladies' man"—a confirmed bachelor who frequently attracted multitudes of beautiful women to keep him company. He was a good-looking, in-shape, successful finance broker who could've had a career with Chippendales if he'd wanted.

He'd never overstepped his bounds with any of the women in their circle of friends, valuing the platonic nature of the friendships he'd made through Annie and Gary. Like the rest of the gang, he was fiercely protective and loyal to their crew.

T.P. trusted Chris and often called on her for advice. They'd cultivated a sort of brother-sisterly banter over the years.

"I can tell you have something you want to talk about," smiled Chris.

"Yeah, actually, I do. Could you read over a letter I wrote for me?"

He almost looked small as he handed Chris a folded-up piece of college-ruled notebook paper from his pocket.

"What is this?" Chris asked suspiciously.

"It's a letter I wrote to Cinnamon," T.P. said. "She was my girlfriend. I think I really love her. I screwed it up though."

"Cinnamon? Her name is Cinnamon."

"I know," T.P. said, almost dreamily. "It's beautiful."

"She's a stripper?"

"She's a lawyer."

"She's a stripper."

"She's not a stripper."

"She's a stripper."

"No, she's not."

"She's a stripper."

"She's a stripper," T.P. conceded.

"You don't marry girls named Cinnamon. Who names their kid Cinnamon? You are dooming your kid from the start. You never hear, 'Please rise for the honorable Judge Cinnamon!' But you do hear, 'Next up on the pole, Cinnamon!' Girls named Cinnamon have parents who should never have been allowed to procreate and hamster wheels where their brains should be."

"Stop being judgmental for one minute and help me," T.P. pleaded. "You're always fast-talking at me like one of those Gilmore Girls. It confuses me. Like how I'm not supposed to call The Dixie Chicks 'The Dixie Chicks' anymore. What do I call them? Who are they?"

"Yes, I can see how that would be stressful. I'm here for you."

"Chris, I really love her. Like Cersei and Jaime Lannister love."

"I'm not sure that's the best metaphor to use here, but okay. You've never actually seen *Game of Thrones*, have you?"

"Please," he said in such an unguarded way that it melted Chris's heart and she secretly rooted for T.P. and Cinnamon's weird love.

162

Chris groaned and started to read the note. She got about five lines in and tossed it back to T.P. with disgust. "These are just the lyrics to Avril Lavigne's 'Sk8r Boi'!"

"She'll understand what it means. We had something really special, me and Cinnamon," T.P. said. "We're just like Ross and Rachel. We met on a tour that took everyone to all of the *Fred Claus* filming locations. One look at her in her shiny gold pantsuit and I knew that she was the one. She's like the Mentos jingle. She got in my head and now I hear her on a loop for days."

"Wow, this is definitely uncharted territory for you. I'm really happy for you, T.P. When do we get to meet her? Wait, why haven't we met her? What did you do?"

"Why do you assume that I did something?" said T.P. He lowered his head. "Okay, I may have gone to poundtown with several other girls recently. I screwed up. In my defense, Cinnamon and I never said we were exclusive. We have an understanding. It's not cheating if we're in different time zones, on a scavenger hunt or haunted hayride, or in a WeWork space."

"It's like Jane Austen wrote your romance. You should be a motivational speaker," Chris said, treading the line between teasing him and being there for him. "T.P.! First off, who says, 'poundtown'? Gross. Secondly, I think your man-bits are like a wildfire that needs to be put out. They're like a Wal-Mart—open twenty-four hours and available to anybody."

"I would be a terrible motivational speaker," said T.P. "I know you guys all think of me as a sexy renegade and studly rebel, but I can't tell others to unleash the beast in them when my beast is a clumsy, happy golden retriever just looking for pats and food."

"Sexy renegade. Yes, that's exactly what we think," Chris said, trying to sound convincing. None of her friends thought that. "A lion doesn't have to tell people it's a lion."

"And fact check, my dearest Chris—I do not apologize for my wanton, unbridled sex appeal."

"I'm not slut-shaming you here. I just hope you get more out of life than your crotch does. And that you get your monthly flea-and-tick treatment." Chris teased him, but she knew he felt bad. It was rare for T.P. to mention any girl he dated seriously. Usually, he had a revolving door of dates that were on an ever-changing rotation for Annie and Gary's game nights.

"At least I'm more genuine than the people who record themselves doing nice things then post it to the internet so they can be online heroes," T.P. sighed, trying to convince himself of his inherent goodness.

"Come on, let's go get some crepes," Chris said, putting her arm around T.P.'s shoulder. "We can discuss the next steps on what to do about Paprika."

"Cinnamon," T.P. corrected her.

"The lawyer," Chris said, leading them out of the room.

The full-length mirror on the wall shook slightly.

Click.

The mirror slowly swung open, as if its left side were on hinges, like a door.

There was something—someone—watching from behind the mirror. From within a hidden room, swathed in darkness. What the room contained, where it lead, its purpose and reason for existing unknown.

Long, bony white fingers gripped the mirror's frame as though it could shatter the glass through sheer anger and force.

The mirror slowly returned to its closed position, as if it had never been opened in the first place.

Click.

CHAPTER THIRTY-ONE

Despite the reservations that nagged the back of her brain, Annie told Cal that he could come back to explore Gull Valley. The conditions were that Rex and Ruby weren't allowed to go in and out of the buildings, as some were still quite dilapidated and had holes in the floors, asbestos that needed to be cleared out, and broken glass, among other dangers.

She'd hang out with her friends while he took his photos. There was something kind about Cal that made Annie want to trust him. But then there was a part of her that wasn't prepared to yet.

Annie met Cal, Rex, and Ruby at the makeshift parking lot. Rex and Ruby seemed thrilled to see her and gave her hugs upon arriving. Rex held his beloved dirty potato in his hand. Ruby was decked out in her Celine Dion memorabilia.

"Annie, we were playing 'Would You Rather?'" Rex said. "Do you know that game?"

"Sure, of course," said Annie.

"Would you rather be a shoe or a unicorn?" Ruby said. "Would you rather be an eyeball or a shoe? Would you rather have a cup of tea or be eaten by a wolf? Would you rather have teeth like a lion or normal people teeth? Would you rather have a watch or fish earrings?"

"Whoa, slow down, guys," said Cal. "Let her answer one."

"Okay," Ruby said. "Would you rather be a kid or a grown-up?"

"Um, a grown-up, I guess," said Annie, her inner thoughts overtaking her mouth as she stared off into the distance. "But I'd love to go back and give my younger self grown-up advice. One day, you're young and playing with your Jem and the Hologram dolls and feel like you too are truly outrageous, and the next you wake up with gray hairs, back pain, and an ever-present sense of anxiety and melancholy. Suddenly, the doctor prescribes you fiber pills and tells you you're at the right age for compression stockings and Depends and you start wondering where the time went. You never went to Spain like you always said you would. You never bought that deserted island with a castle out of a fairy tale or the house by the ocean. You start to wonder if life is just a matrix or a simulation and you're just Jim Carrey in *The Truman Show*—everyone's in on it except you. It's harder and harder to see friends because everyone is so busy and moves farther and farther away, and you try to keep in touch, but everyone's got their own things and worries and it's always stress and pressure. You start to think about the last time you laughed really hard, like really laughed. Soon you sound like all the adults you made fun of growing up and realize they were right when they said you'll understand when you get older. It's infuriating because they're right—you will understand. You tell yourself you won't let things get to you but then replay them all day and all night, and when there aren't any problems in your life, your brain will actively work against you to create and find one, so you can never just relax or have a moment of peace to yourself. And you have to pee like ten times a night, so forget it if you finally got comfortable in bed, that's a fleeting dream."

"Huh?" said Ruby, her little face scrunched up.

"Oh, uh, I'd be a grown-up for sure," Annie righted the ship. "You can eat cake and cookies whenever you want. How about you?"

"A grown-up, so I can yell like Daddy and tell kids what to do," Ruby said. "Would you rather be a heart or a circle? I'd rather be a heart, 'cause a heart can make it on its own."

"You went on a little stream-of-conscious one-woman show there," Cal said to Annie. "You reminded me of my crazy neighbor who would show up at my door at 3 a.m. with a power drill and say he had to fix my enchiladas."

"I'm ranting to a sweet, innocent eight-year-old. I also Google numbers not in my contact list that call me and stay inside on nice days. I've become my Aunt Dolly," said Annie. "I should have a sign on me that says, 'Please slow drively.' I actually saw that sign on a road in Hartwell."

"No, I dig it," Cal said, laughing. "You had a moment. That faraway look in your eyes, I thought you were headed to where Peter Pan lives. It was like the Cliffs Notes version of your mind. 'You must be this tall to ride. Keep your hands and feet inside the ride at all times. Do not operate heavy machinery when talking with Annie. Do not feed the animals.'"

"Would you rather be a lion or a crocodile?" Rex asked Annie, uninterested in what the adults were discussing.

"A lion, I guess," said Annie.

"I'd be a crocodile, because lions would get diarrhea if they ate me!" Rex laughed.

"Stinky word!" Ruby said. "Rex said a stinky word!"

"Hey, let's all calm ourselves down and woosa," Cal said.

Cal, Rex, and Ruby rubbed their ears and said, "Woosa, woosa, woosa." When they finished, he looked over at Annie.

"We passed a hedgehog store in Hartwell. A whole store dedicated to hedgehogs. There's that much call for hedgehog amenities? I call bullshit. It's clearly a front for money laundering."

"Dad!" said Ruby. "No stinky words!"

"Oh, sorry," Cal said. "Daddy will wash his mouth out with soap later. We're not allowed to say 'stinky' words— poop and fart words are bad. Ruby doesn't like them."

"Good to know," Annie said.

"I got you something!" Ruby said. She disappeared to the back of Cal's car.

"I looked your books up," Cal said. "You're pretty prolific. Twenty-eight books? Color me impressed. I ordered the first book in the *Windows of Time* series. You must be very proud of yourself."

"Well, thank you. My agent thanks you for your patronage and percentage," Annie smiled.

Ruby reappeared, clutching a giant, oversize stuffed plush goose. It had X-s for eyes. She held the stuffed goose out for Annie. "This is for you. Her name is Anna Maria. My favorite animals are whales, dolphins, birds, and geese."

"Wow," Annie said as Ruby handed over the goose. "Hello, Anna Maria. Thank you so much, Ruby. This is so thoughtful of you. You know, I have something for you, too."

Annie handed Ruby a compact disc. Liza Minnelli's *Liza With a Z.*

"This is Liza Minnelli. I figured since you love Celine and Barbra, you'll love Liza too. I saw it in a used record store in Hartwell and thought you might like it."

"A compact disc?" said Cal. "I haven't seen one of these in a long time. Annie and I went from albums to tapes to CDs to Napster to streaming."

"I love it!" Ruby shouted, hugging Annie tightly around her waist. "Thank you, thank you, thank you!"

"Okay, Carrot, let her breathe," Cal laughed, putting his hand on Ruby's head.

"We got Dad some stuff, too!" said Ruby.

"Yes, you did," Cal said. "I'm now the proud owner of several packets of Taco Bell mild sauce, a puka shell

168

necklace, a Nicholas Sparks novel, and my personal favorite, my own Irish Spring body wash. Message received, kids. The best part is, they're presents but I paid for them with my credit card."

"You're very generous," said Annie.

"I'm cold, Dad," Rex said, inserting himself under Cal's jacket and hiding inside of it.

"We did this for ten minutes before we left the house, too," Cal said to Annie, motioning to the lump beneath his jacket. "You okay in there, buddy?"

"Mmhmm," Rex said, his voice muffled. "This is my invisibility cloak."

"You know who else I like?" Ruby said. "Taylor Swift, Kelly Clarkson, Lana Del Rey, Katy Perry, Lizzo, and Nelly Furtado. I know they're not new, but they're new to me! Katy Perry has a bra that shoots fireworks."

"Yeah, Carrot, you're too young for a bra, let alone one with pyrotechnics," Cal said, then turned to Annie. "We just watched a video of Madonna singing 'Hung Up' and she emerged out of a giant disco ball. Guess who wants a giant disco ball in their room now? I told her she can put it in the suggestion box."

"It's me!" Ruby said. "I've been practicing and rehearsing my dance routine all week."

"Construction starts Monday," sighed Cal. "I'm project manager. You know, when I was her age, I was obsessed with the revolutionary war. I used to go to the library and read everything I could about it."

"The library?" Ruby said.

"Yes," said Cal. "That's where people got their information before TikTok was invented and were offended by everything. Before the internet, we just believed whatever old wives' tales our parents and friends told us. I truly believed gum stayed in your stomach for seven years. Thanks for that, Aunt Darlene."

"Why do you call her 'Carrot'?" Annie asked. "Ruby, I mean, not your Aunt Darlene."

"Well, when you were little," Cal said, looking at Ruby. "The only thing you'd ever eat was carrots. That's all you liked. You were like a little bunny. So, your mom and I started calling you 'Carrot,' right?"

Annie hoped and prayed that something that sweet was not coming out of the mouth of a demented would-be stalker.

"I brought some stuff for you to look at," Cal continued. "I know you have company and you're really busy, so at your convenience. I can get it out of the car later. Thank you, again, for allowing me to come and look around. I know it's weird, to say the least."

Alice, Laurie, and Nancy saw Annie chatting with Cal, Rex, and Ruby and walked over to join them. Annie introduced everyone. Rex gave a muted hello from underneath Cal's jacket.

"Want to watch me do a cartwheel?" Ruby said.

Annie, Alice, Laurie, and Nancy all agreed enthusiastically.

Ruby's version of a cartwheel was more of an ungraceful, uncoordinated tumble across the ground. Ruby stood triumphantly as the women cheered her on.

"I taught her that," said Cal. "What does the song say, Carrot?"

"I get knocked down, but I get up again," Ruby shouted.

"Ah, the wisdom of Chumbawamba," said Laurie. "Some people turn to Oprah, Socrates, or Deepak Chopra for advice, but Chumbawamba sings the words that we all need to live by and should be stitched on a pillow."

Laurie Hughes was no stranger to cross-stitch. She was Annie's most crafty friend. A master at convincing her kids that their eyes would remain crossed forever if they made a face and were smacked on the back, she also

170

provided amazing salad dressing recipes and balanced her demanding job as a counselor at a non-profit women's shelter with raising six kids. She was a supermom Martha Stewart-MacGyver combo, who loved flowers and could make anything out of duct tape and state fair ribbons. If there were ever a PTA or mother existential crisis, Laurie was the one everybody called.

"Annie said you're doing a book on the history of Gull Valley," Nancy said. "Have you discovered anything particularly interesting?"

Nancy Butler gave up her job in corporate America after two decades of stocks and bonds to go back to grad school and get a degree in music therapy. She had come to the realization that companies don't care about people, even the ones who worked there their whole lives. There was no loyalty, and Nancy had felt stifled and trapped.

She was going to *Eat, Pray, Love* like Julia Roberts. Her children were out of the house, she was single, and she wanted a new direction, so she made the scary decision to embark on a second act in her late forties. She frequently reminded herself that there was the world everyone lived in versus the real world, and wanted the world she lived in to be less cold, angry, and unforgiving than the real one.

"It's been used as a nuclear testing site, a wellness retreat, and before that, a stagecoach route and traveler's inn," said Cal. "But my focus is on The Felicitous and their lives here, where they are now, and the horrible things they did."

"I saw a documentary about them a long time ago," Alice said. "They were seriously terrifying and well-organized. They basically made this place into a fortified castle. They really weren't all about the Chicken Soup for the Soul lifestyle. It made me realize how woefully unprepared I am if there's ever a zombie apocalypse."

"They lost their way," Cal said.

"Do you have any hot chocolate?" Rex peeked out from his dad's jacket.

"We'll get some after we have a look around, okay?" said Cal.

"Can we go explore the woods?" Rex asked Cal.

"As long as you promise to stay close enough that I can see and hear you at all times, and don't touch anything dead or dangerous-looking. And stay on the path. Only the marked trails, okay? There's all kinds of big, deep holes in those woods. And bear traps. And maybe elves and faeries and old bottles of that green ketchup from the 2000s, I don't know. Don't climb anything! Promise?"

Rex and Ruby nodded excitedly. Cal thought of all the places Ruby and Rex could hurt themselves. Among other things, Gull Valley woods was home to abandoned fire towers, outposts, and forest ranger stations that would undoubtedly be lures for kids' curiosity.

"You have to do your magic juju fingers to put a protection spell on yourselves first," Cal said. "If you get lost in the woods, we can't watch *America's Funniest Home Videos* tonight."

Rex and Ruby waved their little fingers in the air, sprinkling the magic all around themselves.

"Ya-da-da-da-da-da!" they chanted.

"How was that?" asked Ruby.

"No notes," Cal said. "Close your eyes."

He pulled insect repellent spray out of his jacket pocket and spritzed Ruby and Rex over their jackets.

"Bugs bite me because they like me," Ruby said. "They like to give me kisses."

"If Dad asks you to pull his finger, don't," Rex said to Annie. "It's a trick."

"I'm not gonna—" Cal said, shaking his head. "Get out of here, you buckethead!"

Ruby and Rex giggled and dashed toward the tree line.

"Make good choices!" Cal shouted. "Stay together! I'll come get you in a little bit! You can't escape Godzilla! Roar! Godzilla is coming!"

"You have wonderful kids," said Laurie. "You know they're not going to listen to a word you just said, right?"

"Yes, I do," Cal said. "But they'll stick together. And we grew up in the '70s and '80s. We survived burning hot metal slides, parents who smoked cigarettes in our faces, jungle gyms made for prison yards, and parents who told us self-esteem and allergies were all in our heads and we needed to shake it off if we fell off of the roof. Rex and Ruby are strong. They'll be all right."

"You're doing a good job, Cal," Laurie said. "I raised my kids with space to let them figure out who they are. They can be whatever they want to be but Lord help them if they grow up to be jerks."

"Thank you. I try. It's all their mother," said Cal. "They are so loving and caring one minute, then ready to rumble the next. The other night, we were watching that Olsen twins movie. The one with Kirstie Alley and Steve Guttenberg."

"*It Takes Two*," said Laurie.

"I just have so many questions about that movie. They're identical strangers, yet somehow look exactly alike? How did neither of the parents not notice the difference between them? What are the odds that they ended up on the same lake, at the same time, when the world is so big? Were they born at the exact same time, so they're exactly the same age? Why am I overthinking an Olsen twins movie? It makes no sense. Anyway, Rex said to Ruby, 'I'd know if you weren't you, if you were a pod person or something had taken over your body and was pretending to be you and I had to kill you,' and Ruby screamed and ran to her room and cried until Rex promised they could watch *Lilo and Stitch*. Then they put on the Phil Collins *Tarzan* soundtrack and had a sing-along."

"Wow, that story was an emotional rollercoaster," said Alice. "Kids are strange. Mine used to steal things from the lost and found box because they thought they were free prizes for them. Whenever I'd tell them something, they'd respond, 'This could've been an email.'"

Alice Fulton worked as a technical manual writer. Her kids were mostly grown and out of the house. She had been divorced from her cheating, good-for-nothing husband for almost a decade. She taught her children not to be anyone's consolation prize, took up kickboxing in her late thirties, believed that life was all about perspective, hated age-targeted ads, and thoroughly believed that there was a special place in hell for people who came into restaurants right before they closed and/or stayed beyond closing time (rightfully so, those people are the worst).

"When my oldest son was in middle school, he had a retainer and would always throw it in the trash at the end of the day," said Nancy. "He thought he would get a brand new one every day."

"Kids are dumb," said Cal.

"Kids don't poop rainbows and sunshine. That's the big secret all the other parents keep from you before you become a parent yourself," Laurie said.

"I'm not good at setting boundaries," said Cal. "I let them watch way too much television. I let Rex watch *Deadstream* the other night. Great movie, but definitely not for kids. Turns out kids like to say they won't get scared, but then they do, and I'm the idiot. It's hard without Mara. She was really good at that stuff. Their Aunt Lyla helps out as much as she can, but it's not her responsibility to raise my kids. I've learned a lot. Especially never to say, 'Ice cream truck' out loud."

"There's five thousand channels to pick from now," said Alice. "It takes longer to decide what to watch than to actually watch it, and by the time I pick, I fall asleep ten seconds into it. First world problems, I guess."

"We're not here to judge," Laurie said. "We all had to do this. You know what they say."

"I'm on a seafood diet," Cal said. "I see food, I eat it?"

"No, not that saying. If you can't beat the fear, do it scared," said Laurie. "Never evaluate your life when you're tired, which you always are when you are raising children. And don't take criticism from someone you wouldn't take advice from."

Eunice waved at the crew from the mess hall. She headed toward them with a grim look on her face.

"Brenda said to get your—" Eunice lowered her voice. "—butts in gear, because the crepes are ready. But she didn't say 'butts.'"

"Well, that's my cue," Cal said. "I'll be around, taking photos and videos, if you need me."

"You don't think that The Felicitous are still around, do you?" Alice said. "I mean, they went their separate ways years ago, didn't they? The members would be in their seventies and eighties now. Geriatrics with canes and AARP cards. They'd need Activia and Metamucil just to do whatever creepy cult rituals they used to do. The rest of them would be ghosts."

Cal was quiet for a moment.

"I will fill you in on more details later, but there's a lot of things happening regarding The Felicitous," Cal said. "In the past couple of years, several former members of the cult, and people connected to them—doctors, nurses, people who wrote reports on them, anyone who spoke out against them—have either gone missing or been in accidents, or worse, killed. And there's a whole online community on the dark web that has websites and information about them. A new generation of young people who are fascinated and bewitched by the ideology of The Felicitous—I mean, their uneducated, nostalgic version of it. But The Felicitous has fans. Someone—or many someones—has been putting flowers on former cult members' graves and at the Hubbell family crypt. And that's not even scratching the surface of the people who were once a part of the cult and their families, who live different lives now. It's all a giant clusterfuck. I'm trying to make sense of it all. There are tons of threads and fragments that are connected to the cult, even after all of this time has gone by. But everything is going in different directions. Like a big game of Tetris—all the pieces fit together, built on top of each other. I just have to find out how. Annie is going to help me with my amateur sleuthing. The Felicitous is gone in theory, but there's still people out there who will never let it die."

"Why do I suddenly feel like we're being watched?" Alice half-joked.

"Is Annie in danger?" said Laurie. Everyone turned to look at Annie.

"No," Cal said quickly. "No, of course not. She's not connected to The Felicitous at all."

"She lives in Gull Valley," Laurie said. "Where The Felicitous used to tie-dye their hippie wear or whatever they did. She's been hearing and seeing things—people— on her property at night."

"Guys," Eunice moaned, as if she were about to explode. "Brenda's waiting."

"Do you want to join us for crepes, Cal?" Nancy said, trying to brighten up the subject matter.

"No, I'm going to make like a tree and go. I want to make sure I'm in shouting distance if the kids need me. And I can take pics on my own. But thank you, I appreciate the offer."

Cal headed down toward the buildings as Eunice waved her hands at Annie, Nancy, Laurie, and Alice to get their "butts" moving.

"Speaking of pictures, I want to get some of all of us," Laurie said. "We're not all together often these days.

I want to do some serious ones and some funny ones. I was thinking, maybe a shoulder train, where we all line up with our arms on the next person's shoulders?"

Laurie demonstrated, causing Alice, Annie, and Nancy to burst into laughter.

"Should we use props, too?" said Nancy. "Giant beach ball? Matching T-shirts from Zazzle with our faces on them? Tongues out, peace signs up, our hands in that 2000s alt-rock nu metal Limp Bizkit pose, with sideways caps? Maybe Photoshop ourselves onto a pumpkin patch or apple orchard?"

"Are my little, old hag, troll friends off of my Christmas card list? Survey says, 'Yes,'" Laurie said.

Annie, Nancy, and Alice hugged Laurie, laughing as they walked.

"How many times have you heard the word 'crepes' today?" Alice said.

"So many," said Annie.

CHAPTER THIRTY-TWO

The whole gang of Gull Valley visitors had assembled at two of the long tables in the mess hall as Annie, Nancy, Laurie, and Alice arrived. Eunice was busy at the food table, making sure the seventeen different types of crepes were kept warm and accounted for. Aunt Dolly, Diane, Brenda, Martha, and Karen flitted and hovered, making sure everyone was getting fed and had drinks.

The room was abuzz with laughter and conversation. Old friends catching up, telling stories, talking, reminiscing. Full of cross-conversations, comfort, and humor that came with the years of friendship.

"Well, thanks for gracing us with your presence, ladies," Brenda said in Annie's direction. Brenda was so tightly wound, Annie expected a spring to pop out of her someday.

"Don't mind her," Diane said to them. "She's upset because she just found out she doesn't have a vibrating bed here. I'm going to put a tranquilizer in her pill organizer. If that doesn't work, we'll just feed her giant sugar cubes like they do with horses and she'll overexcite herself and pass out."

"No hats at the table, kids," Aunt Dolly said preemptively, in case anyone dared. She called these late-fortysomethings her "kids" because they were. She'd adopted Annie and over the past decade and more, she'd adopted Annie and Gary's friend family.

"I found this in the pantry," Karen said, showing off a box of Bill and Ted's Excellent Cereal that had most likely been there since 1991.

"I'll give you a dollar if you eat some of that," T.P. said to Sean.

"A dollar to risk my health and safety to eat something that's probably a weapon of mass destruction now?" said Sean. "Make it a dollar fifty."

"Don't you dare," said Rachel, putting her arm across Sean's chest.

"Did you just 'soccer mom' me?" Sean laughed.

Sean Rhodes was their class clown and court jester. He had a free spirit and massive wanderlust that kept him roaming the world, yet he always came back to be with his friends. Sean wrote a successful travel blog that detailed his exploits at all the places he'd visited—seeing the castles of Scotland, the Northern Lights in Iceland, the lush green hills of Ireland, May Day in Germany, and hundreds of other destinations. His Massachusetts accent made him incapable of saying the word "bananas," properly (he said, "bananers," every time) and once had a rash that was featured in a medical journal.

Karen shook the cereal box. Sean leapt up to get it.

"Nothing can go wrong with this plan," said Rachel. She'd seen Sean do some stupid stuff before, from snorting pixie sticks to trying to start a local luging and bobsled team, but she wanted to save him from the possible side effects of eating radioactive cereal. They weren't in their twenties anymore.

Rachel Webber had kids of her own, so she could live with being called a buzzkill. She was happily divorced and ran her own successful boat tour company out of Boston. Her hobbies included worrying, overexplaining, reading too much into things, taking things personally, thinking everyone was mad at her, overthinking, and wishing she had all the confidence and self-delusion of George Santos. Rachel could turn any room into a panic room. It came from a place of love and had served her well; she was always prepared for any situation, as she'd played every possible scenario out in her head beforehand.

Rachel was working on herself with a therapist. Despite her role as a world-class worrier, Rachel raised well-adjusted children and learned that stress balls were for squeezing, not for throwing at people. She often wondered, what's a "diggity" and how did you know if you had none?

Annie arrived at the crepes table, smiling to herself. The table was set up with plates, napkins, utensils, flowers, and syrups, as if Aunt Dolly and her gals were opening a fancy breakfast restaurant.

"Don't put your hand in front of Annie's food while she's eating," Aunt Dolly warned the others. "You might lose it. Annie used to work at a summer camp every year when she was a teenager. The owners put a limit on how many hot dogs she could eat on Hot Dog Friday because they said she ate too many."

Annie looked sad at the memory. Aunt Dolly patted her arm and said, "It's okay, my brave little toaster."

Wes Carrigan was picking out which crepe he wanted. Wes was Gary's lifelong best friend. Wes had loved Annie right from the moment they met and stayed in touch after Gary's death. He was a single gay man, working as a patent lawyer—not the most thrilling job. Not what Wes expected to have after a youth filled with raves and glowsticks, but he liked the work. He often wondered how awesome it would be to look like Milo Ventimiglia for a day and frequently envisioned himself as Whitney Houston in *The Bodyguard*, imagining young Kevin Costner carrying him to safety in slow-motion as "I Will Always Love You" played.

"Tell me you made a Rooty Tooty Fresh 'N Fruity one, Aunt Dolly," Wes said.

"I did, just for you, Wes, since it was your nickname in high school," said Aunt Dolly.

"Still a savage," Wes smiled, shaking his head.

"Oh, that's right, you're the gay one!" Karen cheered. "My grandson is as gay as a hummingbird in flight. Do you know him? He took me to a Kesha concert last summer. So much glitter!"

180

"Yes, we all know each other," Wes said. "We keep in touch through a big, gay Rolodex."

"Glitter?" Sean said. "Have you heard about the glitter conspiracy?"

"Oh, no, not this again," said Sally, recalling Sean's conspiracy theories on everything from the MKUltra experiments to the way media covered natural disasters and political scandals. She was thankful that Sean wasn't a flat-earther or moon landing-denier. "Sean, do not go to your crazy place. Don't get all weird and bajiggity."

"Nobody knows who's buying all the glitter," Sean said. "It's not drag queens."

"And here we go," Sally said.

"Our government is using the glitter in military operations to kill people," continued Sean. "It's full of chemicals and dangerous toxins. It's in toothpaste and cars. Nobody will tell us who is buying it. There was a worldwide shortage of glitter but no one knows how or why. It can cause problems in electronics and electrical devices, and our military uses it for secret defense projects. You better believe I'm going to talk about it."

"Who's your source? The My Pillow guy?" said Alice.

"I'm just waiting for the men in white coats with the giant dogcatcher's net to come collect you," Sally said to Sean.

"That's a type of apophenia, Sean," said Kit. "Finding connections between unrelated things. It's how we find meaning—seeing patterns in random events, like objects or ideas. Are you seeing spots or hearing voices that aren't there?"

"Everything I say is one thousand percent fact," Sean said. "My imaginary friends and I are perfectly normal."

"Why does nobody pose for album covers with puppets anymore?" Dave said, trying to sway the topic away from unsubstantiated glitter theories. Dave and Sean were best buddies. They'd spent many afternoons getting high and watching *Mallrats* and *Superbad*, but Dave

181

wasn't a fan of Sean's outlandish claims. "You ever notice how people go crazy for bread? What is that? And what's a Timothée Chalamet? It sounds like a paper plate company."

Brenda was calling out for Eunice, shouting over all of the conversations.

"Where is that girl?" Brenda cried. "Probably snorting bath salts and dancing to the *Godspell* soundtrack in a Caldor's parking lot in one of those stupid, faded No Fear shirts. I ask for so little in this life, yet I'm still disappointed by people."

"Here's your spinach and artichoke dip." Eunice burst through the kitchen door and put the plate down on a side table near Brenda.

"Heavens to Murgatroyd, Eunice!" said Brenda. "You barge in here like a moose escaping a velociraptor attack! Go stand on the front lawn with the other lawn gnome and maybe you can finally find a husband to help you pass out your Bright and Shiny survivalist compound pamphlets. I could draw a face on a piece of celery and it would be more useful to me!"

"Should we say something? Stick up for Eunice? I feel like we should step in and do something," Richie whispered, eyes on Brenda. "I would, but I'm terrified of Brenda. My home economics teacher told me to 'Stay cool' in my yearbook and I'm trying to follow through."

Richie McCoy, Jess's husband, was an Eagle Scout as a teenager and ran an advice column in The Boston Globe as an adult. Under the moniker "Miss Petunia," Richie was infamous for dishing out vicious, no-holds-barred advice that became watercooler talk. Though only his friends and immediate family knew his true identity, his other claim to fame was having his picture on the wall of Boston Fish 'N' Chips, where he completed the Whale Challenge and consumed almost one hundred ounces of cod and French fries in one sitting.

182

"I know she is basically an evil crone who eats children like she's the missing Sanderson sister from *Hocus Pocus* and she'd probably harvest my organs and sell them to the highest bidder but I find her dragon-like demeanor oddly fascinating and fabulous and sort of want to be her sometimes," said Jess. "I know fear and respect are two different things, but I think I feel both."

Jess Tapert, Richie's wife, was a well-respected veterinarian in Boston. Sometimes, she wondered if she loved animals more than people, present company and her children excluded. She found that the animals at her office seemed to enjoy EDM music the most so she played it frequently for them, considered New Year's Eve a night for ridiculous amateurs who couldn't hold their liquor, and had an entire category of what she considered "in-flight" movies—films that were good enough for a long plane ride but not to watch in her spare time. Romantic comedies, anything starring Kate Hudson, SyFy channel creature features, things of that nature.

"That woman has definitely buried a dead hooker in the woods somewhere," said Richie.

"The food looks amazing, guys," Annie said, trying to get Brenda off of Eunice's back. "Aren't you hungry, Eunice? We'd love it if you'd hang out with us."

"She should be serving you!" Brenda said, holding up a large spoon in Eunice's direction. "You pick this up. It's called a spoon. And then you put the food on our guest's plate. I swear, I'm going to attach you to a rocket and send you to outer space, where you can contact the other aliens from your planet and Jodie Foster can make a sequel to *Contact* where she discovers you, then you and your people can read her your weird Property Brothers erotic fan fiction! You can tell her, 'Vroom vroom baby, it's been a nice ride!'"

"Oh, it's okay," Annie said, laughing nervously. "I can do this myself. My hands work. You guys can mingle. Go mingle! I'm an independent woman, like Destiny's Child."

Brenda wasn't done with Eunice. "Maybe they'll remake *What's Eating Gilbert Grape?* and you can get cast as the mother. And for God's sake, start using that moisture-wicking T-shirt I bought you. You are covered in meat sweats like a sumo wrestler. You're about as helpful as a non-playable character in a video game."

Eunice snapped, her face full of rage. "I'm going to piss in your J. Lo Glow perfume, you mummified wretch!"

Everyone stared wide-eyed at the interaction. Aunt Dolly, Diane, Martha, and Karen barely registered the exchange, as if it was normal to them.

Eunice set her jaw. "I'm going to put Visine in your prune juice so you shit your dusty bones out, you heifer!" Eunice snarled, her frizzy hair shaking.

"Oh, Eunice, I just love you," Brenda said. "You know when I refer to you as Ugly Betty, it's just my way of expressing myself. You're a good girl. Now go eat your lunch in the laundry room, far away from us so we don't have to watch you shovel food down your gullet like a deranged Magilla Gorilla. I sprinkled some Cookie Crisp on the dryer for you. You can practice your breakdancing in there. Don't forget to use that dandruff shampoo I got you later."

"Okay," Eunice said, as if nothing at all had happened. "Just ring the bell if you need anything."

With that, Eunice bounced away. Everyone exchanged dumbfounded looks. Brenda placed an old, rusty bell the size of a small elephant next to her seat at the table.

"I miss when you could judge people without everyone getting so upset," Brenda said. "We live in a world where green M&Ms are a controversy. Some people will spend their whole lives offended. Let me decide what I'm offended by. I tell my associates that getting their steaks well-done is a sign of lower intelligence—which it is, look it up—and suddenly, I'm Ursula the Sea Witch from *The Little Mermaid*."

"That movie always confused me," Ned said. "Ariel wants to be a part of your world—you know, a world filled with people. It's just proof she's never met the general public. Do you think once she got her wish and saw how stupid, rude, and entitled everyone is, she thought, 'Oh, crap, I've made a huge mistake'?"

Brenda leaned closer to Annie. Annie didn't know if she should be scared.

"Family is important," Brenda said. "I'd know, I've been married four times. My first husband, poor sweet man who ran estate sales, used to watch *Wheel of Fortune* with me every night until I told him I no longer wanted to buy a vowel, if you know what I mean. I didn't need Miss Cleo's Psychic Network to tell me I was justified in leaving him for my skeeball instructor. This is what we call a 'teachable moment.'"

Annie moved to take a seat when Brenda lowered her voice.

"I know how I come across," said Brenda. "But as you age, you have a choice. You get bitter or you get better. I know right now, you're doing what you have to do. We all process grief differently. You're doing the best you can, under the circumstances that you're in. I want you to remember that everything is temporary. People are like tacos—they fall apart but we still love them. You've had enough tragedy for one lifetime, Annie. What I'm trying to say is that if living way out here in the woods is your version of self-care, I will stand behind you and support you however I can. We all will. That's why we're all here. Because we love you. Even when I'm yelling at you, it's only because I love you and want what's best for you. Make sure you say what's in your heart, because no one is guaranteed to be around forever. You don't ever have to apologize or be afraid to say you need us. That's not selfish. You've been through an unimaginable trauma and it's our job to be here for you. But always remember, nobody is coming to save you. You have to save yourself."

Annie was speechless. Brenda being sincere and loving in a conventional way was not a common occurrence. Brenda was a woman who had two photographs on her office desk—one of herself and the other of her with her group of friends. As each of Brenda's friends in the picture passed away one by one, she drew red X-s over their faces and steeled her resolve to be the last one standing.

"Also, remember that as you get older, your feet get wider, so buy bigger shoes," Brenda said. "Oh, Lord, I need an antacid. I'm making myself sick. This conversation never happened."

Brenda left to sit with Aunt Dolly, Diane, Martha, and Karen. Annie nestled herself in the center of where her friend crew sat.

CHAPTER THIRTY-THREE

Cal had been so preoccupied taking photographs and documenting the layout of Gull Valley that it took him some time to realize he hadn't heard his children laughing and yelling in a while. He set out to the edge of the forest, listening for their little voices.

Father of the year, he scolded himself.

He assured himself that the kids were safe. He played in the woods growing up and was fine. They'd just be covered in dirt and grime and need new outfits.

"Rex? Ruby?" Cal called out, stepping into the woods.

"You can't catch me, Dad!" Ruby called from the distance. That was the signal from her to chase her.

Cal only ran under two conditions. One, if someone told him they had a truck full of pizza, and if he could catch up to the truck, he got to have all the pizza. And two, if someone was chasing him. Neither had happened yet. What other reasons were there to run? Every year, he read about people who got hurt at the gym or going hiking or bungee jumping. That's why working out was so dangerous, like deep sea exploration or safari expeditions. Too many variables that could get you killed. He'd stay doughy but mobile in his own way.

Cal picked up his pace on a dirt path that led directly between the trees and foliage. He saw Rex and Ruby up ahead, both laughing and panting in that overjoyed way that kids did when they're having a fun time.

"I see you!" He called out in his best monster voice. The kids both screamed and giggled and ran farther into the woods. Cal was committed to this bit now. He was careful not to step in muddy spots. He didn't like being dirty, covered in smegma and who knows what.

"Can't catch me either, Dad!" Rex proclaimed as he whizzed past Cal to catch up to Ruby. He couldn't see either of his kids through the greenery.

He followed the path into a heavier, thicker part of the woods. Most of the trees had full, lush leaves, letting slivers and fragments of sunlight shine down.

Cal heard the crunching of leaves and breaking of sticks underneath feet in the distance.

He saw someone peeking out from behind a tree. Cal took take a step toward whoever it was when he realized the person was too tall to be one of the kids. He and the stranger were at eye level. As quickly as the person peeked out, they disappeared again.

"Hello?" said Cal. Maybe it was a hiker or one of Annie's friends.

Snapping twigs behind Cal refocused his attention. He shook off a momentary fear and stretched his arms out like he was reaching for the throat of an imaginary victim.

"I'm Godzilla!" Cal bellowed. "I'm coming to get you!"

He heard the kids laughing and running away but didn't see them.

Signs were nailed haphazardly to trees along the pathway—*No Trespassing! Danger! No Entry! Keep Out! Private Property! Stay On Trail! Travelers Advised Not To Leave Paved Road! Reduced Salt Zone! Wrong Way! Road Work Ahead! Men in Trees! Road Closed! Drinking Water Protection Area! Dead End!*

Cal got deeper into the trees, the pathway narrowing in the distance. He kept noticing people emerging from behind trees then hiding immediately. In different sections of the woods, from all sides.

"Rex! Ruby!" Cal tried not to sound worried. "Come on out! We have to go home now!"

No response except for the sound of feet scampering and dashing around him, leaves and twigs crunching and splintering, echoing throughout the woods.

Cal knew it was probably just animals and nature enthusiasts. Although now that he thought about it, he hadn't seen a single animal, or heard any bird calls or noises he'd associate with a forest teeming with members of the animal kingdom.

His line-of-sight caught something unusual and out of place.

A giant section of trees was cordoned off by yellow caution tape wrapped around them, forming a squared-off section. Tacked to the trees were several missing persons flyers protected by laminated covers. Unknown faces stared back at him, their names and the dates they went missing in bold type on the pages.

Cal steadied himself as his mind raced. There were lots of reasons for people to vanish. Animal attacks, people becoming disoriented or injured and succumbing to illness or exposure, or the wish to purposely disappear. He could've stumbled upon something illegal or illicit, like a drug operation or other criminal business. Or it could be a serial killer. Maybe several serial killers. He could be in a serial killer's lair. There were a lot of bad people out there who would sleep just fine at night after ending a human life.

At the top of the center tree was a rickety, weathered treehouse with brittle wooden slats leading up the bark to an opening.

One of the trees had a tire swing hanging from it. There was something wet stuffed inside of it.

An abandoned campsite sat within the confines of the caution tape. A ripped, disheveled tent stood, the frayed tears and lacerations in the fabric flapped against the breeze. Camping gear, long since forgotten, was scattered around the site. A circle of rocks enclosed a fire pit filled with charred wood.

Ziploc bags filled with rotten, moldy food. Waterproof plastic bags with camping equipment, such as ropes, maps, a compass, hunting knives, walkie-talkies, batteries, and matches scattered near broken lanterns and coolers, pots and pans, silverware, binoculars, and torn sleeping bags with their stuffing coming out. A circular manhole cover with the words "O.Z. Gedney" emblazoned into the metal rested against the bottom of a tree.

Cal's mind conjured up several scenarios. Did someone live here? Did something happen to them? It seemed like they left in a hurry. All their stuff was still there. It looked like evidence at a crime scene.

A sheet fluttered in the wind, suspended on a clothesline by clothespins. It was covered in dark, dried-out stains and remnants of whatever waste the wind carries.

He walked around the taped-off section, viewing it from different angles. As Cal strayed farther off of the semi-marked trail and deeper into the forest, he saw something else.

To the right was a seven-foot hill with a metal door on its side. It had a large circular contraption that needed to be unscrewed to open the door, the kind found on a bank vault. The door was marked by a clumpy red paint-like substance, a big smear covering the top above the circle door opener. It wasn't red like blood but looked like some kind of oatmeal paste. The hill was not thick or dense, though the door must have somehow led below the ground, like an entrance to a bunker. Right underneath where Cal stood. He shuddered.

Okay, it was time to go.

One more step forward so he could see what was beyond the hill. Past the hill, deeper into the thick of the woods, was something moving around. Cal caught a glimpse of someone wandering around aimlessly, almost oblivious to his surroundings. Amid the foliage, he saw a bedraggled, gaunt-faced older man covered in gray and brown blankets and rags, pacing and mumbling something

190

to himself. He didn't seem to notice Cal, or much of anything, merely ambling in circles and engrossed in his own world.

That's when the sound started. An intermittent knock that seemed to come from multiple directions, one at a time, as if a call-and-response.

Knock. Knock.

Against the trees surrounding Cal. Like a baseball bat being clacked against the bark. Once, twice, again and again. One knock, then another in reply.

Cal hustled back toward the path. Where were Rex and Ruby? The knocking noises had not subsided. As he walked, he turned to look at the battered tent.

He saw the bottom half of someone standing inside of it, only visible from their waist down. Dirty, black-stained blue jeans and work boots. The top part of the tent, though cut up, obscured his view of who it could be.

Cal picked up his pace, his eyes catching the sheet flapping in the wind. As a breeze swished by, the sheet moved and he saw the indent of someone's face imprinted on the fabric. Someone's face pressed against the white. It was only for a moment, but he saw it. There was someone standing directly behind the discolored sheet, watching Cal.

Cal told himself to be reasonable. This was coincidence. Campers, hikers, people enjoying a day out in the woods. People traveled from miles away to visit the expansive beauty of Gull Valley's forest and had every right to be there.

"Dad!" Cal heard a voice call from far off. The kids were looking for him, wondering where he'd gone. He had strayed far away from the trail.

He sped-walked down the pathway. As he got closer to salvation, the entrance to Annie's property, he felt the eyes on him and heard footsteps all around him in the woods, stalking him.

Cal's heart almost burst with relief when he saw Rex and Ruby at the path entrance, laughing excitedly to see him.

Cal broke his own rules about running and sprinted to his children, hugging them tightly and moving them away from the woods.

"You didn't find us," Ruby said.

"I know," said Cal. "You guys are such good hiders."

"Who's Godzilla?" said Ruby.

"He's a monster."

Ruby's face got serious, her big brown eyes wide.

"He's fake! He's not real. Monsters are not real," Cal said quickly, trying to cover his tracks. Ruby seemed happy enough with this answer.

Cal kept looking over his shoulder, back toward the woods, as they walked.

There was nothing—nobody—there.

As Cal, Ruby, and Rex passed the buildings, Cal made a note to himself to Air Drop pictures to Annie when he got home. They had much to discuss.

The trio passed Jack and Ben taking a break from working on the siding of the storage facility. Jack was on the stoop, smoking a cigarette and drinking a beer. Cal said a quick hello as they walked by.

"Don't smoke in front of the kids!" Ben said to Jack. "Bad role model!"

"They're not our kids," said Jack. Neither Jack nor Ben had kids.

Crack!

A piece of siding crashed down, hanging from its nail. It smashed into one of the windows, sending a split through the glass.

"Fuck!" Ben said.

"Ha!" Jack leapt up. "You said the mother of all swear words! You're the bad role model! Yes!"

192

Ben ignored Jack's celebration and got back on the ladder to secure the loose siding.

Cal, Ruby, and Rex reached the car.

"What's wrong, Dad?" Ruby said.

"Nothing, Carrot," Cal said, getting his kids into the vehicle. "Everything's fine. Let's go visit Aunt Lyla."

CHAPTER THIRTY-FOUR

The crepes party in the mess hall was wrapping up and the reunited friends chattered and joked with each other. The feeling of togetherness and joy was palpable. Annie realized that she hadn't felt this happy in a long time.

Sean was on his second bowl of Bill and Ted's Excellent Cereal.

"Tastes like chicken!" Sean said. "I don't feel so good."

"You're a few pecans short of a pie, aren't you, honey?" Brenda said.

"I like pie," said Sean.

"Okay, this is a very, very important question," Alice said. "Which Chris do you want to be stuck on a desert island with—Hemsworth, Pine, Pratt, Evans, or Messina?"

"Meloni!" said Chris. "No question. Always Meloni."

The rest of the women, and Wes, all enthusiastically agreed.

"You have too much spare time on your hands," Ned teased Alice.

Ned Watkins made his living as a calendar photographer. Lately he'd been dreaming of giving it all up and becoming a driver—any kind of driver with a company car. Maybe for Polar Seltzer. Or Red Bull. He wondered what it would be like to drive the Oscar Meyer Wienermobile. Just freedom on the open road, slinging hot dogs and club soda. He'd imagine himself becoming a keytar player in a jug band, or making candy at the Necco Wafer factory, or working in an artificial flower factory. Something that made him feel less tied down to the daily grind.

194

"You could make a ton of money putting this place on Air BnB, Annie," said Sean. "Can you imagine the ragers people must have thrown here back in the day? All this open space. It feels like another world here. Maybe you and Beverly can get married here, huh, Ned?"

Ned choked on his food. He wasn't expecting the question, though he had considered asking Beverly to marry him. Ned really liked her. Beverly was smart and fun.

"You know me, I'm a party animal," Ned said. "As long as I'm in bed by nine and get the ten hours of sleep a night I require. How about you, Beverly? You want to raise the roof and shake it like a saltshaker Polaroid picture?"

"I was never cool enough to get invited to those kinds of parties," said Beverly. "When I was younger, I worked every night at the video store and went home to go on my *X-Files* fan forums. The only person who ever talked to me was the cashier at Arthur Treacher's in the mall food court, who always wore the same Big League Chew gum T-shirt and told me he'd give me a sign when the apocalypse was coming by giving me free clam chowder."

Beverly Brown lived in a quiet little seaside town and spent her evenings reading on her porch swing and listening to her records. She was the daughter of a sheriff, a member of the local women's choir, and was currently learning how to play the piano. On one random night out a year ago, at a diner with the girls from the singing group, she met Ned when the waiter mistakenly brought her the chili rellenos he'd ordered.

For their first date, Ned had invited her to the Dreamland Theater to see a revival of 1986's *Haunted Honeymoon*, starring Gene Wilder, Gilda Radner, and Dom DeLuise. It was the best first date she'd ever been on.

"Wow," Brenda said. "That was a really sad sentence. You should tell that story during your wedding speech."

"This would be a lovely spot for a wedding," Karen said.

"Ignore them, Beverly," Ginny said. "We're all still learning about boundaries."

"I don't mind," said Beverly. "It's kind of sweet how you guys talk to each other."

Brenda hovered over Alice and Rachel. "And where are your husbands?"

"No husbands," Alice said, throwing out "help me" eyes at the rest of the group. "I don't really need a man in my life to feel okay. I like having my own space and independence. I have me. I'm enough."

"There's a very nice boy named Woody Penderghast who lives in town by Spivey Point," Brenda said. "He's a deputy for the Boston Sheriff's Department. He's single. We could introduce you. People call him Constant Woody because he's so dependable and has always lived around here."

"That's not why they call him Constant Woody," Aunt Dolly said. Diane, Martha, and Karen chuckled.

"He finished fourth in his graduating class at the police academy," Brenda said.

"There were four people in his class," Martha said.

"Good grief, Brenda!" Diane said. "You're like a wet skunk in a paper bag."

"You could be a deputy's wife, just like that show *Law and Order: SUV*. The one with the lady detectives," Brenda said.

"It's *SVU*, Brenda," Diane said. "And the women on that show are detectives, not people's wives. Will you leave these poor kids alone and stop interrogating them? Things aren't the same as when we were young. You lived through the women's lib movement. Equality for all. #MeToo. Watch the news. Not Fox News though. You're a successful businesswoman, don't tell women they need a man to be happy."

"I'm just saying, I bet your mom has a wedding dress saved in a trunk somewhere for you. And a quilt she already has a pattern picked out for when you finally choose someone," Brenda persisted.

"You're not married," Diane said to Brenda.

"You know that my last husband died in a terrible pancake factory accident!" Brenda said. "Thanks for bringing it up. I'm just trying to look out for my ladies. Husbands are nice to have. None of this living in sin or adjusting your tracking. In our day, there was no operator standing by. You stuck with your decision and made it work."

"Haven't you been married four times?" Chris said.

"Well, those rules only apply to poor people," said Brenda.

"We're going to make you go sit in the corner and think about what you say, you human Thighmaster," Diane said to Brenda. "Your kids were raised by the nanny."

"Fran Drescher raised your kids?" Sean said.

"Not *The Nanny*," said Diane. "A nanny. What was her name, Brenda? Do you even remember?"

"Talk to the hand," Brenda said. Diane swatted it away.

"Good for you, ladies," Aunt Dolly said to Alice and Rachel. "The only thing worse than being alone is settling. Don't listen to any of us. We all have the memories of goldfish and say stuff like, 'Things aren't made to last anymore. Nothing's built the same way it used to be.' It's all us waxing nostalgic."

"It's been so long since I've been with a man, I have to use a Dustbuster to clean my lady parts," Karen sighed, then whispered. "Cobwebs."

"Did you mean to say that out loud?" said Diane.

"The closest I get to attractive men these days is my ice tray," Karen said. "The cubes form the shape of Cole Hauser on *Yellowstone*. I miss romance. You may not know it, but back in the day, I was considered a real dish, but Dolly and Diane and Martha and Brenda were always the glamorous ones. All the boys always liked them. They always stayed out late at the church dances and ice cream socials while I was at home listening to my The Mamas and The Papas records."

"Back in our day, if you held a guy's hand, that was the guy you were going to marry," Aunt Dolly said. "Now there's singles groups, video dating, speed dating, online dating. There's a Love Tester machine inside of downtown bars. You've got the bend and snap. You all have options that we didn't. The only reason a husband is useful is to have someone to scratch your back. Men are such babies when they're sick. Present gentleman excluded, of course. I love you all."

"I know you're trying to help, but this is a terrible pep talk," said Annie.

"Do you think Bigfoot lives in these woods?" Karen said. "Oh! Annie, you should write one of those Bigfoot sex books. They're super popular right now."

"Who knows what's in these woods?" said Dave. "Do you know most forests are so large and expansive that they are never fully patrolled or documented? There's massive chunks of land that remain unexplored."

"I was thinking you should start your own YouTube channel about what it's like to live in a ghost town," said Trish. "That would be pretty interesting. You're doing something lots of people dream about doing. Please like and subscribe."

"We could get celebrity guests to visit!" said Wes. "I met Vitamin C once at the Paramus Park Mall in New Jersey. Maybe she'd come."

"Why does everyone want to film everything nowadays?" Aunt Dolly said. "Remember when we didn't have Facegramtok or whatever it is and everyone didn't feel the need to tell everyone how they felt about every subject or film every moment of their lives."

"My grandson asked me the other day, 'Grandma, what app did you use on your phone to listen to music?'" said Martha. "Apps back in our day meant potato skins. We held our boomboxes up to the radio to record songs like normal people."

"What is 'normal' now?" Ginny said. "What's normal for me isn't normal for you. Part of me still wants to be a dance instructor by day and a luchador by night. Wear lavender unitards, feather boas, and Ariana Grande hair extensions and finally get my chance at winning the trophy in a big finale dance-off showdown set to a remix mash-up of Billy Joel's 'Downeaster Alexa' and Vanessa Williams's 'Colors of the Wind.' When I go to bed, I am full of ambition, but then I wake up and think, 'Maybe tomorrow.' You know you're old when you get excited about new appliances and household items."

Ginny Donovan, despite the self-deprecating nature she shared with her friends, was a well-regarded doctor. She worked on a cruise ship for part of the year, which the gang referred to as *The Love Boat*. She still played "punch buggy" in the car, believed the truest test that someone cared about you was if they noticed you got a haircut, kept all the letters former patients she'd helped had sent her, and utilized a practice she called "motivation doughnuts"—quite literally, she rewarded herself with doughnuts every time she completed a daunting task.

"The things I find so thrilling now," said Nancy. "I love gift cards. And potlucks. And Pier 1 Imports. And if I was a professional wrestler, I'd call myself Trisha Yearwood, because she's strong and sassy. My first thought when we got here was how this place would be perfect for a block party. Oh, dear God, who have we become? I think I've lost my commitment to Sparkle Motion. Why doesn't anyone tell you that being a grown-up is just never-ending emails?"

Everyone was laughing.

They were all unaware of the figure standing at the end of the hallway. Silhouetted by the light behind them. Watching and listening.

"Do you remember when you used to do gymnastics, Annie?" Aunt Dolly said. She turned to the rest of the gang. "Annie was a gymnast for a while, until she quit. She had a little farting problem."

"What?" Laurie said. "Wait, Annie. Why have we never heard this story?"

"Aunt Dolly," Annie moaned.

"Yeah," Aunt Dolly continued. "She was eleven, I think, like when she first came to live with me and we signed up. Maybe she was eating something weird that year but she farted a lot during gymnastics. The other girls made jokes about getting her 'fart powder' and we had to switch gyms. It wasn't a problem that persisted forever but it was really bad for a while. It was horrifying at the time but it's hilarious in retrospect."

More laughter. Even Annie cracked up, remembering.

"What is 'fart powder'?" asked Trish.

"Who knows? Maybe something to make Annie less stinky," Aunt Dolly said. She rubbed Annie's shoulder. "My little master blaster. That's why you're lovable."

"You are awful," Annie said to Aunt Dolly. "My sweet Aunt Dolly didn't know what 'bukkake' meant and kept saying it during her Zoom meeting with the president of Outward Bound, when she was going to be a part of their secular program. Plot twist—they never called her back. For a volunteer position, might I add."

"I thought it was a nicer way to say, 'Bullshit!'" Aunt Dolly said. "Well, can't unring that bell. And how are all of you such experts on what bukkake is, anyway? That's nine pounds of nope in a five-pound sack."

"To Annie and fart powder," Ginny said, raising her glass. Everyone raised theirs in honor and clinked them together.

"We should bury a time capsule on the property," said Wes. "To commemorate all of us being here."

"Imagine what we'd find buried around here," Max said. "All the relics and treasures. This place would be a goldmine for ring finders."

Max Pahucki was married to Laurie. He was a proud dad who had more fun at Dave and Buster's than his kids did, a Mr. Fix-It handyman, and professional house flipper. He'd already offered to help Annie renovate and sell Gull Valley, but she wasn't ready at the time. Max had never been inside a Starbucks Coffeehouse, wore a straw porkpie hat like Kolchak, and followed the Pop-Tarts Instagram account so he'd always be up-to-date if there were any new flavors.

"This would be a perfect place for a drive-in movie theater," said Bill. "Or offer tours of the grounds. A Halloween haunted house attraction! There's so much history here."

Bill Leckie was Trish's husband. He was a die-hard movie buff. Since that didn't make him any money, and his free time was spent making Trish go see all the film revivals in Boston, he worked as a fire marshal. He'd actually given Annie invaluable advice about Gull Valley and fire safety when she moved in. Bill was full of useless movie trivia, had made Trish watch *Best in Show* about one hundred and thirty-nine times, and was never going to try overnight oats, no matter how trendy and popular they got.

"This would be an amazing place to film *Naked and Afraid*," said T.P. "I auditioned for that show but they said I was too excited about the 'naked' part."

"I could always have a television crew come film my life here, like Mariah Carey on that episode of MTV's *Cribs* when she worked out in heels," said Annie. "Just kidding. I don't ever want to work out."

Annie laughed for a moment then looked down at her feet. All eyes were on her.

"I was actually considering—in time—turning this place into a victims' retreat," Annie said. "Somewhere that families and friends of people who were killed could come to for help and support."

The room got quiet. Ginny and Alice took Annie's hands in theirs. Nancy and Jess put their arms around Annie. People didn't know what to say. They thought of their friend Gary.

"I think that's a beautiful idea," Diane said.

"Remember when we'd play Catchphrase at game night?" said Richie. "You and Gary weren't allowed to play on the same team because you'd crush us all."

Annie and the gang laughed more. Annie remembered what it was like. She and Gary were infamous for beating everyone at Catchphrase because they knew each other so well.

Gary: That movie you hate!

Annie: The Village!

Gary: That actress you love!

Annie: Nicole Kidman!

Gary: You can't say this word!

Annie: Cumulative!

Gary: Why does this exist?

Annie: Skim milk!

Gary: This song that makes you cry and you don't know why!

Annie: "Here Without You" by 3 Doors Down!

"On that note," Chris said. "We have something for you. For your birthday."

"My birthday isn't for two more days," smiled Annie.

Chris presented Annie with a framed note. It was in Gary's handwriting.

The energy in the room was somber and excited at the same time. Gary's death had shaken all of them, obviously

202

no one more than Annie. Her friends were clearly nervous that giving her a Gary-centric gift could be either beautiful and charming or stir up deep-seated emotions that Annie didn't want to deal with.

Framed inside the glass was a grocery list that Gary had written. Gary loved to use his Peanuts stationery that he'd found at a yard sale, the top of the paper featuring Charlie Brown, Lucy, Sally, Linus, Snoopy, and the gang dancing. Gary's grocery lists were famous among their friends, not only because he was the only person who still wrote them and put them under magnets on the refrigerator, but because they'd have mundane things next to ludicrous things for him and Annie to buy.

Annie stared at Gary's handwriting. Part of her wanted to laugh. The other held back tears.

Toilet paper

Spaghetti sauce

Noodles

Chips

Cookies

Candy

Word of the day calendar

Bunnicula book

Magic show

Night vision goggles

Garbage Pail Kids cards

Beneath the grocery list was a photo of the entire gang at Alice's son's high school graduation party—the last time they were all together as a group before Gary's murder.

"Annie?" Alice said. "Do you like it?"

"I love it," Annie said, holding the framed paper close to her. "I don't deserve you guys."

"Of course you do," Rachel said, as they all went in for hugs.

"Does anybody want an Almond Joy?" Karen asked, interrupting the moment. Everyone turned their attention to Karen, who was waving around loose Almond Joys. She began to hand them out, insisting that everyone wanted one.

"You know what we need to get for you?" Max said. "A game room. Foosball table, air hockey, shuffleboard, arcade games, dartboard, ping pong, beer pong, maybe a dunk tank. I'll have a talk with Mr. Brisket and see what we can do."

"What's our plan for today, anyway?" said Richie.

"Well, I need to steal Annie away for a little while after breakfast," Brenda said. Annie had no idea why. "But you guys can keep yourselves occupied for a bit, no?"

The loud, piercing whistle of a tea kettle riddled the air.

"Did somebody make tea?" Aunt Dolly asked Diane, Brenda, Martha, and Karen. The ladies all shook their heads.

Karen observed Annie's empty plate. "Look at you! You're a member of the Clean Plate Club! Good job."

"Thanks?" Annie said, wondering if now she had to attend Clean Plate Club meetings.

"Eunice!" Brenda calls. "Eunice! Eunice! Stop working on that Björk swan dress you're making and come clean this mess up!"

Eunice hurried into the mess hall, holding a ragged white dress in one hand and a half-stuffed plush swan in the other.

Before Eunice went to grab the tea kettle, the whistling stopped. Everyone was quiet for a second.

"Well, that's unusual," Ginny said. "Is there perhaps a milkman who stops by and would be in your kitchen right now?"

"Go check it out, Eunice," Brenda ordered.

204

"But what if—" Eunice protested.

"Go now!" said Brenda. "You have bad hair and run a *One Tree Hill* fansite. You'll be the least missed."

"I love *One Tree Hill*," Ned said.

Eunice stomped off to the kitchen.

"Wait, before everybody goes off on their own adventures, can we talk about all the stories they tell in town about this place?" T.P. said. "Some guy at the train station told us to watch our backs out here."

"T.P.!" Ginny said, whacking his arm. "Like a bear on an idiot."

"What?" said T.P. "I want to believe."

"Well, I was wondering," Annie said, looking over at Aunt Dolly, Diane, Brenda, Martha, and Karen. "You guys must have heard stories about The Felicitous. Nobody seems to want to tell me about it really. Do you guys know anything about them?"

Aunt Dolly looked nervous, Annie thought. Annie noticed the way her eyes shifted and her gaze slid over toward Diane, Brenda, Martha, and Karen, all of whom seemed on edge.

"We know who they are," Aunt Dolly said. "Or who they were, rather. Are you sure you want to hear all of this? The Felicitous did not spread good cheer, despite their name. I think people just want to forget about them. I don't want to poison your mind with that talk. You live here now, Annie."

"Tell us," Annie said.

CHAPTER THIRTY-FIVE

Ruby and Rex, as they always did, ran up excitedly to give their Aunt Lyla big hugs. Lyla had been a huge help to Cal since Mara died. Cal was grateful for her help and support.

Lyla Balcom was Cal's late wife Mara's younger sister. She worked as an archivist at the county's records office. She never watched movies where the dog was killed, loved escaping to the massage chair at the mall when she needed to be alone, and had been on television twice—once for a high school quiz show and once for an episode of *Total Request Live* with Carson Daly. People often commented to her that she resembled Demi Moore.

Rex and Ruby went to the kitchen to get Go-Gurt snacks, leaving Lyla and Cal in the family room to talk.

Cal looked at all of the pictures on Lyla's walls. Photos of happier times. Lyla and Wade's wedding. Mara and Lyla at York Beach with toddler Ruby and baby Rex. Cal and Mara celebrating Ruby's third birthday.

Cal reminisced at a candid of Rex in Mara's lap with his Play-Doh, holding his hands up and shouting, "Smell it! It's 'Wemon!'" since he couldn't pronounce "lemon" back then. A candid of Ruby eating a muffin—she called all muffins "cupcakes" then.

"That is a very smart pantsuit you've got on there, Lyla," Cal said. "Throw in some shoulder pads and galoshes and it's a party."

"Cal," Lyla said, trying to choose her words carefully. "Are you doing okay?"

"Yeah, everything is awesome," said Cal. "Aside from the fact that I spill everything on myself every time I eat and I eat to fill the empty void inside of me, I'm all good. I think about getting my shit together so much that I actually don't. I think about work and school when I'm home and think about home when I'm at work. I make myself bullshit to-do lists so I can feel like I accomplished something when it's all just menial tasks, like taking out the trash and recycles. I always tell myself, 'I'll take care of this tomorrow,' then tomorrow actually comes and I don't feel like it anymore, and you know how that goes."

"Cal, I'm serious. Do you think it's the best idea to be researching a book about a murderous cult so soon after Mara died? Is it healthy to expose Rex and Ruby to Gull Valley?"

"The kids have no idea what I'm doing. They think it's just happy happy joy joy fun time. I'm learning about where Mara and I came from. Where you came from."

"My parents were out of the cult by the time I was born."

"I discovered something, Lyla. There's an AM radio station that broadcasts coded messages. They're for The Felicitous."

"How do you know that if they're coded?"

"It's a pirate radio station. It's coming from somewhere within Gull Valley. I haven't pinpointed the exact location yet. But I will."

"Cal. Is this what Mara would've wanted? For you or for the kids? She'd want you to move on. You don't know this lady, Annie. You don't know if she's some crazy psycho or maybe she's part of the cult. She could be dangerous. And let's say you're right—there's some uprising among The Felicitous. What if they know that you know about them? What if they follow you home one night? Mara would not want this for you. You're collecting data on former cult members, crime scenes, asylum reports—and for what? Is this going to help you sleep better at night? You should be spending time with the kids, playing racket ball, going on picnics, teaching them that people who wear wool hats and scarves in the summertime look like douchebags, chasing butterflies, things like that. Not casing the neighborhood for a bunch of ghosts. I'm worried that Rex and Ruby are more affected by all of this that you think. That they understand more than you think they do. The other day, we went to put on *Wall-E* and Rex asked if we could watch *Midsommar* instead. I mean this without judgment. I'm here for you. But maybe you should speak to somebody. A professional."

"I have to do this."

"Why?"

"I can't explain it. It's my past, my history. Mine and Mara's. Mara's life meant something. She was wiped out from existence and I'm not ready to forget or move on. I don't want her life to have meant nothing. She mattered. I need to find out where we came from. It was what brought us together in the first place."

Lyla didn't say anything.

"They're planning something, Lyla," said Cal. "I don't know what and I can't prove it yet. They're preparing. Getting ready. I feel it. I don't know how far their power or sway or whatever you want to call it reaches, but there's something wrong in Gull Valley."

"Then why would you bring your kids there?"

"I don't think they'd hurt us. I don't know how to explain it. We're a part of their bloodline. I'm not bringing the kids there in the dead of night. We're there, together, in the daytime with lots of people around. This is not some, 'It's ten p.m., do you know where your children are?' situation."

"That's some sound logic."

Lyla's telephone rang. She held her finger up like, "Hold that thought," and picked up the receiver.

"Who still has a landline phone?" Cal said. "Do you have call waiting?"

"Hello?" Lyla said into the receiver. "Hello?"

After a beat, Lyla looked over to Cal and extended the phone toward him. "It's for you."

"For me?" Cal said. Who would call him at Lyla's house? Who knew he was there? He only had like three friends and they'd simply text him.

"Hello?" Cal said into the receiver.

There was no sound or response from the other end.

"Hello?" Cal repeated.

Still silence and faint ambient noise from the background.

Cal heard the tinny sound of a song playing over the line.

Now I have found a family forever

To fight and love alongside with

There was a time when I felt so all alone

With Bishop Laird, I have found my home

"You've been called upon," a voice—indistinguishable but harsh and clipped—said.

Click.

The caller hung up. Lyla stared at Cal with a worried expression.

"Who was that?" she asked.

"Um, just someone seeing if I wanted to join a flash mob later," said Cal. "They told me to bring my squeegee."

"Cal," Lyla said, but her tone said, "Not funny."

"Squeegees were invented in 1936," Lyla's husband Wade said as he entered from the garage. The sounds of The Clash's "Rock the Casbah" filled the room momentarily, emanating from his workshop.

Wade Holden worked as a salvage broker, specializing in nautical deals, though his company handled all types of sales and distribution. His home office was in his garage. Wade was content not being the center of attention in any situation, hated the sound of people shaking their salads in plastic containers, and bought his underwear at CVS on more than one occasion, to Lyla's horror.

"Why do you even know that?" Lyla said.

"I saw it on *Are You Smarter Than a Fifth Grader?*" Wade said. "Spoiler alert—I am not."

"Can you watch the kids tonight so I can go back to Gull Valley?" Cal said. He knew he was pushing it.

"You're about to get voted off the island. Wade leaves on the ship tonight and I have to work late. We have a million boxes of letters and missives I have to organize and catalog."

"Ah yes, the nerdery waits for no one," said Wade. "And Lyla is their queen."

"Don't you have Chat GPT and generative AI technology to do that for you nowadays?" said Cal. His jokey nature was not being well received. "I mean, I could bring the kids back to Gull Valley with me. Who knows, we might run into some predators. And I don't even mean predators, like wild animals. Maybe they'll encounter an actual Predator from the movie *Predator*."

Lyla threw him an unamused look. "Good luck with that."

"That's one of those code words for 'Fuck you.' Like, 'Bless your heart,' and 'Let me know how that works out for you,'" Cal said. "Lyla, I'm so close to finding something."

"It's not fair that grown-ups have to work endlessly with no break," said Wade. "Where's my summer vacation? Remember when they showed us that movie *The Miracle of Life* in health class? That was no miracle. That was nightmare fuel time. I shit pineapples during that. Nothing they put up on the overhead projector after that could erase those images. They're seared into my brain for all eternity."

"You should be using your time to hang out with your kids," said Lyla. "And go out and make some friends."

210

"Do you know how hard it is to make friends as an adult?" Cal said. "Coordinating schedules because everybody has to work and no one has the same days off, canceling plans at the last minute, kids, life things, see you when I see you?"

"What are you going to do about it? Cry?"

"Well, yes, probably later in private, but not right now."

"Go home and get some rest, Cal," Lyla said. "I know you're family and you mean well. I think you're using all of this cult research as a way to not face reality. Will you just take a couple of days, please?"

"Yes," said Cal. "Sorry for being pushy and not respecting your boundaries. I'm not myself these days. I'll take a couple of days off with the kids. Have some Little Caesar's and watch *Con Air*."

"How about something a little more age-appropriate?" said Lyla.

"Oh, yeah, like *Collateral* with Tom Cruise and Jamie Foxx."

"No, you dummy, like *Encanto*."

As if their little ears heard Cal and Lyla talking about them, Rex and Ruby appeared, covered in Scratch and Sniff stickers. They burst into song, singing "We Don't Talk About Bruno" in exaggerated fashion.

"Look what you've done," Cal said to Lyla.

CHAPTER THIRTY-SIX

All eyes were on Aunt Dolly, Diane, Brenda, Martha, and Karen as they spoke.

"The Felicitous started as a counterculture group, sort of a response to everything going on in the world in the 1960s. Things were changing. The free love movement, war, gender equality, so many new events and uprisings, that sort of thing. They believed in love and peace. They were anti-war and anti-government. Hippies, transients, intellectuals, all kinds of people joined their movement. They wanted to create their own world, away from the confines and rules set by society. They started small but their numbers grew exponentially over time. That's how they ended up in Gull Valley," said Aunt Dolly.

Aunt Dolly took a deep breath and continued. "We all knew about them. We lived in Massachusetts and they were all over New England. You'd see them recruiting in the streets, protesting the government, fighting to be seen and heard. They sold homemade essential oils, fruits, vegetables, handmade jewelry, those kind of things at roadside stands. They had a message of non-violence and harmony. Like a bunch of flower children. That was common in those days. The world was in turmoil and times and views were in a state of change. They thought that man was the enemy, the monster, a destroyer—money, consumerism, ego, violence. They rallied against that lifestyle. They played music and made home videos and had a very open-minded approach to how they wanted to live, which of course rubbed all the more law-abiding folks the wrong way. They were looked at as a group of deadbeats and lowlifes."

"At first," said Diane. "They'd built their own bubble to live in with their own rules and regulations. Hundreds of people lived here, just going about their daily lives.

They gave all their money and possessions to their leader, Laird Hubbell. He was in charge of The Felicitous. Their master and commander. They called him Bishop Laird. Sort of a mockery of organized religion and the strict upbringing many of them had under Catholic childhoods. They were always on the news. People were fascinated by them. They weren't as famous or well-known as people like The Manson Family or the other cults around at the time. But The Felicitous always denied they were a cult—though they were. They each had their jobs and roles within their community—some worked directly under Laird in his circle of trust. There were hunters, gatherers, caretakers, builders, lookouts, guards, enforcers, people who were in charge of medical stations, people for legal battles—everyone was given tasks and goals. Their ultimate objective was to keep this place alive and running."

"Laird Hubbell came from a very affluent and influential family," Aunt Dolly said. "He had money and resources at his disposal. He was a natural-born leader. Seeing videos and hearing recordings of him, you can see why people would follow him. He was good-looking, smart, persuasive, an idealist. But he had spent time in and out of mental wards his whole life. He was broken on the inside. Something in his wiring just wasn't right. And back then, mental health and things of that nature weren't discussed or examined like they are now."

"We didn't have PTSD or self-care back in our day," Brenda said.

"His followers did everything he asked. Nobody came to Gull Valley during that time unless you were a part of The Felicitous. People started to become afraid of them. Rumors started spreading that they'd been involved in bombings at government buildings and even some killings. Laird was using psychological torture and manipulation to keep his followers loyal to him. Brainwashing propaganda, mind games, all kinds of tricks so he'd have total control over them. And it worked. His followers were fiercely devoted to him. They pledged their lives to him."

Annie and her friends barely breathed or moved during the story, alternately intrigued and terrified. Their eyes were locked on the older women as they told their tale.

Aunt Dolly continued. "What people didn't know until later was that when Laird Hubbell was in his early twenties, he'd been in a terrible plane accident with his family and several of his father's business partners. They crashed in uncharted woodland, deep in the forest, and no one could find them or rescue them. They all died except for Laird. Laird was already not in the best mental health, but this completely pushed him over the edge. When they finally located Laird, it had been about a year. He was alive, surviving in the wreckage. He had eaten several of his family members at this point, including his fiancée, Erica. Erica was everything to him. He was madly in love with her."

"It gets worse." Martha took over. "When they finally recovered Laird and took him back home, he started telling people about this thing he saw in the woods. Some kind of humanoid creature that beckoned to him and made him do things for him. Like a spiritual leader in some way. He insisted it was real. He claimed it was the corporeal manifestation of a deity, something that had been alive long before man ever walked the earth. And somehow, even though it was alive—to him—in those woods, he insisted it looked similar to his dead girlfriend Erica. The doctors gave him electroshock therapy and all kinds of arcane treatments that we wouldn't do today, which seemed to quell the voices in his head and the insistence that this thing he saw was real. The doctors said it was an externalization of his grief and trauma, but Laird insisted that this being was real, was talking to him, guiding him."

"After a few years of leading The Felicitous though, and being off of his meds, he started to change," said

214

Aunt Dolly. "He got more paranoid and hyper-vigilant and started instructing people to booby trap the land. Arming the followers with weapons. Telling them that they were isolationist settlers and that anyone not in their group was to be treated as a hostile invader. Convinced the government was after them. He started telling his followers that they worshipped this being. This thing he saw while he was on his own. The Felicitous became darker, more secretive, angrier—extremely hostile and, rumor has it, murderous to anyone they deemed an outsider. People who disobeyed him would be punished severely. There was talk that they were killing hitchhikers and people that wouldn't be missed and that the cult was cannibalizing them. There was never any proof because they'd eaten all of the evidence. No bodies. If anyone tried to leave, they'd be fed to the followers. People would just go missing. Even if there was discord within the ranks, Laird was their leader and people would follow his every word. His commands were law."

"Laird started telling his followers that their goal was to bring this entity to them," said Diane. "They were to worship this thing that he saw in the woods, that Erica-monster thing. His mind had completely unraveled at this point. The female followers were forced to dress like his dead love Erica. She was known to be fashionable and wore very specific dresses—houndstooth, floral prints, birdseye prints, specific stripes and patterns, long sleeved dresses with cuffs and collars, wool, lots of clean black. The male followers were made to dress in the same manner as his father was dressed when he died—a black suit with white dress shirt and tie. So, all these beatniks, mods, and hippies now had to dress this way or risk being ostracized or worse. It became their uniform. No more non-conformity or self-expression. They were carbon copies of Erica and his father. The new recruits had to wear these yellow frocks until they proved themselves to Laird Hubbell—which meant either sleeping with him or killing for him. At this point, his only obsessions were

Erica and the forest incarnation. He was going to bring both of them back."

"Laird was experimenting with dark rituals, like occult stuff and black magic," Aunt Dolly said. "He was determined to resurrect Erica from the dead. At this point, all the women in the clan were expected to sleep with him, so they could make babies to propagate their numbers. He believed—and, in turn, made his followers believe—they could bring Erica back to life through a new baby. Laird forced them to wear human skinsuits on Halloween, because he believed that on Halloween, all the ghosts of the past could roam the earth. That way, The Felicitous would stay safe and honor the dead. They were partaking in sacrilegious rituals, using blood and bones, trying to create an egregore, which is a literal entity that manifests by a collective group thought. Laird believed they could bring this abominable thing forth with the power of their unified minds. So, there they are, making babies to reincarnate Erica, and doing insane blood ceremonies in the middle of the night to bring forth an imaginary creature to life."

"How do you guys know all this?" said Rachel, who had bitten her nails down to nubs during the story.

"We all heard about it," Karen said. "It was a different time back then though. There was no internet or social media. A lot of this didn't come out until decades later. Authorities could never really prove their involvement in crimes. DNA evidence wasn't what it is today. There's been so many medical, scientific, and technological breakthroughs since then. My husband was a doctor at The Calista Island Asylum for many years and had several members of The Felicitous as patients. There were always rumors surrounding The Calista Island Asylum—about horrible experiments and barbaric treatments these people were subjected to. Truly horrific, terrible practices that may have contributed to Laird's mental decline, as well as some of the former patients joining The Felicitous. But that's a whole other kettle of fish."

216

"That's not a kettle of fish, that's a pit of vipers," Aunt Dolly said. "Nothing was ever proven or ever went to court. But there was talk."

"The types of treatments the doctors used on Laird—aversion therapy, electroshock, overstimulation overload, isolation room, lobotomy, shock collar, chemical bath—are the same things he did to keep his followers in line and secure their devotion to him," said Diane. "They did terrible things to him after all of the terrible things that already happened to him. Not that it excuses any of his behavior afterward."

"What happened to them?" Ned said.

"Nobody really knows," Diane said. "One day, they just vanished. Left all of their belongings behind. Laird Hubbell was never heard from again. Some followers escaped back into the world. Most of them disappeared without a trace. Maybe they started new lives under different names. Maybe they died. There were rumors that his disciples really did resurrect Laird's wood monster and it slaughtered all of them and collected their souls. Overnight, their home was abandoned. They could still be out there. What are the residual side effects of being in a cult? Nobody knows where they really went or what happened to them. They could be our neighbors, our friends, our coworkers. We'll never really know."

"Is this a good time to mention that I hate scary stories?" said Bill. "Especially true ones?"

"Here's some helpful tips to survive scary movies—always talk to strangers on the phone, never lock your door, run up the stairs instead of to your car, and always stand near windows," Sean said.

"When did The Felicitous disappear?" Jess said, ignoring Sean.

"Sometime in the 1990s, I think," Diane said. "Laird would've been in his fifties by then, I believe. He'd be the same age as us ladies. Who knows if he's still out there."

"This is all the Cliffs Notes version of events," said Aunt Dolly. "Nobody really knows what happened or the extent of what they did. It'd be easier if we could do this as a slide show."

"Well, Annie, welcome to your new home," Sean said. "You can hang a sign in the window that says, 'Good eats.'"

"Why did none of you ever tell me about all of this?" Annie said, trying not to sound accusatory. "All of you have heard of this cult but none of you mentioned it to me before I bought it?"

"We did, Annie," Ginny said, exchanging concerned looks with her friends. "You were in a really bad place for a long time. I don't think you were listening or processing what we said. You said you didn't care and just had to go away. None of us beat the point into you, but we did tell you."

The rest of the friends nodded their heads in agreement. Annie knew her mental state had been foggy and her determination to move was so strong that she would have done anything to make it happen, so much so apparently that she ignored the stories of The Felicitous.

"What's done is done," said Brenda. "You can't change the past. You can only move forward and make this place your own."

"Why didn't his followers try to stop what was happening?" Wes said.

"They believed in his word, like he was some kind of god," Aunt Dolly said. "He was a false prophet. They'd already been indoctrinated. They thought that this was their family and that's how their family behaved. It was normal to them, almost. At that point, they were so intwined in their world that they did anything he wanted. And those who went against him were made into terrible examples of what would happen if you went against Laird and the group, so I imagine that fear kept many of them in line."

218

"He had to eat his girlfriend—the person he loved the most—to survive," Laurie said, then turned to Max. "You do not have permission to eat me if we are in a catastrophic survival situation."

"Did Laird Hubbell ever describe what the forest monster looked like?" said Kit.

"Oh, yeah, like this," Alice said, holding up a picture on her cell phone.

An artist's rendering of what Laird Hubbell described. Approximately seven feet tall, gaunt and wiry, shiny pale white skin like marble, long black hair—unkempt and shaggy—that fell over its large dark eyes and blood red lips. Extended fingers and jagged, blackened fingertips. Its body was contorted in an unnatural position, as if it couldn't stand completely straight, its bones protruding from beneath its porcelain skin. Its gender ambiguous, its body both old and young looking somehow.

Alice showed everyone a picture of twenty-year-old Erica Keating, Laird's beloved fiancée, laughing and smiling next to Laird. Erica was a natural beauty—long, straight hair and a light that radiated off of her. She was like sunshine. Erica was wearing a paisley-patterned Peter Pan dress with a big white collar.

Somehow, in a bizarre way, that very monster Laird conjured up did bear a strange resemblance to Erica. Beneath the creature's frightening visage and nightmarish countenance, there was something eerily reminiscent of Erica herself—minus Erica's youth, beauty, and smile.

"Well, I'm never sleeping again," Bill said.

"It says here that Laird Hubbell believed the woodsy-thing was a guardian angel who told him he'd been 'called upon,'" said Alice, reading from her phone. "He thought it was some kind of forest spirit that kept him alive and told him what to do."

"Wow, the ultimate deepfake. We were told to pee on jellyfish stings, but that turned out to be a lie," Sean said, then looked at Dave. "I'm still sorry I made you pee on me, Dave."

"That was a weird day," said Dave.

"There was a song they'd sing," Aunt Dolly said. "I can't remember the whole thing. It was so creepy though."

Alice held her phone up again, letting the song play for everyone.

You took me in your arms and I know you care

You showed me the way and will always be there

I was once but a pebble in the rushing river

Now I have found a family forever

To fight and love alongside with

There was a time when I felt so all alone

With Bishop Laird, I have found my home

Your love has called upon me

A love I have never known

"Not creepy at all," Chris said.

"So, The Felicitous spent their time singing and dancing in the hills like they were rejects from *The Sound of Music*?" said Sean.

"Except with more murder and delusion," clarified Kit. "Psychologically, cults usually attract people who feel lost or unseen by society. The leaders prey on this and offer their acolytes acceptance and security, which they use over time to control and exploit them for their own personal needs. It's how abusers operate—isolate people from their families and friends, convince them that they are the only truth, and engineer their insecurities to work in the abuser's favor."

"So, these people went from banging tambourines and braiding each other's hair to cannibalism?" T.P. said. "That seems like a stretch."

"Not really," said Ginny. "Think about it. This was their home, their security, the only place they felt safe. They believed every word Laird Hubbell told them. They followed him blindly, not questioning what they were doing because they didn't want to leave their only safe space."

"The more things change, the more they stay the same," Nancy said. "When people leave cults, they don't know they left a cult."

"Kind of like people in a food co-op," said Sean. After his friends gave him the side-eye, he added, "I thought we were sharing. Just helping Nancy out."

Nancy gave Sean a playful smack on his arm with her spoon.

"Didn't hurt," Sean said. "Do you even lift, bro?"

"A bunch of misfits who felt like they didn't fit in found each other," said Wes. "Sounds kind of like us."

"Wait," Trish said. "So, are The Felicitous still around or not? Are they active? I know you said they vanished without a trace, but that doesn't mean they stopped existing."

"Cal said that there's tons of online communities dedicated to preaching and spreading their message," said Annie. "It's foreseeable that some people still abide by their laws to this day, but it's doubtful that The Felicitous holds the same power or sway over people that it once did."

"The Felicitous are basically ghosts at this point," Diane said. "It's part of the past, where it should stay. Like the riverbed. What once was doesn't always remain. Annie, you're going to make new memories here. Happy ones. This isn't the home of The Felicitous anymore. It's your home."

"Here, here!" Annie's friends said, cheering and clinking their glasses.

Annie bit her lip as her stomach churned. Just how buried was the past here?

If The Felicitous truly were a memory.

CHAPTER THIRTY-SEVEN

Jack couldn't remember where he left his tool kit. He searched his brain and retraced his steps to find it but came up empty.

"Where was the last place you had it?" Ben asked.

"If I knew that, I'd know where it is," Jack huffed.

Jack had already checked several of the buildings. He made his way into the church, but Ben wandered away, not really interested. Jack touched his Saint Christopher's medallion necklace as he entered.

A foul, pungent odor smacked his nose as soon as he opened the doors. There was a rotten, sour smell permeating the inside of the church, carried on a slight wind that flicked at Jack's face.

There were no open windows in the church. Where was the breeze coming from? And that smell...

He spotted his tool kit on the pulpit. As he made his way to the front of the church, the smell grew stronger and more overpowering. Like something—or many somethings—had died in the vicinity, and recently.

Probably animals trapped in the woodwork or between the walls. Rats maybe, dying after they'd eaten poison and gone home to their nests. In the years he'd been fixing up houses, he'd seen plenty of dead animals. He'd hang some air fresheners up on his next visit.

His tool kit was empty—its contents scattered all along the floor, as if they had been tossed and discarded. Jack stooped down to collect all of the tools, feeling a gust of rancid air wash over him.

It was coming from inside the confessional. Jack opened the right-side door of the confessional, inspecting it. His hammer was on the seat.

Another wave of putrid-smelling air blew past. Jack looked down.

There was a trap door inside the confessional, its cover slightly open.

Jack was instantly curious. A little frightened, but lots of old settlements and structures had secret rooms and fruit cellars. He wondered if anyone even knew that trap door was there.

He carefully removed the wooden cover, the smell of decay and decomposition even stronger. His curiosity got the better of him.

There was faint light coming from within the hole in the ground and a small staircase leading down. Jack thought for a moment but made his way into the pit below.

The passageway was large and wide enough for Jack to stand up straight and move around freely. The walls were made of dirt, soil, and rock, covered in decades of handprints, dust, grime, and various other filth that came with age and neglect.

A long hallway extended in both directions. The corridor was lit by reflective orange and white construction barrels, the kind used for traffic and highway repairs, with slowly blinking orange lights flicking on and off... on and off...

On the wall, written in a dark color, was one word—

Erica

Jack was dumbfounded and excited by his discovery. How far did these tunnels go? Where did they lead to? What was underneath the buildings of Gull Valley?

He was disquieted once he saw the outline of something at the end of the passage, obscured by shadows. Someone, or something, standing in the far distance—too far from Jack for him to make out who they were or what they were doing.

Jack had seen enough horror movies to know not to call out a hello.

"Who's down here with me?" a man's voice, sorrowful and pained, cried out from the opposite direction of the silhouette.

Jack spun around, backing up toward the staircase, and listened.

Silence. The faint clicks of the blinking orange road lights.

Screech!

From the darkness, only a hundred yards from where Jack stood, emerged a man.

A man with his eyelids sewn shut. Dressed in a yellowed, burlap-style nightgown of sorts. Sallow skin, emaciated, dirty bare feet, feeling his way against the wall. The man looked more like a humanoid abomination than human.

"Who's down here?" the man repeated, his voice moaned.

Jack turned to run up the staircase.

Once he did, he was face-to-face with a tall man in a black suit, wearing a black executioner's hood with a white X painted above the eyeholes.

Before Jack could react, the executioner drove a hunting knife into the side of Jack's neck. The executioner retracted the blade immediately, leaving Jack stumbling up the staircase. Jack's neck wound shot blood out with every heartbeat.

Jack looked up at the trap door opening. Ms. Click stood there, looking down into the tunnels.

"Ms. Click," Jack groaned, struggling for strength. "Ms. Click, help me."

Ms. Click stared at Jack with dead eyes.

Jack screamed as Ms. Click covered the entrance with the square wooden trap door cover, leaving Jack to bleed out alone.

CHAPTER THIRTY-EIGHT

Before Annie could entertain her guests, there were some things she wanted to check on. Cal had texted her a dozen times with photos and stories of strangers in the woods. She planned to call him later on. In her experience at Gull Valley, she knew there were always people milling about in the woods, so she didn't want to sound the alarm quite yet.

Annie placed the framed photo gift on her desk, smiling to herself.

Part of her realized she had become the girl who convinced herself that everything strange going on was just the wind, blamed bizarre happenings on coincidence or happenstance. Was she ignoring crucial, damning evidence of something wrong? She couldn't trust herself. And Gull Valley was a unique situation—a public forest, though her property was private. She didn't really know Cal well enough to decide on him yet. He had his own trauma.

Annie regarded the pile of Gull Valley photographs on her desk. She'd sort through them later.

She sat in front of her computer when the thought hit her.

George Squires.

She'd forgotten to mention George to Cal. Realistically, George was probably who Ruby and Rex encountered in the woods; the one who said weird and creepy things to them.

To be sure, Annie pulled up several hours of trail camera footage and fast-forwarded through it.

She slowed the tape down to see Rex and Ruby wander by. They were talking to someone who was just off-camera. The person never came into the purview of the camera. All Annie could see was a shadow.

She typed "The Felicitous" in her search bar and scanned the news articles. She saw several items about people once connected to Laird Hubbell and the cult. Reports as recent as a few weeks ago, detailing break-ins, robberies, and sightings of strange, cult-like activity experienced by people around the New England area. The word, "*Erica*," left at several crime scenes. Accounts of people who had gone missing or been murdered.

A report on three men—Gil Abbott, Trent Langdon, and Zeke Penhall—who set out four months ago to film a documentary about strange occurrences in Gull Valley. They hadn't been seen since.

The families of Dr. Arthur Wainwright, Dr. Andrew Liu, Dr. Meghan Chittle, and Dr. James Salehi—all once doctors for members of The Felicitous—had been slaughtered or disappeared within the last year. The news articles characterized the incidents as "home invasions."

There were hundreds of videos posted online by people who claimed that they had encountered The Felicitous—or at least suspected they had. Annie clicked on some of the links. Most of the videos were short and had no clear-cut answer or tidy resolution as to what the cause of their mysterious experiences actually was.

In the first video, a woman's dog growled and barked angrily at something unseen in the darkness of her back yard. Hidden in the darkness, the vague outline of a person was barely visible.

Another video captured an unknown person wandering through the woods at night as the sound of singing or chanting echoed in the distance.

Another was of someone waking up in the middle of the night to the sound of unseen people ransacking their home as the recorder called 911.

Annie watched several dozen more of the videos—the sound of a baby crying deep in the forest late at night;

finding the E and K symbol scratched on to trees and other objects in nature and spraypainted on signs and doors; hearing people moving about in their basement; a group of unrecognizable people performing a ritual around a fire in the woods; a bunch of people using a Ouija board to summon the spirit of Laird Hubbell; ghost hunters who snapped the image of a face staring back at the camera from within gaps of the wood in a rickety, old barn; a group of urban explorers traversing through an abandoned asylum as voices and noises whispered in the darkness, until the person recording screamed and ran as if someone—or something—was chasing him.

The last video segued into a new one. Annie squinted to see through the grainy feed and darkness. It was an unseen person wandering around a group of buildings in the middle of the night.

The recorder stopped as the sounds of voices and footfalls were heard faintly in the distance. The person recording ducked down, their camera focused on a section between two of the houses.

Annie realized that this person was recording in Gull Valley. The video showed guest houses two and three. From between the buildings, a group of people in suits and masks appeared.

They were carrying something behind them, dragging it across the ground. It looked like burlap sacks, filled with something.

Something that was still moving.

The video quality was too low and dark to properly discern what the people were doing and what was in the sacks.

Abruptly, the video ended.

Annie reclined in her chair. What would she do without Google? She didn't know enough things to live without it.

Annie typed in "Mara Reardon" into the search bar. A few small articles about Cal's late wife Mara popped up—

a one-vehicle car accident. Mara had driven off of the road and into a large tree. No foul play suspected.

Her mind had been reeling for days. She needed this break with her friends.

She recalled one of her lowest points after Gary's murder. Annie had been consumed by the idea of revenge.

She had seen several online comments on social media from people defending the murderers. Social justice warriors who, like the murderers themselves, blamed everything else except the people who actually committed the act. People who defended the killers.

Annie had contemplated whether she should find those people, as well as the family of the murderers, and kill them. Like a vigilante but justified. The thought washed over her so regularly that she realized she had to get away.

Those notions had faded away a long while ago. Gary's murder had changed Annie on an inherently molecular level. For a long time, it was hard for her to watch happy people. She had become a shell of herself and she knew it.

Annie laughed to herself at the toxic positivity and "helpful" advice she'd received from acquaintances— *You're strong! You got this! There are other people who have it way harder than you! Think about all the good things you have! At least you have the memories of Gary. Why don't you just try being happy? Gary's at peace now. Being sad won't change anything. Gary would've wanted you to move on. Go on dates! There's plenty of other fish in the sea! You still have your own life to life! Don't dwell on the negative. Have you tried not being sad?*

And, of course, Annie's personal favorite—*Thoughts and prayers.* She had a strong suggestion where people could put their "thoughts and prayers."

Annie never knew how awful people were at comforting someone during a real crisis. Part of her understood—what could someone say? They didn't make

Hallmark cards for that. *"Sorry about your husband's murder!"*

The other part of her thought it was best not to say anything instead of saying something stupid, insensitive, and unhelpful. Though Annie realized that people would always play a part in their own suffering, she did not agree that it applied when it came to her distress and sadness over her husband's violent, vicious murder.

Thankfully, Annie's friends and family had never said such idiotic things to her, but there were throngs of people she knew that loved to vomit their terrible, useless, uninformed opinions and thoughts on her.

For the moment, Annie didn't want to focus on the cruelty, stupidity, terrors, and injustices of the world. She hit a few keys on her computer and ABBA's "Waterloo" began to play.

Annie was interrupted by a soft knock at her door.

"Anne, my dear," Aunt Dolly said from behind her. "I didn't want to startle you."

"Hey, Aunt Dolly," said Annie, swiveling around in her chair to face her.

"Why are you hiding in here? You have a big group of people who love you waiting to spend time with you."

"There's a Nigerian prince in my DMs who really needs my help and money, I'm just getting the details. He needs me to send several Amazon gift cards, my social security number, and my mother's maiden name. It seems totally legit."

"You know what's funny about getting older? Men become silver foxes but when women age, people treat them like they should be sent to the woods and live like shunned witches. My memory isn't what it used to be. I tell the same stories over and over. But let me have that— it's all I can remember. My body in youth has not equated to my body in old age. I grunt every time I sit down or stand up. I take every letter of the alphabet in vitamins. Nowadays, I just want to listen to my *Pure Moods* CD and avoid anyone obnoxiously youthful. They should just give me a punch card for my colonoscopies at this point. The tenth one is free. But the good news is that life doesn't end at fifty."

"Well, for some of us," Annie said, thinking how Gary would never make it to fifty. She shook her head, as if to shake the thought away. "Ah, I remember being a kid and thinking high schoolers were so cool. Then I got to high school and thought being a college student was where it's at. Then I decided that being an adult was the crowning achievement. Nobody tells you that we're all a bunch of idiots, all people are awful, and you're never as smart as you think you are."

"That's the big secret—we're all figuring it out as we go. None of us actually knows what we're doing."

"Aunt Dolly, you get more done in a day than people half your age. You've lived. I hope I can accomplish that. I'll only start worrying if you become one of these people who constantly needs the heat on at seventy-five degrees."

"Stop using logic on me. I just want to vent and be dramatic. I won't be around forever. One of these days, we'll have to talk about everything I want to leave you."

No! I don't want all of your insane trinkets and knick-knacks and special edition Beanie Babies.

"Aunt Dolly, do you remember how you and Diane, Brenda, Martha, and Karen took all of us kids to Diane's beach house in York every summer? You guys would order cake from that cake slice delivery service, and we'd all sing 'Almost Paradise' on the deck, and watch *Hey Dude* on Nickelodeon, and Karen would say things wrong—like 'Take a short walk off a long pier!', and you'd get us all pedicures, and Diane would tell us spoilers about what was going to happen to her character on the show, and we'd play hide-and-seek and ghosts in the graveyard then go splash in the water like we were Madonna in the 'Cherish' video. At night, you'd tell us ghost stories about Boon Island by the fireplace. Those were the greatest times of my childhood. Did I ever say thank you for everything you did for me growing up?"

"Why are you getting all mushy, Annie?"

"It was the happiest time of my life until I met Gary. I don't think I ever cried and laughed so hard at the same time as I did in those summers. You gave all of that to me. I could've just been the wasted daughter of two junkies, but you made sure that didn't happen to me. You made it so my life wouldn't be constant sadness, loneliness, and fear. I didn't know if I ever said, 'Thank you' to you for it all. For everything."

"Annie, you are the light in my life. Don't ever forget that. You needed me. I did what was best so you could have a better life. We did have fun, didn't we?"

"You changed my life."

"Well, you changed mine, too. And you're welcome. I wish I could have helped your mother more. And just because you're being so sweet and nice, don't think I changed my mind about you living out here like a frontier woman." Aunt Dolly shook her head and recalibrated. "Why did I come in here again? Oh, Brenda and the girls request your presence. Brenda did something I know you're going to hate, so make sure your face doesn't do that thing it always does, where you can't hide your emotions at all, no matter how hard you try."

"I thought that's what faces were for, but okay."

"Come on. Don't keep Brenda waiting. Remember, this is a woman who orders coleslaw as her side dish instead of fries or anything else, so we already know she's unhinged. She's the only person I know who actually makes and eats porridge."

"I asked Brenda who her idol was once and she said Dolph Lundgren in *Red Scorpion*."

Annie closed her laptop and followed Aunt Dolly.

CHAPTER THIRTY-NINE

"Jack!" Ben called. "Jack?"

He'd seen Jack go into the church but hadn't seen him since. Ben threw open the church doors, letting the outside light illuminate part of his surroundings. The church was always so dark.

"Jack, where did you go?" Ben called out again.

The doors closed behind him just as Ben's eyes adjusted to the low light.

There were people sitting in the pews. They were faced forward toward the pulpit. Ben could only make out the outlines and vague details of their backs and heads. There were about a dozen people, spread between the left and right pews.

Slowly, their heads began to turn, as if they were asleep and Ben had awakened them, alerting them to his presence.

"Hello?" Ben said tentatively, though his brain was saying, "What the fuck?"

When the people in the pews craned their necks enough for Ben to see them more clearly, he shuddered.

They were all wearing crudely-made masks—alien, cat, cherub, dog, Frankenstein's monster, ghost, ghoul, mummy, former president Lyndon B. Johnson, astronaut Neil Armstrong, princess, sea creature, skeleton, vampire, werewolf, witch, wizard, zombie. Masks that he'd seen in old photographs from Halloween nights in the 1950s and '60s, the kind someone bought at a local drugstore from a man in a white uniform behind a counter.

None of the people moved. They stared at him through the eyeholes in their masks. They didn't even seem to be breathing.

Something fell behind Ben, causing him to whip around to see what it was.

Nothing.

When Ben turned back to the people, they were all standing up, still in the pews, facing him.

"Who are you?" Ben barely squeaked out.

"We are your past, present, and future," the people said in unison, almost a robotic whisper of voices blended together. "We are bound together as one. We are the light and the darkness. We are the true owners of this land. We have been called upon in the name of Bishop Laird. You are right to be afraid of us."

The way their words echoed and reverberated around the church made it sound as if their voices came from every direction, surrounding him.

Ben pushed on the church doors. They wouldn't move. He'd been locked in from the outside. He threw all of his weight onto them, banging at the wood.

Whack!

Ben buckled when he felt the blow of a hammer to the back of his head.

The masked people approached, one by one stepping out from their pews and headed directly toward Ben. He ran around to the side of the church, frantically searching for an exit.

Ben stumbled toward the pulpit, screaming in horror.

He came face-to-face with a rotted, skinless body propped up in a large, ornate chair, dressed in a gray suit and robe combination. The corpse had clearly been dead for a long time; decrepit and decomposed, mostly a husk of a human covered in dust and gore. It had a manmade crown of flowers and sticks rested atop its hairless, soot-covered skull.

Ben looked behind him to see the masked people approaching him from between the pews, down the aisle, headed right for him.

The ghoul carried Jack's severed head in his hands, swinging it as he walked.

Something arose from behind the chair.

A humanoid construct, a man rebuilt with animatronics, whose body and face were stitched together with the skin from others and electrical parts—like a human robot. Wide eyes covered by infrared goggles, patches of hair and skin in places they shouldn't have been (or missing where they should have been), wires and gadgets molded into its body, gray and spotted skin besieged by lesions and cuts.

It was human—but a human that had become a depraved science experiment.

Slash!

Before Ben had a chance to react, the monster ripped Ben's throat open with the sharp, jagged nails of its left hand.

Ben stumbled back to the floor, grasping at the gaping wound that tore his neck wide open. He gurgled, choking on his own blood.

As the life drained from his body, he stared at the dark church ceiling. Long enough to see all of the masked people hover over him, their faces blocking his view.

The masked people watched silently as the light in Ben's eyes faded out.

CHAPTER FORTY

Annie ran into Eunice in the upstairs hallway. Brenda had instructed Eunice to sage the entire household. Eunice had a giant clump of stinky herbs tied together, lit up, as the smoke filled the corridor.

"You don't have to do that, Eunice, but thank you," said Annie.

Eunice paused. "Brenda said I have to. It's her good deed of the day."

"People who have to tell you they're good people usually aren't. Also, on this edition of life advice you didn't ask me for—The customer is not always right, big hair holds secrets, we don't always get closure, and the threat of the Bermuda Triangle was greatly overdramatized when I was a kid. Thank you for coming to my TED talk."

Eunice chuckled. "You ever have imaginary arguments in your head with people? Like, you think of a great comeback or what you should've said. Or you just play the conversation over and over in your mind?"

"Yes, all the time. Eunice, why do you work for Brenda? You could probably do anything else."

"Well, we grew up in your neighborhood. My mother was a single mom. My dad took off when I was young. There were five kids in the family and my mom had to take care of all of us. Brenda knew my mom from around the neighborhood and heard that she couldn't afford to send me to college. Brenda paid for my entire college education, so I wouldn't end up stuck. Brenda has no idea that I know that. She asked my mom to never tell and to let me think my mom paid for school herself. In a weird way, I owe everything to Brenda. So, I let her boss me around and treat me badly, but I kind of like that she treats me as badly as she does everyone else. It makes me feel included, in a weird way. She makes fun of me and says I have bad posture and that I like Coldplay unironically and that I'm the reason they make ten-pound bags of cereal marshmallows, but it doesn't get to me the way she wants it to. I know her secret. That Brenda isn't all venom and bile. She doesn't want people to think of her as soft. She had to be hard to make her way in business, surrounded by men. She'd kill me if she knew I was telling you this. But because of her, I have a chance at a different future that my mom never had."

"What do you want to be when you grow up, Eunice?"

"Happy."

"Anne Danielle Porter, get your butt down here!" Aunt Dolly called from downstairs.

"Coming, Aunt Dolly!" Annie said, linking her arm with Eunice's and heading down.

Neither Annie nor Eunice saw the masked people come from within several of the upstairs room. One in a black suit and expressionless beige mask that looked like porcelain skin at the end of the hallway, the others a cherub and the ghoul. The three intruders watched them descend the staircase. They moved to the railing and peered down at the women as they obliviously walked away

CHAPTER FORTY-ONE

Sloane Doyle had finally made it to Gull Valley.

She hugged Annie so tightly that Annie thought she'd never let go. They stood in Annie's living room in the main house, surrounded by Aunt Dolly, Diane, Brenda, Martha, Karen, and Eunice.

"I'm sorry, I'm sorry, I'm sorry," Sloane said, pulling her long, dark hair out of her face. "I wanted to be here sooner. I had work things I could not get out of."

"You are fine, Sloane," said Annie. "You're here now."

"Where is everybody?"

"Oh, I sent them all away," said Brenda. "I told them to keep themselves busy for a while. We have other things we need to take care of right now."

"Well, that's mysterious," Sloane said. "What are we doing?"

"You'll see," Brenda said. "I have a visitor on the way. She should be here any minute."

"Sometimes I think about that little bee girl from Blind Melon 'No Rain' video and how she was so happy and went around dancing everywhere," said Sloane. "What ever happened to her? I wish I could go through life like that."

"Sloane, if you're going to hang out with us, I'm going to need your stories to be more interesting," Brenda said.

"Ignore her," said Annie. "Brenda's upset because she read what we all wrote about her in the slam book."

Sloane was unfazed. "I was listening to a podcast on my way over. It was all about people who trained themselves to have the willpower to control their emotions and addictions. Like, this one guy was obsessed with Wii and it cost him everything—his job, his relationships, his sanity. And one day, he just willed himself to stop. Just like that. It's an incredible, uplifting story. He has so much confidence now."

"What is this word 'confidence' you speak of?" Annie said. "I'm not familiar with that concept."

"Oh, God," Brenda moaned. "You're like the sad, boring nice girl who sits by herself every day at lunch that we'd all feel bad for in a movie, but in real life, we wouldn't sit with either. You're the 'I Like Turtles' girl of Annie's friend group. I bet when you do laundry, you mix up your hangers so none of them feel left out when you hang things. You and Eunice should have a playdate. You can start a Go Fund Me for a road trip to see the world's biggest ball of yarn and discuss how everyone should get a participation trophy 'cause we're all winners!"

Eunice waved wanly at Sloane.

"Why wouldn't you sit with her?" Annie said, putting her arm around Sloane.

"Who wants to be friends with a girl with no friends?" Brenda said.

"Brenda? Yoo-hoo!" a woman's voice called out from the front door.

"Ah!" Brenda said. "There she is. Come on!"

"You'll get used to her," Diane said to Sloane as they all followed Brenda. "And if not, you'll learn that none of us really like her that much either."

There she was, in all her glory. Standing in the doorway of Annie's house.

Madame Fructuosa, county-wide famous psychic. Annie recognized her immediately from her late-night public access commercials. Madame Fructuosa deemed herself a clairvoyant, oracle, seer, empath, medium, feeler to all the elements; reader of palms, tarot cards, crystals,

238

and tea leaves. She claimed to be versed in scrying, communication with the dead, and was the creator of unboxing videos on her very own YouTube channel. She never met dowsing rods she didn't like.

If a Zoltan magic fortune teller machine on the beach boardwalk came to life, it would manifest as Madame Fructuosa.

Annie was not amused. She exchanged perplexed, mirthless looks with Diane, Aunt Dolly, and Sloane.

"I was told there would be laundry service provided for me," Madame Fructuosa said, pointing to two giant laundry bags on the floor next to her.

"Eunice," said Brenda, her eyes on the bags.

Eunice grabbed the bags and hurried off to the laundry room.

"This is my surprise?" Annie said. She would've preferred cash. Or cake.

"Sorry," Aunt Dolly said, resigned to what was about to go down.

Madame Fructuosa, a robust woman in her sixties, looked like the cover of an astrology book. Her outfit was the result of a Bedazzler fight that she lost, vibrantly colored and woefully mismatched with garish plaids, paisleys, stripes, fake gems, leopard prints, and part of the plastic sheet from a Twister board game. Multicolored barrettes and clips in her hair, chunky gaudy jewelry, make-up applied with a paint roller, several necklaces that clinked together as she moved, and the tops of Pringles cans cut off to make bracelets.

Brenda introduced everyone to Madame Fructuosa.

"Please refrain from flash photography," Madame Fructuosa said, as if they were fans looking for an autograph. She paused, taking in a dramatic breath. "My senses are overwhelmed by the amount of energy here. There are so many voices calling out to me. Speaking through my spirit guide, Wanda. I can hear them. They're saying—oh, my God, you were on *As the Wind Blows*!"

239

Madame Fructuosa completely lost her train of thought and ditched her overacting as soon as she saw Diane.

"When Contessa Wilhelmina was attacked by her evil clone Lucretia, who used brain control on her to blow up the local candy shop in order to save the town and Johannes Prescott III, president of the transmission fluid dynasty, destroyed the satellite that was controlling the clone, and Wilhelmina found out it was orchestrated by her vengeful niece Aramintha, who had faked her own death after everyone thought a pack of leopard seals mauled her!" Madame Fructuosa gushed. "That was brilliant! You should've won the Daytime Emmy for that."

"Thank you," said Diane. Sometimes Diane missed being on the show.

"Wanda, are you seeing this?" Madame Fructuosa said to her imaginary spirit guide in the sky. "I'm reading your auras. I can see the colors that surround you all."

Madame Fructuosa paused where Brenda stood and shivered. "So cold."

Annie exchanged irritated looks with Aunt Dolly. Aunt Dolly shrugged, as if saying, "Brenda's trying to help."

"You can thank me later," Brenda said to Annie.

"Oh yeah, I'll send the banana peel and oven mitts thank you basket right over," Annie said, moving away from Brenda.

"I hear you," Madame Fructuosa said, her head following the imaginary voices in the atmosphere. "There's a place where the voices are strongest. The energy is more urgent. Follow me."

CHAPTER FORTY-TWO

Annie, Sloane, Aunt Dolly, Brenda, Martha, and Karen stood behind Madame Fructuosa as she went outside. Madame Fructuosa scanned each building, putting her fingers up to her temples, her mind searching for where Wanda directed her to go.

"What is it, Wanda?" she said. "What do you hear? What do you see? I don't understand. Use your words."

Madame Fructuosa led the women to the church, ignoring the birds tweeting and the sunshine around her. Her mind was full of dark thoughts and images.

"In here," she said. She pushed the church doors open, letting the building fill with light.

Rachel, Laurie, Max, Jess, Richie, and Ginny were exiting their temporary sleeping quarters and saw Madame Fructuosa's procession. The quintet quietly joined, standing next to Annie and Sloane.

"The thing they worshipped in this church was not holy," Madame Fructuosa said, entering the structure. The rest of the group followed her inside.

"What's going on?" Ginny whispered to Sloane.

"I have no idea," said Sloane.

"Who is this woman?" Max said.

"She's a sensitive," Sloane said.

"Oh, so she cries easily?" said Max.

"No, she sees ghosts," said Sloane.

"Oh, okay," Max said. "Wait, what?"

"Silence," Madame Fructuosa instructed. "I need to hear Wanda. She's showing me things. She knows what happened in this place. Where do I go, Wanda? What is it you're trying to tell me? I'm open to your world. My mind is free and empty and ready for guidance."

Your mind is definitely empty, Annie thought.

"I need you all to believe with me," said Madame Fructuosa. "Put all of your energy and light into the universe so Wanda's voice will come through loud and clear. Think of it like a doorway—the more you believe, the more it will open and show us what we seek. Let the light in, Wanda."

Everyone remained quiet, watching the so-called psychic put on her parlor tricks and magic show.

"Two new souls," Madame Fructuosa said. "Two new souls have joined them. The people who came and went through here, through this land. Their voices call to me from beyond this mortal coil. So much pain. Anger. Death. Punishment. Fear. What, Wanda? What are you saying? Not all of those to fear have crossed over. Wanda is telling me we need to go into that room."

Bang!

A crash from within the secret room.

Madame Fructuosa pointed to the locked doors. Annie reached into her pocket and produced the keys.

"In there," the psychic said for emphasis.

Annie put the key into the lock, hoping it would work. The key fought against Annie's effort at first.

"I don't believe in ghosts or monsters," Annie said under her breath. She didn't convince herself.

From within the locked room, the chords of a song began. Tiffany's "Could've Been," tinny-sounding and muffled, played through the air.

The flowers you gave me are just about to die...

Annie pushed against the door. It burst open with a groan. Everyone entered except Rachel, who stayed behind in the door frame.

The song emanating from the locked room grew louder, though the record began to skip.

...just about to die...

...just about to die...

...just about to die...

Aunt Dolly found the light switch on the wall and clicked them on. Annie and her friends held back their gasps when they saw the room in its entirety.

...just about to die...

Among the items in the room was a 1950s-style jukebox—curved arch, neon pink and blue façade, big glass window full of vertically-stacked records.

...just about to die...

...about to die...

...about to die...

Max stepped over to the jukebox and smacked it. The song stopped playing.

Annie and her gang surveyed the room. Madame Fructuosa placed a small digital recorder on a shelf.

"For EVP's," she said. "Electronic voice phenomenon. We can't always hear what the spirits are trying to communicate to us."

"This looks like a serial killer's lair," Richie said. "One of the nice things about the city is I never have to go into mysterious, locked rooms."

Jess gave him a tilted-head look that said, "Not the time, Richie."

"I'm not afraid," said Richie. "I've got my Chuck Norris action jeans on."

"People always think there's no serial killers in the country, but that's not the case," Laurie said. "My useless knowledge of random serial killer facts from years of listening to true crime podcasts has finally come in handy."

"Hey guys!" Rachel called from the doorway. "Are you okay in there? Should I call for back-up? Are you killed? Is it a bear or a masked psycho or a ghost?"

"Which one would you feel safer with?" said Ginny. "How would it be a bear?"

"It's just a room," Jess said. "Come on in, Rachel."

"I never thought 'Could've Been' could sound terrifying," said Laurie.

"Remember if anything happens, yell 'Fire!'" said Rachel, not entering the room. "Nobody comes if you yell 'Help' but they all come if you yell 'Fire!' That gets their attention."

"Look at this place," Aunt Dolly said.

"It's a shrine to The Felicitous," said Diane.

The room was a makeshift museum, dedicated to the cult's history and effects. Boxes were piled on top of each other, forgotten relics from the past relegated to storage. The cult's old uniforms and masks. Strange medical supplies. Birth and death certificates.

Unremembered toys, electronics, clothing, shoes, discarded papers, photo albums, old newspapers and magazines, furniture, sheets and comforters, lawn gnomes, sporting equipment, manila envelopes, wall phones, jewelry, cards, stuffed animals, car parts, cleaning supplies, artwork, vases, Tupperware, board games, musical instruments, luggage, film canisters, and filing cabinets strewn all over, stacked and assembled haphazardly like a deranged game of Tetris. Flypaper and air fresheners hung from the ceiling, giving off a sickly pine-scented smell.

That wasn't all.

Mannequins dressed in the outfits of The Felicitous lined the walls. Mannequins in black suits and ties and white shirts, the others in the 1950s and '60s-style dresses that Erica Keating, Laird's fiancée, wore.

The E/K symbol was etched and drawn all over the walls, on plaques and boxes, and stitched into clothing.

In the center of the room, against the back wall, was a wax figure in a glass case of Laird Hubbell. The wax had warped and melted over time but it was him. Dressed in his ever-present gray suit and robe combination. The wax statue's feet were secured onto a board with a placard that read, "Bishop Laird."

"This must be where the Laird Hubbell fan club meets," Max said.

Taxidermy animals on plaques aligned the wall, looking down on the visitors. Notes and songs written by cult members spread out over a desk. News articles about The Felicitous on the walls, pinned into the wood. Pictures of the past—the cult members laughing, dancing, playing, being together. Reports on every aspect of the cult—from stories about the Hubbell family to recollections by its members after their world fell apart. Photographs of the former cult members, taken without their knowledge, as if they were being spied on. Journal articles about Dr. Arthur Wainwright, Dr. Andrew Liu, Dr. Meghan Chittle, and Dr. James Salehi, the main caretakers of several members of The Felicitous when they were patients at The Calista Island Asylum.

Two daguerreotypes—one of Laird, one of Erica—hanging next to each other over a hand-painted mural drawn by the cult's members, depicting smiling, happy people with joined hands. Next to that were children's drawing of laughing suns and kids feeding goats and sheep.

Someone took the letter keys from a typewriter and placed them into the wall like an avant-garde art project. Photo IDs and passports in shoeboxes. Melted candles stuck to the floor. Diary and journal entries from The Felicitous. A framed black-and-white photograph of the Hubbell family hung next to a similar portrait of The Felicitous, Laird's other family.

"Cults are like religion," said Ginny. "They make people feel better about themselves. Give them a sense of superiority and belonging. Makes them feel like their lives have meaning. Helps take away the fear of the afterlife. You put a bunch of outsiders together in a cult— think about how that affects them physiologically, psychologically, emotionally, mentally, even physically."

"Yeah, somebody definitely put a pox on your house, Annie," Laurie said.

"I feel like I'm in a really bad, corny B-movie right now," said Annie.

Annie, Sloane, and Jess stopped before a mosaic on one of the walls. Someone had created a large, imposing caricature of the thing—that creature Laird believed he'd seen in the woods and made his followers worship—made from sticks, leaves, and found earth. The thing loomed over the women, as if it were ready to come alive and snatch them away.

"This is their storage unit, hidden away from society," Sloane said. "Until they can come back out."

"Is there anyone here?" Madame Fructuosa said. "I'm picking up on many vibrations. Would anyone like to speak to us? Please talk to me. I am a friend. We mean you no harm. Do not be afraid. Tell us what you want us to know. We come in peace. Our hearts and minds are open and ready to receive your story. Why are you still here? You can speak to me through Wanda."

The only sounds were of everyone's breathing.

"I feel him here," Madame Fructuosa said.

"Who?" Annie said, trying not to sound frantic. She didn't want to buy into any of this. "Laird Hubbell?"

"Yes, I hear you," said Madame Fructuosa, not to Annie but to the ether.

"Who do you feel?" Aunt Dolly said. "Is he inside you?"

246

"No," Madame Fructuosa said. "He's all around me. All around us."

Madame Fructuosa stared at a dead bat on the wall. It had been nailed into the wood. It didn't look like it had been there for very long.

"What is this?" Martha said, standing over a box full of dynamite and explosives. Behind the boxes were several sealed black barrels.

"We'll have to get someone to come take this away," said Diane. "That is definitely dangerous. Don't touch it, Martha."

"Those are barrels of lye," Aunt Dolly said, pointing. "It helps disintegrate bodies. And it's in soap. In smaller doses, of course."

"I took a Buzzfeed quiz the other day," Karen said. "Which *Sex and the City* character are you? I'm a Charlotte. Sometimes when I'm all alone in the house, I do the *Bird Box* challenge and see if I know my way around. Do you like crossword puzzles?"

"Karen, did you take the wrong allergy pill again?" Martha said, taking Karen's hand in hers.

"I'm so sneezy," said Karen, looking dreamily into space.

"Remember, you take the orange one? Which one did you take?" said Martha.

"The blue one."

Martha groaned. "Okay, we're going to put you to bed. You have that Zac Efron pillow your granddaughter gave you to sleep with."

"Let's go scuba diving," said Karen. "An ounce of prevention is worth a pound of cure. How many ounces are in a foot?"

Martha helped Karen toward the doorway, talking softly to her, encouraging her voyage to bed. Karen's eyelids slowly opened and closed as they walked.

"I'm going to go watch *Steel Magnolias* and have a good cry," Karen said. "You know, Karen used to be considered such a pretty name. Now it's been ruined by all the mean, bad haircut ladies. I'm not a bad haircut lady, am I? Night-night."

Once Karen and Martha were out of view, Brenda turned to everybody.

"She won't even remember this tomorrow," Brenda said. Her face became very serious as Madame Fructuosa closed her eyes and put her hands out in front of her.

There was an old rocking chair in the corner, situated next to a coat rack full of oilskin garments. The chair swayed back and forth slightly, as if someone was sitting in it.

"Identify yourself," Madame Fructuosa said to the empty space in the rocking chair.

Annie, Sloane, Aunt Dolly, Brenda, Jess, Richie, Laurie, Max, and Ginny froze in place.

"Tell me your name," continued Madame Fructuosa. "What is it you want with us? Why are you still here, spirit? Do you know you have not gone into the light?"

Madame Fructuosa's eyes fixate on the ceiling, like she was going into some sort of trance.

"Hush, Wanda," she said. "I know. I know. I hear you. Just wait. The veil has been lifted. The realms between our world and the next is thinnest here."

The creak of the rocking chair was the only sound in the room.

"Wanda sees things from the netherworld," Madame Fructuosa said. "We'll see if she can make believers of you and help open your minds to the world of the dead. When I was a young girl, I fell into an iced-over pond during a snowstorm. When I awoke, Wanda was with me. She walks with me through the realm of the dead."

Madame Fructuosa became entranced again.

248

"Yes, Wanda," she said, eyes back on the ceiling. "Oh, 'Non-living.' I'm sorry. To the world of the non-living."

She returned her gaze back to us. "Wanda doesn't like the term 'dead.' She says it's offensive. She also says that one of you isn't wearing any underwear."

Richie raised his hand, both impressed by Wanda's statement and amazed that she called him out.

"Richie," Jess said, shaking her head.

"It's trying to communicate with me. Speak up, spirit," Madame Fructuosa said. She looked at Annie. "You're staying in his old room, I think. He wants to communicate with you."

"Can we call the *Long Island Medium*?" said Richie. "Please say yes!"

"Why do you say that?" Annie said.

"Because she gets so emotionally involved and you can tell she really cares about the people she helps," said Richie.

"No, not you," Annie said. She looked at Madame Fructuosa. "You. Why do you think he wants to communicate with me?"

"We know there are things out there beyond this mortal domain. And these buildings have stood for hundreds of years, witnessing suffering and traumas. The land around it has seen things and has soaked up the bloodshed in its soil. This land has not forgotten what happened here," Madame Fructuosa said. "They're showing me things. They were experimented on. Horrible, awful experiments. They did terrible things here. They summoned things that should never be disturbed. Opened portals and doors that they never closed. It's all still here. Some things that were never even human. Are you a ghost or a spirit? Wanda, tell them to answer me."

"What's the difference? Between a ghost and a spirit?" said Annie.

"Ghosts are tied to the location where they died, usually in a violent or tragic way. Sometimes they don't know they're dead. A lot of times they have unfinished business here on earth and can't rest," said Madame Fructuosa. "Spirits are more abstract or metaphysical. It's someone's soul that lives on even though their physical body is gone. They can visit people at will, like those they had an emotional connection with in life. But the things they conjured here—I can't tell what they are. They're evil."

The group remained silent and motionless, not knowing if everything was grotesquely funny or terrifying.

Tap!

A tapping noise came from one of the water pipes. A long, deep groan from within the belly of the building. Sounds of the church settling, pushing against the air from outside.

"Why do you remain here?" Madame Fructuosa called out, wandering around and touching items as she walked. "You are no longer among the living. This is not your home any longer. It's time for you to cross over, to be with your loved ones. I can help you. You are free to move on to the next world."

The lights flickered.

"What is it, Wanda?" said Madame Fructuosa. "What, Wanda? I can't hear you. Why?"

Bang!

A loud knock against the wall, followed by several bangs against the sides of the church. Everyone spun around, searching for the source of the noise.

Bang! Bang!

More knocks and blows slammed against the room, the walls, the boxes, all around them yet they were unable to locate their origin.

"There are so many lost souls here," Madame Fructuosa said. "I feel their anger, hate, sadness. There's so much loss, rage, jealousy, vengeance. They were tormented in life. Now they are trapped here. Wanda is showing me their faces. We have what they want."

"What do they want?" said Laurie.

"Life," Madame Fructuosa said. "We have life. They don't."

"I am not having fun," said Jess.

"They're trapped between this world and the next one," said Madame Fructuosa. "They aren't allowed to reside among the living but they don't want to be dead. They aren't free. They're captive. Confined and locked up in a state of purgatory. A void, an oblivion of nonexistence."

"Holy fuckballs, we're the red shirts on *Star Trek*," Max said.

"Someone is standing next to me," said Madame Fructuosa. "It's not Wanda."

Madame Fructuosa looked over to an empty black space next to a stack of boxes. Everyone's buttholes were so puckered that they feared their anuses would go inside their bodies.

"Who's there?" Madame Fructuosa said. "Who hurt you? Why won't you leave here?"

Everyone stared into the black abyss. Waiting. Breath held.

"There's someone in that corner," Madame Fructuosa continued. "Right over there. He's staring at us. He's been crawling up and down the walls. He wants you to know that he doesn't want you here. This is his house. You are all trespassers here. He said you are taking what belongs to him and his family. He will do whatever he can to make you leave. He's hurt people before. He's looking right at us."

They all backed away from the corner, standing in a huddle in the center of the room. There was nothing visible in the corner, only darkness and floating dust particles. Everyone squinted to make out any shape or form but couldn't see anything except murky blackness.

"Can you see him?" Madame Fructuosa said. "Show yourself to us."

"You really don't have to," Ginny said softly.

"Shh," said Madame Fructuosa, stepping closer to the dark. "He's not the only presence here. There are many. What are they saying, Wanda? They aren't friendly. They're so angry you're here. They're watching us. Do you see them? They're all around us."

The air was filled with what sounded like whispers and conversations in hushed tones. Several voices, layered over each other, speaking faintly, their words unintelligible.

Richie grabbed Jess's hand, squeezing it tightly, not letting go as she tried to shake it off.

"Easy, Franken-grip," Jess whisper-yelled, wrenching her hand free.

Strings of lights lining the walls sprung to life, illuminating the room. Nobody was near any of the light switches or plugs.

"He's right there," Madame Fructuosa said into the dark space.

They gazed into the blackness.

A pair of stark white eyes opened, staring back at them from the dark.

Boom!

All of the tops of boxes surrounding them burst open simultaneously, as if unfurled by several unseen hands all at once.

"And we're done here," Annie said, making her move to leave.

As soon as she took one step forward, a stack of boxes crashed to the ground, spilling files and pictures at her feet. Madame Fructuosa picked up some of the photos and papers, stuffing them in her pocket.

The group hustled in unison out of the room.

Before they left, everyone saw the deep, jagged scratch marks dug into the doors. Like someone—or something—had been locked in the secret room and tried to claw their way out.

Madame Fructuosa followed unhurriedly. Annie swore she heard Madame Fructuosa say, "Good night," to whatever she had been speaking to.

Martha left Karen sleeping soundly in her bed. Before she left, she shut all of the curtains to keep the afternoon sun from overheating Karen's small room.

Karen was completely oblivious to the people that stood around her as she slept. Masked intruders who gathered around her bed, staring at her as she slumbered.

The five strangers stood motionless, silent, watching her.

Watching and waiting.

CHAPTER FORTY-THREE

Annie, Sloane, Ginny, Laurie, Max, Jess, Richie, and Rachel gathered in Annie's dining room. They looked completely shell-shocked by what they'd witnessed.

"Well, that was an unexpected parlor game," Richie said, breaking the silence.

"Parlor trick is more like it," said Ginny.

"You all saw that, right?" Jess said. "Those eyes?"

"You saw something or you want to believe there's some presence here so we all conjured up some psychosomatic ghost episode?" Ginny said.

"This is not in our heads," Laurie said.

"Laurie, I love you," Max said. "Ghosts aren't real."

"You know me better than that, Max," said Laurie. "You know I would never make something like this up. You were there."

"Of course I do, my sweet babboo. But we don't really know this charlatan psychic lady. Maybe this is what she does," Max said. "Maybe she tricks people into seeing things that aren't really there. Preying on our fears of the dark and death. It happens all the time. When the ghostbusting grannies leave tonight, we'll go back to where we saw Casper the not-so-friendly ghost and see."

Laurie shot Max an unamused look.

"Have I mentioned today how beautiful, wise, and amazing you are, my dearest wife?" Max said. "And did I mention your hair looks lovely today and that I love you? You are the wind beneath my wings. You complete me."

"Good save."

"Let's break this down," said Ginny. "What really went on in there? Madame Fructuosa, hostess to the dearly departed, gave us vague and non-descript scenarios and words to exacerbate the fear we were already feeling. In a new, unexplored area in a dusty, rickety old church. Sound carries in strange ways. There's your disembodied voices right there. The eyes? A trick of the light. Masterminded by a woman wearing seventeen clashing patterns. That's it. Science. Annie moved to a big, spooky, desolate, isolated old ghost town in the sticks. That already generates irrational fears and worries in our minds. All our psychic network friend did was exploit them."

"Really?" Rachel said. "That's all you've got? That's your easy explanation for everything? You won't even entertain the idea that there could be otherworldly activity here? That's very cynical, Ginny."

"People who live out in the middle of nowhere usually do so for a reason," said Sloane. "Who knows what in the name of Kirk Cameron's weird balls happened in that church before Annie moved in."

"There's no such thing as ghosts, Sloane," Max said. "It's a concept invented by people who are afraid of dying so they created this idea that there's this magical spirit world we go to. People are real. Ghosts are figments of people's imaginations that have perfectly logical, reasonable, if not always obvious, explanations. And so moviemakers, horror writers, and ghost hunters can make money. Ghosts are fake."

"New England has a bloody history," said Rachel. "Old houses have history. People have died here on this property. Is it so far-fetched to think a spirit might still be here, attached to this place?"

"That's quite a leap, Rachel," Ginny said. "The other morning, I knew I had put the Windex away under the sink, but I found it on the counter later. So that wasn't me? That was a ghost?"

"Yes," Rachel said.

"You know I believe in spiritual things," said Max. "There are other planes of existence and realms that we don't see or feel. I believe in past lives. But I also believe in coincidence and timing. Annie is busy cleaning out all the clutter in this place. We've got cult talk on our minds because their things are right in front of our faces."

"Doesn't Demi Lovato sing to ghosts now?" Richie said.

"It was an optical illusion," said Ginny. "Your mind trying to make sense of the darkness. Sailors call it Fata Morgana. A mirage you see on the horizon. It's not the exact same thing but a similar principle. People want to make sense of everything. You were already scared so it's only natural that you'd have an overreaction. It's human nature."

"We all had a scare," Sloane said. "We went in with high expectations and convinced ourselves of more going on than there actually was."

"I prefer low expectations," said Richie. "Low expectations are my sweet spot. That way I never have to pick anyone up from the airport or send a care package."

"For the sake of not being completely freaked out for the rest of the weekend, I'm willing to chalk this up to being easily influenced and impressionable, being in a strange and slightly spooky new place," said Laurie.

"I'm all for cautious optimism," Rachel said. "But are we safe here? How do we get rid of them? I saw his eyes. How am I supposed to forget about that? It's like saying, 'Don't think about the color yellow.' That's all you'll think about."

"Lots of self-delusion and repression," Jess said.

"The good news is that ghosts aren't always like they are in the movies," said Sloane. "Most of the time they're just lost, confused souls who have unfinished business here on Earth or just don't know they're dead. Or can't accept it. Ghosts can't hurt you. Don't be afraid of the dead. Be afraid of the living. These ghosts may be angry, but I think that if we talk to them, they'll leave. They believe that this is their home and you are all interlopers. Don't let it ruin our weekend. We're just passing through. They're harmless. They won't bother you if you don't bother them. Maybe don't go snooping around in people's houses. There's so much more fun to be had this weekend. You need to forget about this and enjoy what's to come. Ignorance, as they say, is bliss."

"I think Madame Fructuosa set this whole thing up," said Max. "The right combination of wiring, lighting, special effects, audio and visual manipulation. All she was missing was a crystal ball. She was maneuvering our fear for her own amusement. It's all a hoax she probably recreates for all the tourists and then has a big laugh about them behind their backs."

"She went to all that trouble to mess with us?" Laurie said. "That's either incredibly mean or incredibly clever. I don't know if I'm mad at her or completely impressed."

"It can be done a lot more easily than you think," Max said. "Some well-placed mechanics and cues and a susceptible audience, and you magically get a ghost show. It's Grand Guignol theater. There's probably a WikiHow detailing the whole thing. One of us would have seen if there was actually someone down there. We freaked out based on the power of suggestion and Madame Fructuosa got a sadistic thrill from it. Remember that movie *Hell Night* with Linda Blair that we watched at the grindhouse theater for Gary's fortieth birthday party? The characters constructed all those elaborate scare tactics and that movie is from 1981. Psychic lady's got forty years of engineering advancements on her side."

A collective sigh of relief washed over the group.

"There is one," said Ginny, holding up her phone. "How-to step-by-step instructions on setting up a haunted house."

"What would we do without you, Mr. Wizard?" Jess said.

The mood between everyone lifted considerably.

"Let's look at this from another angle," said Richie. "Let's say for argument's sake that ghosts are real. Why would they prefer haunting a dusty attic or grimy basement? They wouldn't spend their limbo in some gnarly secret church room. They're going to hang around the things in life that made them happy and that they had some connection to."

"What about the ghosts that can't control where they go or who they haunt?" Rachel said. "The ghosts of New England. I never thought 'mean old psycho-biddy lady gets her jollies frightening guests with a phony house of horror' would be on my worry list, but here we are."

Madame Fructuosa cleared her throat, the chunky jewels and bangles on her wrists clanging together. She stood in the doorway.

"Many years ago, I went to a house where the family claimed their son was possessed by a very powerful, violent entity," Madame Fructuosa said. "They were like you. Non-believers at first. We stayed with the family and recorded all kinds of horrifying noises and events. The son was wild like an animal, speaking in languages he didn't know and displaying almost otherworldly strength, levitating, self-mutilating. He said that something, some spirit from another world, kept talking to him, making him do things. The son had taken a relic from a sacred place on a family trip and that's when all the bad things started to happen. Nobody believed them or us. People called us fruitcakes and weirdos for being there, for believing."

A hush fell over the room.

Madame Fructuosa continued. "We captured all kinds of paranormal activity and tried to convince the authorities that this was real. One night, things were quiet, so we left to get some rest. When we came back, we found the son, covered in blood. He had torn apart every member of his family with his bare hands. They had to sedate him with ten times the normal amount of tranquilizer. It took six grown men to subdue him."

258

"Couldn't he have just been mentally ill and violent?" said Richie.

"No," Madame Fructuosa said. "Ghosts."

Madame Fructuosa reached into her pocket and handed Annie a bunch of photos.

"He told me to give these to you," she said. She turned to the group. "A closed mind doesn't catch rainbows."

"Are we catching rainbows or ghosts?" said Richie. "Or are they somehow related? Rainbow-colored ghosts. Doesn't seem practical. Then everybody would see them. Leprechauns would hide their gold in them. They'd be on every float at the gay pride parades. Gay ghosts! How would we get rid of them? Dance around to Pink and say, 'Toy boat' five times fast?"

"Richie," Jess said, sending him a disapproving look.

"Give it time," Madame Fructuosa said. "They'll show themselves to you soon. I have to go. Thank you for having me. I left the tape from the EVP with Brenda. Goodbye, everyone. Have the day you deserve."

Before she left, Madame Fructuosa stopped and whispered in Annie's ear. "It's not your fault."

What does that mean? Annie thought.

Madame Fructuosa exited, leaving the stack of photos in front of Annie. Annie slid them into her jeans pocket.

"You ever notice how in movies and television shows, characters order food, and when the food comes, something always happens and they have to rush out so they leave all of it?" Max said, trying to break the tension. "What happens all that food? Does it all just get thrown away? I don't understand."

Max got a few laughs. He put his arm around Laurie.

Annie's mind was elsewhere.

CHAPTER FORTY-FOUR

Alice changed into her hiking boots as Trish and Bill waited for her in the common room of guest house number three.

She checked herself out in the mirror, stopping when she noticed something peculiar.

Her bed—previously made—was unkempt. There was a person's outline in the sheets, an impression and indentation on the mattress. As if someone had been sleeping there.

Scratch.

Alice stopped when she heard the scraping sound coming from within the wall. She tried to pinpoint the source—slow, methodical scratching, barely audible.

"Alice," Trish said from the doorway, causing Alice to jump. "You done putting on your Lady Gaga meat dress? You look beautiful, as always. Hey, what's wrong?"

"Nothing," Alice laughed at herself. "Let's go before Bill turns into a gremlin."

"Don't get him wet, don't feed him after midnight, and no bright lights," said Trish. "I know the rules."

"Isn't it always after midnight, technically?"

Alice and Trish walked into the hallway to see Bill staring out of the screened-in door at something.

"Hey, Bill?" Trish called out. "What are you—"

Bill moved to the side as Alice and Trish approached. On the other side of the screened-in door was a pudgy, older man carrying a briefcase. He was dressed in a tattered brown suit and an orange ascot.

"Hello," the man said, smiling widely, exposing brown, crooked teeth. "My name is Marvin Sturges and I'm selling..." He looked down at his briefcase. "...Encyclopedias."

Alice, Bill, and Trish regarded the odd man with trepidation. Trish instantly put her foot against the bottom of the door, in case the man tried to force himself inside. Marvin Sturges was so old and frail, she doubted he could, but just to be safe.

"We don't need any encyclopedias, but thank you, Marvin," said Trish. In her work as a lawyer, she had gotten used to clients whose mental health was unsteady.

"That's where they used to hang the traitors," Marvin said, pointing over to the tree line. "The people who went against the group. They'd hang them up from the branches and let the birds peck their eyes out. They'd leave the bodies up for everyone to see as a warning."

Alice, Bill, and Trish were silent. What was there to say?

"Is there someone we can call for you?" Bill said. "Someone to come and get you?"

"Oh, no, young man," said Marvin, pointing back toward the forest. "I live there. I'm never alone that way. I have lots of friends to keep me company. They say that water is a conduit for the undead, but the riverbed is all dried up now. I can still hear them at night, speaking to me. I dug a pit in the ground because I heard a voice calling out to me. But there was no one there, in the earth. Sometimes, I think I died and this is hell."

Trish dialed the emergency line on her cell phone. She put the phone to her ear but heard nothing—no ring, no sound, no beeping.

"That won't work here," Marvin said, glaring at her phone. "Things here aren't the same as they are where you come from. I have to go now. I have so much to do. Please tell Annie I stopped by."

261

Bill almost stopped Marvin from going, but Trish lightly grabbed his arm. Alice, Bill, and Trish watched as Marvin slowly walked away, headed toward the trees.

"How did he know Annie's name?" Alice said.

"He's probably some local whackjob from Hartwell who doesn't have much to do in his retirement," said Bill. "A lonely old man. It's nothing to worry about."

"He left something on the porch," Alice said, opening the screen door and picking up an old, brown bottle.

"Please don't let it be a Gwyneth Paltrow vagina candle," said Trish. Alice showed her the bottle.

"It's a witch's bottle," Alice said. "Traditionally, it would have urine and hair and nail clippings in it, but this one seems to be full of pins and needles and rosemary. And red wine. Old New England superstitions. I had a Wiccan cousin who used these in white magic rituals. It's supposed to offer protection against witchcraft and evil spirits."

"What do you think was in that briefcase?" said Trish.

"Probably a collection of shrunken heads, voodoo dolls, and daily mailers from the Piggly Wiggly," Alice said.

"You should wash your hands," Bill said to Alice. "Who knows where that's been. Use the dish scrubber."

Alice realized she didn't know what she was touching and tossed the bottle back outside, rushing to the sink to clean herself.

"I don't see him anymore," Bill said.

"Then he's still there," said Alice.

"Bye, Marvin," said Trish. "Let's not do this again."

CHAPTER FORTY-FIVE

Madame Fructuosa bid her goodbyes to Brenda and went to find the laundry room to retrieve her washed wearables from Eunice. While she wandered past the buildings, lost in her own thoughts, the steady sound of a man's voice wafted on the air.

She couldn't make out what the man was saying, but the incessant droning of his flat and serious tone gave her pause.

Madame Fructuosa stopped in front of a building with a wooden plaque that read "Main Office." The man's voice was coming from within. She felt a sense of dread and curiosity, as if she shouldn't enter but was compelled to.

The office was loaded with filing cabinets, electrical equipment, and the type of supplies and amenities found at base headquarters, like an old school, mustard yellow-colored telephone on the wall and large, weathered desk.

There was a large section missing from the corner of the floor, surrounded by tools and wooden slats, in the process of being rebuilt.

On the shelf was a rickety AM radio from yesteryear. The giant knob on its face was clicked on. The sound was coming from the dusty speaker.

The man's voice was unchanging, as he read out what seemed to be coordinates to certain locations. In between each methodical reading of numbers, he would speak. Every word he said sounded like general information someone could read on a placard or a type of proverb. It didn't make sense to Madame Fructuosa.

Who was that transmission for?

"In the darkness, you shall be the light," the man said over the static and broadcast interference. A hum and a vibration repeated in the undercurrent of his speech.

Madame Fructuosa stared at the massive pile of soiled, damaged stuffed animals in the corner of the room as the man on the radio continued to talk.

"Those who you cannot change shall be made to see the truth," the man spoke as Madame Fructuosa got closer to the stuffed animal heap.

There was a person looking back at her, hidden among the plush toys. Only the person's face was visible, the rest covered by fake fur and overly-cute mammals. It was a woman.

It was Eunice, Brenda's assistant.

"Eunice?" Madame Fructuosa said. "What are you doing in there? Are you all right?"

Eunice didn't respond. She simply kept her gaze straight ahead. Madame Fructuosa wondered if this was some kind of joke or if Eunice did this as a coping mechanism for comfort. Madame Fructuosa reached out to move some of the stuffed animals away from Eunice.

The entire stack tumbled forward, spilling around Madame Fructuosa.

Along with Eunice's head.

Madame Fructuosa had no time to scream when Eunice's decapitated head stopped rolling at her feet.

"If you encounter an enemy, strike them down with force and no mercy," the man's voice on the radio said.

Madame Fructuosa gasped when she saw someone staring at her from the open space in the flooring. Mostly hidden by the uneven wood that remained, but visible enough that she could make out someone in a mummy mask peering at her from beneath the floorboards.

She didn't see the stranger in a black suit and skin-colored, expressionless mask, like a demented wax figure, behind her. But she felt as the barbed wire wrapped

264

around her neck, their spikes piercing her skin, causing rivulets of blood to run down her dress. Madame Fructuosa crumpled to the floor, bloody and defeated.

Madame Fructuosa's last vision was of the man's cold, black eyes boring holes in hers.

CHAPTER FORTY-SIX

Annie told her friends to explore Gull Valley while she checked on some emails and took care of things she needed to. She wanted to get her head back into a clear space.

When she got to her room, she found Aunt Dolly there, holding a humidifier in one hand and a jug of water in the other.

"What are you up to, Aunt Dolly?" Annie said. "Haven't we had enough crazy for one day?"

Aunt Dolly poured the water into the humidifier.

"It's holy water," Aunt Dolly said. "To keep the bad spirits away. I got Father McKinley to bless this for me."

Annie couldn't control her eye roll. "There's always room for more crazy, I guess."

Aunt Dolly plugged the humidifier in. "I may have given up my vows but I still have my faith. There are things in this world we can't explain. This will keep the evil at bay."

"I'm sure it will," said Annie. "Very scientific. I can feel the ghosts fleeing in terror as we speak. We didn't even need proton packs."

"Is this what you kids call 'negging'?" Aunt Dolly said. "You say mean and negative things but you really mean, 'Thanks'? Never mind. Either way, we're going to make some spicy wings for later. Come join us. Karen is entering a spicy wings competition and we thought we'd practice."

Annie laughed. "Okay. I'm happy that you're here, Aunt Dolly."

"Me too, my curly fry," Aunt Dolly said, leaving Annie alone with the hum of the humidifier and the comforting but misguided idea that somehow its mojo would magically rid Gull Valley of all its ghosts and spirits.

The walls in Alice's bedroom were lined with dozens of photographs. They were nameless people with unfamiliar faces to her, but she paused for a minute while retrieving a hoodie to look at the pictures more closely.

One black-and-white photo in particular, which Alice estimated was taken some time during the 1960s, captured her attention—a father and mother standing on either side of their adult daughter, who was seated in a plush chair. They presented as a well-to-do, upstanding family, dressed as if they were headed to or coming back from church; the father in a suit and tie and the two women in archetypal demure, classic dresses associated with the time period.

Alice wasn't sure though. She could only make an educated guess about who they were, what their stories were, and what kind of people they had been when the photograph was taken.

She was sure of one thing—she did not like the picture. Or the foreboding, sinister feeling it filled her with.

The faces of the people in the photo had been scratched away. As if their existence had somehow been cursed and erased by unseen hands; their visages destroyed and stolen by a sharp instrument wielded in anger and rage.

Alice wondered why someone went to all the trouble to scrape away their faces then reframe and hang their picture.

She suppressed a shudder and lifted the framed photograph off of its rusty nail. She placed it on the ground, turning the mutilated faces against the wall.

CHAPTER FORTY-SEVEN

After nightfall, Annie and her friends set up a giant bonfire in the center of the gorge. The night air was cold and unwelcoming but they were having so much fun that they didn't notice.

Aunt Dolly and her girl gang had made spicy wings and pepperoni pizza macaroni and cheese for dinner. They were in the mess hall cleaning up while Annie and her crew drank beer and wine coolers around the roaring fire.

The bonfire was enclosed with large rocks. Everyone had grabbed thick, long tree branches and brush to create a monstrously raging blaze. The red and orange flames lit up the pitch-black darkness of the night sky, making it difficult to see anything past the burning inferno.

Dave and Sean were mildly high on gummies and dancing around the fire as Paul Anka's "I Don't Like to Sleep Alone"—which Aunt Dolly put on before she went to do dishes—played on portable speakers connected to a laptop.

"This is too slow," Sean said. "We need something more appropriate for the venue."

Sean clicked a few buttons and The Cure's "A Forest" began to play.

"You can see every star in the sky out here," Dave said. "You don't get that view in the city. All this space, freedom, air, stars."

Sean put his arm around Dave, adjusting the portable neck fan he wore. "It's beautiful. It's very romantic if you think about it."

"Is it bad that I'm fully prepared that the two of you will run away together someday?" Sally said.

"You're always my number one, Sally," said Dave. "Sean and I have a bromance, but I don't think he's ready for this jelly. Speaking of, we're working on Sean's online dating profile. Any thoughts?"

Sean showed everyone the in-progress dating application on his cell phone.

"Hm," Richie said. "How about this. 'Like Angelina Jolie, I too am a great humanitarian and plan to adopt not 1 but 4 Cambodian babies, who will be named Blair, Tootie, Natalie, and Jo, even if they are boys. They will attend the Eastland School for Girls in Peekskill and work in my sweatshop for seven cents an hour making slime and raising sloths. Take that, Maddox Jolie-Pitt! According to Sally Struthers, the most trustworthy person on the planet, adoption from a third-world country costs the same price daily as a cup of coffee. I definitely have the extra cash flow since I only drink hard liquor, although I may have to stop shooting heroin as much. On our first date, we'll do off-road recovery then a couples sensory deprivation tank, where you can teach me the months of the year.'"

"You're hired!" Sean said, trying to type out what Richie said. "It's like you saw into my soul."

"Why is it so hard to meet people nowadays when there's too many people everywhere?" Wes said.

"Yeah," Dave said. "And you're a snack, Sean. That's what the kids say, right? A 'snack.' What else do the kids say? You'd be a 'good' date. That's the right way to say that, right? The kids say, 'Good'?"

"I thought you'd have lots of dates, Wes," said Sean. "Isn't that the best part about being a gay dude? There's penises everywhere and you're all always horny?"

"Yes, that's exactly what it's like, Sean," Wes said, not taking any offense to Sean's teasing. "Just constant dicks in your face. We're all ready with our assless chaps, Bud Lights, and lube in case we stumble upon a new dick."

"How does scissoring work?" Sean said. "Doesn't that hurt your balls when you do it?"

"Dear God," Wes said. "This is what happens to people our age who grew up playing games called Smear the Queer. I'll show you some videos later to show you how it actually works, okay, Sean? I'm sure Annie has a copy of *Shaving Ryan's Privates* here."

"Awesome," said Sean. "I love the gays."

"Try being a woman in your mid-forties and dating," Alice said. "It's getting to the point where I wonder how to get a sugar daddy or a generous and wealthy benefactor. I'm too old to be the ward of someone with an estate, right?"

"That's a really great plan," Nancy said. "Alice, any man would be lucky to have you."

"How are we all grown-ups now?" Jess said. "All we wanted when we were kids was to be adults. Now look at us. I want my money back. It's a scam. That salad I ate last week did nothing for me. There's no book fair for adults. It's all a fraud."

"The only time I get alone time is when I put on my imaginary shower concerts," Nancy said.

"I spend all my time apologizing," said Rachel. "We're always saying, 'Sorry,' for things that we had no control over. So many sorries, over and over. Sometimes I apologize for apologizing."

"Being an adult is just being tired all the time," Trish said. "And turning down the volume of the radio so you can see the road better when you're driving."

Annie missed all of this. Her friends together, laughing and making jokes, making fun of each other, talking about their lives.

"The best part of us getting older is watching our kids grow up," Kit said. "I can't believe how time works. To us, a year is gone in a day. But to the kids, a day feels like a year."

"The next generation," Annie said. "And my favorite people."

"My kids are your favorite favorites though, right?" said Alice jokingly.

"I love all of my nieces and nephews equally," Annie said. When everyone wasn't looking, Annie mouthed, "But yours the most," to Alice.

"I'm going to need more alcohol if we're going to get all maudlin and sad," Sean said.

"Do you remember the D.A.R.E. program they used to try to sell us?" said Ginny. "All that Just Say No business. I used to go to school in my D.A.R.E. shirt while everyone else was huffing paint behind the bleachers. Meanwhile, the D.A.R.E. people were telling us where and how to get drugs and how if someone smoked pot once, they'd end up in a gutter begging for change and turning tricks for 7-11 slushies."

"I miss the '80s," Alice said. Everyone laughed and cheered, raising their drinks in agreement.

"What about now, though?" Rachel said. "We have each other. We're healthy, safe, and happy—not a challenge, universe—and we're all here together."

Everyone fell silent for a moment, thinking about Rachel's statement.

"To the next fifty years," T.P. said, raising his drink for another cheers.

As the friends cheered again, there was a face illuminated in the firelight. Someone standing by the fire, hidden by the darkness and flickering shadows. Someone not in Annie's friend group.

"Who's that?" Chris said, interrupting the merriment. She tried to hide the fear in her voice.

Someone darted past the bonfire, obscured by the blackness beyond the roaring flames.

"Who was what?" Ginny said.

"I saw someone over there," Chris said, pointing past the fire toward the tree line.

"It's just a trick of the light from the fire," Sean said.

"No, I think I saw someone standing over there, almost like they were trying to blend in with us," Chris said.

"I saw it too," Laurie said. "There was someone there, near the fire."

"This better not be a joke," said Bill. "Are you guys being serious?"

"Let's go check it out then," T.P. said.

"No, let's not," said Rachel. "Let's stay here where we're safe."

"There's a fine line between courage and stupidity," Alice said. "We're all together, and I'm sure Chris saw something, but it could've been a camper or a hiker or something."

"Maybe it was the Blair Witch," Sean said. "Or someone from The Felicitous."

Sean, Dave, and T.P. walked past the fire toward the tree line.

"Be right back after these commercial messages," T.P. said.

"Guys, don't go out there," Annie said. "Stay here where it's safe. It was probably just a strange anomaly. The fire bends the light and makes shapes against the contrast of the dark."

There was no answer from Sean, Dave, and T.P. as they searched the grounds beyond the fire.

"Dave," Sally said. "I need you in one piece."

Everyone was quiet as Sean, Dave, and T.P. walked farther away from the safety and light of the bonfire.

"Do you see anything?" said Ned.

No answer. Everyone waited with bated breath for any response. Sean, Dave, and T.P. appeared back by the fire.

272

"There's nothing out there," Dave said. "Could've been an animal curious about the fire."

"Can we go back to getting our groove on now?" said Sean, loading up "Dare" by Gorillaz, followed by Smashing Pumpkins' "Tonight, Tonight," and shaking his bum.

"I think the scary stories from today are getting to everyone," Steve said. "This place does get really dark at night."

"There's nobody here but us," T.P. said. "We're safe and sound."

"I saw someone," Chris said.

"I swear, all this Felicitous talk has gotten our imaginations running wild," said Kit.

"I don't know, Kit," Jess said. "I seem to remember a certain friend who has an overwhelming and irrational fear of killer robots."

Kit gasped. Her face was serious as she spoke. "I watched this horrible movie in the '90s with atrocious CGI. It was about this killer robot murdering his creator's friends and family. I was actually terrified. I don't even remember the title but then when I saw *The Terminator* and *Chopping Mall* years later, I felt my fear of killer robots to be justified. The robot in *Chopping Mall* exploded that girl's damn head!"

Everyone erupted with laughter, not directed at Kit's pain and suffering, but the kind of laughing when friends know each other well.

"The movie is called *Evolver*, by the way," said Jess.

"You saw it? Do you see how terrifying this robot is? So cold and efficient and relentless? Listen, that robot removed a jack and a guy got crushed under a car and I got shivers. So diabolical. The point is that he was getting away with these murders and attempted murders!" Kit said.

Everyone laughed harder.

"We couldn't survive this kind of onslaught from Evolver. If he wanted us dead, we'd be dead," said Kit. "He's not high-tech like M3gan but he got the job done. With every kill, he evolves. That should've been the tagline. It was the first of many movies to instill a healthy fear and distrust of autonomous robots. I'm still pissed at you guys for making me watch *M3gan*. That creepy, freaky dancing, psycho hose beast, nightmare doll. I didn't sleep for a week."

"That sounds like a very reasonable fear, Kit," Ginny said. "I love that this random movie caused you to forever fear robots."

"Go ahead, laugh at my pain," Kit said, chuckling. "Don't come over to my house for protection when the robots take everything over."

"I'd take a killer robot over a killer person any day," Max said.

"I used to have this recurring dream that someone was standing at the foot of my bed while I slept, sawing at my achilles heel," said Laurie. "I think everyone has these deep fears that we can't explain. We don't know where they come from or why certain things scare us more than others."

"You're never afraid, out here all by yourself, Annie?" said Beverly.

"I'm afraid of a lot of things," Annie said. "But what am I going to do? I'm still figuring it all out."

What would Claire Danes do?

CHAPTER FORTY-EIGHT

Aunt Dolly, Diane, Brenda, Martha, and Karen tidied up the mess hall and put the last of the leftover food away. They stood in the large kitchen, drinking wine coolers.

"I love this," Aunt Dolly said. "All of us together again. I actually saw Annie smiling. It's been so long since I've seen that."

"She needs to suck it up and get on with her life," said Brenda. "Life is pain. You have to get used to it."

"There's that compassion we've grown accustomed to, Brenda," said Diane. "You definitely missed your calling by not working at a suicide hotline or with sick children. You need to curb the whining and verbal assaults for the weekend. Only positive vibes from here on out. You got that, lady?"

"Okay, okay," Brenda said. "I get it. I'm an old grump. I will be a saint from here on out."

"We love you, pumpkin, but nobody believes that," said Diane. "Your superpower is that you can find something wrong with anything."

"That is not true," Brenda said. "There's lots of things I don't have any issue with."

"So, you'll go on that cruise with us then?" Karen said.

"Cruise?" said Brenda. "Cruise? Do you think I want to go on a cruise? So we can crash into an iceberg or a coral reef and the ship can sink and flip upside down in the open ocean and leave us stranded in the middle of nowhere so sharks can eat us. Or we get that weird cruise ship sickness that everybody gets because nothing's clean or sanitary. Or one of us can fall off the ship in the middle of the night and no one will notice until morning, when it's too late. Yeah, that sounds fun. Let's go."

"I rest my case, Your Honor," Diane said.

"You can bring Eunice along to clean your room," Martha said. "Where is Eunice, by the way?"

"I texted her and told her to take the night off and go into town," Brenda said. "Maybe she'll meet some other weirdo who's into Winnie the Pooh and wants to dance around tiki torches and play with marionettes or whatever kooky stuff that girl is into. She's the only twentysomething I've ever met who swoons when Kenny G. comes on the radio."

"That's uncharacteristically nice of you, Brenda," Diane said. "Did you take the wrong meds today?"

"She said something about a cowboy poetry night in Hartwell," said Brenda. "I don't even want to know what cowboy poetry is. As long as she doesn't call me and make me listen to it, she can go be free."

"There used to be a time when we'd call each other on the phone," said Karen. "Nobody calls each other anymore. The old days when people wrote each other letters. Now we just send texts. It's so impersonal."

"Hey, we call you," Diane said. "We always call each other."

"I wish you'd tell my kids and grandkids to," Karen said. "They only call on my birthday or if they need something. When you get old, you become invisible. Nobody pays attention to you anymore. You've outlived your usefulness. You don't matter. You're not a hot, young thing any longer."

"We have each other," Aunt Dolly said. "No matter what. We've been together all these years and I don't care how old and invisible we are, we'll make people pay attention to us."

Aunt Dolly, Diane, Brenda, and Martha moved in to hug and comfort Karen.

"Okay, enough of that," Brenda said.

The lights in the cafeteria flickered on and off. On and off.

"What is going on in there?" said Diane.

The ladies walked toward the cafeteria as the lights continued to click on then off. They made it to the doorway from the kitchen to the tables.

They strained their eyes to see in the dark.

Someone was sitting at one of the long cafeteria tables, facing their direction. The person's breathing was heavy and labored, a crackle-filled wheezing.

"Hello?" Aunt Dolly said.

"Don't go in there," Karen said.

Another deep, raspy breath cut through the air. It sounded like a drawn-out death rattle.

"Who's there?" said Brenda. "Identify yourself!"

The lights turned back on, flooding the room in bright, fluorescent yellow.

There was nobody there.

The women exchanged baffled, frightened looks.

"What if it was—" Karen said.

"It was one of Annie's friends," Brenda said, cutting her off.

"But what if—" continued Karen.

"It was a prank," Brenda said. "A really dumb one."

Karen didn't look so sure.

CHAPTER FORTY-NINE

Gull Valley was quiet.

It was late at night and Annie's friends were sound asleep in their respective rooms. Annie made sure they'd properly extinguished the bonfire and that all the guest houses were securely locked up for the night.

Annie stood outside, alone but not alone. She looked up to the stars in the sky.

"I wish you were here with me, Gary," she said to the ether. "Everyone came here to see me. There are so many things I want to talk to you about. It's just not the same without you. I'm not sure what I'm doing and I wish you were with me to talk about it. I hope wherever you are, you're happy. I think about you every day. I miss you."

There was no reply from the night, as Annie expected. She hoped Gary heard her.

T.P. was in the shower, soaping his face and rinsing the shampoo out of his hair. He was never able to go to bed without showering first.

He covered his face with his hands, scrubbing away the dirt from the day.

T.P. was oblivious to the figure standing on the other side of the shower curtain, its outline vaguely noticeable through the fabric.

The figure reached his arm out, pressing his hand against the shower curtain, closer to T.P.

T.P. jumped back when he saw the curtain moving. Soap got into his eyes. He frantically washed his eyes out with the streaming water, wondering if he simply imagined someone being there.

He shut the water off and leapt out of the shower and into his bedroom.

"Sean!" T.P. said. "What are you doing in my room?"

"Great penis!" said Sean, looking at T.P.'s naked body up and down. "No homo."

"What do you want, you creep?" T.P. said, covering himself with a towel.

"I ripped my pants and you're the same size as me," said Sean. "Can I borrow a pair?"

"Yes, go in my bag," T.P. said, motioning to his suitcase. "How did you rip your pants?"

"I told Dave I could light my fart on fire and my pants split open."

"Serves you right. Will you go now, please? I want to go to bed."

Sean grabbed a pair of jeans out of T.P.'s suitcase. "Thanks, these are great. See you in the morning, beer can."

"Get out!" T.P. said, shutting the door behind Sean.

A dozen masked strangers gathered under the cover of darkness, surrounding guest house number three.

The one in the vampire mask opened the front door and let the others inside.

The guest house was dark and silent, all of its inhabitants sleeping soundly.

The masked strangers walked down the hallway and chose rooms. They moved and worked in unison, their motions purposeful and muted, acting with a hive mind and common goal.

At the vampire's nod of approval, the masked strangers dispersed and opened the bedroom doors to observe the slumbering occupants.

None of the sleeping guests had any clue.

Alice was fast asleep in her room at guest house number three. She left the window open a crack to allow the cool night air into the room. Her bed was directly beneath the window.

She didn't stir as a hand reached in through the open space of the window. Someone hidden in darkness stood outside, stretching their arm out through the gap.

The masked figure put his hand as close to Alice's face as he could without touching it. She was unaware of the intrusion, her eyes closed and her mind in dreamland.

Tap!

Alice was jolted awake when she heard the thump on the glass of her window.

She was alone.

Bill had been a sleepwalker since he was a teenager. Trish had gotten used to it over the years and he only sleepwalked on rare occasions as he got older.

Trish didn't stir when Bill got out of bed, still in a dream state, and walked past the two masked strangers in their room. He was completely asleep, not responsive to outside stimuli.

Bill was a lower-half nudity sleeper. He wore a white T-shirt to bed but nothing else. He wandered out of his and Trish's room, past all of the intruders who had taken up temporary residence in the guest house, and walked straight for the front door.

When he reached the outside, there were six strangers in a semi-circle around Bill. He still hadn't opened his eyes or regained consciousness. He stopped walking, standing in a wobbly pose, as the strangers regarded him.

"Is this where you get the garlic bread?" Bill said, his mind in another realm.

"You're asleep and this is all a dream," the wizard-masked person said in a steady voice. "You won't remember any of this tomorrow. Go back to bed. We're not ready for you yet."

Bill mumbled something unintelligible, swaying slightly.

"Go back to your bedroom," the wizard said. "We have so many things planned for you. But not now. You have to wait."

Bill mumbled again then turned on his heel, back into the guest house. He climbed back into bed with Trish, still mumbling and no wiser to the presence of the strangers.

Nancy slept on her side with her back to the door. She did not hear the sound of someone opening it and standing in the doorway, watching her.

The figure remained silent and still, filling her doorway. Nancy didn't move. The figure lingered there for several minutes.

As if shocked back to reality, Nancy awoke and rolled over. She felt as if her body sent shockwaves through her, her neurons firing at full capacity, ordering her to awaken.

Her door was open. No one was there.

Nancy got up and shut the door. She climbed back into bed and pulled the covers tightly around her.

She did not see the masked stranger crouched down at the end of her bed, watching her as she drifted off to sleep.

CHAPTER FIFTY

Beverly couldn't sleep. Ned was snoring next to her like a wildebeest. Once Ned was asleep, that was it. An atomic bomb wouldn't wake him.

She tossed and turned, trying to make sleep come to her. It wasn't working. She had always struggled to sleep in new places. It was an unfortunate indisposition she had dealt with since she was a child and wouldn't go to slumber parties.

She sat up when she realized the bedroom door was wide open. She knew they had shut it before bed. Somehow, she hadn't noticed that it didn't stay closed.

Beverly got out of bed and put her jeans and sneakers on. She figured she might as well go for a stroll and see what there was to snack on in the mess hall.

When she got outside, she saw Annie sitting by the extinguished bonfire. Beverly didn't know whether to say hi and risk bothering Annie or if she should just leave her alone.

"Hey," Beverly said softly. "I didn't want to scare you."

Annie turned around and smiled. "Hi. What are you doing up? I thought I was the only one who was on a vampire's schedule."

"I'm not a great sleeper," said Beverly. "You either, I take it."

"I can never relax. It's not who I am. I don't know why I am weird. Like, I always order everything bagel ice cream even though I know I don't like it. But somehow, every time, I think this will be the time that I actually like it. I have no explanation for myself."

"Does anybody know why they are the way they are, really?"

"Does anybody know just what the fuck?" Annie said, laughing.

"I'm really sorry about Gary. I wish I could have met him. From everything Ned has said, he sounded like an amazing guy," Beverly said. She instantly regretted bringing up Annie's dead husband.

Annie didn't seem phased. "He was."

"Well, I didn't want to bug you or anything," said Beverly. "I was hoping for something to eat and maybe a book to read."

Annie pointed to one of the buildings. "The library is right there. I can't promise that the books in there aren't covered in mold and dust but there's a ton of things to read."

"Thanks. I hope you can get some sleep tonight."

"Yeah, you too," Annie said. She stood up, ready to go to her room. She said good night to Beverly and they parted ways.

CHAPTER FIFTY-ONE

Steve woke up to see Kit standing next to one of the vents in their room. Her ear was pressed closely to the slats in the vent.

"What are you doing?" Steve said, still groggy.

"It sounds like someone is talking," Kit said. "Like a conversation. There's whispering coming from the vent."

"Kit," said Steve. "We're in the middle of nowhere. It's just animals outside or noises that the wind picked up."

"I heard it," Kit said. "There were two voices. A man and a child's, I think."

Kit and Steve fell silent and listened.

"There!" said Kit. "Did you hear that?"

"No, I didn't," Steve said. "We watched *The Conjuring* the other night and you're scaring yourself. I'm going back to bed. I love you."

Kit stayed at the vent for a few more minutes and assured herself that she was simply hearing unfamiliar noises in an unfamiliar place. It was normal and natural to be spooked in an isolated, foreign location.

Neither Kit nor Steve was aware of the man in the suit in the interstitial space between the wall of their bedroom and the outside of the house. He carried on an animated conversation with the ventriloquist dummy on his hand, dressed exactly like him, as if the dummy were alive.

The man and his dummy lurked in the narrow space, chatting away like old friends. Their voices seeped through the louvers of the vent, faintly carried over the air.

Kit slid back into bed, close to Steve, and stared at the vent suspiciously until she drifted off to sleep.

CHAPTER FIFTY-TWO

Beverly perused the books on the shelves in the library and settled on Teri Hatcher's autobiography *Burnt Toast: And Other Philosophies of Life*. Teri Hatcher would give Beverly comfort and guidance in her sleepless state.

Beverly tensed at the gusts of air that kept washing over her. The library door and windows were closed. She wondered where the air was coming from.

She saw a faint light coming from one of the shelves against the back wall. The shelf itself looked as if it were pushed farther out than the other shelves.

A secret room behind a bookshelf! Like in a Gothic novel, Beverly thought.

Beverly walked over to the shelf. The light and breeze were both coming from behind it. She debated for a moment, wanting to check out what was behind it but wondering if that was the smartest idea.

Her curiosity overcame her. She pulled the bookshelf open. Behind it was a long, winding staircase leading to the source of the light.

Beverly left her Teri Hatcher book on the shelf and turned her phone light on, taking each step gingerly. She wondered if Annie knew about this hidden room.

The pungent odor of copper and old meat filled Beverly's nostrils. She figured there must be dozens of dead animals from over the years who were trapped inside without a way to escape.

She reached the bottom step and saw the massive corridors and tunnels before her, spread out in every direction with no end in sight. Beverly looked up to the top of the staircase. The bookshelf door was still open.

She wanted to see what was down there.

Beverly moved forward. The tunnels were quiet and tranquil. Candles and battery-powered lights lined the hallways, fastened into sconces and contraptions mounted to the dirt walls.

"Beverly," a voice whispered from deep in the darkness.

"Nope," Beverly said, headed back to the staircase.

The stairs were blocked by an old woman in a black dress. Her breaths came out like strained, crackling wheezes.

"Who are you?" Beverly said.

The woman didn't answer. She stared at Beverly.

Beverly ran in the opposite direction. The walls of the tunnels seemed to close in on her. She passed by several more forks in the corridor and side rooms.

The old woman hadn't followed Beverly. She was far away from the staircase. Her mind raced. She had to find a way out of there.

Beverly was in a darkened corridor. She shone her light on the ground before her.

In the illumination of the light was a pair of muddy shoes.

Beverly moved the light up to get a better look at what she saw.

A masked man in a suit was sitting in an old chair that was pressed up against the wall. He wasn't looking at her. He stared at the wall across from him.

Beverly took a step back. The man slowly turned his attention toward her. In one swift and stiff motion, he stood up from the chair and faced Beverly. He held a barbed, tactical machete in his right hand.

Beverly ran. She didn't know where to go or how to escape. The sounds of people talking and footsteps seemed to come from all of the corridors around her.

"Help!" a voice called from down the hallway. "Help us!"

Beverly crept toward the voice, afraid it was a deception to trap her. Her mind raced, wondering who these people were and what they wanted.

She came to a room that was built like a jail cell. Behind two separate walls of bars were two thirtysomething-aged men, both looking frail and malnourished. Their clothes were in tatters. They looked like they hadn't showered or eaten in weeks.

A third man, Zeke Penhall, was barely alive and tied horizontally between two traffic and construction barriers, his body suspended off the ground.

"Help us!" one of the men, Trent Langdon, cried out to Beverly once he saw her. "They're coming back for us! We've been down here for months. Help us, please!"

Beverly didn't know what to think. Trent pointed to the set of keys hanging on a nail in the wall.

"Get us out of here!" the other man, Gil Abbott, said. "Hurry! Before they come back!"

"Lower your voice!" Trent said.

"What is this place?" Beverly said, unlocking the cell as the men wildly rushed out from their containment.

"We came here to film a video and they took us," Trent said.

Both men, now freed, screamed and lurched back at whatever was behind Beverly.

"We're sorry! We're sorry!" Trent said, falling on his behind and backing away.

The sound of an engine being revved cut through the air as Beverly spun around to see a masked stranger holding a large chainsaw in the air.

"No, no, no, no, no!" Gil said. "Zeke! No, no, no!"

The stranger brought the blade of the chainsaw down on the tied-up man, cutting him in half at the waist. The man split in two, both sides of him still tied to the barriers. His internal organs spilled out to the ground.

Beverly and Gil bolted past the masked stranger. Trent looked up at the stranger, tears streaming down his face.

"Come on, get up!" Gil screamed at Trent.

Another masked stranger emerged from one of the side rooms. Trent stood up, his eyes on the man with the chainsaw.

Trent didn't see it when the stranger behind him held up the garden shears. Shocking pain raced through him when the shears pierced through the soft part of the back of his skull, the blades jutting out of his mouth.

The stranger with the garden shears grunted as he snapped the blades wide open—still lodged inside of Trent's mouth. Trent's head burst with blood and viscera, his head bisected at the jaw.

Beverly screamed for her life as Gil pulled her down through the corridor. They pressed themselves against the wall, trying to hide in the darkness.

The entire corridor was lined with corpses. Dozens of dead bodies in various states of decomposition and age were propped up against the walls, dressed in suits and 1950s dresses, their vacant eyes open and staring into nothingness. Beverly and Gil squeezed in together between two of the corpses in an attempt to blend in and remain unseen.

"They put us in the oubliette," Gil said. "It's where they leave you until they need you."

Neither Beverly nor Gil saw the figure moving among the rows of bodies, hidden within the corpses. The figure quietly stepped out from the cover of darkness and dead things.

Beverly and Gil sank themselves into the shadows between the corpses. Beverly put her hand over Gil's mouth to silence his heavy breathing.

They froze as they saw the figure walking toward them, inspecting each of the bodies that filled the corridor. He wore a white mask streaked with multi-colored paint.

The figure stopped directly in front of Beverly and Gil. They both stopped their breath and stared out into the darkness, hoping and praying that the figure didn't notice that they were alive.

The figure paused for a moment, as if contemplating. Beverly swore he could hear her heart beating. Then he moved on to the other corpses.

Beverly and Gil waited until the figure turned into a side room to breathe again. They stayed in place, unable to move or speak.

Beverly used her eyes to indicate to Gil that they needed to go. They waited until they heard no movements or footsteps and cautiously extracted themselves from their hiding place.

Gil pointed at a side room a few hundred feet away and walked in front of Beverly. They stopped in their tracks when a noise, like the sound of a large rock rolling, sounded out through the passageway.

The top half of Trent's head landed at their feet, having been rolled their way from the darkness ahead. Gil let out a terrified howl.

Beverly covered his mouth and pulled him in between a pair of bodies against the wall.

"Shhh," Beverly said. "You have to think. How do we get out of here?"

"You don't," a voice whispered from the blackness.

Gil lost control of his senses and sprinted down the corridor, leaving Beverly alone.

One by one, the corridor filled with masked strangers emerging from every side room doorway and open hallway.

Beverly heard the sounds of Gil screaming and struggling from the depths of the darkness as the strangers got closer and closer to her.

Beverly screamed as she realized there was no escape.

CHAPTER FIFTY-THREE

Annie had the best night's sleep she'd had since she moved. Having her friends and family there gave her a sense of peace and happiness that she hadn't felt in a while.

She had slept with the giant stuffed goose, Anna Maria, that Ruby and Rex gifted her. When she woke, she took her time to shower then wrote a few paragraphs for her upcoming novel.

Annie blasted Skid Row's "Youth Gone Wild" and danced away her feelings. She was happy but sad; thrilled to feel the love from her people but unable to let go of the sorrow and anger that lived inside her. She thought about how the music she loved from her younger days helped shape her life; how she didn't connect with songs now the way she did as a kid. She thought about how she had to stop comparing her life to other people's; their successes and achievements came with their own struggles, challenges, and responsibilities, just like hers did.

We're all just trying to survive.

She thought about ghosts. Real ones, imaginary ones, the ones that lived inside her head. She wondered if the ghosts of Gull Valley would let her find peace.

Around noon, Aunt Dolly and Sloane let themselves in with the keys Annie gave them. Aunt Dolly wanted to know if Annie was planning on joining her friends in the mess hall to eat the breakfast spread Aunt Dolly and her girls had prepared.

"I'll be there in a few," Annie said.

"You know what?" Aunt Dolly said. "You do what you need to. I'm here if you need anything."

Annie opened her closet and gasped.

Hanging on the inside of the closet door was a floral dress that had belonged to her mother. Attached to the dress was a birthday card.

"What is this?" Annie said. "This was Mom's. She was buried in this dress."

"I don't know," said Aunt Dolly. "That can't be the same dress, Annie."

"Were you guys in here earlier?" said Annie.

"Nobody would play a joke on you like that," Aunt Dolly said. She moved forward to inspect the dress more closely. Annie could tell by Aunt Dolly's expression that it was not a replica of her mother's dress.

"What does the card say?" Sloane said.

Annie opened the card. The writing was unkempt, the ink red.

"'Dear Annie, You are always a part of us. The best gifts are ones from sacrifice. May your birthday bring you new life.' It's not signed."

"Annie," Aunt Dolly said, her voice steady and low. "I don't want to hurt your feelings but do you think that maybe your subconscious is doing some of these things? As a response to trauma. I think we should call Dr. Crews."

"I didn't write this," Annie said.

"Annie, look at your hands," said Sloane.

Annie held her hands up. Her fingers had faded red marker stains on them, partially washed off by her shower.

Annie couldn't believe her eyes. She had gone crazy. She was gaslighting and scaring herself.

"You're okay, Annie," said Aunt Dolly. "I'm going to make you a plate and we're going to talk this over. You're going to be all right. These things happen."

"Where did my mother's dress come from?" Annie said, trying not to burst into tears.

"I don't know," said Aunt Dolly. "It's okay. We'll talk about all of this. You get ready for the day. I'll tell your friends not to wait for you and to go entertain themselves today. Don't beat yourself up. This isn't your fault. We can overcome this."

Annie nodded, trying to push all her negative thoughts out of her head. Aunt Dolly left. Sloane stayed behind in case Annie needed any comforting or a sounding board.

"Not the birthday party we were hoping for," Sloane said. "Say it with me. Kittens, mittens, reversible hats, Baby Yoda, the comforting sound of rain. Kittens, mittens, reversible hats, Baby Yoda, the comforting sound of rain."

"That's your mantra, not mine," Annie said, trying not to sound too snappish.

Sloane put her arm around Annie. Annie sat at her desk and looked down at the photos from Madame Fructuosa.

"What are you going to do?" said Sloane.

"I'm going to do what nobody in horror movies ever does and leave," Annie said, with a weary and resigned sigh. "This is all too much. I have been through enough. I'm going to pack the few belongings I have and stay with Aunt Dolly until I can figure out what I'm doing next. Someone on Zillow will surely want to buy this hellhole. Maybe Cal will want it. I can't do this anymore. Cults, ghosts, murder? I moved here because I wanted peace. You know what they say—those who forget the past are condemned to repeat it. I'm not forgetting. I'm getting out. Maybe it's all in my imagination, maybe there's something really happening here. I don't want to stick around to find out. It's all so ridiculous, I almost want to laugh."

"Laughter is the best medicine," said Sloane. "And antibiotics."

Annie looked down at the pictures before her. They were clearly members of the cult, dressed in their Laird

Hubbell-designated uniforms. People smiling with their children, tending to their gardens, dancing, laughing, pretending to be normal.

Her chest seized when she saw one of the pictures. It was of a dozen or so members of The Felicitous happily standing together.

Annie picked the photograph up, giving it a closer inspection. She couldn't believe what she was seeing. All of the scary story cliches happened to her at once—her blood ran cold, a chill ran down her spine, her hair stood on end, she got goosebumps, she was shaken to her very core, her heartbeat quickened in her body. Annie held the photo out to Sloane.

"That's my mother and father," Annie said.

CHAPTER FIFTY-FOUR

Cal Reardon was home in his office. He left the door open so he could hear his kids playing. Rex and his potato were pretending to be judges at the imaginary beauty pageant fashion show Ruby was putting on with her Barbie dolls. Ruby was the special musical guest at the made-up ceremony, singing Barbra Streisand's "Send in the Clowns" with reverb and sound effects on her magic pink karaoke microphone.

One entire wall of Cal's office was dedicated to pictures, news reports, and various files, details, and sightings of the members of The Felicitous. Like he was an FBI or CIA agent, tracing the facts and speculation, trying to tie it all together. Blueprints and maps of Gull Valley. Photos and contact information for previous cult members who were still alive, the families of those who weren't, and statistical timelines of events from Laird Hubbell's birth to the creation of the cult and their numerous activities and proclivities.

How far did The Felicitous reach? How many people still chose to answer their call? How far would those people go?

Cal thought back to a conversation he had with one of the surviving cult members, Joel Pendleton. Joel's words rang in Cal's head.

"We didn't care about anything but our survival," Joel told Cal over a Zoom call months ago. "We thought in our hearts and souls that everything we were doing was right. The power of our convictions was greater than the fear of the consequences. We didn't see ourselves as malevolent. We thought we were changing the world and we believed in Laird's philosophies so wholeheartedly that we would die for it. We were righteous. We thought we had truth and justice on our side. We lived how we thought everyone should. We thought if people saw what we did, understood our goals, that they'd understand and change their ways, be more like us. We wanted to spread the word. We were going to make people see and hear us, even if they didn't want to. No measures were too extreme. Those are the most dangerous kinds of people— ones with absolute certainty in their beliefs and no fear."

It was maddening. Cal felt like he was losing his sanity at times. He pondered throwing every piece of data into a giant burn barrel and forgetting it forever. Would Mara have wanted him wasting his time like this? He had a good job and great kids. That should have been his focus, right?

But Cal had to know. He had to know where the members were and why they did the things they did. And if they were still doing them. He wanted to know where he and Mara came from.

Cal had accumulated many Felicitous-related items over the years—Erica Keating's diary, files from The Calista Island Asylum for the patients who stayed there before (and sometimes after) they were a part of the cult, personal effects and paperwork pertaining to Laird Hubbell and his doomed family.

None of that seemed worthwhile at the moment. Cal wondered if he needed to let it all go, let it remain buried in the past, let himself move forward so he could heal and feel happiness again.

"Rex, Ruby!" Cal shouted, grabbing his coat. "We're going to Grandma Kay and Grandpa Al's. Daddy has something to take care of."

CHAPTER FIFTY-FIVE

Aunt Dolly searched through the multitude of books in the library. There were so many to sort through. Some first editions, many classics, works of literature that spanned over a century. The books were worn and musty, some covered in mold. The library was one of the few buildings in Gull Valley that seemed to be unchanged over the years.

Aunt Dolly did not see the intruders that hid and darted between the stacks and shelves, observing her as she perused the myriad of books at her disposal.

"Aunt Dolly," Annie said, startling her.

Aunt Dolly turned around to face Annie. "What's up, buttercup?"

Annie held the photograph up so Aunt Dolly could see it. Annie couldn't control the emotions she felt—a cauldron's mixture of rage, anger, sadness, frustration, and betrayal.

Aunt Dolly immediately recognized the people in the photograph as Annie's parents and Aunt Dolly's own dearly departed sister.

"I don't know what to say," said Aunt Dolly.

"You lied to me my entire life," Annie said, her jaw set. "That's why you and the ladies know so much about The Felicitous, isn't it?"

"Let me explain."

"Don't say, 'Let me explain.'"

"Sometimes we lie to protect the people we love."

"This is more than a lie, Aunt Dolly. This isn't like when I was a kid and you told me the tooth fairy was real or when I was a teenager and you told me that if I had unprotected sex, God would kill a puppy."

"I'm sorry, Annie. I did it because I didn't want to hurt you."

Annie glared at Aunt Dolly. "That's why my parents were the way they were, isn't it? It's why they took drugs and drank and couldn't function and be good parents. They were fucked up and damaged because they were part of The Felicitous."

"Annie, it's a lot more complicated than that."

"Tell me! Tell me the truth now. I deserve to know. I deserve to know who my parents really were. Do Diane, Brenda, Martha, and Karen know the truth?"

"Yes, they know. All of us know. We wanted to shield you from that world and the reality of who your mom and dad were."

"Did my parents kill people? Did they participate in all of the bad things that The Felicitous did?"

"Your mother and father were troubled long before they joined The Felicitous. They left the cult because they didn't agree with the direction Laird Hubbell was taking things in. They ran away one night in the middle of the night. You were just a little girl at the time. They did it to protect you from the cult. They knew if they were caught trying to leave or spoke out against anything Laird and his followers did, you'd all be killed. And when they started a new life, under different names to hide from The Felicitous, they had severe trauma and psychological damage. They lived in constant fear and they didn't have the resources or fortitude to handle the aftermath. They weren't equipped. I never wanted you to know this. I never wanted this day to come. I never wanted you to feel like this."

"You've been lying to me my whole life."

"What good does it do you to know all of this? What does it change, Annie? I didn't want you to have to carry this burden. That was your parents' lives, not yours. I

300

didn't want their choices to affect who you could become. I know it sounds wrong and cruel. I know. But it was for you, so you could not have the specter and weight of what they'd done drag you down."

"That's why you didn't want me to move here. You knew that I'd find out the truth."

"I was shocked at the one-in-a-million coincidence that this was where you'd chosen to live."

"All these years, you all knew the truth about where I came from and never told me. I grew up thinking my parents hated me and I was the albatross around their necks. That they were how they were because I had ruined their lives."

"I'm so sorry for not telling you the truth, Annie. And I'm so sorry that you blamed yourself for the way your parents were. It was not your fault, not any of it. They both had issues long before you ever came to us. We tried to help them. We really did. It was too much for your mom and dad, living with the fear that the cult would find them and hurt you. They couldn't deal with the things they'd seen and done, and the drugs and drinking helped them forget. None of it was ever because of you. Ever. You were the best thing that ever happened to them. You didn't have it easy growing up and I was afraid this would make everything worse."

Annie's mind spun. She was putting the pieces together in her mind. Painful memories came flooding back to her.

"Aunt Dolly, is Laird Hubbell my father?"

"What?"

"You guys told us that he was sleeping with his followers. Was my mother one of them? Is Laird Hubbell my real father?"

"I really don't know the answer to that, Annie. Your father was your father, for better or worse."

"I don't know if I believe you."

"This is going to take some time for you to come to terms with. I'm here for you, no matter what. You're not alone in this, Annie. You take all the time and space you need to deal with what you're feeling."

"Stop being so nice! I'm so mad at you right now, Aunt Dolly. I'm so hurt by you. What else? What else do I need to know that you haven't told me?"

"I'd say that's about the long and short of it."

Annie was quiet. Aunt Dolly took a tentative step toward her.

"What can I do to help you?" Aunt Dolly said. "Do you want a hug? Do you want to scream? What do you need right now?"

"I need to be alone for a bit and think," said Annie. Annie slumped her shoulders in defeat. "I'm not staying in Gull Valley. You win. The Felicitous wins. Whatever is going on here, it's all too much for me. I'll leave tomorrow. We'll let everybody have a fun day today and do birthday cake later but tomorrow, I'm out of here."

"You know you always have a place with me."

"Yeah, I know. I know, Aunt Dolly."

Annie left Aunt Dolly standing alone in the library.

As soon as Annie got out into the open space between the buildings, she looked up toward the sky and shook her head, cursing the gods she didn't even believe in. Her entire existence, her whole world, everything she thought she knew about her family—all sideswiped and exploded.

Annie didn't want to think about it. But she knew she would, replaying it over and over. She had so many more questions for Aunt Dolly but needed to breathe in and out first.

CHAPTER FIFTY-SIX

"Annie!" Cal called out from the distance. "Hey, Annie!"

Annie put her "Everything is okay" face on and forced a smile at Cal. She wasn't going to be rude to him but most of her just wanted everyone to leave her alone.

"Hey, Cal. What are you doing here? Where are the kids?"

"Oh, they're home watching *Scream,*" Cal joked. Immediately noting Annie's shock that he'd leave his underage kids home alone to view a violent horror movie, he quickly added, "Just kidding. It was *Scream 6.* I'm just kidding again. They're with their grandparents. Mara's folks."

"Did you want to be a stand-up comedian at a certain point in your life, Cal?"

"No. Why do you ask?"

"No reason."

"Over the years, I've wanted to be a crocodile wrestler, ultimate fighter, cannoli maker, kick-the-can referee, Jell-O wrestling announcer, or world-renowned back-up singer for Justin Timberlake. That being said, I'd love to be Justin Timberlake. He's a very pretty man. I don't care if it's gay for me to say. I'm comfortable with my sexuality. Although if I was him, I think I'd just spend all my time slapping my ham."

"You get comfortable with people really quickly, don't you, Cal?"

"I haven't even told you all about my back-ne yet."

Annie didn't want to show her impatience with Cal. She wasn't angry with him. She was just angry. She wasn't going to take out her emotions on anyone. She was used to pushing down her feelings and pretending everything was okay. That seemed to be how most people got through their lives anyway.

"What is it that you need, Cal?"

Cal held up a VHS cassette tape. "You got some time to watch this?"

Written on the sticker on the side of the VHS tape were the names of several 1990s nighttime soap operas— *Melrose Place*, *Beverly Hills 90210*, *Pacific Palisades*, *Savannah*, *Central Park West*, and *Models Inc.*

"We're going to watch old episodes of *90210*?" Annie said. "I already know that Donna Martin graduates."

"Ignore the label," said Cal.

Annie knew that the movie theater was set-up to play various types of media. She recalled seeing a VCR among all of the various equipment.

"What's on there?"

"You'll see."

CHAPTER FIFTY-SEVEN

Dave and Sean were at the front of the line of friends, each with a GoPro strapped around their heads, traversing through the woods to get to one of the mountains that featured a cave that they were dead set on seeing while they were in Gull Valley.

The cave opening was at the top of a steep incline up part of the mountain, a well-worn pathway guiding their journey. The entrance was several hundred feet from the ground.

"Don't look down," Wes said to Alice, Bill, Sally, and Trish, who were behind him on the walk.

"You can see all of Gull Valley from up here," Dave said. Everyone turned to see Annie's homestead sprawled out in the distance, past the acres of trees and dried riverbed.

"Dave always wanted to explore a cave," said Sean. "Ha, that rhymed. I'm a poet and didn't know it."

The cave opening loomed in the foreground. The group climbed the rocky path to make it to the entrance.

"I've heard rumors that a lot of caves are a hideaway for deep underground military bases, long since abandoned and forgotten," said Sean. "That they have adverse effects on humans when they are exposed to it. The strange vibrations, like a giant microwave, cause auditory and visual hallucinations, intense feelings of fear, oppressive heat, and subliminal messages and sounds when subjected to it, used as a deterrent to keep trespassers away. These same tactics could be used to simulate a haunting. Those who have searched and found this cave spoke about the intense feeling of fear and dread they felt before and after exploring it."

"Are you suggesting that may be why all this weird stuff has been happening with Annie?" Alice said. "Or that's the reason The Felicitous went from 'Let's be flower children' to 'Let's kill everybody and burn down the world,'?"

"The Felicitous is kind of like a weird allegory for life itself, if you think about it," said Trish. "They started out with the best intentions and full of hope and promise, then life came along and smacked them down and twisted them into something bitter and angry. I mean, look at cults in history—Heaven's Gate, Waco, Jonestown, The Weather Underground. They all thought they were doing something special and world-changing and it never ends well."

"Kind of like orcas," Sean said. "They look all playful but they just want to sink your boat."

"The world is fucked anyway," said Wes. "It doesn't matter what we do. You could be having a great day, eating ambrosia salad at the inflatable theme park, and inevitably some dildo in a Kid Rock T-shirt with unresolved anger issues, a fourth grade education, and a massive sense of entitlement who thinks cutting lines and harassing innocent low-paid workers is all right will come along and ruin it, because everyone these days is so full of rage and stupidity."

"I'm sorry that happened to you, Wes," Sally said.

"It's okay," Wes said, pushing the memory out of his mind.

"I almost kind of get it, you know," said Bill. "Wanting your own land, to live by your own rules, to not have to cater to the social responsibility of society. I can see why people would want to be a part of something they believe so strongly in."

"I get it in a weird way, too," Wes said. "Except the whole 'murder and mayhem' part. That's where they lose me."

"Did you know that the phrase, 'Don't drink the Kool-Aid' is actually incorrect? The people at Jonestown drank Flavor-Aid," Alice said.

"Leave it to Annie to go all *Girl, Interrupted* and move to Murderville," said Sean. He didn't mean it as a dig against his beloved Annie. More of a resigned observation.

"We have cults on the brain right now," Bill said. "Can we address the fact that none of us are in our twenties anymore and this hike is hell on our knees?"

"These days I have to think really hard before I bend over," said Wes. "I have to weigh the options of how I'm going to get back up. If I have to get on my knees for something, I have to roll myself back into position and have something to hold on to in order to get myself back up."

"Oh, Wes, not being able to bend over must be horrible on your dating life," Sean said. "That's why you would never be a good soldier. You'd be too busy asking when the showers were. 'Is it shower time yet? How about now? Come on, guys, let's go shower!'"

Everyone laughed. Their faces became more serious as they made it to the ledge where the cave face beckoned them.

Dave clicked on his flashlight to illuminate the inside of the cave. Large chains soldered into the cave ceiling swung back and forth. The ground was wet and muddy. A faint, noxious smell carried on the air from within the cave.

Wes, Trish, Alice, Sally, and Bill exchanged hesitant looks.

"You first, Dave," said Bill.

Dave and Sean stepped inside the cave, their lights shining on the wet stone and rock that surrounded them.

"It looks pretty deep," Dave said. "Watch your step."

307

Dave and Sean went farther in, their silhouettes becoming less visible to Alice, Sally, Trish, Bill, and Wes.

"What's in there?" Wes called.

"Cave stuff!" Sean called back. Sean spoke to Dave next. "Did you ever see that movie *The Descent*, where they go into the cave and the crawlers come for them?"

"Remember we talked about appropriate times to bring things up, Sean?" said Dave, trying not to let his nerves best him.

They approached a curve in the tunnel of the cave, letting their lights guide them. There was enough space for them to move about freely.

"Whoa, it stinks in here," Sean said. The rancid odor in the air became increasingly pungent.

The sounds of dripping water and their footsteps echoing mixed in with unidentifiable noises. Perhaps cave creatures? Dave had seen videos of strange things that lived inside caves. He didn't want to meet any.

"What's that?" Sean said quietly.

Up ahead, a faint light from around the bend.

"Do you think someone lives in here?" Sean continued. "I've read about people who live in caves because they have nowhere else to go."

"I really appreciate how all the things I tell you really sink in and you learn from them, Sean," said Dave, ready to push Sean in front of him if it was indeed a cave creature.

Dave debated internally about whether to proceed. He decided that if that was someone's makeshift home, they'd turn tail and get out of there quickly.

"Well, go on," Sean said to Dave, giving him a little push.

Sean's light flashed over the word *Erica* smeared on the cave wall.

Dave took a deep breath and proceeded around the bend, Sean right behind him.

Dave and Sean almost vomited once they saw.

The entire cavern was covered in human and animal bones, half-eaten innards, blood, and bodily fluids. Several dozen bodies, ranging from freshly killed to heavily decomposing, strewn across the expanse—some wrapped in clear cellophane, others splayed out like a Christmas ham.

A rack made of tree branches, shaped like a giant X, was fastened into the ground, standing straight up. A dead man was tied to it, his body splayed open, his eyes milky white.

It was an animal's lair. At least, Dave hoped it was an animal. But Dave knew that animals didn't wrap their prey or fasten them to makeshift stands.

A cacophony of screams, wails, moans, and screeches rang out at full volume from deeper within the cave. What sounded like several voices howling and caterwauling, not in sync with each other, but total sonic chaos. The voices ranged in decibel levels, some like a low bass and others like a shrill squealing. The voices of people who were all being tortured and defiled at the same time, their inner horror unleashed. Some calling out words and phrases but Dave and Sean couldn't make out anything they were saying. Popping and hissing noises from the darkness only made the agonized screaming sound more horrific.

Something started to emerge from the dark corner, its eyes fixated on Dave and Sean.

Neither man waited. They turned to run.

Snap!

Sean kicked something on the ground when he went to flee. His foot triggered a booby trap of some sort.

Slam!

A manmade device—made from glass shards, large nails, and various sharp instruments secured onto several boards and wooden beams attached to a long wooden pole—burst from a spring on the wall.

It landed directly onto Sean's face and torso, pinning him against the cave wall and slicing through him in dozens of places.

Dave was caught between trying to dislodge Sean and the thing slowly approaching from behind him. Sean's eyes had already begun to close, as his wounds were so severe. Dave screamed in frustration, running away from the beast that crept up on him.

Dave saw Wes, Bill, Sally, Trish, and Alice at the entrance to the cave.

"Go, go, go!" Dave yelled at them, waving his hand for them to start running. Despite their confused faces, they did as he instructed and exited his view, headed back down the mountain trail.

Dave looked behind him into the cave as he reached the opening. Whatever the thing that was following him was, it stopped at the spot where outside light hit the darkness. It slinked back into the black, still watching Dave but hiding in the shadows.

Alice, Bill, Sally, Trish, and Wes made it to the bottom of the mountain. They saw Dave at the edge of the cave mouth, saw him staring away from them.

"Dave!" Sally yelled. "What's going on?"

Dave looked down at them, sighing for a moment.

Bam!

Something pushed him off the ledge. Dave didn't see it coming. It was so fast; a flash of a figure rushing from the darkness and shoving him.

Dave's GoPro captured the fall—Dave barreling toward the ground, slamming against the rocks below in front of his friends with a sickening crunch.

Dave's friends screamed and swarmed around him as he landed. He hit the ground so hard that blood spurted out in giant red clouds. His eyes were wide open, staring at the sky, though he was barely alive.

"Dave!" screamed Sally. Her husband, the man she loved most, lay before her in a heap of broken bones.

"What is that?" Wes said, pointing up at the cave ledge.

Something lorded over them from high above. A figure dressed in black. It disappeared from view too quickly to get a good look at.

"Oh, my God, Dave," Sally cried over him.

"Where's Sean?" said Alice.

"Look out!" Trish said.

Alice and Trish pulled Sally off of Dave with only seconds to spare.

Splat!

A large boulder crashed on top of Dave, obliterating him. His organs and blood exploded all around them, all over his friends. Dave had been flattened.

"Sally, come on," Trish yanked on Sally's arm so that they could run.

"Wait," Wes said. "Where's Sean? Sean!"

Crash!

Sean's mutilated body crashed down in front of them. Alice, Bill, Sally, Trish, and Wes screamed, backing away.

Before they ran, they looked up to the ridge and saw several masked people gathering—and beginning to walk down the trail toward them.

"This way!" Bill shouted, heading the brigade. He shoved brushes and branches aside to clear a path.

Bill ran ahead of the rest of them but lost the pathway. In their panic, they had veered off course from the main trail.

He didn't see the tripwire low on the dirt ground, strung between two trees.

Bill's foot caught on the wire, sending him careening forward.

Into a pit of sharpened wooden sticks, dug deep into the earth, that had been hidden by grass and fallen tree limbs. Bill was impaled completely through by dozens of makeshift weapons, falling face-first into the trap.

Sally, Alice, Wes, and Trish continued running, stopping at the ridge, looking down to where Bill fell to his death.

The last thing Bill heard as he lay dying was his wife Trish screaming his name.

CHAPTER FIFTY-EIGHT

Annie and Cal were joined in the movie theater by Chris, Ginny, Steve, Kit, Jess, Laurie, Max, Nancy, Rachel, and Richie.

The theater itself was old-fashioned, with red plush seating (around thirty-six seats), blood red curtains hanging over the stage, a white screen, and a projector booth on the second level.

Annie and her friends sat in the front rows of the cinema while Cal stood before them.

"Do you remember the show *Penrod and the Squirrels*?" said Cal.

The group nodded; yes, they recalled.

"Oh, I had their Christmas album growing up," Nancy said.

Penrod and the Squirrels was a popular cartoon that ran from the late 1960s until the mid-eighties. Considered an American classic. A mammoth, timeless institution that still spawned toys, albums, movies, comics, books, cosplay, and copious merchandise. Three squirrels who were adopted by a human man and lived like regular human children, dressed in colorful clothing, and navigating the ins and outs of then-modern-day life. Like so many television shows of that era, there were "very special episodes" designated to teach moral lessons.

"I found an old episode of it on YouTube that relates to The Felicitous," Cal continued. "The episode called 'Erica' focused on The Squirrels'—Penrod, Clancy, and Alonso—school friend Erica, who was a good student, chaste and law-abiding, went to church and Sunday school, and listened to her parents. That is, until the traveling minstrels came to town. The rogues and rapscallions, the ragtag scruffy hippie types with their promises of counterculture and free love and anti-war views; preaching their anti-family and anti-American views as they played their instruments and wandered from town to town like Gypsies, seducing innocent townsfolk, robbing and stealing, trying to confuse God-fearing folk with their lies and deceptions. Erica became deeply enamored with them and their lifestyle, leaving behind her family and friends to join them on the road."

"Children's entertainment was really a different vibe when we were kids," said Steve. "The things we were allowed to watch. *Red Dawn*, *Indiana Jones and the Temple of Doom*, *Jaws*, *E.T.*, *Return to Oz*."

"We all turned out all right, didn't we?" Richie said. "Our parents had no idea what we were watching. We had *The Secret of Nimh* then we discovered grunge and Bridget Fonda and Parker Posey. My inner child is okay."

Cal wasn't done. "Months passed and Erica returned to school. But now she was a shell of herself, always wearing a white-and-yellow sundress and a light orange straw hat with pink ribbons that tied around her chin. Her eyes were drawn like swirling pinwheels, her speech dreamy and affected, her goals and values ruined by the scoundrels and wretches she associated with. Her legacy tainted, her worth now decimated in the eyes of good, decent townsfolk. The Squirrels learned a lesson that day. They would not end up like Erica."

"Cal," Annie said, reaching her limit of cult talk. "Why are you telling us this?"

"The episode only aired once," Cal said. "The television network received so many complaints about the heavy, kid unfriendly nature of the program that it was banned from repeats. Then came the second wave of complaints. Kids across America were claiming to see Erica at their window. In their rooms. Under their bed. In their closet. Behind their bedroom doors. Her eyes like pinwheels, her dress dirty and stained with blood. Her pale white skin and long auburn hair. Calling to them, telling them to join her and her new friends, singing their

314

minstrel song. But she wasn't a cartoon. She was flesh and blood. Or whatever the kids were telling their parents. An entity. A thing. A ghost or spirit. Yet tangible, real, whole."

"Okay, so it's all a very poorly disguised parable for The Felicitous," said Kit. "Nice touch using the name Erica. A little too on the nose."

"So, basically, a children's cartoon became anti-cult propaganda and scared the Fruit Roll-Ups out of the nation's kids," Chris said.

"Come on, Cal," Ginny said. "Think of the time period. We had the Vietnam War, the Manson Family, a nation in turmoil. Just like it always is. Nothing's changed, I guess. But back then especially, the episode was a morality play. A condemnation of 'the other' and anyone who challenged the values and beliefs of good Christian people. Erica was a 'good girl' who was swayed into a pagan lifestyle, a deranged sect who corrupted her All-American ethics and loyalty. The episode was an urban legend used to keep girls in line, like the 'babysitter and caller upstairs' story. Mired in xenophobia, rooted in the need to control any acts of disobedience by rowdy kids."

"Fearing a scandal and loss of revenue, the higher-ups at the network ordered all copies of the episode destroyed. However, like so much lost media, a copy survived. As viewed by modern audiences, the animation was crude and amateurish, like so many '70s cartoons compared to the breakthroughs of today's graphics. Erica's pinwheel eyes were merely spinning black circles drawn over large white orbs. Yet it was terrifying back then. It would be terrifying now, seeing a mesmerized, dazed woman reaching out to you, the whites of her eyes twirling and twisting. They say if you watch the episode, Erica and her friends will come for you. She will wait for you. If you don't join her, she will kill you and take your soul. You will forever be a part of the traveling minstrel group, dead or alive. You will never escape."

"That's how I felt about The Wiggles," said Max.

"What's your point here, Nancy Drew?" said Annie. It was official. She'd run out of patience.

"I figured it out," said Cal. "I know what they're trying to do. The Felicitous. They want to resurrect Laird Hubbell and Erica Keating."

"But nobody knows if Laird Hubbell is actually dead or not," said Rachel.

"If he's alive, why has no one heard from him?" Cal said. "That's what this is all leading up to. The former members of The Felicitous who are still believers have new recruits, new followers, and their plan is to bring Laird Hubbell and Erica Keating back from the dead."

"How?" Annie said. "Why? It's ludicrous. That makes absolutely no sense."

"What cults make sense?" said Cal. "Really? When you think about it? Like any religion or set of beliefs. Christians believe there's some magical man in the sky who is all powerful yet does nothing to stop war, violence, famine, plague, disease, or poverty. Some cults believe an alien race is coming for them to take them away to a distant planet. It's not ludicrous if they really, truly believe it. There are people who believe that birds and manatees are secretly government spies."

"Wait, they're not?" said Max.

Annie sighed deeply. She didn't know whether to be afraid or annoyed.

"There's more," Cal said. "One of the writers for the show—his son was a member of The Felicitous and wrote the episode after he left the cult. There's coded messages in the episode for the other cult members. Those pinwheel eyes Erica has? When you look closely at them, you see the symbol on the thing my kids found in the woods, the symbol that The Felicitous used. Laird Hubbell was obsessed with the occult and dark magic. Why? Because he believed he could bring his beloved Erica back to life. Long story short—"

316

"Too late," Richie said.

"Now that they're both gone, his followers think they can bring both Laird and Erica back and pick up where they left off," Cal finished.

"What idiot really thinks that is going to work?" Annie said. She didn't mean to sound so angry but she could barely contain it anymore.

"Not idiots," said Cal. "Believers."

"Are you going to play the tape or what?" Chris said.

Cal went to the projection booth as Annie exchanged bewildered, exhausted glances with Nancy, Rachel, Jess, Laurie, Ginny, and Chris. Richie and Max both shrugged.

Cal sat next to Annie as the show started.

CHAPTER FIFTY-NINE

A screen capture started the episode, clearly put there by the studio, in white lettering against a black backdrop.

PENROD AND THE SQUIRRELS (SEASON 20, EPISODE 15: "ERICA"; ORIGINAL AIRDATE: AUGUST 23, 1983).

The group watched the video, enthralled by the proceedings. Three squirrel friends singing, laughing, and dancing, then confronted by the insanity of an unnamed, unspecified, watered-down analogy for a cult.

The episode played out before them on the screen. Pixelated and fuzzy, most definitely a bootleg from a different era.

Annie stared at the screen so hard she forgot to blink.

Penrod: Hey, Erica! Where have you been? We haven't seen you around school lately.

Erica (her eyes like pinwheels, gazing off in the distance): I made some new friends. You wouldn't believe the things they've shown me. You wouldn't believe the things I've seen. Why don't you come with me after school and meet them? Father has so much to tell you.

Penrod (cautiously): Sorry, Erica, we have band practice after school and then our dad is coming to pick us up.

Erica (the pinwheels in her eyes slowing down to focus on the squirrels): Maybe we'll stop by your house one night. I know where you live.

Some of Annie's friends laughed nervously, a tension release. It was an uncomfortable, weird episode to watch—thoroughly inappropriate for children. It was no wonder it was only shown on Saturday morning one time.

The episode drew to a close. The credits were abruptly chopped off midway through the videocassette and another show popped up.

The Felicitous behind-the-scenes. The video looked like a documentary filmed on a handheld, out-of-date camera or camcorder.

Smiling, unaffected cult members dancing together and laughing, participating in activities, singing in circles of harmony. Quick edits and cuts, flashes of people's faces gone by too speedily to make out who they were.

A young woman with long, flowing hair speaking to an off-screen interviewer. She was dressed in a flowery, loose gown. Her smile beamed widely, her hair glowing in the sun.

The screen caption read:

Temperance Winters

Known as "Bramble"

"Everyone is so happy here," Temperance said in a dreamy, otherworldly way. "We get up every day and are filled with so much love and joy and peace. The outside world doesn't touch us here. As Bishop says, 'At this moment, you're the youngest you'll ever be and the oldest you've ever been.'"

"What about the accusations that you and the fellow members of The Felicitous are involved in certain violent crimes?" the interviewer, still unseen, asked.

Temperance smiled even wider. "People have to die so that Erica may live again."

The interviewer was silent.

"A war is coming," Temperance said, her tone becoming graver. "Bishop has been persecuted for speaking his truth. He's given us so much. The world wants us to love money, power, fame, success. We don't want your lies. Bishop wants to protect us all. People like you don't listen to his words. But we know. We're

prepared. We will take those with us who believe in our word. We will be the ones standing after the apocalypse that's coming."

"What apoca—" the interviewer's voice was cut off as another portion of whatever was on the tape began playing.

Annie decided she was done for the day. Done with cult talk. Done with all of that. She stood up and quietly left the theater. Her friends nodded at her in understanding but stayed to watch what was next.

Annie let the heavy doors close behind her and stopped in the theater lobby, next to the rusted popcorn machine and empty glass snack counter.

Inside the theater itself, her friends watched as the recorded events unfolded.

Annie pushed open the doors to the outside world, letting the sunlight hit her face.

She stopped dead in her tracks.

There were five masked strangers standing around the doors, as if in waiting for Annie to arrive. They each held sharp weapons in their hands. A cherub, an alien, a zombie, a ghoul, and LBJ.

The zombie was holding a sharp knife against Sloane's neck as he held her to him. Sloane's pleading eyes were locked on Annie.

Cal threw the doors open in pursuit of Annie, stopping suddenly as Annie had. What was going on?

"Annie—" Cal started. His breath caught in his throat when he saw the masked men and Sloane. He instinctively put his arm out in front of Annie, as if to protect her.

Cal and Sloane looked at each other for a quick moment.

"Lyla?" Cal said to Sloane, dumbfounded.

The zombie lowered the knife as Sloane stepped away from him. Her face changed from fear to control.

320

"I told you to stay away from here, Cal," Sloane said.

CHAPTER SIXTY

T.P. and Ned trekked deep into the forest to test out T.P.'s drone. They followed it as they watched everything it captured on the monitor.

Amid the dense, lush foliage, they passed over a small, abandoned hut, some random hikers and campers wandering the woods, and several animals frolicking and foraging.

"You all right about Beverly leaving?" T.P. said.

"Yeah, I understand," said Ned. "Family emergency. She left me a note and said she tried her hardest to wake me but I'm a heavy sleeper. She had an Uber come get her in the middle of the night. She's going to call me later."

"I can barely get my phone to work out here."

"Yeah, me too. I just hope everything is okay with her and her family. She must have left in a hurry because her handwriting looked super weird. I don't think she even turned on a light when she wrote the note."

"Keep me posted. You really like her, huh?"

"I do. It's crazy. She's really cool. I like who I am when I'm around her."

Ned seemed done with the subject, a little sad that Beverly wasn't with him at the moment.

"You think about the way history is retold and recounted," said Ned. "How many mitigating factors go into the truth before it just becomes a fairy tale? How accurate are the stories about The Felicitous really? I mean, at this point, we have no actual proof of anything except that they once lived here. Look at Dracula. He's based on Vlad the Impaler, right? But how much of what Vlad the Impaler did is accurately represented by Bram

Stoker's novel? Side note—May 26th is World Dracula Day. Did you know that?"

T.P. realized he was in for one of Ned's rants. So many of his friends liked to rant. T.P. knew whatever he said wouldn't derail that train, so he decided to add his own comments and see if Ned would notice.

"I set aside fifteen minutes a day to cry," said T.P. "I put on sad records and let it all out. Then I go back to my day like nothing happened. That's how I perfect my time management skills."

Ned continued on. "Look at famous people in history that we think are so terrific. Gandhi slept next to prepubescent girls to test his willpower. Mother Teresa believed pain and suffering was a gift from God. Columbus didn't purposely discover America and caused a massive genocide!"

"I try not to be the best at my job because good workers are only rewarded with more work," T.P. said, still being ignored by Ned. "Average workers get left alone. People say that work is a family but if that's true, I'd rather be adopted by a family of rabid weasels. If I knew as much about anything academic as I do about movies and TV, I would've been a doctor by now. I stay up thinking about every little thing at night. I get the Liberty Mutual song stuck in my head for days. I worry that social media has caused irreparable damage to society and the effects on people's minds and behavior can never be reversed. But I can't say these things because then people won't think I'm manly anymore."

"What?" said Ned.

"What?" T.P. said, brushing Ned's query off. He knew Ned didn't hear a word he said anyway.

The drone reached an area where the trees were burnt, blackened, and dead. As if a raging fire had destroyed a minor subsection of the greenery. The trees remained but without any branches or leaves; the area surrounding it was scorched and dead.

"Did you ever hear the story of the tree witch when you were a kid?" said Ned. "My brothers and sisters swore that there was an evil old woman who stole babies and kidnapped children who lived inside the trees in the woods."

"That's a really riveting story. I can't wait to hear how it ends."

"She kills kids, T.P. There's no other ending."

T.P. and Ned followed the path toward the fire-ravaged area, curious to see it up close. The trees, though no longer thriving, still reached almost as high as the blooming ones around them. It was a majestic sight.

"There's somebody over there," Ned said.

T.P. looked to the tree line, where the destroyed trees met the still-growing ones. There were several figures moving in and about the woods, all headed toward something deeper in the forest.

"Probably campers or hikers," said T.P.

T.P. sent the drone over the area where the people walked but couldn't get a clear view through the greenery.

Plunk!

Something hit the drone, sending it crashing to the ground. T.P. shook the monitor, as if that would solve the problem.

"What happened?" said Ned.

"I don't know. We have to go get it."

"Remember Madballs? I always thought that would make a great swear word. 'Ah, Madballs!'"

T.P. and Ned went into the thick of the woods to find T.P.'s drone. The monitor had a tracker in place to pinpoint the area.

Both men stopped when they heard a rustling sound coming from their side. Not close by, but close enough that they saw something through the trees.

Smack!

T.P. and Ned narrowly dodged a severed deer leg. It landed with a wet splash at their feet. They searched the area to see who or what threw it at them.

"I don't want to believe," T.P. said, correcting an earlier statement.

"T.P.," Ned said in a hushed voice, pointing.

Several masked strangers stood together, shovels on the ground next to them. There was a circular hole dug into the ground. The people lifted up a sheet-and-rope-wrapped corpse and lowered it vertically into the pit in the earth. The white sheet engulfing the body was adorned with bulbs of garlic and withered flowers. Although they couldn't see who it was concealed inside the white sheet, the unmistakable shape of a human figure was silhouetted beneath. Ned hoped whoever was in there was dead, but he couldn't be sure.

The people dropped the body into the soil. A provisional grave marker stuck out of the ground next to the hole.

Neither man could hear what the strangers were saying, but it sounded like some kind of chanting or ritualistic spell being spoken as the body was swallowed by the earth. One of the people filled the hole up with dirt.

All of the strangers looked up.

Directly at Ned and T.P.

The strangers all took steps forward, toward the men. Ned and T.P. ran into the forest, for once quickly and silently assessing and agreeing that they did not want to meet these people up close.

T.P. hid behind a large tree as Ned took off in a slightly different direction. Ned stopped running, scanning the area around him, hearing the strangers' footfalls as they searched for him.

Ned looked down at his feet. He'd stepped on a red stone marker on the ground.

Ffffft! Ffffftt! Ffffftt!

Ned's body was pierced by arrows coming at him from every direction, set up in traps among the trees. The marker he'd stepped on had triggered the springs on each apparatus, turning him into a giant pincushion.

Ned shuddered as he fell to his knees.

Fffffttt!

An arrow soared through the air and directly into Ned's open mouth, its tip jutting out of the back of Ned's head.

T.P. watched on in horror, unable to do anything to save his friend. He covered his mouth to quiet his gasping breaths. The strangers retrieved Ned's body and dragged it away into the woods.

Once T.P. felt that he had a chance to run for it, he made a tentative move to run again.

He didn't stand a chance.

The noose tightened around his neck as he was lifted into the air, his legs kicking out from beneath him, finding nothing to gain footing on. He struggled against the rope strangling him, turning his face blue. His eyes began to bulge as he tried to pull himself up toward the tree branch the rope was slung over.

A large beast of a man with wild hair and enormous build—looking like some untamed mountain man—stepped out in front of T.P. The man grabbed T.P. by the legs and pulled down as hard as he could.

Snap!

The sound of T.P.'s neck breaking reverberated through the forest.

CHAPTER SIXTY-ONE

Ginny, Laurie, Max, Rachel, Steve, Kit, Nancy, Jess, Richie, and Chris continued to watch the movie unfold on the screen before them.

A sterile white hospital room. Harsh white light, trays of metallic medical equipment, peeling lime green paint on the walls. Doctors and nurses in starched uniforms performing surgery on a patient strapped down to an operating table. The patient mumbling something to himself as the doctor inserted a giant metal rod into the man's eye.

None of them noticed as each of the rows behind them began to fill up as the strangers entered quietly, deliberately, taking seats in the theater behind the friends.

In a small dark room, a television set played. The picture was staticky and distorted, as were the voices coming from it.

In front of the television, illuminated by the TV's light, were two wide-eyed strangers sitting on a couch. One was shaded purple, the other red. They looked like damaged, misshapen science fiction experiments on humans that went horribly wrong.

Their heads slowly turned in tandem, away from the images on the television, to stare directly into the camera—staring at the viewers, with their expressionless, inky black opaque eyes, as if they were aware that they were being watched.

The tape stopped there. The screen went white. The theater was still dark aside from the beam of light from the projection booth.

There were a dozen intruders collectively gathered in the theater, unbeknownst to Annie's friends.

The Neil Armstrong-masked stranger sat directly behind Max. In one silent, steady motion, Neil forced a machete through the back of Max's seat. The blade shot through Max's body, soaked in blood.

Max looked down at the object sticking out of his chest in disbelief.

The lights in the theater went up, temporarily blinding the friends.

Rachel's terrified scream first alerted everyone to Max's gory demise, then to the fact that they were not alone.

"What the fuck?" Richie said, pulling Jess close to him.

Everyone leapt to their feet and scrambled toward the white movie screen. Laurie stayed behind, cuddling Max's lifeless corpse and weeping.

"Laurie!" Rachel said.

The strangers stood up, slowly advancing on the friends.

Rachel and Steve bounded forward to pull Laurie away from Max's body. One of the strangers reached out to grab Laurie but missed her by a fraction of a second.

Ginny led the group to the side of the movie screen, behind the heavy white vinyl. On the other side of the vinyl were the shadows of the rapidly approaching figures.

The ghost emerged from the gap between the screen and the curtain.

Chris saw a toolbox on the ground next to construction equipment. She quickly grabbed a screwdriver and brought it down on the ghost's head, impaling the ghost through the eye.

The ghost fell to the ground. A second later, the figure stirred and clamored to his feet, lunging at Chris.

"You can't be alive!" Chris screamed, driving the screwdriver into the side of the ghost's head. That put the ghost down for good.

The others grabbed whatever weapons they could find in the toolbox while Nancy pushed at the emergency door, finally busting through.

"This way!" Nancy yelled.

They ran out of the theater toward the main house as the sun was setting in the sky behind them.

CHAPTER SIXTY-TWO

The sound of the woodchipper was making Brenda's head hurt. First Eunice went off and wasn't answering any of her text messages or phone calls, then Dolly broke the news to them that Annie knew the truth about her parents. It had not been the fun day she'd hoped for. She didn't even get a thanks from Annie for Madame Fructuosa's visit, and that didn't come cheap.

Karen was still asleep in her room, while Diane, Martha, and Dolly kept Brenda company in the common room of their temporary lodging, playing backgammon and gin rummy.

"That's it," Brenda huffed. "Enough is enough. There's no need for Mr. Brisket to be running that thing right now. I can't even hear myself think, for God's sake."

Brenda followed the hum and buzz of the woodchipper, stomping her feet as she walked. Mr. Brisket was going to get an earful. Unless he was an attractive older man. Then Brenda might let him off the hook, provided he took her somewhere nice to eat. Though she doubted any of the towns surrounding Gull Valley knew from haute cuisine. She'd be lucky to get a McDonald's Fish-O-Filet.

Brenda rounded the corner behind one of the buildings as Mr. Brisket and the woodchipper came into view. She opened her mouth to scold him but stopped in revulsion.

Mr. Brisket stood at the woodchipper, his gloved hands shoving mutilated bodies into the grinder. Blood and mush made from internal organs sprayed over the ground. There was a pile of people she didn't recognize, all dead and rotting, at the side of the woodchipper.

Mr. Brisket looked over at Brenda and gave her a slow, inhuman smile. Brenda staggered back, her brain struggling to make sense of what she was seeing.

He stepped toward her, leaving two legs sticking out of the grinder.

Alice, Sally, Trish, and Wes came screaming and running in from the road.

Mr. Brisket had a bone saw in his hand. He approached Brenda methodically, each step designed to give her terror and him pleasure.

Alice grabbed Brenda and helped her run to safety, back to Brenda's guest house. When Aunt Dolly, Diane, and Martha saw what a state Brenda, Alice, Wes, Trish, and Sally were in, the women jumped up in panic.

Bang!

Mr. Brisket whacked at the door with his bone saw. Once, twice, again, again.

Trish covered her arm with an afghan and smashed the "In Case of Emergency" glass case, pulling out a fire axe. She held it tightly in her hands.

Mr. Brisket peeked into the hole he'd made in the doorway. He smiled sinisterly as his face filled in the open space surrounded by jagged wood. He reached his arm through the hole to unlock the door.

Wes, Alice, and Sally rushed forward to stop Mr. Brisket. Trish pounced, pushing past everyone.

"I'm going to give you something to remember us by!" Trish said as she brought the fire axe down on Mr. Brisket's head.

Mr. Brisket instantly fell backward, his skull split open and pouring blood. His eyes stared widely at the sky, though the life was draining from them.

Martha, Diane, and Aunt Dolly looked on in horror, completely confounded as to what transpired.

"What on God's green earth is going on?" Aunt Dolly said, confused and horrified by the chaos and bloodshed. Diane and Martha huddled next to Brenda.

"Have you all gone mad?" said Diane.

"Someone tell us what is going on, now!" Aunt Dolly said.

"Lock this place up, now!" Wes ordered.

"I have to go check on Karen," said Martha.

Everyone scattered to make sure the windows, doors, and any other entryways were secured.

"Someone's out there," Alice said, listening intently.

Kit, Steve, Laurie, Ginny, Nancy, Chris, Rachel, Jess, and Richie were running past the guest house when Alice threw the door open and demanded they come inside.

"Patch this door up," Diane said, rummaging under the sink for tools. She found a kit with a hammer and nails. She needed wood. In her rush, she grabbed the coffee table and smashed it as hard as she could against the wall, grabbing the pieces and sticking them over the hole in the door.

Ginny and Alice were in the last bedroom in the guest house, making sure the windows were shut and locked. Ginny paused for a moment, tilting her head slightly.

"Alice, there's someone in this room," Ginny said.

As if on cue, the zombie-masked stranger stood up from behind a plush chair, poised to strike Alice.

"Alice, there's someone in this fucking room!" said Ginny.

Alice spun around to dodge the zombie's grasp as it lunged toward the women. As Alice staggered back, she slammed the door to the room shut.

Ginny yanked the mirror off the wall and smashed it over the zombie's head. The zombie lost his balance for a moment, allowing Ginny to strike him again.

Alice picked up a piece of the broken glass, covering her hand with her sleeve, and jammed the shard right into the front of the zombie's neck.

The door burst open. Nancy was in the doorway, a look of shock and disbelief on her face. She held a large kitchen knife in her hand.

"I was coming to help," said Nancy. "I'm into survival."

The zombie slumped forward in a pool of his own blood. The mirror shard pushed farther into his neck.

"We have to find everybody else," Steve said.

Those who remained—Aunt Dolly, Diane, Brenda, Martha, Karen, Alice, Sally, Trish, Rachel, Steve, Kit, Jess, Laurie, Ginny, Chris, Nancy, Richie, and Wes— gathered in the common room, stockpiling any and all weapons they found in the house.

"Where's Annie?" Aunt Dolly said.

"We don't know," said Kit. "They killed Max."

"Bill, Sean, and Dave are dead, too," Wes said. Sally and Trish looked away when Sean spoke of their husbands.

"Has anybody seen Sloane, T.P., or Ned?" said Nancy.

"We just have to hope they're okay for now," Richie said.

Bang!

The cultists began to throw things at the guest house. They knocked at it, hit the sides, took shots at it, even if only to let everyone inside know they weren't safe or alone.

Bang!

Bang!

Bang!

The cultists surrounded the house, smashing their weapons at the wood and windows. Everyone inside was trapped as the sounds echoed and reverberated. The house shook against the onslaught.

The noises stopped.

"What are they doing?" said Wes.

"What do we do now?" Rachel said.

"Nobody's phones are working?" said Jess. "I can't get any reception or bars."

"They've blocked everything," Laurie said. "They've made sure we can't reach anyone outside of here."

"Where did they come from?" said Sally. "Who are these people?"

"The Felicitous have returned," Aunt Dolly said. "I don't think they ever went away. I think they were waiting for this. They want to finish something they started so many decades ago. I should have never let Annie come to this place."

"I'm going to go double check on the back bedrooms," Diane said. "We can't let them in. We're safest here. We have to protect ourselves."

"I'll go with you," Nancy said, following Diane down the hallway.

Bang!

Bang!

Bang!

The banging, knocking, and assault on the outside of the house began again. This time, even more intensely and frantically.

Nancy gripped the knife in her hand while Diane held on to a hammer. They inspected each bedroom one by one, looking under beds and examining the locks on the windows.

"All clear," Diane said.

They went to check the bedroom directly across from the one they were just in. They didn't see the dirty rug rising off of the ground behind them.

Rising, rising...until it stood tall, covering up whoever was hiding beneath it.

Diane and Nancy went back into the hallway, headed toward the common room. The rug-covered figure slowly, gingerly stalking behind them.

"Behind you!" Steve shouted from the end of the hall.

Nancy and Diane spun around in time to see two long arms extended out toward them. The women did not hesitate.

Nancy began stabbing through the rug, drawing copious amounts of blood with each jab. Diane beat the figure over the head with the hammer. Over and over, until the person beneath toppled over.

Nancy rushed to the bedroom where the rug came from.

There was a trap door in the floor, wide open. Warm, musty air flowed out from the opening. Diane and Ginny appeared behind her.

"That's no fruit cellar," Ginny said, slamming the wooden cover back over the trap door while Nancy and Diane moved the bed over it so no one could access it from below.

"This whole place is a trap," Diane said.

CHAPTER SIXTY-THREE

"Annie," Sloane said gently. "Annie."

Annie groaned, rubbing her neck. She couldn't remember how she passed out or where she was.

When she opened her eyes and saw Sloane staring back at her, she was filled with rage and anger.

Then Annie saw the rest of the room.

She didn't recognize any of it.

A dirty, dusty, putrid-smelling dugout.

Annie was seated at the head of a large dinner table. The table was covered with bright, swirly "Happy Birthday" logos and symbols. Happy Birthday balloons floated in the air above her, tied to chairs around the table.

The room had been decorated with birthday party favors. Streamers, noisemakers, a banner, swirly pink-and-white straws in paper cups, unicorn plates and napkins, party horns, glitter sprinkled across the table.

Sloane had dressed Annie in a "Happy Birthday" tiara and sash.

Annie saw the party guests.

Rotted, decayed corpses in each seat around the table. Dressed in festive, vividly-colored party hats. Their eyes and bodies stuffed like scarecrows with straw, sawdust, and various rocks, stones, and sticks. Annie had no idea who these people were.

She did recognize one person at the table. Marcie Squires, George's granddaughter, was lifelessly propped up next to the other bodies.

Annie almost screamed but it came out as a panicked squeal. She realized she was zip tied to her chair. Annie struggled against the restraints.

"It's almost your birthday, Annie," Sloane said. "You should be nice to your party guests. They're here to celebrate. We brought them out just for you."

Annie didn't say anything. Her mind raced. She had to get out of this situation. She didn't even know where she was. She was looking at her friend Sloane.

Her friend? Not her friend.

Sloane put a gloppy, sloppily-made birthday cake in front of Annie. It had several half-melted candles haphazardly placed in the icing.

"Your cake got a little dirty," said Sloane. "Sorry for that. It's really hard to keep a clean house underground. Do you want a piece? I'll cut you off a piece."

Sloane picked up the cake cutter.

"I don't want cake," was all Annie managed to get out.

"But you're always hungry," Sloane said.

"You're not Sloane Doyle, are you?"

"God, it took you two years to figure that out. No. I'm not Sloane Doyle. There is no Sloane Doyle. Like Tyler Durden, she doesn't exist and is just a figment of your imagination. Or, well, my imagination. Except I don't have a split personality."

"What was all of this for?"

"Wow, I really thought you were smarter than this, Annie."

One of the corpses slumped down in its chair a little, startling Annie.

"Don't mind him," Sloane said. "He may be a little drunk on punch."

"Where's Cal?"

"He's with my friends."

"Where are my friends?"

"Also with my friends."

"What did I ever do to you?"

"You didn't do anything, Annie," Sloane said. "It's all about timing. Your birthday, your bloodline, it all marks the perfect confluence to let Erica back in through the portal. Through you. In essence, most of this is not your fault. Though yes, most of your friends and family are going to have to die and you'll blame yourself. We were going to wait to kill them because it's more powerful after your transformation but some of them got too curious. And you know what they say—curiosity killed the friend crew. They're above ground right now, huddled together because they think they're safer if they stick together. But we've got this whole place rigged. They're breathing in toxic gases as we speak. Soon, they'll get sleepy."

"You fucking psycho. You crazy bitch."

"That's the best insults you can come up with? Do better, Annie. I expect more from a writer."

"Did you kill Gary?"

Sloane paused. "Sadly, not my doing. Turns out, you really do have horrible, awful luck. You were really born under an unlucky star. That was chance, random happenstance. It worked out perfectly for me though, because it gave me the opportunity to pretend to be a real estate agent and get you to sign a fake deed claiming that Gull Valley was all yours. It was so easy to convince you to buy our home. You were so sad, so distraught, so vulnerable. You never even checked my credentials, my backstory, any of it. You so willingly trusted me and believed everything I told you. It almost makes me feel bad for you. Being so naïve and ridiculous and all. It's kind of pathetic, if you ask me."

"You want to talk ridiculous and pathetic? Look at what you're doing. I'm tied up for the birthday party from hell—great fucking loser cake, by the way—and you're a

338

lapdog to a dead cult leader who dressed his followers like they're in a Woolworths catalog."

"You shut your filthy mouth!" Sloane picked up the cake cutter and held it in front of Annie's face. "Laird Hubbell was a visionary. He was a genius. Do you know what those doctors did to him? The experiments they performed on him? What he went through? What he did for all of us?"

"Yeah, he sounds like a real winner. Sexual predator, murderer, obsessed with his dead girlfriend, thought some mystical monster spoke to him in the woods. What a precious snowflake. He was fucked in the head long before those doctors ever got to him."

"I will cut your fucking tongue out," Sloane said, brandishing the cake cutter closer to Annie's face.

"I'm not afraid to die, Sloane." Annie wondered how much of that statement was bravado and how much was the truth.

"You're not going to die, Annie. You're going to be a host. You'll be you but not you. Erica is going to live inside of you. After midnight, once it's officially your birthday, you will be the new home for the body and soul of Erica Keating."

Annie couldn't help but laugh. A mirthless, tired laugh, but a laugh nonetheless.

"That's the stupidest fucking thing I've ever heard. You wasted all of this time and money on this plan and it's a goddamn joke."

Sloane laughed as well. Hers was more rueful. "You have no idea, Annie. You don't know what we've seen and what we've done. You should hear the noises people make when we kill them. You should hear them beg for their mothers, for their gods, for us to spare them. Every drop of blood we've spilled is for him. We've planned this for so many years. Tonight, we finally get to see our dreams come true. To bring our leaders back."

"You don't even know you're insane, do you?"

"I'm not insane. I'm right."

"So, all this time, you were just messing with my head until it was time for the main event? Making me think I was crazy? Making me believe Gull Valley was haunted."

"We like to have our fun."

"What's the recruitment for The Felicitous like, Sloane?" Annie said. "Must love murder and rearranging corpses for entertainment. Bring your own knives. Must be willing to ignore all logic and reason and abandon rational thought. Underground accommodations cozy but skanky and dark."

A shadow darkened the doorway between the dugout and the next portion of the tunnel. A monstrously large man with huge hands and giant build filled the space, staring at Annie.

"The Felicitous literally went underground, didn't they?" Annie said, one eye on the enormous beast-man in the doorway. "That's why no one ever found them. All those years, they built this tunnel system beneath Gull Valley and killed passersby to survive. They eradicated themselves from society, from their home, and lived in this bunker like animals."

"The time has come, Annie. They won't be living down here much longer."

It all began to connect for Annie. "They killed and cannibalized people. They inbred to keep their numbers up and have people who could go out into the world that had no identification or fingerprints on file. That way, they could carry out crimes and never be caught or found. Everyone had forgotten about Gull Valley. They all thought it was haunted. But it wasn't ghosts—not really— but the ghosts of the past using legends and fear to keep their land."

"This land is ours. No one can take it away from us. And they never will again."

"Mr. Brisket and Ms. Click aren't really caretakers."

"They are, just not the kind you thought. The helping hands of The Felicitous reach far and wide. You really shouldn't put so much trust in people, Annie. I'm actually surprised you do, what with all the bad stuff that keeps happening to you."

"Yeah, this whole week will make another great entry for my dream journal."

Sloane cut a piece of cake for Annie, putting it on a plate in front of her. Annie tried to loosen the zip ties to no avail, to wriggle her wrists from their prison. She had to save her friends and family. She had to escape her hellhole.

"Why kill all of my friends and family? People will notice they're missing. People will come looking for them."

"They'll never find them. The blood of those closest to you has more power. Besides, you're the one who always tells me women should support women. We may not kill all of your girlfriends—some will make excellent mothers to the next generation of The Felicitous."

Annie shuddered at the thought.

"You killed your sister."

"I did. I had to. She wouldn't listen. It was so easy to make it look like an accident. She had so many problems as it was. Mara wasn't interested in belonging. You know what it was like to grow up in her shadow, listening to my parents go on and on about The Felicitous, always being treated like I was less important than Mara because Laird Hubbell wasn't my father?"

"Laird Hubbell was no father."

"But he is, Annie. He's your father. I really thought you might be more excited about this, Annie. You're going to meet your real father tonight."

"What?"

341

"You didn't know? I know. I have the DNA test results to prove it. You're not a Porter, you're a Hubbell. That's why your bloodline works best for Erica."

Annie swallowed her disgust and shame. She didn't want to believe Sloane, who had already been proven to be a pathological liar. Somewhere in Annie's heart though, she knew Sloane wasn't lying.

"We have to get you dressed for the festivities tonight," Sloane said.

Annie wrenched her hands free from the zip ties. She grabbed the cake and threw it at Sloane. Sloane dodged it.

"Where do you think you're going?" said Sloane.

Annie didn't know. She took off running into the tunnels. She heard Sloane and the beast man's footsteps following behind her as she fled into the unknown.

CHAPTER SIXTY-FOUR

Annie tore down the long stretch of tunnel without a clue where she was headed or where it led. She desperately searched for an exit, a ladder, a way out. She ran past several darkened corridors and side rooms, not wanting to think of what lurked inside them, her mind solely focused on escaping.

Sloane and the giant man lost her once she took a right and they took a left. Annie had lost them for now, but she had no way of knowing how the labyrinthine maze below Gull Valley worked. It seemed to stretch for miles.

Smash!

Smash!

Smash!

Annie didn't see the giant man but heard him smashing the lightbulbs that hung down each passageway, bathing the corridors in heavy darkness.

Annie felt a slight breeze blow past her. She tried to pinpoint its source. That would lead to a way out.

As she rounded a corner, she paused and covered her mouth, attempting to get her bearings.

Annie slid into one of the many side rooms.

It was a torture chamber.

Dead bodies were bound by their wrists from chains in the ceiling, strung up by the dozens. They had been eviscerated, mutilated, and defiled. Some were hung upside-down like beef.

Past the group of corpses, Annie saw someone in the corner. A person was close to the ground, bent over and leaning over something.

343

As Annie's eyes adjusted to the darkness, she saw the pale creature-like human eating the flesh and meat of a body on the ground. It hunched over its prey like a feral animal, smacking its bloodstained lips as it ate. Annie knew it was human yet it didn't look or seem human.

It turned immediately toward her, sensing her presence. Its black eyes burrowed into hers, its face contorted in rage and anger that its meal had been interrupted.

Annie screamed and ran.

She stopped in what appeared to be some kind of makeshift hospital room, like a replica of the one Laird Hubbell once stayed in. There was a strait-jacket crumpled on the ground, a gurney with leather restraints, jars of medical supplies lining rickety shelves and tables, shelves lined with glass beakers and jars full of unknown substances, and old-fashioned, outdated medical tools and equipment scattered on metal trays and about the room. A bucket marked "Hazardous" was filled with viscous fluid, blood, and other waste. A drain in the center of the floor was clogged with coagulated blood and other grisly matter.

Like a twisted version of a morgue, several bodies lay on gurneys, wrapped in burlap sacks. Many of the sacks were soaked in blood.

Perched atop a dirty examination table was a dead abomination of a man. Of several men, and perhaps some women—they had been sewn and stitched together, Frankensteined out of several people's body parts, stuffed and propped up to look alive. A grotesque, hideous experiment.

Annie held back her disgust and looked around quickly. She grabbed an antique scalpel inside a doctor's medical bag on the floor.

Annie peered out into the corridor and listened for Sloane and the giant man's presence. She heard rustling and thumping in the distance but couldn't pinpoint where the sounds came from.

Annie didn't see the person in the burlap sack sit straight up behind her, as if rising from the dead. Another rose right after the first. Then another. Then another.

Annie was oblivious to the people in the sacks sliding off of their gurneys, still covered in burlap. Their feet touched the ground, standing up and stepping toward Annie.

Only when Annie heard the soft sound of dirt crunch beneath a shoe did she turn around to see four undefined people creeping closer to her.

Annie stifled a scream and darted out of the room, following the origin of the draft through the corridor. She had to find a way out.

CHAPTER SIXTY-FIVE

Diane's eyes fluttered as she felt herself getting sleepy. She noticed everyone else around her seemed to be lethargic and slow-moving.

They hadn't heard any noise from outside. As if the cultists had other things to do and moved on. But that couldn't be the case. However, maybe temporarily they had other culty things to do and left Diane and the crew alone for the moment.

In the meantime, Diane realized that something was in the air, quite literally. Something was wrong, making everyone around her lose their wits and suck away their energy.

"We need to get some air in here or move to another location," Diane said to everyone. They resisted and required explanation at first but Diane persisted.

The group—Brenda, Martha, Karen, Chris, Sally, Trish, Kit, Steve, Laurie, Jess, Ginny, Alice, Rachel, Nancy, Wes, and Richie—was to head for the roller-skating rink while Diane and Aunt Dolly would run for the car and drive into Hartwell for help.

Diane quietly opened the door and peered out into the darkness of the night. There was nothing, nobody, outside. Faint animal noises and a slight wind.

With whatever weapons they could find, they cautiously exited the guest house. Out into the night.

"I don't see anything," Diane whispered, heading the charge.

"Be careful," Brenda said to Diane and Aunt Dolly. "Come back in one piece."

Once they were outside but still on guard, Diane and Aunt Dolly grabbed each other's hands and hurried toward Diane's car.

The rest of them took watchful steps toward the skating rink.

None of them saw the figures standing on the roof, looking down on them.

One leapt down, tackling Richie in the process.

"No!" Laurie said, kicking the cultist as he raised a knife over Richie as they tussled on the ground.

Laurie jumped on top of the cultist in fury. She stabbed his back, sides, neck, and body repeatedly, filled with anger and hate against him and his people for killing her friends, for killing her beloved Max.

The cultist looked like chopped meat after Laurie's frenzied attack.

The other cultists disappeared from view.

"Laurie!" said Chris. "Laurie, he's dead. Come on, let's go!"

"We have to move now," Nancy said.

The cultists began showing themselves from in between the buildings, on top of the structures, and at the distant tree line.

"We're outnumbered," said Ginny. "Move your asses, now!"

Jess helped Richie up off the ground as the group sprinted to the skating rink.

As they did, another cultist ran at them with an axe in his hands. He swung wildly, leading the charge against Annie's friends. The cultists swarmed them from all sides, some at full speed runs. Dozens of masked strangers came from every direction, headed straight toward the friends.

The axe-wielding cultist sliced Wes's back. Wes bellowed in pain as his friends used the opportunity to overpower the cultist. The cultist dropped the axe.

Alice picked the axe up and slammed it down on the cultist's shoulder. The cultist's severed arm flopped to the ground.

Nancy picked up the chopped-off arm and beat the cultist with it.

Whack!

Whack!

Nancy let loose, walloping the cultist with his own hacked off arm and shouting a string of obscenities in her anger and fear.

"Nancy! Nancy!" Sally said, pulling Nancy with the rest of the group. "Come on, let's go!"

The cultists weaved in and out of the friends as they ran. Kit and Steve were blocked off by a pumpkin-masked cultist. Steve grabbed Kit's hand and they darted off into the night.

The cultists launched a full-scale attack on the friends—striking at them with their bladed weapons, attempting to tackle them, surrounding them as their prey.

A cultist reached for Brenda. She kicked him in the balls. He fell to his knees.

"Don't fuck with me, junior!" Brenda said, kicking him in the face. Martha and Karen grabbed Brenda's arm and yanked her to safety.

The rest of the group made it inside the rink, slamming the doors shut behind them. Many of them were wounded and bleeding.

CHAPTER SIXTY-SIX

The skating rink was dark and silent inside. The group made quick work of barricading the doors, piling anything they could find against them. The cultists pounded on the door, trying to break through.

"Check for windows and open doors," Laurie said. "Anything they can get in through."

"Laurie, are you okay?" Karen said, putting her hand on Laurie's back.

"Do as I say, now!" Laurie said.

Everyone scattered to do a safety check throughout the rink. Karen stood with Laurie for a moment.

They were interrupted by the sound of A-Ha's "Take on Me" blasting over the speakers. The overhead LED lights and mirror balls turned on, bathing the room in an artificial, glittery glow.

"Someone's in here," Rachel said from the back doors.

Jess and Rachel stopped once they saw T.P. crouched down in the dark corner, facing away from them, as if he were hiding.

"T.P.!" said Jess. "You're alive! Come with us! Everyone is together!"

It wasn't T.P.

It was someone wearing T.P.'s clothes, using the darkness to hide. The fake T.P. turned slowly toward them, clearly enjoying tormenting them, then stood up to face them. His satisfied smile could be seen from beneath the sea creature mask he had on.

In each of his hands was a sharp, shiny hunting knife. He pointed the knives, poking at Jess and Rachel, like he was playing a game. The sea creature-masked man enjoyed himself.

Rachel and Jess backed up. Without anywhere to run, they had the choice to run out the back doors—behind which, undoubtedly, several more deranged cultists awaited—or take care of this guy themselves.

The sea creature sliced the air in front of them, almost cutting Rachel. Once. Twice. The next one contacted Rachel's skin, slicing her arm.

Jess grabbed a pair of roller skates from a shelf and hurled them at the sea creature. He dodged them but it gave Rachel enough of a chance to strike.

Rachel picked up a discarded, broken mirror ball and smashed it over the sea creature's head. Jess forcefully brought the fire poker in her hands, taken from the guest house, down on the man.

"Die, you son of a bitch!" Rachel said.

The sea creature slashed at them, cutting Jess in the leg. Blood ran down in small streams from beneath his mask.

Jess shoved the fire poker through the sea creature's torso.

Sally and Nancy ran toward the DJ booth to shut down the music and neon lights. They opened the door to the booth, screaming at the putrefied corpse that was propped up inside, as if it were spinning records.

Nancy kicked the body out of the way as Sally flicked switches. The music and disco lights ceased. The rink flooded with regular lighting.

Wes did a head count and shuddered. "Wait, where are Kit and Steve?"

CHAPTER SIXTY-SEVEN

Diane got the car started, thanking the universe for small victories. The doors and windows were locked. They were belted in and ready to go.

"Diane, hit the pedal," Aunt Dolly said, her eyes widening as she stared out the windshield.

The cultists surrounded the car, smashing at the windows and attempting to break in.

Diane peeled out in reverse, knocking some of the cultists to the ground. She sped off down the dirt road toward town.

Neither woman saw as the figure in the back slowly climbed over the seats, soundlessly getting closer to them. Creeping, crawling toward them.

Diane and Aunt Dolly were distracted and panicked. They didn't notice the approaching threat.

"Does your phone have service?" said Diane.

"Not yet," Aunt Dolly said, staring at her cell phone.

Diane caught a glimpse of the person in her backseat. Aunt Dolly screamed as the figure reached out and clasped its hand over her throat.

Diane swatted the hand as Aunt Dolly tore at her neck, trying to free herself from his grip. Aunt Dolly attempted to bend his fingers back but his hold was strong. Aunt Dolly choked for air.

Diane hit the gas. The speedometer hit eighty miles an hour.

Diane slammed the brake. The car came screeching to a halt, sliding down the dirt road, fighting against gravity.

Smash!

The cultist ejected forward through the windshield. Glass shards burst everywhere, raining on Diane and Aunt Dolly.

The cultist lay flat in the road before them. Once he stirred, Diane set her jaw.

As the cultist began to stand, Diane pushed her foot all the way down on the gas pedal and mowed the man down.

The cultist burst like a blood-filled piñata. His insides exploded to the outside, covering Diane and Aunt Dolly in gore. The masked maniac flopped to the ground as the car surged forward and Diane ran him over for good measure.

The women looked at each other, covered in blood and guts. They almost had to laugh.

Rookie mistake—always check the backseat, Aunt Dolly thought.

CHAPTER SIXTY-EIGHT

Kit and Steve, separated from their friends, weaved in and out of the darkness to avoid being seen by the cultists. They managed to slip undetected into the woodshop garage.

Kit put her finger to her lips to say, "Don't speak." Steve nodded.

Steve quietly shut and locked the door behind them. They didn't turn on any lights. Their eyes adjusted slowly to the darkness in the garage.

Kit and Steve searched over the contents inside the woodshop. Shovels, tools, construction equipment, a table with a vice. The entire building was overstuffed with boxes and various hardware, gadgets, and implements, making it difficult for them to negotiate a clear path to traverse. A beat-up refrigerator stood against the back wall.

Several tools and sharp implements hung on the walls. A chainsaw and an axe were missing, as evidenced by the white outline drawn in where they would have normally been stored.

They heard someone running by the window and pressed themselves against the wall to avoid being spotted.

"We're going to see our daughters again," Steve said quietly.

He turned to make sure nobody else was in the garage with them. As he did, he accidentally knocked over a vintage radio that was perched upon a stack of boxes.

When the radio slammed to the ground, it sprang to life. The Police's "Every Breath You Take" warbled out of the ancient, dusty speakers.

Steve hurried to click the radio off, fumbling for the proper button to restore the silence. Kit checked out of one of the windows to make sure they hadn't given away their location.

Neither one of them saw the figure that rose from within a collection of the boxes. He was completely covered by shadow, his outline barely noticeable in the darkness.

"What do we do now?" Kit said, desperately attempting to get reception on her phone.

"We wait for Dolly and Diane to come back with help," said Steve. "We stay here and arm ourselves in case any of those lunatics find us."

Creak...

The fridge door opened slowly, the dim light from inside illuminating portions of the room.

Kit and Steve held back their revulsion as the fridge door revealed that the shelves and racks were stuffed with human body parts and organs. A human head was in the center of severed limbs and jars filled with viscous liquids.

Kit lurched forward and slammed the fridge door shut. It slammed with a loud bang. She backed away, afraid she had given away their position.

"I don't see anyone out there," Steve said, sighing a breath of relief.

"Have they been here all this time?" Kit said. Steve didn't answer.

There was a window behind Kit and Steve, past a cluster of boxes and magazine stacks. Neither heard the masked cultist raising the glass, leaving enough space for him to crawl through.

Kit and Steve were alerted when the blast of cool air breezed past them.

The cultist was halfway through the open window.

354

Steve sprung forward and slammed the window shut on the cultist. The cultist was trapped midway in between the garage and the outside.

The cultist slashed a knife at them, narrowly missing Steve.

Kit grabbed a nail gun and held it at the cultist's head, firing once. Twice. Three, four times. The cultist slumped down, his head riddled with nails.

"Kit!" Steve said, pushing her aside as the cultist behind her was poised to strike.

The cultist knocked back against the fridge, sending the door open and rattling the contents. Limbs, jars of blood and fluids, and the head jostled and tumbled out to the ground.

The cultist stabbed Steve in the arm with his knife. Steve kicked him in the knee. The cultist groaned, his knee broken, staggering back and swinging his knife at them.

Steve grabbed the fridge door and smashed it in the cultist's face. Kit brought an axe down on the cultist's head, splitting it open down the middle.

They pulled back, out of breath.

Kit saw the cultist outside before Steve did. The cultist's masked face was pressed up against the window. He slapped his hand against the glass, letting them know he found them.

Kit and Steve heard the sound of more cultists surrounding the garage, banging on the walls and shattering the door down with their weapons.

The doors and windows smashed as cultists pummeled their way inside. Kit and Steve had nowhere to run.

CHAPTER SIXTY-NINE

Annie heard the echoes of people walking and talking throughout the tunnels. She followed where she thought the breeze came from. Her insides were gripped by fear. She tried to calm herself and stop her body from shaking.

You have to focus, Annie repeatedly told herself.

She saw the outlines of two of the cultists headed toward her. Unsure if they saw her or not, she slipped into one of the various side rooms to hide.

The room was already occupied. The children who had knocked on her door earlier that week were playing with grimy toys. They still had their masks on—an astronaut, a vampire, a ninja, a dinosaur, and a robot.

At first, they didn't regard Annie pressed against the wall, staring at them. They continued to play with their dolls and cars and Legos, which Annie realized were all stolen or left behind by people the cultists had most likely murdered.

The room was full of skeletons dressed in the cultists' attire. Propped up around the room, mixed in with mannequins posed in chairs and scattered about.

The children continued to ignore Annie. She stepped past them as they played, her eyes on the next passageway. She watched for any sign that they took note of her presence, yet they were engrossed in what they were doing and simply ignored her existence.

She slid past the children and into the next alcove.

Before she did, she looked back at the children.

They were all staring at her. Completely aware of her intrusion.

"Shhh," Annie said. "I'm a friend."

The children looked at her quizzically. Annie began to back out of the room slowly.

"It's okay," said Annie. "It's okay."

The astronaut rang a bell, as if to alert the others to her.

Fuck!

Annie darted into the alcove. A room filled with candles and photographs of Erica Keating. The walls adorned with testimonials, love letters, pictures, and clothing, all dedicated to Erica.

A wax figure, made in Erica's image, sat on a throne against the wall. She was dressed how Laird Hubbell remembered her best—1950s Peter Pan dress, smart black shoes. Atop of the figure's head was a wig made from a scalped victim, the hairline caked in dried blood.

It was Erica's tomb.

Annie had an idea. She listened for any signs of movement from the rooms and corridors around her. She heard the approaching cultists coming.

There was no exit out of the room. She would have to go back the way she came but she didn't have time.

Annie heard the footfalls getting closer and closer. There was only one thing to do. She hurriedly went forward with her plan. There was no time to waste.

Once the cultists reached Erica's tomb, they filled the room, blocking Annie's only way out.

Annie was waiting for them. She had changed out of her clothes and into Erica's dress and—gag—put on the scalped hair. This was her bid for escape.

The cultists stared at her through the eyeholes in their masks. Annie tried to gauge if her gambit worked. Their eyes didn't give anything away. Were they feeling wonder and amazement at their beloved Erica's return from the grave?

Annie tried to suppress her fear and disgust as she spoke.

"You did well," Annie said, pretending to be Erica although she had no idea what Erica sounded like. She tried her best to sound commanding and authoritative. "You brought me back."

The cultists were silent.

"I have come back from the other side to tell you that you are safe and loved and I live again," Annie continued, making that shit up on the spot.

The cultists were still silent.

"Bishop and I want you to take me outside to the world," said Annie. "Let me breathe the air and see Gull Valley for myself. We have so much work to do together."

The cultists were buying it. Several of them dropped to their knees, crying.

"You have made Bishop and me proud," Annie said. "But now it is time for the next chapter. We must give the world our message and tell them what we've done here. No more blood needs to be shed tonight. You may rest now."

Annie went for it. She stepped forward. The cultists parted to allow her past, some holding back the urge to touch her as she walked by.

"Bring me outside," said Annie.

Several of the cultists ran ahead of her to lead her toward an outlet.

You're almost there, Annie. Stay the course. They think you're her. Holy shit, are they all idiots? Am I that convincing or do they so desperately want to believe? Don't give yourself away.

They directed her down a pathway leading to a ladder built into the side of the rock wall.

"I will be back for you," Annie said to the cultists. "Wait for me here."

She began to ascend the ladder, pushing against the trap door over her head. Light shone in from the room

358

above her head. Annie made it halfway up before she heard Sloane's voice.

"It's showtime, Annie."

CHAPTER SEVENTY

Annie felt the tug on her legs, sending her crashing to the floor. She swung the scalpel wildly at the crowd around her, trying in vain to fight them off. She slashed a couple of the cult members, drawing blood.

One of the cultists threw a gunny sack over her head. Another wrestled the scalpel from her hand.

She felt herself being dragged away down the dirt passageway as she kicked and screamed, away from freedom and light.

Annie felt the hand over her mouth through the sack, filling her lungs with something vaporous that was meant to make her pass out.

Annie wrestled herself out of the gunny sack and barreled down the corridor, the cultists close behind her. She pulled the scalped hair off of her head and tossed it as far as she could away from her.

A light from overhead!

Annie sprinted up the metal rungs nailed into the wall, slamming the trap door shut behind her. She heard the cultists right on her heels.

She was in a room she'd never seen before—darkly lit, musty. She pushed a trunk over the trap door. The wooden slats shot up and down as the cultists pushed on it, trying to reach Annie.

Seated in a weatherworn, vintage brown recliner was the desiccated corpse of an old woman. She was positioned at a desk in front of a sewing machine, as if in death she was doing the activities she did in life.

The walls were adorned with symbols and missing persons flyers. The wallpaper was peeling off of the wall, revealing names and part of a family tree scribbled in black marker. At the top, it read, "Hubbell." Other parts had the names of members of The Felicitous.

Boom!

The trap door bounced up and down again. Annie slid the dead old woman's desk next to the trunk, sealing the opening off even farther.

Annie realized she was looking through the other side of a two-way mirror. She was in guest house number two. Looking right into Chris's room. She pushed on the mirror, running through the empty house.

As soon as Annie made it into the hallway, she heard the front door of the guest house open. She ducked into one of the bedrooms, knowing that it was one—or more—of the cult members approaching.

Annie heard multiple sets of footfalls and people tearing the house apart searching for her. She shut the door behind her and went to the window, slowly opening it, fearful it would make a screech or noise and alert the intruders to her location.

Swoosh!

A cultist outside passed by the window. Annie immediately pressed herself against the wall. The cult member didn't seem to notice her—at least she hoped.

She couldn't jump out of the window with someone lurking there. She considered under the bed but that's the first place someone would look and she'd be trapped. She carefully crept under the window and to the closet.

Annie ducked inside the closet, hiding in the corner behind all of the clothes. She waited.

Almost instantly, she heard the bedroom door open and someone walking around the bedroom.

Then quiet.

The closet door opened.

An arm reached in to rummage around. Sorting angrily through the clothes. Hangers clacked together. Annie pressed herself as far against the closet wall as she could. Had she been seen?

The masked stranger lost interest, closing the door again.

Annie waited until she heard the footsteps fade away.

Quiet again. Annie held her breath, listening intently.

Listening, waiting.

"I know you're in there," a man's voice called out from the other side of the closet door.

Annie froze up.

"I'm in here, too," another voice said.

Annie's eyes struggled to adjust to the darkness. She shuddered when she saw.

Someone else was in the closet with her. On the opposite end. Staring directly at Annie.

Bang!

A masked cultist launched himself forward at Annie. She screamed and reached for the doorknob, running out of the closet and straight into the other cultist.

The man in the closet grabbed Annie's hair and pulled her back as the other cultist held her arms. Annie fought to wrest herself free.

Annie threw her entire body backward, knocking the cultist at her back against the wall. She jumped forward, causing the cultist in front of her to let go of her arms. They both toppled to the ground.

The cultist behind her had whacked his head against a shelf and attempted to regain equilibrium.

Annie wrestled with the cultist on the floor. She kneed him in the gut, kicking him, pushing him off of her. She was next to an end table. She grabbed the bedside lamp and smashed it over the cultist's head, screaming at him.

"You!"

Smash!

"Can't!"

Smash!

"Sit!"

Smash!

"With!"

Smash!

"Us!"

Smash!

The cultist's head was a mess of brain matter, bone, and blood.

And on my new carpet, too, Annie thought.

The cultist gurgled and stirred, as if willing himself to get back up. As Annie backed away, the cultist staggered to his feet, some of his teeth falling out of his mouth as he did.

The cultist tried to speak but all that came out were blood-soaked babbles and sentence fragments.

Behind Annie, the other one had recovered and knocked Annie onto the bed. He raised a dirty sickle over her, grumbling something at her from beneath his dime store Halloween mask.

Annie reached up and ripped the mask partially off of his face. It temporarily distracted him and obscured his vision.

It was a young man—perhaps only early twenties, fresh-faced and All-American looking. Like an all-state college football player.

Annie used the moment to her advantage. She drove both of her fingers into his eyes, pushing as hard as she could.

The cultist screamed and backed off of her, swinging the sickle wildly at the air as Annie rolled off of the bed. His eyes were bleeding a little.

Annie's eyes landed on the large fish mounted on a plaque on the wall. On its long, pointy nose.

Annie leapt up to rip the fish from its display, turning the fish's sharp nose toward the cultist and ramming him with it.

The cultist screamed out loud as the pointy tip sliced through his torso. Annie used all of her force to drive the pointed nose through the cultist's body. She charged forward, sending the cultist backward, where his back smashed against the wall.

Pinned there by the long-dead, stuffed fish.

Annie didn't hear anyone else in the house. She knew she had to find weapons. Leaving all of the lights off, she slowly crept her way toward the kitchen.

CHAPTER SEVENTY-ONE

The roller-skating rink was as sealed up as they could get it. The remaining group—Jess, Richie, Trish, Sally, Nancy, Ginny, Chris, Rachel, Alice, Martha, Brenda, Karen, Wes, and Laurie—holed up in the diner seating in the concession area.

Chris made her way past the counter and into the area where the roller skates were stored. There was a loaded shotgun behind the countertop. She grabbed it.

She passed the shelves of empty shoe cubbies, headed toward the back of the building. There was an office in the back with its door shut.

Chris listened at the door for a moment before she pushed it open. Inside was a desk covered with old papers and a small couch.

A cot was set up in the corner, covered with a heavy green blanket. There was something beneath the blanket.

Something human-shaped.

The mass began to writhe and move slowly.

Chris raised the shotgun. She reached out to pull the blanket back.

She yanked the blanket off of the cot and staggered back, horrified.

It was the decayed, rotted corpse of a stranger—milky white eyes, bone and insides exposed, discolored skin. Rats covered the body, eating the flesh and meat, squiggling in and out of the bones and holes in the body.

Chris held back her scream.

Something in the corner of the room moved behind her.

A person stepped out of the darkness closer to Chris. A tall, thin man with gaunt features and pallid skin—like a walking corpse or a zombie. He reached out to touch her.

Chris heard the creak of the floor and spun around to see the man.

Bang!

She fired the shotgun instantly, hitting the man and sending him reeling back against the wall. His blood splattered over the walls behind him.

"Chris!" her friends yelled for her.

Alice, Ginny, and Nancy ran into the office, taking in the gruesome scene and the aftermath of Chris's kill.

"Come on," Nancy said, pulling Chris away. "We got you. Are you okay?"

Alice, Ginny, and Nancy brought Chris back to the rest of the group, where she explained what had happened.

"This thing has enough bullets to take down a herd of buffalo," Chris said, showing everyone the shotgun.

"We have to stay alert and make sure no one else gets in here," Laurie said. "Have we checked all the side rooms?"

Everyone nodded. They had done a thorough search.

"What do we do now?" Rachel said.

"We can't just wait here for them to find their way inside," said Nancy. "We have to find whatever weapons we can and be ready when they come for us. They will."

"We have to fight back," Wes said. "We have to survive."

"We're not professional fighters," said Karen. "We don't know how to fight."

"We'll improvise," Alice said.

Everyone got quiet. Taking in the living nightmare that surrounded them.

"I don't hear them out there anymore," Martha said.

"What do they want?" said Ginny. "I keep thinking about this. Are we just in the wrong place at the wrong time? Do we have something that they need?"

"Remember what Cal said," Laurie said. "The Felicitous thinks our blood will help bring back their leaders."

"We have to find Annie," Brenda said. "She's out there all by herself. She's the one they really want."

"I'll go," Chris said, hands on the shotgun. "If any of those creepy assholes make a single move toward us, I will shoot a hole them you so big, they'll be used as pool rings."

"We can't just go running out in the open like sitting ducks," said Richie. "We're expendable. They want us dead. We're just in their way."

"We can't just sit here and wait," Sally said. "We have to fight back. I'll go with you, Chris."

"I will, too," said Alice. "Chris, Sally, and I will go. You guys keep your eyes out and be our lookouts. We'll go and try to find Annie and Cal and whoever else we can. We can go out the back door and hide in the shadows between the buildings."

"I'm coming, too," Wes said. "Safety in numbers."

Everyone exchanged unsure glances. Were they willingly marching to their doom?

"If you don't find them, you hurry back here," Brenda said.

Alice, Chris, Sally, and Wes nodded.

CHAPTER SEVENTY-TWO

Annie exited the guest house as quietly as she could. She saw the lights in all the buildings shining out through their windows into the darkness of the night.

Where did they all go?

She was a part of their master plan. They didn't want her dead. Yet. They wanted her alive to take part in whatever ultimate goal they sought.

Maybe I should just let them take me and they'll leave my friends and family alone, Annie thought.

She walked down the center of the road, in between each of the rows of buildings.

As she passed each house, on both sides, the doors swung open, revealing the silhouette of one—or more—standing in the doorway. One by one, as she went past, the doors would swing open and there was a cult member, unmoving and watching her.

Annie shuddered.

"Annie," they whispered. "Annie...Annie...Annie."

Their voices became louder and louder as Annie walked faster and faster. Door by door opened, revealing another person bathed in backlight.

Annie ran down to the dried riverbed. She saw some of the cultists lumbering her way now, following her. With each house she passed, more of the cultists appeared and began trailing her from all directions.

The riverbed, though completely barren, had artifacts and remnants from when it was a tourist attraction. A rack of canoes, a couple of beached boats, swimming equipment, snorkels, and diver's masks.

Annie ducked down and hurried inside the triangular canoe rack, peering out of the open slots to see a few cultists wander by, searching for her.

She put her hand on the rope that tied all the canoes together and waited.

A large man in a smiling, blonde princess mask stood in front of the canoe rack. Annie could hear his heavy breathing through his ancient plastic mask.

"Don't you want to be free, Annie?" the princess-masked man said. Annie wasn't sure if he'd even spotted her or if he was speaking with the hope he'd found her. "Don't you want to be a part of something greater that yourself? You'd be making the greatest sacrifice. You'll be a hero, Annie."

He reached his hand into the space between two of the canoes, nearly touching Annie's hair. Annie backed away, ducking down in the darkness.

"She's here," the princess-masked man said to two cohorts.

Annie looked to the side and saw one of the cultists standing at the end, peeking into the underside of the canoe rack.

She pulled the rope in her hand. The canoes crashed to the ground, knocking down the princess-masked man and another cultist in a wizard mask.

Annie ran for the forest.

CHAPTER SEVENTY-THREE

The word "black" did not properly describe what the woods looked like at nighttime. There wasn't a strong enough word to convey just how dark Annie's surroundings were. She didn't want to use her cell phone flashlight. It would alert the cultists to her location.

She was stuck. Hands out in front of her, fumbling around to not crash into a tree or trip on a root or fall in a hole. Slivers and glimmers of moonlight shone through the trees, giving her a direction to go in.

Annie heard the skittering and crunching of the cultists dashing and darting throughout the forest. Around her, close by, not quite aware of exactly where she was but in the same vicinity.

She paused in her tracks when she saw George Squires, the old man who warned her that all of this was going to happen, wandering aimlessly through the trees, as if he was lost. He was completely nude, his old body sagging and drooping.

"George?" Annie whispered. "George!"

George lifted his head toward her.

It wasn't George.

It was someone wearing a George skinsuit.

George's face draped over another man's. Hollowed out eyeholes, loose skin, bloodstains where the skin had been cut.

The fake-George reached his arms out and lumbered toward Annie, moaning. Annie didn't wait. She darted farther into the darkness, farther away from human life and light.

All the trees looked the same. She'd been swallowed up by the darkness of the woods. She was a part of its opaque terrors and secrets now.

She had her phone but there was no reception. She needed her car keys—they were in the house—but she wasn't going to leave her friends there to die. Maybe if she went into the woods, away from Gull Valley, they would follow after her and leave her people alone.

She didn't even know if everyone was okay.

She stopped to hide behind a tree as mere feet away, a cultist with a machete walked around, searching for her.

"Come out, little rabbit," the man said in a purposefully taunting voice.

As soon as the man stomped off into the trees, Annie bolted in the opposite direction.

A light!

Annie saw the faint glow coming from within a shack in the distance.

"Oh, God, please help me!" Annie said.

She burst through the door. Though the outside of the house appeared worn down and old, the inside was brightly colored in pastels, each room with a different light, creamy color—pink, blue, yellow. Like a marshmallow lived there.

The main room was set up like a quaint, 1950s-style living room—vintage, outdated couch, coffee table, box television set, cuckoo clock on the wall.

"Hello?" Annie said.

The adjoining room was a dining room, similarly adorned in a 1950s theme. Faceless mannequins dressed in obsolete fashions from that area were seated around the dinner table, like a family gathering for a meal. A Chantilly berry cake was placed in the center of the table on a cake plate.

Annie heard clicks, fuzzy static, and electronic humming emanating from the back room. She knew this wasn't a safe place. Still, she carried on.

The next room was filled with television sets. At least two dozen, stacked on top of each other, their cords like snakes on the ground. The monitors all showed different scenes—some old TV shows, some music videos, some security footage, some videos of The Felicitous.

Past that, in the farthest room, was where the clicking and humming originated from. A large metal desk stocked with radio and recording equipment, microphones, cables and wires, all connected to a broadcast system.

The room was cluttered with cell phone jammers. Some connected to larger, manmade electronic contraptions; a makeshift jammer meant to block all calls throughout Gull Valley.

A tape played on a loop, sending a transmission and signals out to whoever the intended listeners were. The sound of a monotonous voice reading numbers aloud and giving vague instructions over the airwaves.

Annie stood silently, taking it all in. She didn't see the figure standing behind her in the doorway.

"You're a part of all of this, Annie," Ms. Click said. "This is your legacy. Your purpose."

"Why do you guys all talk like that? So seriously and self-importantly?" Annie said, facing Ms. Click. "This is all a joke. You have wasted your lives on this insane nonsense. For what? For nothing. You killed all these people for nothing."

"People die every day, Annie, and no one cares. What's a few more for a good cause?"

"Why? Why do you believe all this?"

"Everyone believes in something. There's a new world coming," Ms. Click said. "You were so easy to manipulate. A few ghost texts from your dead husband, some mind games, all we had to do was maneuver through the tunnels and trap doors and hidden rooms. That's all it took and you were convinced the place was haunted. You made it so easy for us."

Ms. Click held up a portable drill. She revved it for effect.

"I really do like you," Ms. Click said. "You'll be an excellent vessel for Erica."

Annie didn't dodge Ms. Click's advance fast enough. The drill bit ate into Annie's upper arm, drawing blood. Annie screeched in pain.

"It's just a flesh wound, dear," said Ms. Click.

"Stay back," Annie said. She picked up the nearest thing she could find. A metronome from the desk.

"I'm not afraid," Ms. Click laughed.

Annie smacked Ms. Click across the head with the metronome, sending her stumbling backward. Annie rushed past her, back out into the forest, again into the cold night. She made it a few hundred yards when she stopped herself.

Only inches away from a giant hole in the ground. Full of mutilated bodies. A body pit.

Annie put her hand over her mouth to keep from screaming or vomiting.

Dozens of dead people, thrown atop one another, scattered like garbage. Soon to be buried and forgotten.

Annie gasped. She swore she saw someone move in the pit.

An arm shot up from within the menagerie of corpses. Someone still alive. Some luckless hiker or camper who had nothing to do with anything that was happening.

Thwack!

From the dark, a hatchet. Thrown directly into the head of the half-alive person in the body pit. Now the person was all-dead.

Someone shoved Annie into the pit. She landed on top of the tangled mess of mangled, massacred corpses. Annie

struggled to get out, slipping and sliding in gore and
bodily matter. She crawled over the bodies to get to the
side of the hole, reaching up and grabbing handfuls of
dirt.

A cultist loomed over her, staring down at her in the
body pit.

One by one, more cultists arrived. Completely
surrounding the pit.

Looking down at Annie through their masks.

CHAPTER SEVENTY-FOUR

Chris, Wes, Alice, and Sally made it out of the roller-skating rink, weaving in and out between the houses. They hadn't seen any sign of life—the ones they wanted to save or the ones who wanted to take theirs.

They saw two cultists up ahead, leaving one of the buildings.

Wes opened the door to the nearest building so that they could hide. It was the library. Alice, Chris, and Sally slipped in behind him.

Sally locked the door.

"We'll wait here until they pass," said Wes.

"We should go to the garage," Chris said. "There will be sharp things there."

"Sharp things?" Sally said.

"Weapons," said Chris.

"Where do you think Annie and Cal are?" said Alice.

"This is the worst trip I've ever been on," Chris said. "I wasn't aware that we had to prepare for combat when we visited. I wish I knew Tae Bo."

They shared a tired laugh.

Clunk.

A book fell to the floor. From a far-off, high shelf.

Clunk.

Another.

Clunk.

And another.

They weren't alone.

Click.

An unseen hand pressed play on the speaker system. An audiobook narrator read Michael McDowell's "The Elementals" aloud. The reader's words bounced off of the bookshelves and hung in the air.

"Time to go," Alice said.

Two cultists blocked the door, silently materializing out of the shadows.

"Guys," said Sally, her grip on the knife in her hand tightening.

The aisles filled with masked cult members who did not speak or make any sudden moves.

"Here's what's going to happen, you creepy, donkey-dick-licking, brainless sycophants," Chris said, pointing the shotgun at them. "You're going to back your stupid, gross, dumbfuck asses up and as far away from us as you can or I'll remove you like a wart."

A moment.

Screech!

A cult member jumped out from the shadows, slashing at the foursome with an antique, bladed medical tool.

One of the cultists lunged for Chris and the gun.

Bang!

She fired and instantly took half of the cultist's head off.

Alice shoved the rolling ladder, connected to the shelves, straight into the cultist. He went soaring back, knocking over a stack of magazines and newspapers.

Several more cultists advanced. Chris reached high onto the top of a nearby bookshelf, shoving it on top of them. The cultists fought against the weight of the wood and books.

Sally grabbed Wes's arm and pulled him toward Alice and Chris. The foursome was encircled by approaching cult members, running through the aisles.

Wes knocked books into the cultists' path as they chased him, hoping to slow them down.

Alice, Chris, Sally, and Wes made it to the back of the library.

No exit door.

They were trapped. With the cult members rapidly gaining on them.

All of the lights went out.

Gull Valley was enveloped in deep, endless darkness.

Brenda, Martha, Karen, Nancy, Rachel, Laurie, Jess, Richie, Trish, and Ginny were swallowed by the dark in the roller-skating rink.

Everyone grappled for their cell phones, clicking the flashlights on.

A row of masked cultists stood before them, illuminated by the light.

CHAPTER SEVENTY-FIVE

Annie and Cal were chained to two of the fire-ravaged trees in the section of forest that had been destroyed by flames. Two trees closest to the edge of the part of the forest that still bloomed.

The moon hung high in the sky, shedding some light down on them. The woods were completely silent. The animals had gone quiet. Only the sound of Annie and Cal's heavy breathing reverberated through the night air.

A giant bonfire was lit and raging.

The cultists—at least two dozen in number—were gathered in a circle around Annie and Cal, holding torches in one hand and weapons in the other. Sloane remained at the head of the circle, directly in front of Annie and Cal.

Cal had a bloody wound on his head. He looked over at Annie with sad, defeated eyes, like he blamed himself for everything that was happening.

"It's officially your birthday, Annie," Sloane said.

Annie and Cal desperately tried to break free of their restraints. Unless they could climb all the way to the top of the dead trees, there was no hope.

"Tonight, we bring our masters, our leaders, back from beyond," Sloane addressed the cultists. She held a book, bound in human skin, in her hands. Like a grimoire. "We've been waiting a very long time for this. It's time to spread the word of The Felicitous to the world. It's time to resurrect the ones who will guide us."

"No!" Cal shouted at the cultists. "She's lying to you! She wants you to believe in things that aren't true. Laird and Erica are dead and gone. You can live your lives without them. You can be free."

Sloane stared into Cal's eyes, not blinking.

"How could you do this, Lyla?" Cal said. "What about Ruby and Rex? What about your family? The people we love? Why would you do this?"

"I already have a family," Sloane whispered as she stabbed Cal in his side. He screamed in pain. "You're going to see tonight."

"Why, Lyla? For what? Mara would be ashamed of you," Cal said, wincing in pain. He spat blood at her. "None of this is real. This is all a fantasy in your head. What are you going to do when they realize that?"

"Tonight, we make believers out of doubters," Sloane said.

Sloane backed away and joined the other cultists in the circle.

Annie and Cal watched the tree line as something slowly emerged from the darkness.

A thing steadily came into view, only illuminated by the light of the fire.

A large, spindly humanoid creature of some sort. Like nothing Annie nor Cal had ever seen before.

Tall, lanky, emaciated, grotesque. Pale, alabaster skin so white it was practically see-through. Long, dirty dark hair and sharp-clawed fingernails. It smelled like rotted meat and decomposed flesh.

Laird's monster.

It was real.

Somehow, it was real.

The Felicitous had brought it back from whatever hell it came from.

Annie and Cal couldn't believe what they were witnessing. Neither could the cultists, who beheld the sight of the creature with awe, amazement, joy, and wonder. The cultists weren't afraid of the thing. Like Laird, they worshipped it.

The creature remained at the tree line, as if it were averse to the fire.

"Come forward," Sloane said, barely able to contain her ravenous excitement. "We offer these lives to you. So that you will give us the lives of Laird Hubbell and Erica Keating. So that they may live again and share their teachings."

The creature tentatively stepped closer to Annie and Cal.

Closer.

Closer.

"You'll be with Gary and Mara again soon," Sloane said to Annie and Cal. "Reunited in the afterlife. With the ones you love and miss the most. Your bodies will remain here, home to Laird and Erica. Everything is going to be all right."

Annie had no words. The fear that surged through her body made her fight harder against her shackles. The tree was impervious to her resistance. The chains on her wrists wouldn't break.

Lyla read passages from the grimoire as the creature closed in on Annie and Cal.

Closer.

"To the rebirth!" Lyla said.

"The rebirth!" the cultists repeated.

The creature was practically face-to-face with Annie and Cal. Its mottled hair, acrid breath, bony body, black eyes mere feet away from them. It regarded each of them as if it were deciding who to slaughter first.

Closer.

"They're yours," Sloane said to the creature.

The creature unleashed a wild, uninhibited scream into the night air. Annie and Cal fought back their tears, not wanting to resign themselves to their imminent fate.

The creature bared its jagged, decrepit teeth at Cal. Cal was face-to-face with the monster. The creature smelled him, almost as if regarding him or checking him out, before it sunk its jaws into Cal's neck.

Cal screamed as the creature ripped chunks of flesh and gristle from his neck. Cal's blood splashed and sprayed in full, voluminous spurts, soaking Annie.

The cultists watched on in wonderment.

Cal's neck had been ravaged by the creature. His head bobbled and teetered, barely holding onto the rest of his body.

The cultists ran forward with cups and buckets to catch Cal's blood.

Annie let out an anguished scream, still trying to smash the chains on her wrists.

There was a small stump sticking out of the tree. Annie lodged it in between her wrist and the shackles, cutting herself in the process.

She looked up to see the creature staring right at her. Its pale white face had become red and wet. It stepped toward her, its next meal.

The blood from Annie's cut lubricated Annie's hand enough to slide it from out of the shackle. Now free, she jumped back and whipped the chain still attached to her other hand at the creature.

Sloane and the cultists rushed at Annie, aware she had broken from her restraints.

The cultists surrounded Annie. The creature lurked in front of her, its eyes bloodthirsty and wanting.

Annie swung the chains at the advancing enemy. Annie had her back against the towering bonfire. Nowhere to run.

Sloane stood before her, defiant and self-satisfied.

"You're not leaving, Annie," said Sloane. "We're not done here. Without memory, there can be no retribution."

"We're done, Sloane," Annie said. "Or whoever you are. You can stay here with your new friend."

"There's no way out of this, Annie," said Sloane.

The cultists remained silent, standing with Sloane.

Annie reached into the bonfire, her hand burning as she grabbed a flaming chunk of wood and slashed at everyone with it.

"Get back!" Annie shouted. "Get away from me!"

The creature, averse to the flames, skulked back into the darkness of the tree line.

Annie panicked. There was no way out of this. She was heavily outnumbered. What could she do? She was surrounded. She had to do something.

Annie dropped the piece of wood to the ground.

"Good girl," said Sloane, putting her face in Annie's.

That was all Annie needed. With every ounce of her might, fighting back her terror, she reached forward and grabbed Sloane by her collar.

Annie spun Sloane and flung her into the bonfire.

"I don't want to be friends anymore, Sloane!" Annie said.

Flames engulfed Sloane as the fire burned and melted her. The cultists hurried to retrieve Sloane as she screamed like a banshee. The cultists were so distracted by saving Sloane that they almost completely ignored Annie.

Growl!

The creature reached from the darkness and pulled a screaming cultist into the depths with it. It tore at the cultist, feeding on blood and meat, squealing and smacking its lips as it ate.

Once it finished with the first cultist, it yanked another into the woods with it to feast on.

This was her chance. Annie made a run for it. Into the woods. Into the night.

382

The cultists hunted her down. They were all around her, running in tandem with her through the trees, chasing her without fear.

She was of no use to them anymore. She'd ruined their ritual. Now she was expendable.

Annie slapped branches out of her way, dodging and weaving between the trees and through the brush, hoping and praying that she was on the right path back to Gull Valley.

"Annie!" the cultists shouted her name, mocking her. "Nowhere to run, Annie!"

Annie saw the buildings up ahead. She gained a second wind and rushed for cover. As she ran, an idea came to her.

She ran to the main house.

CHAPTER SEVENTY-SIX

Annie didn't have time to wonder if everyone she loved was okay. She had to fight back, to survive. That was all she could focus on at the moment.

As soon as she entered the main house, locking the door behind her, she heard noises coming from the living room. She wasn't alone.

Click.

Pffft!

Click.

Pffft!

Annie grabbed two knives from the kitchen drawer, one for each hand, and crept down the dark hallway toward the living room.

Three people sat motionless on her couch. Annie was behind them. They stared straight ahead a slide show played out over the wall.

An audio recording played as the slides appeared and rotated. It was the playback of the EVP session Madame Fructuosa had conducted earlier. Annie heard voices that weren't hers or her friends in the background of the recording; voices they hadn't heard at the time.

Each slide remained lit up hazily upon the wall for a few seconds then the slide projector switched the image.

Every slide was of The Felicitous. Pictures of the cultists laughing, dancing, singing, communing with nature and each other...

...And of them mutilating screaming victims, breaking into dark houses, slaughtering strangers, and performing dark rituals.

Annie didn't want to take another step forward. She held the knives tightly in her hands, ready to strike from behind. She paused.

Ned and T.P. were two of the people on the couch. They were dressed in the yellow frocks that new converts to The Felicitous were forced to wear.

Annie covered her mouth when she realized they were both dead. She didn't recognize the corpse seated next to them.

Her attention turned to the window. She saw a man running around outside. She didn't know who he was but he looked disheveled and terrified.

Gil Abbott was outside, having escaped from the tunnels he had been held captive in. He was standing in view of the window, unsure of which way to run.

Annie saw several cult members approaching him in the distance. He didn't notice.

Annie lunged forward to open the window. It had been nailed shut. She banged her hand on the glass, trying to get his attention.

"Behind you!" Annie screamed. "Run! Behind you!"

Gil didn't hear her at first. It was too late for him. By the time his eyes met hers and they recognized each other's terror and fear, the cultists were already on top of him. He was completely surrounded.

"Behind you!" Annie said again, even though it was futile.

Gil screamed as the cultists stabbed his flesh with their sharp weapons. He disappeared among the mass of cult members who descended upon him.

"Behind you," Annie said quietly and in defeat.

At that moment, the third man on the couch—the one Annie didn't know—stood up directly behind her.

Creak.

Annie heard the noise of the floorboard and turned around to see the man. The cultist had a completely black mask over his face, covering everything but his wide, white eyes. He held a dagger in his hand.

Annie raised her knives to strike but the man pushed her back against the window. She dropped both knives as the wind was knocked out of her.

Annie lifted her hand to block the cultist's dagger slash. The blade of the dagger went through her hand. Annie screamed in pain as the cultist retracted it.

Annie dodged the cultist's next slash and bolted up the staircase. He chased after her, his footfalls heavy and angry on the stairs. Annie barely made it to her bedroom.

She threw the door closed behind her but was blocked. The cultist's arm was in the gap, waving the dagger at her and missing. Annie pushed her weight against the door. Her eyes zoned in on the welcome gifts Aunt Dolly brought her.

Annie grabbed the bear spray and shot it directly into the cultist's eyes. He screamed and backed away, clutching at his face and dropping the dagger in Annie's bedroom. Annie slammed the door shut and locked it.

Thank you, Aunt Dolly.

The cultist banged at the door, cursing her and yelling. Annie ran to the side of the bed to retrieve her bat, Jason Statham. She wrapped her bleeding hand with duct tape.

In all the commotion, Annie never saw the person standing in the corner of her room, watching her every move, covered by shadows.

The figure raised a double-sided axe high over her head. Annie, out of the corner of her eye, saw the movement and ducked as the cultist brought the axe down. The axe lodged in the wall.

The cultist, a young woman in a brightly-colored faerie mask, lunged for Annie. Annie grunted and swung Jason Statham at her. The bat connected with the cultist's head, sending her careening backward onto the blade of the axe. The blade pierced through the faerie cultist's torso, spraying blood everywhere.

The knocking and banging at the door had stopped. Everything was quiet.

Ding-ding!

The sound of the bell Brenda used to call Eunice.

Ding-ding!

Someone rang the bell from farther down into the house.

Annie gathered a few more of the items Aunt Dolly had given her. She had a plan. If she could ever get out of the main house.

Annie opened the door as gingerly as she could manage. She peered down the hallway, searching for signs of unwelcome guests.

Someone was watching her from around the corner, hidden by the wall next to the staircase. She could only see part of their ghostly white face, peeking out at her. Annie retreated back to her bedroom, shutting and locking the door.

Annie lay on the ground, looking through the crack between the door and the floor. There was nobody there.

Her body felt the vibrations of footsteps in the hallway. She didn't move.

She watched as two booted feet walked past her bedroom doorway, dragging a mauled, rotted corpse behind it. Annie had no idea where the cultist was taking the body but she knew someone dangerous was on the other side of the door.

She stood back up as quietly as she could. Her only option was to get on the roof and jump down to the ground below.

CHAPTER SEVENTY-SEVEN

The cultists came from every building, every shadow, the woods. They'd gathered the remaining survivors—Alice, Brenda, Chris, Ginny, Jess, Karen, Kit, Laurie, Martha, Nancy, Rachel, Richie, Sally, Steve, Trish, and Wes—and marched them into the church.

Annie's friends were tied together with rope and duct tape. The cultists shoved them into pews.

Ms. Click stood at the pulpit, beneath the battered, damaged statue of Jesus. Behind her, dead bodies were arranged in various poses and stances; some held up by rails and support beams. Beverly and Sloane's husband Wade were among the corpses.

"You all are a part of The Felicitous now," Ms. Click said.

The cultists responded in unison, uttering an indistinguishable chant.

The church filled with members of The Felicitous. The cultists were comprised of various walks of life—old and young, former members and new, children, the lost and the found. Some looked like science experiments gone wrong, clearly the people who had been medical projects operated on by either the doctors at The Calista Asylum or the cult members themselves.

There were at least sixty members standing before Ms. Click, forming a perimeter around Annie's friends. They were rapt with attention to Ms. Click's every word.

"Laird Hubbell saw things the common person couldn't," Ms. Click said.

As she spoke, members of the cult went on stage to act out her words, as if performing a twisted, gore-soaked play.

"A plane crash brought him to a deserted area where no one could rescue him, no one could hear his cries. His family killed, his hope shattered. He lost his one true love, Erica," Ms. Click continued. "That's when the forest god appeared."

The sickly, pale creature stood in the church doorway, taking up most of the frame. It lumbered toward Ms. Click and the cultists.

"Bishop Laird heard its word and survived," Ms. Click said. "He brought the message back to all of us. We are not cattle or sheep. We saw what Bishop Laird envisioned. A community, a family, a place where we were free to be who we are. But the world wouldn't have that."

Annie's friends struggled against their restraints as covertly as they could. The cultists kept their eyes locked on them.

"There is no God," Ms. Click said. "There is no devil. The Felicitous is the truth. We are the only ones who know what is real. You are all here to witness the rebirth."

The creature moved past Ms. Click and the cultists, leaning over one of the corpses. It began to feed as Ms. Click spoke.

"They opposed us," said Ms. Click. "They tried to stop us, to silence us, to take away our home. No one can stop us. Our voices will be heard again. Tonight, you will be our witnesses to the resurrection. You will help us spread the word and take back what is rightfully ours. No one can stop the vengeance that is coming, the justice we will wreak on those who defy and oppress us. There is no salvation for what's coming."

The cult members behind Ms. Click pantomimed and overacted silently, their movements overexaggerated and sweeping. Annie's friends watched on in horror. It would have been unintentionally funny if it wasn't so horrifying to watch the depths of their madness; how entrenched in their psychosis and delusions they were.

"They called us crazy," Ms. Click said. "They said we were insane, misguided, weirdos, hippies, freaks, heretics, brainwashed. They laughed at us. They made fun of us. They didn't see the truth. They are the sheep. They didn't listen to the words of the one and only true prophet. We showed them. We warned them. No one listened. Nobody ever listens. We have devoted our lives and souls to Bishop Laird. Nothing is going to change that. No one is going to stop that."

The doors to the secret room burst open. Annie stood in the doorway.

"Hey, shitfucks!" Annie screamed from the doorway to the secret room. "You cockwranglers! You sloppy, wet buttlickers! You crusty, cheesy-ass sheepherders! Come here! Over here! This way! I'm in here! Let them all go and you can have me."

Annie had snapped. It was clear to the cultists and Annie's friends.

The masked cult members walked toward Annie. The cultists parted, revealing Sloane, the side of face burned and hair singed. She scowled and clutched a knife in her hands.

"I like your makeover, Sloane," Annie said.

"I'm going to make your pain last," Sloane hissed.

"I give up," Annie said, holding her empty hands out. "If you let them go, I will do whatever you want. I have nothing to live for anyway. The one man I truly loved more than myself is gone. I don't want to go on anymore. I'm tired. My life has been one tragedy after another. I don't want to do this. I will be your sacrifice."

"You think we're stupid enough to fall for this trick?" said Sloane.

"It's not a trick, Sloane," Annie said. "You know me. I don't know you really, but you know me. I came to Gull Valley to end everything, be by myself. Erica can live on through me. I'll go peacefully with you. If you let my friends leave here."

"What if we just kill you?" Sloane said.

"You could but then you failed."

"What if we just say we'll let your friends go, kill you, then kill them anyway?"

"'What if's' are a special kind of torture."

Annie backed farther away, fully inside the secret room. Loretta Lynn's "In the Garden," her mother's mania song, played on the jukebox.

"Let them go, Sloane," Annie said. "I have nowhere to escape to. You've won. I'm all yours."

"We'll be back for you," said Sloane to Annie's friends.

Sloane followed Annie into the secret room. The cult members and the creature trailed behind Sloane. Ms. Click remained with Annie's friends. Sloane shut the door behind her, locking it.

Annie faced the cultists and Sloane. "This is what you wanted. I'm ready."

Annie closed her eyes and waited for Sloane to approach. Annie stood in front of the wax figure of Laird Hubbell.

"You're just a meat and blood bag, Annie," said Sloane. "I own your soul."

Sloane stepped closer to Annie, neither trusting nor believing Annie's words. After a few steps, she looked down.

The entire floor was covered in lye. From the barrels Annie and her friends had discovered earlier.

"It's okay, Sloane," Annie said, lighting the flare that Aunt Dolly had given her earlier. "We don't all get a happy ending."

Annie threw the flare to the ground. It lit the fuse to the dynamite, which Annie had spread out over the lye on the ground.

Annie leapt inside the glass case surrounding Laird Hubbell's wax figure, covered herself in blankets, and crouched down behind the statue. She secured a gas mask, which she had hidden there, over her face.

Boom!

Boom!

Boom!

The room exploded and lit up like a billion fireworks. Fire and flames ate everything in its path, including Sloane and the cult members. They cultists screamed and wailed, howling at their bodies consumed by flames that melted their flesh.

The fire set off the sodium hydroxide in the lye. Though lye itself wasn't flammable, it emitted poisonous gas when burned.

Sloane pounded on the glass door where Annie hid, slashing a knife at it. She clutched her throat, her eyes burning from the fumes. Annie threw the door open, reached out, and zapped Sloane with the stun gun Aunt Dolly gave her, then shut herself back into the encasement.

"Eat my farts, Sloane!" Annie said, then lowered her voice to mock Sloane's mantra. "Kittens, mittens, reversible hats, Baby Yoda, the comforting sound of rain."

The church roof caved in. Giant wooden beams crashed down on some of the cult members and in front of the only doorway in or out. They were all trapped.

Just how Annie had planned it.

Annie watched through the cracked glass encasement of Laird Hubbell's wax figure as Sloane and the cultists simultaneously suffocated on the gas and burned like paper in a fireplace. They fell like dominoes, clutching their throats and running around like headless chickens, trying to find a safe place to hide from the blazing inferno.

There were none.

The creature burst from the flames, smashing its clawed hand against the glass. Annie ducked down, crawling behind the wax statue, her eyes wide in the circular lenses of the gas mask.

The creature released an inhuman shriek as flames enveloped it and the gas seeped into its lungs. It collapsed to the floor, blood oozing from its eye sockets.

The heat from the fire began to melt Laird's wax face. Annie watched the fire ravage the cultists and Sloane.

She had accepted that this would be her end as well.

CHAPTER SEVENTY-EIGHT

Aunt Dolly and Diane arrived with the police and fire department in tow. The firemen doused the church with water from the firehose as the police rounded Annie's friends up, directing them to safety.

The church was half-burnt down. Police officers and firefighters yelled back and forth to each other. One of the officers shouted something about several dead bodies in the fire.

"The woman that was with us," Kit said, referring to Ms. Click. "Where is she?"

Nobody knew. Ms. Click had escaped the explosion, just as Annie's friends had. The closed doors from the secret room allowed them enough time to get out before the fire spread. As Annie's friends always had, they protected each other and worked together to escape the inferno.

Aunt Dolly and the survivors stared at the raging blaze. The firefighters had not found Annie yet.

"Annie," Aunt Dolly said, unable to stop her tears.

Laurie and Sally stood next to Aunt Dolly, putting their arms around her.

From the wreckage, using the pathway made by the rivers of water, Annie emerged. She threw the gas mask to the ground as she escaped.

Aunt Dolly ran to her and hugged her like she'd never hugged anyone before.

"Are you okay?" Aunt Dolly said, inspecting her.

"Rarely," said Annie.

"How did you get out?" Aunt Dolly said, tears streaming down her face.

"There is a trap door beneath the glass case in the church," Annie said. "I didn't know if I could pull it off but here I am."

"You were always a fighter," said Aunt Dolly.

Annie's friends gathered around her, hugging her and each other.

"You're safe now, Annie," said Aunt Dolly.

"I didn't get them all," Annie said.

Annie, Aunt Dolly, and their friends received attention from EMTs and medical professionals as the police officers and firefighters worked. Annie's friends retreated to the main house, needing rest, food, and water.

Annie didn't stop watching the fire until the sun began to rise. She waited to see if anyone else escaped from the church. There were no signs of life, other than the people working the scene.

Annie felt a sense of relief although her body buzzed with overactive nerves and disbelief in what she had endured.

Aunt Dolly draped an afghan around Annie's shoulders.

"There's a lot of handsome firefighters here," Aunt Dolly said. "Oh, look at him."

"This is definitely not the time, Aunt Dolly," said Annie.

"I know," said Aunt Dolly. "You're going to be okay, Annie. We're going to get past this."

"Maybe," Annie said. "Someday."

"The things you've seen," said Aunt Dolly, almost more to herself.

Annie was quiet. The fire was black smoke and ash, billowing up toward the orange sky. Only a shell remained of the church.

"So, you going to put this place on the market?" Aunt Dolly said.

"Sure," said Annie. "Nineteen buildings, pretty views, comes with its own maniacal cult. I'll include that in the listing."

Annie saw Sloane's grimoire on the ground. She picked it up and threw it into the fire.

Annie knew she would never really be okay. Nothing would ever really be okay. What choice did she have though? She wanted to live. She had family and friends to love. She had friends' kids to watch grow up and become who they were meant to be.

She would be okay enough.

That's all she could do for now.

CHAPTER SEVENTY-NINE

It had been three months since Ruby and Rex went to live with their Grandma Kay and Grandpa Al, their mother Mara's mother and father. Though neither Ruby nor Rex disliked living there, as they were given lots of love and attention, they missed their parents.

Ruby was choreographing a dance routine to Debbie Gibson's "Shake Your Love"—Annie had sent her a special divas playlist—while Rex played with his Marvel action figures. There was a knock on the front door. Grandma Kay had always told them not to answer the door for strangers, even though they lived in a small, safe town.

Ruby and Rex nestled up beside Grandma Kay when she opened the door.

Ms. Click, who none of them knew, stood on the porch, smiling brightly. She wore a floral print dress and black shoes.

"Hello," Ms. Click said. "My name is Roberta Huld. I just moved in next door and wanted to introduce myself."

Grandma Kay opened the door for Ms. Click. "Oh, hello! So nice to meet you. I'm Kay Balcom. These are my grandchildren, Ruby and Rex."

Ms. Click bent down to say hello to Ruby and Rex. As she did, her necklace dangled in front of them. On the chain hung an E and K charm. Grandma Kay did not notice it. Ms. Click tucked it back under her collar.

"Won't you come in, Mrs. Huld?" Grandma Kay said. "I'm making lasagna. My husband Al and I were just about to sit down to eat before we go play a round of golf."

"That's very kind of you," Ms. Click said. "Please, call me Berta."

Ms. Click followed Grandma Kay into the living room. Ruby and Rex went back to their playtime.

"I can't stay long," said Ms. Click. "My family will be visiting very soon. We have a lot of plans. Family is very important to me."

"I understand," Grandma Kay said. "Family is everything. Will you excuse me for a moment? I have to check on my lasagna. Please make yourself at home."

"Yes, of course," Ms. Click said.

Once Grandma Kay exited the room, Ms. Click walked to the back door. She stepped out into the large back yard, surrounded by forest and green bushes. Ms. Click surveyed the woods.

Ms. Click whistled, letting the sound carry over the air.

From somewhere within the depths of the forest, someone whistled back.

THE END.

ABOUT THE AUTHOR:

Matt Forgit lives and writes in New England. His interests include spending time with friends and family, annoying his better half, trying to be a cool uncle, scary stuff, movies, television shows, music, reading, eating, board games, creepy folklore, urban legends, spooky history, abandoned places, castles, islands, cabins in the woods, being near the ocean, and the 1970s, 1980s, and 1990s. He is terrible with social media, dreams of owning a haunted bed and breakfast atop a cliffside overlooking the sea, hopes that someday *Chopping Mall: The Musical* becomes a reality, and doesn't normally talk about himself in the third person. For updates, random thoughts, horror recommendations, and general nonsense, please like and follow the Matt Forgit Author page on Facebook.

ACKNOWLEDGEMENTS:

Hi Grandma! Hi Aunt Nancy!

James Sanguinetti, Lisa Stout, Lucia Mohamed, Meghan Buckley, and Melissa Capezio—You deserve all of the glitter, unicorns, double rainbows, and cake in the world for how above and beyond you've gone to support me and this book. Thank you to the moon and stars and back. Like Bon Jovi sings—I'll be there for you, these five words I swear to you.

The amazing, incredible, wonderful, brilliant people who give me their time, love, encouragement, and support—Anna Maria Skiotis, Steve Galuna, Sofia Maria and Diana; Colin and Olivia Capelle; Dad and Kay; Danielle, Harry, and A.J. Providakes; Drew, Kassie, Carver, and Sailer McConville; Erica and Brian Sheldon; Gina Newell; Jessica Raymond; Jessica, Andy, Leah, and Naomi Simon; Jim Paul; Julie and Jake Forgit; Katie, Gavin, Owen, and Simon Allen; Kerri Allard; Maribel Palin; Matt Keller; Megan Ruggiero; Mia Turner; Paul Buckley; Phoebe Sexton; Roberta Townsend; Ryan, Sara, and Emerson Hastings; Shannon, Ryan, and Ryder Vogt; Shannon White; Stephanie Iscovitz, Frank Valdez, Frankie, and Cece; Tami, Travis, Mirren, and Porter Harless; Toni and Steve Weymer; my awesome nieces, nephews, cousins, aunts, and uncles; and my friends, family, friend family, and friends' families.

The brave, smart, capable, strong, trailblazing, resilient, and resourceful final girls who inspired and comforted me when I was younger (and still do)—Adrienne King, Amy Steel, Caroline Williams, Courteney Cox, Dana Kimmell, Daphne Blake, Ellie Cornell, Gillian Anderson, Heather Langenkamp, Jamie Lee Curtis, Jennifer Love Hewitt, Jill Schoelen, Kate Hodge, Kelli Maroney, Kimberly Beck, Linda Blair, Lisa Wilcox, Louise Robey, Marilyn Burns, Nancy Drew, Neve Campbell, Olivia Hussey, Sarah Michelle Gellar, Sigourney Weaver, and Velma Dinkley.

My most heartfelt appreciation and gratitude to everyone who buys my books and shares positive, enthusiastic, warm-hearted, and thoughtful messages, posts, and reviews. May The Felicitous never knock on your door.

From: Sloane Doyle <sdoylebroker@hotmail.com>
Sent: Monday, October 2, 2023 2:27 PM
To: Custom Contact List: 'The Gang'
Subject: RE: Shh! Annie's Surprise Party!
◼Gull_Valley_Map.jpeg
◼Slumber_Party_Assignments.docx

Hi Everyone!!!

I know it's been a bit, but I wanted to reach back out as we're getting closer to the BIG DAY! Annie has NO IDEA and I am SO EXCITED to have you all meet me in Gull Valley to surprise her!

When you get here make sure you park around the back of the main house so Annie doesn't see your car.

I also drew up a fun map of Gull Valley so you know where to park and so that you can get a lay of the land (attached). I also thought it may make sense to list out who will be crashing in which of the guest houses (This list is also attached ☺). Open to swapping of course! But this way you can drop your stuff off and GET THE PARTY STARTED! I will meet you all there later in the evening after work.

Feel free to text me if you get lost at all! It's 5 miles from Hartwell, if you hit the Buckley Gas Station you've gone too far!

Can't wait and see you soon!

Sloane
207-281-0202

Slumber Party Assignments

Annie (obvs) will be in the Main House

Guest House #1:
- Aunt Dolly Haskell
- Diane Fenwick
- Martha Gaines
- Brenda Mulhern
- Karen Belmont
- Eunice Trout (Brenda's Assistant)

Guest House #2:
- Trish Vaughn & Bill Leckie
- Sally Forster & Dave Sanders
- T.P. Mitchell
- Sean Rhodes
- Rachel Webber
- Chris Sawyer
- Ginny Donovan
- Wes Carrigan

Guest House #3:
- Beverly Brown & Ned Watkins
- Laurie Hughes & Max Pahucki
- Jess Tapert & Richie McCoy
- Alice Fulton
- Kit Granger & Steve Collver
- Nancy Butler

Other people you may see around Gull Valley:
(don't be scared if you see them)
Mr. Brisket: GV Groundskeeper
Ms. Click: Estate Sales
Jack Henderson: Local Handyman
Ben Russell: Local Handyman

Laundry Room

Main House

Parking →

Mess Hall

Generators

TO HARTWELL →

Library

Main Office

Infirmary

Woodshop

Made in the USA
Middletown, DE
11 October 2023

40599148R00230